DELICIOUS!

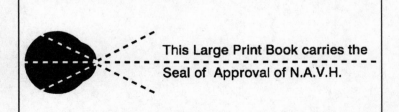

DELICIOUS!

RUTH REICHL

THORNDIKE PRESS

A part of Gale, Cengage Learning

GALE
CENGAGE Learning·

Farmington Hills, Mich • San Francisco • New York • Waterville, Maine
Meriden, Conn • Mason, Ohio • Chicago

GALE
CENGAGE Learning·

LIBRARY OF CONGRESS CATALOGING-IN-PUBLICATION DATA

Reichl, Ruth.
    Delicious! / by Ruth Reichl. — Large print edition.
        pages ; cm. — (Thorndike Press large print women's fiction)
    ISBN 978-1-4104-6794-2 (hardcover) — ISBN 1-4104-6794-5 (hardcover)
        1. Life change events—Fiction. 2. Hiding places—Fiction. 3. World War,
    1939-1945—Ohio—Akron—Fiction. 4. Letters—Fiction. 5. Large type books.
    I. Title.
    PS3618.E5239D45 2014b
    813'.6—dc23   2014009467

Published in 2014 by arrangement with Random House, Inc., a Penguin
Random House Company

Printed in the United States of America
1 2 3 4 5 6 7 18 17 16 15 14

*To the memory of Marion Cunningham.
I miss her every day.*

GINGERBREAD

"You should have used fresh ginger!"

The words flew out of my mouth before I could stop them. I glanced at Aunt Melba to see if she was upset, but she was looking at me with undisguised admiration. "Why didn't I think of that!"

"And orange peel." I wanted her to look at me that way again.

"Any other ideas?" Aunt Melba was rooting around in the vegetable bin.

She emerged holding a large knob of ginger triumphantly over her head, then went to the counter and began to grate it, sending the mysterious tingly scent into the air. "How come you didn't say something *last* year?"

"Would you have believed me?"

She swiped at the thick red curl that had fallen across her right eye and grinned ruefully. "Ask advice from a nine-year-old?" She reached out and tousled my hair. "Now

7

that you're ten, of course, everything's changed."

"You make this stupid cake every year." My sister was annoyed. "It's never very good. Why don't you just give up?"

"Because it's the only kind of cake your father likes." Aunt Melba reached for one of the beautiful ceramic bowls on the shelf above her. "And your mother always used to make it for his birthday. I'm trying to keep tradition alive."

"You should have asked Mom for the recipe." Genie was a year and a half older than me, and she had opinions.

"I did. But she would never give it to me. My sister was funny that way. And then it was too late."

"We're going to get it right!" They both turned to stare at me; I wasn't exactly known for self-confidence, but I could taste the cake in my mind. Strong. Earthy. Fragrant. I remembered the nose-prickling aroma of cinnamon when it comes in fragile curls, and the startling power of crushed cloves. I imagined them into the batter.

Aunt Melba was grating the orange rind now, and the clean, friendly smell filled her airy kitchen. The place was a mess; eggshells were everywhere, the counter was covered with splotches of sticky batter, and bags of

8

flour spilled onto the floor. Ashtrays filled with half-smoked cigarettes were scattered among the ceramic plates and bowls Aunt Melba had made; she was famous for them. In the middle of it all sat a couple of forlorn cakes, each missing a tiny sliver.

Aunt Melba put the new cake in the oven and we began to clean up. The scent of gingerbread whirled through the room and out the window into the Montecito hills. Down below, the Pacific sparkled. "It smells pretty good," said Genie hopefully.

Alas, this cake was doomed to join those abandoned on the counter. "What now?" Aunt Melba sounded discouraged, but she searched my face as if I had the answer. I liked the feeling.

"Cardamom!" I said, mustering all the authority I could.

"Cardamom? How do you even know about cardamom?"

"She practices," replied Genie, a slight edge to her voice. Smart and beautiful, she was used to taking charge. "You should see her."

"Practices?" asked Aunt Melba.

"Yeah," said Genie. "She's always sniffing the bottles in the spice cabinet."

I didn't know she'd even noticed. At first it was just curiosity; why did fennel and

9

cumin, identical twins, have such opposing personalities? I had crushed the seeds beneath my fingertips, where the scents lingered for hours. Another day I'd opened a bottle of nutmeg, startled when the little spheres came rattling out in a mothball-scented cloud. How could something so delicate have such a ferocious smell? And I watched, fascinated, as the supple, plump, purple vanilla beans withered into brittle brown pods and surrendered their perfume to the air. The spices were all so interesting; it was impossible to walk through the kitchen without opening the cupboard to find out what was going on in there.

Aunt Melba gave me the oddest look. "And you remember them?" She was crushing cardamom pods, and the deep, musky scent zipped around the kitchen.

"More," I said, "use more." How could you ever forget the smell of cardamom? Or cinnamon? Or clove?

I don't remember how many times we made that cake. Each time Aunt Melba thought it was good enough, I insisted that she try again. I had made a discovery: Having the flavors in my head meant I could re-imagine them, put them together in entirely new ways. I wanted to keep doing it forever.

The kitchen was in chaos, but now each

cake was better than the last. Late in the afternoon, Aunt Melba mixed the sixth or seventh batch of batter; this one had crushed peppercorns, sour cream, and orange zest. I greased the pans, Genie put them in the oven, and Aunt Melba set the timer. Just then the room began to shake. It was one of the earthquakes that I like — the roller-coaster kind that feel as if the earth is merely shrugging off the blues. None of Aunt Melba's precious plates broke, but when we opened the oven, we found that our cake had crashed.

The next day, we tried the recipe again. "No earthquakes now," Genie whispered as she put the pans into the oven. This time the cake was high and brown, the spices so delicately balanced that each bite made you want another. It was rich, moist, tender. We brushed it with bourbon, added a fragrant orange glaze, and it was perfect.

"This is even better than your mother's." Aunt Melba reached to caress my cheek; her palm was so soft. "It's a gift, you know. Like an ear for music. You got it from her. She used to do that thing you do, sniffing spices. Did you know that?"

I didn't.

Everyone was always telling my sister how much she resembled our late mother. Not only was Genie brilliant and beautiful, she was also artistic, popular, and most likely to succeed at almost everything. I was the shy one, sitting in my room, writing little stories. No one had ever said I was like Mom in any way.

But I had inherited her gift. Now that I knew it, I hugged the knowledge close.

BOOK ONE

Book One

ELEVEN YEARS LATER

When Jake Newberry asked me to cook for him, I froze.

"Something wrong?" He swept a strand of silver hair out of his eyes and gave me his famous cool blue stare.

"I'm not applying for a position in the test kitchen." I tried to keep the disappointment from my voice; the job had sounded so perfect. "I thought you were looking for a new executive assistant."

"I am." Then he added, "Didn't anybody tell you I ask every candidate to cook for me?"

How had I missed that?

Jake reached down and patted the big yellow dog at his feet; the dog wriggled with pleasure, and I found that oddly reassuring. "Look, Billie." Jake offered an encouraging smile. "You seem like a good fit for *Delicious!* You worked on *The Daily Cal*. It sounds like you know your way around a

15

kitchen. And you're even willing to leave school to take the job. I like that; it shows how much you want it."

I'd spent hours working on an explanation for dropping out; it had never crossed my mind that he'd consider it a plus. "You've said all the right things." He looked down at the pile of manuscripts on his desk, and when he looked up again, his smile was crooked. "You Googled me, right?"

"Would you want an assistant who didn't?"

"Good answer. But that just proves my point. I don't find interviews all that revealing."

Every article I'd read about Jake mentioned that he was a non-corporate guy, which was one of the reasons I'd applied for the job. Working at *Delicious!* sounded like joining a club, entering a little world of its own, and that's exactly what I wanted. Needed. I'd spent hours preparing for this interview, studying Jake, chasing down every detail. Now it appeared that hadn't been enough.

"What's wrong with interviews?" I was playing for time. I really didn't want to cook.

"Isn't it obvious?" He was truly great-looking; the photographs captured his all-American looks, but they didn't catch the

16

humorous way his lips turned up or the watchful intelligence in his eyes. "You tell me you love the book, but, then, you're hardly going to say you hate it."

He'd lost me. Book? I had no idea what he was talking about.

"Ha! Another piece of the puzzle slides into place. You *don't* know much about magazines, do you? In this business, magazines are always called 'books.' I don't know why. What I do know is that every writer who comes for an interview is madly in love with this book. Then I ask what they're reading, and they serve up the usual suspects: *The New Yorker,* and the most challenging bestseller on the current list."

He pointed an ebony letter opener at me. "I have to admit, throwing Brillat-Savarin into the mix was a clever move on your part; nobody's ever come up with that before."

Not all that clever: It hadn't taken much to find out he'd written his college honors thesis on the great French gastronome.

Jake was studying me, and I couldn't help wondering if he'd be easier on me if I were one of the pretty girls, or at least a bit more stylish. Aunt Melba had insisted that I buy a black skirt and a white shirt, but I hadn't bothered trying them on and the skirt was a little too short; now I tugged at it, trying to edge it closer to my knees. But it turned out Jake wasn't concerned with the way I looked. "I'm trying to figure out if you knew I'd ask what you had for dinner last night."

It had been a lucky guess, but if *I* were the editor of a food magazine, that's a question I'd be asking. So I Googled around and discovered that Jake had a passion for Japanese food. Then I found some obscure new place in the East Village specializing in Kitakata ramen and went in for a big bowl of clear fragrant broth filled with broad, chewy noodles.

"Sounds great!" he said, when I described the tiny restaurant and the eccentric chef who ran it. "I've never heard about that place, and I can't wait to try it. Thanks. The thing is . . ." He stopped for a moment to let a noisy truck go by. *Delicious!* occupied a grand old mansion, and on this hot September morning Jake had all the windows open. I looked around, noting what a mess the place was; there were so many stacks of manuscripts, it had been hard to find a place to sit down. "Here's what I've learned about you: You do your homework. That's good. But all it really tells me is that you're smart and you want the job. We could talk all day and I'd still have no idea if you're right for *Delicious!* But cooking's different; it doesn't lie. Is this a problem? Just humor me, okay."

There was no question mark on the end of that last sentence. If I wanted to work for Jake Newberry, I was going to have to cook.

Why hadn't I anticipated this? Because there *was* a problem: These days, simply thinking about cooking could bring on a panic attack.

Already I felt the clammy sweat popping out all over my body. Not now! I thought, willing myself to stand up, reminding myself to breathe. "Anticipatory panic is the worst part," the therapist had said, and anxiety was pouring over me, making me woozy, as I followed Jake out of his office.

I tried to concentrate on the dog, who was running before us, jauntily waving his tail. In that moment I would have given anything to be him, to be so carefree. Go away! I pleaded with the panic, but now it entered me, expanding like a huge balloon, filling my body with agitation. My hands were shaking and the nausea was coming on, but Jake didn't seem to notice. "I'm always eager to find out what people will make for me."

"Gin—" I began, grateful to be talking. It might help. But Jake waved me quiet.

19

"No, no, don't tell me. I like to be surprised."

I followed him up the stairs, so focused on the panic that I barely registered the graceful carved oak banisters and soft wooden floors. Concentrate on the recipe, I told myself, trying to repeat the ingredients in my head: oranges, cardamom, pepper, sour cream. The words were slightly soothing; maybe it would be okay. But then we were at the kitchen and Jake was opening the door. The scent of sugar, flour, and butter wafted toward me, and it was so familiar that I felt the blood rush from my face as the dizziness claimed me. The panic was inside, choking me, and outside too, a great wave crashing over me.

"You okay?" Jake's hand was on my arm. I knew I'd gone white.

"Fine. I'm fine." I put my hand out and grabbed the counter, trying to steady myself. From somewhere far away I heard Jake say, "Okay, then. This is Maggie, our executive food editor. She'll make sure you've got everything you need." Then he was gone.

All I wanted was to lie down on the cool floor, but I glanced up, trying to focus on the woman in front of me. She was old and painfully thin, with a straight nose and short black hair that looked as if she'd chopped it off with a carving knife. She glared at me and muttered, just loud enough for me to hear, "Why's Jake wasting my time? He'll never hire her."

Her unexpected meanness was like an electric shock, and it jerked me backward, jolting me into the moment. The effect was so immediate and so strong that the dizziness receded. It was like a miracle; I almost laughed. What was the worst thing that could happen? I'd faint? Scream? Make some kind of fool of myself? I straightened up, looked her in the eye, told her I'd need ginger, eggs, and oranges, and began ticking off the spices. She silently pointed to the refrigerator, the cupboard, the spice cabinet — staccato little jerks, as if she begrudged me every motion. The blood began to return to my head, and now I could feel the sweat drip down my face. I swiped at it with a paper towel when Maggie's back was turned. Then I opened the refrigerator and reached in, grateful for the rush of cold as I grabbed the eggs. The nausea was still there, but it was bearable now, and the departing panic had left relief in its wake, so strong it felt almost like elation. I'd have a terrible headache later on, but I was going to get through this.

Maggie stomped off to the next counter,

where a tall, older cook was rolling out pasta. The room was crowded — at least eight other cooks were in there — and the scent of baking cakes, roasting meats, and caramelizing onions filled the air. I gathered my ingredients and began to relax into the rhythm of the kitchen, slowly slipping into that flow where I was all alone. I grated orange peel, concentrating on the way the cool oil felt on my fingertips. I picked up a knob of ginger, losing myself to the rain-forest fragrance as I slowly shredded it with my knife. The scents swirled around me: cinnamon, cardamom, pepper, and clove.

Captured by the cooking, I picked up the pace, my spoon ringing against the bowl, my body vibrating to the familiar moves. I was so into sifting flour, greasing pans, and pouring batter that I didn't even realize I was talking as the cake went in the oven.

" 'No earthquakes now'?" Maggie's voice was belligerent. "What the hell does that mean?"

"It's a California thing."

She sniffed derisively and stuck out her sharp chin. She seemed to be searching for a cutting remark when someone shouted, "Taste!"

The word reverberated through the room, galvanizing the cooks. They all dropped

22

what they were doing and went charging toward the sound, forks held out before them, like knights heading into a joust. They descended on a roast one of the cooks had just pulled from the oven, each jockeying for the first forkful. There was a moment of silence as they stood chewing, then a sudden rush of words as they deconstructed the dish.

"Needs more salt."

"Reminds me of that Paula Wolfert dish, the one with warka."

"Why'd you use achiote?"

Ten minutes later, they were still talking. I opened my oven door, and as the carnival scent of gingerbread came spilling out, they all looked toward me before resuming the conversation.

I turned the cake out of the pan and let it cool for a few minutes. I had just finished glazing it when Maggie stalked over. "How long do you let it cool?"

"I like to eat it while it's still a little warm."

"Taste!" she bellowed. I jumped back as the outstretched forks came rushing toward me.

"It smells incredible," said one of the cooks.

Maggie, a practiced jouster, shoved his fork aside. "*I'll* take the first bite," she said, lopping off a chunk. She put it in her mouth and her lips twisted, as if she'd swallowed a mouthful of vinegar. For a minute I thought she hated it. But then she said, reluctantly, "Oh, God, this is fantastic. Jake's going to love it."

SPRING CHEESE

Dear Genie,

It was the gingerbread, of course; when Jake tasted it, he said anyone who could turn the world's most banal cake into something so compelling — he actually used that word — belonged at *Delicious!* He said he had to hire me if only to get the recipe.

As if I'd give it to him!

Everything's happened so fast. Two weeks ago I was heading back for senior year, and now I've got a job in New York, an apartment, a whole new life. If I let myself think about it, I get terrified, so it's a good thing I'll be busy: Jake said I'll sometimes have to work till after midnight. And the pay's so low. Dad says he'll cover my first year's rent, which is pretty serious, considering how much he hates me dropping out of school. And how much he's going to miss me. Aunt

Melba keeps texting me, reminding me to call him. She thinks he's going to take this hard, but, then, she's always worrying about Dad.

I found the most incredible place, a fifth-floor walk-up on the Lower East Side. It's like the place I've always dreamed of, so perfect I sometimes think I must have conjured it from my imagination. It's tiny, but there's tons of light, and it's in a great old neighborhood. If I keep the windows open, I can hear people's voices as they walk down the sidewalk, and if they're loud enough I catch intriguing little snatches of conversation. It goes on all day and all night; there's always something happening on Rivington. I love that.

My first night here, I went out at midnight — midnight! — to grab a bite at the little Chinese place on the corner. Then I went to the bookshop. Even that late at night, it was filled with people who looked like they led interesting lives.

I just wish you were here to share this. I feel so lonely. And then there's the question of clothes. I'm heading off to my first day of work, and I'm hopeless. All those mornings I watched you get-

ting dressed — if only I'd paid attention.

Miss you.

xxb

Stately, gracious, old, the Timbers Mansion seemed to soak up all the sunshine on
the street. I walked slowly up the soft stone
steps, taking in the worn bricks and faded
marble columns. A hundred years ago, in
1910, when *Delicious!* magazine moved in,
Greenwich Village must have been full of
houses just like this, but now the mansion
was the last one standing on this narrow
tree-lined street.

Inside, the high-ceilinged lobby was dark
and cool. The guard at the antique desk
glanced up. "First day, right?" He waved
me toward the staircase. "Jake's expecting
you. Second floor."

The day of my interview, I'd been too
nervous to notice much, but now I looked
around, taking in the details. How amazing
to be working in this gorgeous old house,
surrounded by marble, carved oak, and
chandeliers. There must be a fireplace in
every room, and ancient windows with wavy
handblown panes captured the sun and
drew it inside.

Jake was waiting on the second floor

beneath a silver chandelier. His dog was there too, leaping ecstatically to greet me as if I were his favorite person in the world. I reached down to pat him, but he jumped up, put his paws on my chest, and tried to lick my face. I laughed.

"Good thing you like dogs." Jake pulled him down. "That temp they sent was terrified of Sherman." He tugged gently on the dog's silky ears. "But you didn't think much of her either, did you, boy? The woman was a disaster. Poor Billie's got no idea what a mess she's walking into."

I liked the sound of that; it was bound to make me look competent. As he led me down the quiet hall, I imagined a desk piled with papers reaching to the ceiling, imagined myself efficiently creating order out of chaos. I figured the sooner I could please him, the sooner he'd start throwing small writing assignments my way.

Jake gestured at the closed doors around us. "By ten, most of them will be here." He said it apologetically, as if his entire staff had failed the work-ethic test. At the moment the empty corridor, with its thick carpet and graceful torch-shaped sconces, felt more like a fancy hotel than a place where any work got done.

The illusion ended when we got to my

"office," which was a dreary little cubbyhole, sparsely efficient, with nothing but a desk, a phone, and a computer. Jake didn't stop, so I followed him through into his office, blinking at the sudden burst of light pouring through the large arched windows.

Sherman went to the desk, circled three times, and flopped down beneath it. I looked around, studying my surroundings. The room was an even bigger mess than last time — books, manuscripts, and newspapers were scattered everywhere. It smelled like leather and lingering wood smoke; apparently the fireplace worked. There was a round table in front of it, heaped with books and magazines that probably hadn't been touched in the ten days since my interview.

Jake sat down in the chair behind the desk. "Sit down, sit down," he said, waving vaguely.

Where? The scuffed leather sofa beneath the windows held even more manuscripts and magazines than the table did. The two deep armchairs weren't any better; they too were piled with manuscripts and folders. I glanced at the little end table, but the bronze elephant sculpture on it had sharp edges. In the end I went over to one of the chairs and perched on an armrest.

Jake looked amused. "You go to orientation?"

I nodded.

"So you know this is just a trial period? That it'll be three months before the job's official?"

I nodded again. He was watching me, waiting. When the pause got uncomfortable, he said, "Your letter of recommendation mentioned that you're kind of quiet."

I am. Genie's always talked enough for both of us.

"Your professor also said you're an eloquent writer and a, quote, awesome, unquote, cook. You looked so uncomfortable when I asked you to cook, I was sure he'd gotten that wrong. You went completely white. I admired your pluck for going through with it, but frankly I wasn't expecting much. Then you made that gingerbread. . . ."

"Even Maggie seemed to like it."

Maybe I shouldn't have said that. His eyes narrowed, moving over me. I sat up straighter; I'm tall and I have a tendency to slouch. Dad's always trying to persuade me that I'd be pretty if I'd do something with my hair or buy better glasses, but he's my father, so of course he thinks that. I tugged at the cuffs on my white shirt and smoothed

30

the loose khaki pants. "She said you'd never hire me."

"Maggie says that to everyone. She's allergic to change." He fiddled with the ebony letter opener and added, "And as you clearly noticed, she's got something of a mean streak." He stood up abruptly. "C'mon." He made for the door. "I'll take you around and introduce you."

By now the doors were all open, and we went into one office after another: executive editor, managing editor, articles editor, fact checker, copy editor. . . . It was a blur of names and titles, which made it easy; all I had to do was shake hands and say hello. Everyone seemed friendly and slightly harried. No small talk required.

The last door on the hall remained closed, and Sherman began to paw at it, trying to nudge it open with his nose. "Give it up, pal." Jake pulled the dog away. "Sammy's not here."

I traced the letters on the old-fashioned brass nameplate with my finger. " 'Samuel Winthrop Stone.' "

"Travel editor." Jake gave the dog's collar another tug. "C'mon, Sherman, Sammy's in Morocco. No smoothie for you. Maybe you'll have better luck in the kitchen."

At the word "kitchen," Sherman pricked

31

up his ears and raced for the stairs. "This dog is so smart." Jake said it softly, as if worried that Sherman might overhear. "He loves smoothies, and he knows exactly who the suckers are. Paul even brought in a special little juicer just for him."

I followed them up the stairs. "The art department's on four," said Jake, pointing. I followed his finger, noticing the graceful plaster swags and garlands decorating the walls. The Timbers Mansion really was beautiful; if Genie were here she'd be reaching for her sketch pad. "Library's up there too, but you don't need to worry about that: It's been locked for years. Down here" — we'd reached the third-floor landing and he turned left, sweeping me into an enormous cream-colored room — "is the kitchen, which you've seen, and the photo studio, which you haven't."

The photo studio must once have been a ballroom. Even now, with lights dangling from the ceiling, thick electrical cords snaking along the floor, and half a dozen tripod-mounted cameras, it clung so stubbornly to the past that I could easily imagine an orchestra tuning up for the next waltz. As we watched, the door to the kitchen opened and a woman inched out backward, carefully sheltering an arrangement of vegetables.

"That's Lori," Jake whispered. "She's a food stylist — and our best baker." Taking tiny steps, she edged into the middle of the room and very slowly lowered the plate onto a pedestal in front of a huge cloth-covered camera.

"Valente?" Jake called, and a short, solid man surprised me by emerging from beneath the cloth. He shook my hand briefly and then ducked back inside the camera. Jake and I watched Lori fussing with the plate, moving microgreens and midget carrots first one way, then the other. She picked up a tiny brush from a tray sitting on a nearby table and fastidiously applied olive oil, then added flecks of cheese, one by one, with a pair of tweezers. From beneath the cloth, Valente directed the precise positioning of each tiny morsel.

"Move the parsley to the right, Lori," Valente ordered. She pinched up a minuscule bit of green with her tweezers, moving it an infinitesimal fraction of an inch.

Suddenly the door flew open and Maggie came charging in. At the sight of her, a spark of adrenaline shot through me; was I going to have to see her every day? Buoyed by the breeze, the parsley leapt into the air, and as it floated back down, Valente appeared again. "Damn it, Maggie," he shouted, "now we have to start over."

"Oh, sorry." She was unconcerned. Valente snorted and pulled the cloth back over his head. She turned to Jake. "Do me a favor? I need really good anchovies, and Thursday's cornered the market on menaicas." She made a face, doing that thing with her lips that made her look as if she'd swallowed vinegar. "Again. If I send a messenger it'll take all day. Do you think the new girl could . . . ?"

Jake seemed embarrassed, reluctant to ask me to run this errand but even more reluctant to turn Maggie down. He shrugged and turned to me. "Do you mind? Thursday's the chef at The Pig."

"I've heard of her." You'd have to be a hermit not to know about America's most famous female chef. "Her picture was on *Eater* this morning; Patti Smith threw a big party at The Pig last night."

"I know; I was there." Jake handed me a twenty. "Grab a cab. It's not far, just into Chelsea, but it'll be faster."

Fifteen minutes later I was standing on 16th Street, so far west I could see the Hudson River. From outside, The Pig looked like

34

any other scruffy tavern. I'd been expecting something fancier, or at least more exotic. In the famous Annie Leibovitz picture "Midnight at The Pig," the restaurant has a dark, gritty glamour. The photographer had caught Keith Richards lounging across a scarred wooden table, surrounded by eccentric friends. The picture always made me think of Paris in the twenties — you wanted to be there — and I'd anticipated something with a bit more style.

I banged on the door until a tattooed man with a nose ring finally let me in. It smelled like spilled whiskey, and daylight had drained every bit of romance from the room. "Thursday's in back," said a man with a ponytail from behind the bar, jerking his head toward a swinging door. He tossed an empty bottle into a giant garbage can. It clattered noisily to the bottom.

I gave the battered door a push. The kitchen was dim and much smaller than an average California kitchen, so crammed with industrial equipment that there was barely room to move. Thursday was standing at the stove, swathed in a cloud of steam. She was elegantly beautiful, with an ash-blond braid reaching almost to her waist and big black-lashed eyes that hovered somewhere between gray and blue. "I'm —"

35

I began.

"Taste this." Thursday thrust a large wooden spoon into my mouth. Her eyes watched closely as I swallowed. She had fed me a fluffy cloud, no more than pure texture, but as it evaporated it left a trail of flavor in its wake.

"Lemon peel," I said, "Parmesan, saffron, spinach." She held out another spoonful, and this time, at the very end, I tasted just a touch of . . . something lemony but neither lemon nor verbena. It had a faint cinnamon tinge. "Curry leaf!"

"I'm impressed." Her hands were on her slim hips and her voice was — what? Sarcastic? "But I didn't mean it as a test. I just wanted to see if I'm getting anywhere with this new gnocchi."

"That's an amazing combination. The saffron's brilliant — it gives it such a sunny flavor. But what made you use curry leaf? I never would have thought of that."

"It kind of came to me at the last minute. So you think it works?"

"Yes! But maybe you should use a little more?"

I blushed; who was I to be giving Thursday Brown advice? But she was tasting the gnocchi, rubbing her lips together in that way that chefs do. "You think so?"

I was about to ask if I could taste it again when she cried, "Sal!" with such delight that I looked over my shoulder. A tall, broad man in a baseball cap was standing in the doorway. He had the look of a plumber come to fix a leak — blue jeans, work boots, and a plain blue work shirt. He was probably fifty, but his face had a curious innocence. When he removed his cap, a thatch of thick, graying dark hair sprang joyfully upward. Thursday scooped up another gnocchi. "We were tasting my new gnocchi." She thrust one into his mouth. "What do you think? She — what did you say your name was? — thinks I need more curry leaf."

"I didn't, actually. Billie Breslin."

Thursday looked at me now, really taking me in. "So you're Jake's new assistant? That should work out well. I bet there isn't one person in a hundred — no, a thousand — who'd know there was curry leaf in there."

"Curry leaf?" Sal tasted again. "There isn't one person in a thousand who's even heard of it." He was studying me the way Thursday had, as if he were trying to see into my mind. "One taste and you could tell it was there?"

"Yeah. Curry leaf doesn't taste like anything else. It's like there's an echo of

37

cinnamon right behind the lemon."

Sal reached into the pot and scooped up another gnocchi. "You're right!" He sounded truly excited. He turned to Thursday. "And she's right about using more too. But if you ask me, you're using the wrong cheese. That's the fall Parmigiano — am I right? — and it's too rich. You need the spring cheese. I'll send you some."

Definitely not a plumber.

"I need that cheese right now!" She turned to look at me again. "Sal knows more about cheese than anyone in this city. Why don't you go with him? Fontanari's isn't far, and he can give you my cheese. By the time you get back I'll have figured out where I put those anchovies."

I hesitated. "I really should get back. . . ."

"You're new to New York, right?"

I nodded.

"Then you need to see Sal's shop. Fontanari's is incredible; every cook should know it."

"I'm not a cook."

"You *aren't*?" She peered at me as if she'd just encountered a rare specimen in the zoo. "With that palate? Then what the hell are you doing at *Delicious!*?"

"Oh, leave her alone, Thursday," said Sal. "You're embarrassing her."

I smiled gratefully. "I'd love to come with you, but Maggie wanted me to bring the anchovies right back."

Thursday crossed her arms. "She'll wait. I don't even know where I put the damn jar. Go on, now!"

She made little shooing motions with her hands, and resistance seemed futile. I followed Sal out the door.

"That's right." Sal gave me a cheerful smile. "No point in arguing with a chef. They're all bossy, but Thursday's the worst. Did you know she once worked at *Delicious!*?" He glanced down at me. "I can see from your face that you're wondering how that turned out. Well, let me tell you, it was pretty bad. Thursday was just out of culinary school, but even then she had to have her own way. She and Maggie . . ." He whistled. "All I can say is, when it comes to Thursday, there's no point in arguing. You might as well give in at the start. Where you from?"

"Santa Barbara —"

"Now, me, I'm from right here." To my relief, Sal was as talkative as he was kind; I wouldn't have to say a word. "My family shop's been on the same corner in Little Italy for a hundred years."

"Little Italy?" I tried to remember where that was.

"Just a couple of miles," he said comfortably. "A good walk that will take us past some of the finest food in the world. Coming from — where'd you say you were from? This is going to be a treat for you."

"Santa Barbara. Maybe we can take a cab?" I pleaded.

"A cab?" He sounded scandalized. "To go a couple miles? If you're going to be a New Yorker, you'll have to learn to walk. It's the only way to get around this town. Besides, this way I can give you my personal tour."

Sal walked through the streets as if they belonged to him, utterly indifferent to the concept of straight lines. He meandered, breaking off in the middle of a sentence to beckon me across the street and point out the attractions of some shop. Everything from hats to hardware captured his curiosity. The nightclubs and restaurants of the Meatpacking District were still sleeping, but once we got to Bleecker Street he stopped every few feet to peer into the windows of bookstores, toy shops, and art galleries. The neighborhood aged as we walked south, and as the shops grew more venerable he paused to breathe in the aroma of old bakeries and to appreciate salvage shops, cutting a zigzag path so we missed nothing. I'd never met anyone like Sal; his knowledge was encyclopedic, and he seemed to know everyone we passed. Part of me knew I should get back to the office, but he was taking so much pleasure from this walk that I found myself irresistibly drawn in, sharing his pleasure, enjoying the moment.

"Joey! Great to see you!" Crossing Seventh Avenue, Sal had spotted a policeman. "Where you been? It's been a while. Please don't tell me you're buying your salami somewhere else."

"The line at your place is always so long." The cop actually looked guilty.

"Not for you." Sal put his arm around the policeman's shoulders. "Never for the boys in blue. Come see us soon, okay? My sister, Theresa, misses you. We all do."

Every panhandler got a dollar and a "Good luck to you." "Rosalie — that's my wife — thinks I'm too soft a touch, but I say, there but for the grace of God. I'd rather be a fool than hard-hearted." He swiped a hand across the upturned nose that made his face so amiable.

"There's Benny!" He waved me across Carmine Street. "You have to meet him. I bet you don't have any real butchers in Santa Barbara, and Benny's one of the greats."

He led me proudly into a shop that looked

41

as if it had been here, unchanged, for at least a hundred years. There was sawdust on the floor, and the clean forest scent hung in the air, mingling with the mineral aroma of good meat. Framed in bouquets of parsley, the various cuts were proudly displayed in a tall refrigerated cabinet. Sitting on top was a huge old-fashioned roll of pink butcher paper; an antique dispenser of twine dangled above it. Photographs of customers were everywhere, and a huge calico cat sat curled on a bench, purring loudly.

The man behind the counter had a blood-stained apron wrapped around his mountain of a body. He looked like an aging prize-fighter, and everything about him — body, hands, even his feet — seemed thick. But when he smiled, I saw that the gap between his teeth made him less formidable. Sal pushed me forward. "Meet Billie. She's just gone to work for Jake."

Benny held out a mammoth hand. "Come on back here." He swept me behind the counter and through a heavy wooden door. It was dark and cold in the meat locker, and I found myself staring at a quarter of a steer hanging from a hook. "Look at that loin!" Benny swung the carcass onto a scarred slab of wood. "Do you know where the T-bone ends and the porterhouse begins?"

I shook my head. He began cutting up the animal, and I stood watching, mesmerized. I'd never seen a real butcher work, and Benny was as precise as a surgeon as he showed me how the muscles met, his knife flashing down with incredible speed, carving up steaks, roasts, and chops. Benny's whole appearance changed when he had a knife in his hand, each motion so sure and economical that the bulky torso became graceful. It was like watching a bullfight, without the thrilling terror of the kill.

Benny held up a long loin of prime aged meat, its exterior hardened into a crust the color of withered roses. Picking up a thin blade, he trimmed the crust off with a single pass of the knife. The meat beneath was bright red and heavily marbled with fat. "Some people think that wet-aging in Cryovac is just as good as dry-aging. Sure, it's cheaper. Sure, it's easier. But the only way you get a respectable steak is you let it hang a few weeks. Me? I like twenty-six days, but some like it longer. Concentrates the flavor. No other way to do it." He sheared off the thinnest sliver. "Open your mouth."

It was like nothing I'd tasted before, the rich slice melting onto my tongue, its texture so soft I barely needed to chew. The

43

flavor, on the other hand, was potent, filling my mouth with the slight tang of iron. "I don't think I've ever eaten anything more wonderful."

Benny beamed.

"You're lucky, kid." Sal touched my arm. "The old-time butchers are dying out. Take a lesson when it's offered. That's why you came to New York, right?"

"Yeah," Benny chimed in. "This is the Neanderthal approach, but it works. And New Yorkers, thank God, they appreciate an artisan."

"Benny's amazing," I said when we were back on the street.

"He doesn't always open up like that. Benny's stingy with his talent, but I think he saw something special in you. You want to know the truth? It was a treat for me too; that's the first time he's let me watch him butcher an entire hindquarter."

"Do you know everyone in every shop in this neighborhood?"

"Pretty much. I grew up here. I travel a lot — buying cheese for the store — but I'm always happiest at home. People will tell you food is better over in Europe, but don't you believe it. We've caught up; these days the place to be is New York."

"I wish I could spend all day just following you around. I want to meet everyone!" I looked down, guilty, at my watch; I'd been gone two hours.

"Don't worry" — he gave my arm a re-assuring pat — "not far now."

He kept walking, turning serenely onto Prince Street at a leisurely pace. But then he spotted someone on the next corner and began to trot down Thompson Street. "It's Kim!" He urged me to keep up. "She makes the best chocolates in the city. You have to meet her!"

I love chocolate.

Up ahead, an elegant Asian woman was standing in the door of a shop, waiting. "Sal!" Her voice was as delighted as that of a child who has sighted Santa.

"Meet Jake's new assistant. Billie Breslin. Kim Wong."

"Welcome." She opened the door to a quaint shop filled with sparkling glass cases, then reached for my hand and tugged me inside. The shop was dark and dramatic, the chocolates laid out on velvet and lit like jewels. It was the perfect setting for this delicate, bird-like woman with a face like carved ivory.

"I know you're a chocolate lover. I can always tell. I'm about to temper the chocolate. I have my own method; want to watch?"

"Could I?" Inside my head, a little voice was reminding me that I had to get back to the office, but it was drowned out by the scent of chocolate, which flooded all my senses with a heady froth of cocoa and coffee, passion fruit, cinnamon and clove. I closed my eyes, and for one moment I was back in Aunt Melba's kitchen with Genie.

I opened them to find Kim dancing with a molten river of chocolate. I stood hypnotized by the scent and the grace of her motions, which were more beautiful than any ballet. Moving constantly, she caressed the chocolate like a lover, folding it over and over on a slab of white marble, working it to get the texture right. She stopped to feed me a chocolate sprinkled with salt, which had the fierce flavor of the ocean, and another with the resonant intensity of toasted saffron. One chocolate tasted like rain, another of the desert. I tried tracking the flavors, pulling them apart to see how she had done it, but, like a magician, she had hidden her tricks. Each time I followed the trail, it vanished, and after a while I just gave up and allowed the flavors to seduce me.

Now the scent changed as Kim began to

dip fruit into the chocolate: raspberries, blackberries, tiny strawberries that smelled like violets. She put a chocolate-and-caramel-covered slice of peach into my mouth, and the taste of summer was so intense that I felt the room grow warmer. I lost all sense of time.

Sal was waiting outside, talking on his cell phone, but when he saw me he slipped it into his pocket. "You liked her chocolates!"

"She's a sorceress. That rain chocolate — it tasted the way the air smells just before a storm. I want to know how she does it. I identified hyssop and maybe myrtle and a bit of cassia, but then it got away from me. God, she's amazing!"

"Cassia, hyssop — you're really something. I wish my daughter had your talent for flavor. But" — he sighed — "Toni's a lawyer, and I'd bet she's never even heard of hyssop." He gave me a slightly guilty look. "Don't get me wrong; Toni's the most wonderful daughter a person could ask for. But she's never had an interest in our business."

Sal sounded so sad that I said impulsively, "I think my father feels the same way about me. He's a lawyer. My mother was too. Dad's the nicest man in the world, but I know he's disappointed. He would have

47

liked me to follow in their footsteps." Embarrassed at having said so much — too much? — I stared down at my watch again.

Sal reached out and covered it with his hand. "Don't worry." His voice was sympathetic. "Jake's a good guy. And" — he was watching me with a kind of compassion I found hard to interpret — "he'll understand that you saw an opportunity and seized it. Jake appreciates curiosity. And these are all people you should know if you're working at *Delicious!* Wait until you see our store!" He led me east past bakeries, butcher shops, and Chinese grocery stores. "Just a couple more blocks." He spread his arms wide, taking in the shops around us. "Aren't you glad you came to New York?"

His love for his city was so compelling that I found myself inhaling the aromas wafting from every door — roasting ducks, soy, dried mushrooms — with special pleasure.

"When we were growing up, my sister and I knew everyone on the block. But the neighborhood's changed. Good people, still, but mostly Asian now. Here we are!"

He turned in to a crowded shop, and the deep, pungent smell of cheese wrapped itself around us. I smelled garlic and tomatoes and, somewhere, the rich ancient scent of olives. Bottles of clear green olive oil and dark-purple vinegar glistened like stained glass, while hams and salamis dangled from hooks in the ceiling. Huge loaves of bread balanced precariously on the shelves behind the raised counter, and great bunches of herbs hung from the rafters. It was like walking into a small Italian village, a kaleidoscope of scent, sound, and color that shifted each time another person came in.

I'd never been inside a store like this one, never imagined a room filled with great wheels of cheese stacked so high they towered over me. There must have been three dozen people, all talking at the same time, their babble resonating like a flock of exotic, excited birds. An old lady with a cane reached to touch Sal's arm, and he bent to murmur Italian endearments in her ear. A little girl handed him a drawing, and he swept her off her feet, both of them laughing as he swung her into the air. An elegant old gentleman said in heavily accented English, "I've been waiting. You're the only one who cuts my cheese right," and Sal replied, "You know my sister, Theresa, always gives you extra." As he escorted me through the crowd, he whispered, "I want you to taste the cheese, so you understand why Thursday should be using the spring Parmigiano."

I'd forgotten about Thursday. "But I need to get her the cheese! She said she was going to wait."

"Relax." He was reaching for the nearest wheel of cheese, a huge round, nearly two feet tall. He gave it a good thump. "This is the spring Parmigiano."

And before I could stop him, he was off.

By this time I would have followed him anywhere. He showed me how each wheel was stamped with the month and year, and then he cracked the first one open to reveal its pale cream-colored interior. He chipped off a hefty shard and handed it to me. I took a bite, and my mouth filled with the hopeful taste of fresh green grass and young field flowers welcoming the sun.

"That's the spring cheese." Sal was cracking the next wheel, which was stamped with an autumn date; he chipped off a little piece. The color was deeper, almost golden, the texture heavier and nubbier. When I put the cheese in my mouth it was richer, and if I let it linger on my tongue I could taste the lush fields of late summer, just as the light begins to die.

Sal sliced off a slab of winter cheese and put that into my mouth. It felt different on my tongue, smoother somehow, the flavor sharper. "It's like a different cheese." I was savoring it. I tasted again; there was a familiar flavor. "It tastes like hay!"

"Yes!" Sal was openly delighted. "I *knew* you were going to be able to taste how different this cheese is! Most Americans don't even notice, but that cheese is so different that, back in the old days, it was sold under a different name. The Parmesan made from December to March, when the cows were in the barn, was called 'invernengo' — winter cheese — because the flavor is so distinct." He looked genuinely happy, as if he had met a kindred spirit, and I thought how hard it must be to care so much and have a clueless clientele. "Now I want to take you into the back kitchen and introduce you to my wife, Rosalie. She'll show you how we make the mozzarella."

I wasn't about to pass that up. But I glanced at my watch again, thinking that even Jake wasn't going to appreciate how fully I had seized this opportunity. "I might need a marketable skill. If they fire me" — I was only half joking — "will you give me a job?"

"They're not going to fire you." He picked up an apron. "But if they do, there's a place for you at Fontanari's."

But the mention of the magazine seemed to jog his memory. He looked up at the clock. "It's after three! You'd better get the Parmigiano to Thursday right away. I hope she's not too upset." He handed me a package. "If you have any trouble, tell Jake to call me. But I meant what I said: You can always have a job here." He gave me a shrewd look. "I know it's not your first choice, but it could be worse. We pay a lot better than the slave wages they hand out over at Pickwick Publications. You wouldn't have to stay all night either. And you'd learn a lot."

"Thanks."

Sal put his hand on my arm. "Got any friends in New York?"

"I just got here."

"If you find that you're lonely on the weekend, we can always use an extra pair of hands. I like you, kid. Don't be a stranger."

Thursday is a small woman, and every review mentions she has eyes like pansies and enormous charm. But she was scowling when I got back to The Pig. "I was hoping to use this today." She held out her hand. "I should have sent a messenger. I expect Maggie was hoping the same." She shook her head. "Wasn't this your first day on the job?"

"Yeah," I said. "I guess I blew it."

She gave me an enigmatic look and went back to stirring her pot.

The cab I'd managed to hail crept through traffic, and I sat there wondering if I still had a job at *Delicious!* Probably not. Working at Fontanari's wouldn't be so bad. I could always temp. Maybe I could even try to freelance. It had been worth it; I wouldn't trade this day away for anything.

On the other hand, I'd just blown the best job in New York. I was a total idiot.

I reached the Timbers Mansion in a schizophrenic state and went racing up the stairs. I barreled into the kitchen with such force that the door almost sent Maggie, who was standing behind it, reeling into a counter. Surrounded by a semicircle of cooks, she rubbed her arm and peered accusingly at me. I handed her the anchovies and turned to go.

"Wait!" Maggie's voice was imperious. She had set the jar on the counter and stood staring at her watch. "Congratulations. You've clocked the slowest time in *Delicious!* history."

"Excuse me?"

"In the eight years we've been sending people off to take the Sal Test, no one's ever stayed away this long."

"The Sal Test?" There was a beat as all

the cooks looked at me expectantly. "What are you talking about?" My eyes moved from one face to another, trying to understand what was going on. When I finally got it, a wave of laughter swept through me, mingled with relief, indignation, and disbelief.

"Are you telling me you *planned* that?" I said when I was finally able to speak. "Thursday was in on it? Benny? Kim? They *all* were?"

Maggie nodded. "A waste of everybody's time, if you ask me," she said sourly. "But Jake doesn't want to be surrounded by what he calls 'corporate widgets.' He appreciates 'curiosity.' " She even used air quotes.

I laughed again. Sal had been telling the truth. Something occurred to me. "Does anyone ever manage to escape?"

"Most do." Her voice implied that if I had any sense, I'd have been among them.

"What happened to them?"

"Jake paid them for their time, thanked them very much, and told them they wouldn't be happy here." She walked away. "Oh, yeah," she called over her shoulder, "thanks for the anchovies."

"Did you even need them?"

But she was gone.

"No," said a pretty cook with a heart-shaped face. "She's got two jars in her refrigerator." She had straight black brows sitting like dashes above widely spaced brown eyes, and they were raised now, as if she was trying to make up her mind. Then the brows relaxed and she held out her hand.

"I'm Diana. Maggie would never tell you this, but after you left the shop, Sal called Jake. He told him you have an extraordinary palate. He said he didn't know how Jake had found you, but he should not, under any circumstances, let you go. He said you belong here. Welcome to *Delicious!*"

GUARANTEED

"Did you get those approved?" The creative director was standing at my desk, staring critically at the daisies I'd bought at the corner deli.

Richard Phillips was the most attractive man I'd ever met. His olive skin, emerald eyes, and chiseled cheekbones gave him the languid, unshaven arrogance of a model, but he wore quirky old clothes, which softened the impact of his beauty. The smile was even more effective; I watched warmth transform his face, taking him from sexy to sweet as it traveled from his mouth to his eyes.

"Don't you know we have rules about these things? Daisies in the Timbers Mansion . . ." His face was so serious, I couldn't tell if he was teasing me.

"Rules for daisies?"

"Oh, yes. Martha Stewart has nothing on us." He flicked his blue-black ponytail over one shoulder. "Stop looking at me like I'm speaking Martian."

"I don't understand."

"If you worked over at her book, you'd have to get every photograph and flower approved. You hadn't heard?"

"Even family pictures?"

"Especially those." Head cocked to one side, he was focused on the daisies again. "I mean, it's true about Martha. I don't think Jake would care if you stacked a pile of used tires on your desk. But now that you mention it" — he scribbled something on a piece of paper — "we *should* have standards." He handed the paper over. "Call this number, ask for Sharon, and say you're a friend of Sammy's."

"The travel editor? I haven't even met him yet."

"You will. He can't stay in Marrakech forever. You'll learn it never hurts to say you're a friend of Sammy's. He knows everybody, and everybody loves him." He executed a lazy 360 around my little space; when he faced me again, he was holding the daisies. "Tell Sharon to send you something small and intriguing once a week. Put it on Jake's expense account. He'll never notice." And he dropped the daisies in the trash.

"I just bought those!" I protested.

He wiggled his fingers at me and disappeared into Jake's office. Diana had told me that everybody at the magazine had a crush on Richard, and not just because he was such a beautiful man. He was also talented and so calm that I found talking to him very easy.

But I knew he was not for me. With a sister like mine, you learn to limit your expectations. Genie had star power even when we were children, and by the time I was a teenager, every guy we ever met was so busy looking at her slanting violet eyes and curly blond hair they barely noticed me. She and Richard would make a dazzling couple; I was picturing it when the phone began to ring.

"Jake Newberry's office. May I help you?"

"I'm looking for the recipe for my mother's famous coffee cake," the caller began. "I'm pretty sure it came from an issue in the fifties. It was very rich and contained a lot of nuts."

"What kind of nuts?" I asked.

"Maybe pecans," she replied. "And there might have been a layer of marzipan running through it? Or maybe I'm remembering that wrong. But it was a great cake, and I promised to bring it to brunch tomorrow."

"If you tell me how to reach you, I'll see

what I can do." I hung up the phone. "How am I supposed to find it from that ridiculous description?"

"Don't waste your time." I jumped; I hadn't seen Richard come out of Jake's office. "Most of these people are crazy. Take the easy way out."

"I should ignore her?"

"You should ask Maggie. She knows by heart almost every recipe we've ever printed. I'm on my way to the kitchen. Come along; I'll protect you." He took my hand and pulled me out of my chair.

Sherman had followed Richard into my office, and I reached down to pet him. "Come with us, dog," I called. Sherman made the office feel so friendly. "Maybe someone will make you a smoothie."

With Richard at my side, I was less afraid of facing Maggie, but when we got upstairs, she took one look at us and said, with real venom in her voice, "You know I don't like that creature in my kitchen!" I gasped; it seemed a little harsh, even for her.

"It's not like I sent the dog an invitation," Richard replied, and I let out my breath, realizing she hadn't meant me. "Is it my fault if he followed me? Blame it on Paul and his magic smoothie machine." Sherman, who obviously had no fear of Maggie, took this

59

as his cue to go trotting off in search of sustenance. "Billie's wondering," Richard went on, "if you remember a spectacular coffee cake from the fifties that had a lot of nuts —"

Maggie was answering before he'd even finished the sentence. "The Fountain's Famous French Nut Cake. October 1956. Tell whoever wants the recipe that the timing's right; you *must* cream the sugar into the butter for as long as it says. If you get lazy, it's not lethal, but it's pretty leaden."

I was impressed in spite of myself. "Thanks," I said.

She finally deigned to acknowledge my presence. "Don't think I'm going to answer every reader question. I've got better things to do. That's why we hired you." She stomped off before I could come up with a suitable retort, dragging Richard in her wake.

"Don't take it personally, Gingerbread Girl." Diana had materialized at my side. "She's mean to everyone." I looked down at her feet; she was short and always wore wildly inappropriate high heels in the kitchen. Today's pair were blue suede. "You get used to it. But I'm glad you're here; I've been wanting to ask about your gingerbread.

It's the best thing anyone's made for Jake's stupid test since that red salad of Richard's."

"What kind of red salad?"

"Roasted beets. Radicchio. Swiss chard. Red onions. A dollop of sour cream. Gorgeous. Brilliant. Jake put it on the cover. But what I want to know is where you got your recipe."

"I made it up."

The eyebrows rose in surprise. "Really?"

"Yeah. When I was ten. For my dad's birthday."

I could tell from Diana's face that she didn't believe me. "Ten?" She gave a skeptical sigh. "Okay, if you're such a genius, tell me what's missing in this." She handed me a spoon. "I'm meant to be making the world's richest chocolate ice cream."

Yes, the ice cream was rich, but a bit cloying; the sugar was playing hide-and-seek with the chocolate. "You need a little less sugar and a pinch of salt. And I'd throw a quarter cup of cocoa powder in with the melted chocolate."

Diana's eyebrows did that dash thing again. She stuck her finger into the bowl and licked it thoughtfully. "I think you may be right about the chocolate."

I dipped my finger in; I *was* right. "You

used good chocolate, but you can get better cream, right? I bet Fontanari's sells great cream; it'd make a huge difference. I could pick some up for you."

Diana punched me lightly on the arm. "I guess Maggie's got a point."

"About what?"

"Thursday apparently told her you don't cook, and Maggie thinks you're wasting our time. But what you're really wasting is your talent. Sal's right about your palate, and I bet you'd be an awesome cook. Not my business, of course."

How could I even begin to tell her?

"Anyway, it's not you." Diana had sensed my discomfort, and she looped back to Maggie. "She's always mean to Jake's assistants. You'd think she'd be over him by now; it's such ancient history."

"They used to have a thing?" Google hadn't mentioned that. I looked to the far end of the room, where Maggie was standing next to a man I assumed was Paul, pointing down at something he was stirring in a pot. She was a lot younger than I'd thought at first, probably in her fifties, and she had great bones. If I tried hard, I could see her as one of those artsy beatnik girls who wore black turtlenecks, black tights, and black ballet slippers.

"It was a long time ago." Diana had followed my gaze. "Back around 1980, when Jake was really hot. They even had a restaurant. I think it was called Maja. That's all I know, but you should ask Sammy when he gets back. He knows all our secrets, and he loves to gossip. You'll see; we have much more fun when he's around. He —"

She broke off as someone shouted, "Taste!"

Tossing me an apologetic look, Diana joined the other cooks as they descended on a dish that had just emerged from the oven. Then they all began to talk at once.

"Have you tried roasting this beef at a lower temperature?" It was Lori, the stylist. "I'd bring it down twenty-five degrees."

"Put more liquid in the pan, Paul." One of the cooks was poking at the bottom of the pan. "Your onions are dry!"

"I'm not sure about the seasoning." Diana pursed her lips. "Marjoram with beef?"

"I like the marjoram," said another cook — I still couldn't keep them straight — "but what's the other flavor in there? The one that's closing my throat?"

"Fenugreek." Paul held out a handful of tiny rust-colored pebbles. "Too weird?"

I listened, thinking how lucky I was to have landed in the one place on earth where

63

recipes were taken this seriously. The cooks tested these dishes almost to absurdity, redoing them again and again, using a pinch more of this or a tiny bit less heat, trying to make each dish as perfect as possible. They were all dedicated to getting it right, and when I was here among them, it made me wish I were cooking again. But although the panic was letting me be for now, I knew it wasn't gone. I could sense it out there, always waiting, and I was not about to invite it back into my life. For now, just being here was enough.

"Okay." Maggie took control. "Try it again, Paul. Lower temperature. More liquid. Reconsider your seasonings. Got it?"

The taste was winding down. I whistled for Sherman, who trotted toward me, tail waving like a flag. No point in giving Maggie another opportunity to attack.

Back on the second floor, I went into Jake's office, trying to decode his expression. Irritation? Should I not have taken Sherman to the kitchen? Maybe I'd been away from my desk too long?

"I was just asking Maggie for help with a recipe."

"Good idea." Jake nodded. "She's a font of *Delicious!* information."

"But wouldn't it be easier if you gave me the key to the library? Then I could look things up." And stay away from Maggie.

Jake shook his head. "Not going to happen. In the old days, they had a full-time librarian. But long before I got here, that position was eliminated. The place was a shambles: People'd been taking books and not returning them or just leaving them in piles on the floor. It was such a mess we decided to lock it up. And it's going to stay locked until we can afford another librarian. Which," he added gloomily, "is not likely to be anytime soon."

"I'd put everything back where I found it," I said.

"I'm sure you would." Jake gave me a conciliatory smile. "But if I let you in, I'd have to let everyone else in too. So, no, I'm sorry, you're going to have to depend on the database."

"And Maggie," I said glumly.

"That's not what I want to talk about. You've been here two weeks," he began, so hesitantly that I got nervous. Was he about to tell me the trial wasn't going so well? "And it's time you tackled one of the most important parts of your job. What do you know about the *Delicious!* Guarantee?"

" 'Your money back if the recipe doesn't work'?"

Jake nodded. "So you've heard of it."

"I always assumed it was a gimmick."

"Oh, it's real. When the first Arthur Pickwick started the magazine, he wanted to make a splash. It was a hundred years ago, and back then everybody was trying to make recipes more efficient. But nobody'd ever come up with the idea of *guaranteeing* them. *The New York Times* called it one of the most brilliant public-relations ploys of all time. Everybody assumed Young Arthur would put an end to it when he took over, but he decided not to mess with success."

"Don't you end up refunding an awful lot of money?"

Jake shook his head. "The truth is, we rarely send anyone a refund."

"So it *is* a trick!"

"Not at all. The offer's real. But most people can't follow instructions. They think they're making our recipe, but what they're really doing is inventing their own. What *you* have to do is go through the recipe with them, step by step, and try to figure out where they went off the rails."

"That sounds like fun."

"I hope you're still saying that a week from now." Jake handed me a pile of letters.

"But that's highly unlikely. As you can see, most of the people who write in don't even own computers, which says a lot about who they are. My last assistant loathed the Guarantee."

I picked up the first letter, which was from a Little Rock matron who'd sustained a severe risotto disaster. Jake was right: When I called, it turned out she'd used Minute Rice. Mrs. Amanda Bienstock had substituted baking powder for baking soda in her cake ("Really, what's the difference?" she complained). As for the woman whose batter had overflowed, causing enough smoke to bring out the fire department, she'd seen no reason why a recipe for a dozen cupcakes wouldn't fit into a six-inch cake pan.

John Kroger of Boulder, Colorado, was a different case. In a calm voice, he told me he'd followed the instructions to the letter. "When it said to toss the salad," he said earnestly, "I did just that. And, believe you me, it wasn't easy getting all that lettuce into the bowl from the other side of the room."

I couldn't dispute his point. I promised him a refund and picked up the next letter.

"I am absolutely furious about the scallop mousse in the current issue," wrote a Mrs. Cloverly from Cleveland. "It is simply vile."

On the phone, her querulous voice conjured up white hair and a pasty body muffled in a voluminous apron. "I have made a great many dishes in my life," she informed me, "and this was, without any doubt, the vilest of the lot."

I tried to sound sympathetic. "I'm so sorry, let me find that recipe." I punched it into the database and up it came, along with ecstatic four- and five-star reader comments.

"I would never have believed," a reader wrote, "that scallops, cream, a couple of eggs, and a splash of wine could make anything so divine."

Mrs. Cloverly had indeed gone off the rails.

"This is the first complaint we've had about that recipe —"

"Most people are just too lazy to call!" I pictured her shaking a finger at the phone. "But that is a dreadful recipe, and I consider it my duty to warn other cooks away. A magazine that once employed James Beard has no business running such trash. And I'd like to point out that those ingredients were very costly. I expect you to honor the *Delicious!* Guarantee and refund the money that I spent!"

"Let's see where the problem might lie," I

began. "Let's start with the scallops: What kind did you buy? The large sea scallops or the little bay kind?"

"Oh, really!" Her voice was chilly now. "I would never purchase scallops. They are far too expensive. I substituted canned clams."

"Any other substitutions?" I inquired. "Perhaps you used half and half in place of heavy cream?"

"Don't be ridiculous!" Now she was cross. "I never have cream in the house; it is far too rich. I always use powdered milk."

"Of course." I could almost see her kitchen as she talked. It would be small — maybe a double-wide trailer, with one of those half refrigerators and a tiny stove. She sounded so sad. "I don't imagine you had any wine on hand?"

"I used water. But I did add a bit of lemon juice to give it some zip."

Trying to imagine how this bizarre amalgamation might have tasted, I suffered a complete failure of the imagination.

"It was vile," she told me. "Simply vile. Will you stand behind your Guarantee?"

What was I supposed to do? "May I put you on hold?" I asked. "For a moment?"

"You must be new." Her voice had grown suspicious. "That other girl never put me on hold."

"Never?" Just how often had Mrs. Cloverly called? "It will be only a moment," I said.

"Never mind." Her voice filled with weary resignation. "I know what you're going to say." A bitter note crept in. "One more institution that lies to the public and refuses to honor its promises."

She sounded so lonely, so filled with despair. "Send us your receipts, Mrs. Cloverly," I blurted out. "We want everyone to be satisfied with the recipes in *Delicious!*"

"Really?" She sounded shocked. "Are you sure?"

"Yes, ma'am." But as the words came out of my mouth, I suddenly saw the truth: Mrs. Cloverly was one of Jake's decoys. I had fallen into another trap.

"Why, thank you very much, dear." She sounded so triumphant that for a moment I almost believed she was for real. "It's good to know there are still people who believe in honoring their promises. You have yourself a blessed day."

"You too, Mrs. Cloverly." She'd overdone it with the blessing bit.

"Cloverly?" Richard had come in to inspect the new flowers, and he reached out an elegant index finger to pet a hydrangea. "Did I just hear you offer her a refund? Big

70

mistake."

"That's what I figured," I sighed. "I totally blew it, didn't I? She's another one of Jake's tests."

Richard looked puzzled.

"You know, like the Sal Test," I prompted. "Another way to find out if I'm right for *Delicious!*"

Richard's face cleared. "Not even Jake could dream up Mrs. Cloverly. What I meant was that now she's going to call twice a day. And all I can say is, good luck to you."

Jake appeared, leaning his long body against the doorframe. "Did I hear 'Cloverly'?"

"Yes." Richard was laughing. "Billie offered her a refund."

"You did what?" Jake looked horrified.

"I didn't know what else to do." I repeated the conversation, and Jake laughed so hard that Richard had to pound him on the back.

"Oh, Billie," he gasped when he could finally breathe again, "I'll be eating out on that story for weeks! Worth every penny that we'll pay her."

"But we can't refund everybody's money!" I said.

"Why not? Do you have any idea how much cheaper this is than hiring a PR firm? And I told you, the Guarantee is all about

71

public relations. But you've just encouraged our most incorrigible caller, and, believe me, you're going to regret it. The woman is relentless."

NOWHERE

Dear Genie,

I love this city so much. Some weekends I just get on the subway and get off in random neighborhoods, walking the streets, going in and out of bakeries and butcher shops. One day I went out to Jackson Heights and almost convinced myself I was in Delhi or Mumbai: The streets smell as if they've been curried, there are sweets shops everywhere, and men on the street sell paan, which turns your teeth bright red. I went into a supermarket where there were whole aisles of spices I've never seen before — kokum and black salt and mango powder. Getting out like that helps with the loneliness, but I find myself looking wistfully at all the paired-up people, wondering if I'll ever be like that again. The weekends can get long.

Weekdays are another matter — no

time to think. Jake never leaves till after nine, and I can't leave before he does. Last week, when we closed the issue, we were there till almost two in the morning. Jake ordered dinner in for us, but most nights I pick up takeout from Ming's, the little place on the corner, climb the stairs, turn on the TV, and fall asleep with the chopsticks in my hand.

Being the new girl at work makes me kind of edgy; they've all known one another forever, and it's hard to find a way in. But I think I'm starting to make a friend. Diana's one of the cooks, and she's been stopping by my desk to ask if I want to go to lunch or to suggest a quick drink after work. At first I thought she was being kind, but now I think it has something to do with the Sal Test. He told everyone about my palate, and she's intrigued; she keeps kind of testing me, which I find very funny. But I like her: She has a terrific sense of humor, and she doesn't seem to give a damn what anybody thinks. All the other cooks come to work in old clothes and sensible shoes, but she's always showing up in vintage clothes, very high heels, and lots of makeup. Would you think she was silly? You might.

Tonight she's taking me to friends-and-family night at some new restaurant a friend of hers is opening in Alphabet City. I guess her boyfriend didn't want to go. The place is called Nowhere. Stupid name, right? Like Who's on First? Hope it's fun.

I thought I should bring something as a thank-you for the dinner, and this afternoon I was passing a thrift store and saw a velvet beret in the window. I thought she might like it, but now I'm not so sure. What was I thinking? Me buying clothes for someone?

Dad and Aunt Melba seem to be doing okay without us. But Aunt Melba's driving me crazy; she keeps reminding me to call Dad, as if he couldn't pick up the phone if he wanted to talk to me.

Miss you. Miss you. Miss you.

xxb

Nowhere was aptly named, which was a relief; when you're by yourself, it's a lot less embarrassing to walk into a small nondescript restaurant than a big glitzy one. I perched on a stool at the minuscule counter in the front, put the gift-wrapped beret down next to me, and hoped Diana wouldn't be too long.

I tried pretending I was a restaurant critic, swiveling on my stool to scope out the small storefront. The owners hadn't done much besides cram in some booths they must've found in an old fifties diner. I got the feeling they'd begrudged the white paint on the pressed-tin ceiling and the sander for the soft wood floors. I ordered a glass of white wine and picked up the menu.

Fried pig's ears. Braised duck hearts with snails. Pork-snout terrine with pickles and toast. Grilled rabbit livers with bacon. Whole grilled mackerel. Lamb burgers. Breaded pig's tails . . . "As you can see," said a voice behind me, "my friend Tom's a nose-to-tail guy."

Diana was wearing a short plaid skirt with a tight black sweater and high black boots. I gestured apologetically at my worn khakis and frayed oatmeal sweater.

"You look fine. I'm overdressed."

"I love your skirt." I handed her the package before I lost my nerve. "This might go with it." Giving people presents is such an intimate act; you're basically telling them who you think they are, and if you're wrong, it's over.

But when Diana unwrapped the package, she went straight back to the ladies' room. And when she returned, she was wearing

76

the little velvet hat and a huge smile.

"God, it looks great on you," I said.

"I know! How could you tell?"

"I don't know. It just kind of reminded me of you."

I'd surprised her — in a positive way, which is what happens when you get a gift right. It was going to be a good night. I picked up the menu and began to read it out loud. "Will people really order this stuff?"

Her eyes opened wide. "In this neighborhood? Sure — the weirder the better."

"Nobody in Santa Barbara would eat pig's tails or duck hearts —" I was starting to say when the chef came out carrying a platter, and my words spluttered to an apologetic halt.

Tom was short and wide, with tattoos everywhere, even across the back of his shaved head. "Try my pig's ears." He set the platter on the counter. I picked up one of the crisp disks and found it was as crunchy as a potato chip, with a wonderful chew. We munched our way through the entire pile while the bartender kept our glasses filled with the cool, easy-to-drink wine. I began to reconsider the decor; it was rather cozy.

"Bet you can't guess the secret ingredient

in my lamb burgers." Tom handed us each a slider.

Diana took a bite. "Miso?" she guessed. Tom shook his head.

I bit in. "Fish sauce!" It was definitely fish sauce.

Tom looked at Diana. He rubbed his bald head. "Your friend's a big improvement on your usual date."

Diana swatted him. "Tom thinks my boyfriend's a pill."

"I don't think Ned's a pill," Tom objected. "Ned *is* a pill."

"Is he?" I asked when Tom had retreated to the kitchen.

"Nah." Diana twisted the ring on her finger. "Ned's an engineer, and you know how they are; they live on burgers and pizza. None of my food friends get what I'm doing with a guy who's not into food. But I don't see the point in being with someone who's just like you." She took a sip of her wine. "You seeing anyone?"

"Seriously? The only people I know here are the people at work. And you might have noticed that they're all old, gay, or female."

"Or Richard."

"Or Richard. Who is definitely out of my league."

She didn't contradict me.

"Besides," I continued, "with my hours, where would I find the time? You kitchen people work nine to five, but down in editorial we sometimes stay all night."

"Crazy hours," she admitted. "But I don't understand why you don't do a little something with yourself. You wear the dreariest clothes. And you could get cooler glasses —" She stopped and put her hand over her mouth, horrified. "I can't believe I said that. Too much wine. Sorry. I'm so sorry."

"No, it's okay. You're only saying what you think."

"No. It was definitely not okay. But there are things I don't get. You don't *seem* conceited, but maybe you don't care what people think of you?"

"That's funny," I told her. "I just wrote my sister that *you* don't seem to care what people think of you. I envy that. With me it's different. Genie's so beautiful that nobody ever looked at me, and it never seemed worth trying. Now I wouldn't even know where to start."

"Older sister?" I nodded, and Diana gave me a look that was filled with sympathetic understanding. "I guess I got lucky. Four older brothers. They always made me feel like I was the most wonderful creature in all of New Jersey, like they were privileged to have me in the house. My parents had a fit when I said I wanted to go to culinary school instead of college, and my brothers all stood up for me. My oldest brother, Michael, even offered to pay for it; he knew it was all I'd ever wanted to do." She hesitated a moment and then said quickly, as if she was afraid she'd lose the courage, "So can I ask another rude question? How come someone with a palate like yours doesn't cook?"

"I can cook." The words came out in a whisper. "In fact, my sister and I had a bakery."

"You had a bakery? No shit."

"Yeah, Cake Sisters. We started it when we were really young."

"You sold that gingerbread!" She was triumphant, like someone who'd just slid the missing piece of a jigsaw puzzle neatly into place. "That's where the recipe came from! You said you did it when you were ten."

I nodded. "That's how it all started. We made the gingerbread cake for my dad's birthday, and people began asking if they could buy one. The next thing we knew, we had a business. My sister decided we should branch out, and she invented the Giant Hostess Cupcake Cake. Then Aunt Melba had the idea of selling them in pairs, one a little smashed, like they always are in the supermarket."

Diana rubbed her forehead. "Cake Sisters. Cake Sisters. Could I have read about this?"

I shrugged. "It's possible. We got a lot of press: *Bon Appétit,* the *L.A. Times, The New York Times.* They liked taking pictures of my sister. She designed the cakes and I worked out the recipes. The first year we each created a signature cake. Genie's was called the Goddess: really tall, all white on the outside, wrapped in mountains of coconut and whipped cream, with a passion-fruit heart."

"And yours was called the Shrinking Violet. Unassuming on the outside but pretty special once you worked your way in." She reached over and squeezed my wrist.

"Wish I'd thought of that. You'd understand if you knew my sister." By now I was a little drunk. "One year Genie came up with Melting Cakes. You know, like flourless chocolate, the kind that are melted in the middle? They were gorgeous neon colors, and I made the flavors intense — blood orange, blueberry, lime, hibiscus, and caramel. But it was our wedding cakes that really made us famous. All different, and nothing like anything else out there."

"But you don't have the bakery anymore. What happened? You sell it? Or did you poison someone and have to flee the state?"

"We started Cake Sisters when we were so young. And then . . ." I shrugged. "We grew up."

"You should tell Maggie. Bet she'd lighten up."

"No!" The word came out louder than I'd intended. "You can't tell anyone. Promise me that."

Diana looked at me strangely. She had to be wondering. . . . Maybe she'd Google us. Would that be so bad? "Okay, Gingerbread Girl" — she swiped her index finger across her heart — "your secret's safe with me." Just then Tom plunked down a plate of roasted pineapple, asking if he'd used too much rum.

We stayed late, drinking endless glasses of wine. We talked about the people at the magazine and about her boyfriend. She asked if I was sorry I'd dropped out of school. That was an easy answer.

"I've always liked to write, and I figured I should just do it. Get on-the-job training. Now all I have to do is figure out how I can get Jake to give me an assignment."

Diana waved her hand. "No worries; make

it through the trial period and he'll start shoving assignments at you till you scream. He likes having his assistants write for the book."

"I'd heard that; it's why I took the job. Then I saw that the last one — Sarah? — never had a byline, and I began to worry that it wasn't true."

"Sarah was a disappointment; none of us liked her very much. Particularly Jake. But you're different. Sal was right: You're one of us."

"Thanks." I had another glass of wine, feeling more hopeful than I had in quite a while.

"I should get you drunk more often," she said as we walked out the door. "This was so much fun. Let's do it again, soon."

I went to bed that night feeling like I'd finally made a friend in New York. Or at least a start.

But in the morning I felt awful. My head was pounding, my mouth was dry, and I was still wearing the clothes I'd worn the night before. The day yawned emptily before me.

I drifted out the door and clumped down the stairs. The weather was gray, the streets filled with that Sunday morning silence that makes you feel like everybody else is home with people that they love. I thought about Diana, home with Ned. I wondered what Dad and Aunt Melba were doing and if they were doing it together. Passing a newsstand, I glanced at the headlines. The papers were still talking about the rescue of the Chilean miners earlier in the week, and the feel-good stories were all about them being reunited with their families after sixty-nine days underground. Somehow that made me feel even more alone. I went into the bookstore on Prince Street, but my heart wasn't in it, and I left with empty hands. I kept moving, surprised when I found myself in front of Fontanari's. My feet had known all along where they were going, but my head had just caught on.

I tried to go inside, but it was after noon and the little shop was so crowded that the door would open only a crack. Even from out here I could smell the pungent, nose-prickling aroma of salami and the rich, milky perfume of cheese, and it was so enticing that I gave the door a hard push and edged inside. There was yet another scent now teasing my nose, and when I looked up I saw the strings of bright-red chilies dangling from the rafters.

It was as clamorous and cozy as a cocktail party, everybody deep in conversation. I stretched up on my toes, trying to see over the heads to the counter in the front of the store, just as Sal looked up from the customer he was serving. His face relaxed into a delighted grin. Putting his knife down, he pushed his way through the crowd.

"Folks" — he sounded so happy — "we got lucky. Help has arrived." He propelled me through the throng and whisked me behind the counter. His sister, Theresa, gave a little nod, as if she'd been expecting me.

"But what do I do?" I was utterly bewildered.

"First" — he was matter-of-fact, as if the question was idiotic — "you go into the back kitchen and wash your hands." He held up a plain white apron. "Then you put this on. Then you ask the next customer what he wants. And finally you give it to him."

"But I don't know how to slice salami or cut cheese!"

He took my hand. "It's not exactly rocket science. Just do what I do; you'll be fine. Rosie." He towed me into the back, where a pretty woman in her late forties with silver-streaked black hair stood making mozzarella. "This is that girl I told you about from *Delicious!* Billie, my wife, Rosalie."

Rosalie was a compact woman, with big breasts, comfortable hips, and a tiny waist.

Her smooth hair was pulled into a bun at the nape of her neck, and she was wearing an apron of impeccable whiteness. She was the cleanest person I'd ever seen.

"I'm very happy to meet you." She had come over to the sink where I was washing my hands. "Sal can't stop talking about the day you spent together." She lowered her voice to a whisper. "Don't tell him I told you, but he'd have been so disappointed if you hadn't come back. Let me see that apron."

I looked down, embarrassed, at my rumpled clothes, but she took no notice. She twitched the apron down, straightened it, and retied it so snugly that I felt neat, covered, contained. "That's better." She clicked her teeth in satisfaction. "Is your name really Billie?"

"My real name's Wilhelmina."

Her eyes lit up. "Much better! A name for a queen. That is what we will call you. Sal says he's offered you a job. I hope you'll say yes. And from what I know of Mr. Pickwick, I imagine you could use the money." She tucked my hand into the crook of her arm, escorted me to the counter, and pointed at a stocky woman with short gray hair in the front of the line. "Jane" — she gave me a little push — "this is Wilhelmina's first day, so be nice." In a stage whisper she added, "Jane was the great love of Sal's life."

Jane's eyes danced with amusement. "You should know that this great love affair ended before we reached the first grade." She looked me frankly up and down. "Sal's letting her work?"

"He trusts her palate." Rosalie said it with finality, as if no other explanation could possibly be needed.

"Then I'm impressed." Jane gave me a small salute, and I realized that what I had taken as Rosalie just being nice was more than that: Sal really did want me to be here.

Rosalie patted my arm. "Jane's a fussy customer, but don't let that trouble you. She'll want you to show her every single ball of mozzarella before she makes her choice —"

"I will not!"

"And she'll watch like a hawk when you slice her prosciutto," Rosalie continued. "Not to mention demanding tastes of so much cheese she won't need lunch." Jane huffed slightly at that. "But" — Rosalie gave my arm another pat — "you take your time and you'll be fine."

That seemed to be the Fontanari mantra; as the day progressed and the crush of customers grew more intense, Sal refused to rush. When he spied a small, slight man with pure white hair and skin so translucent you could see the tracery of blue veins beneath it, he cried, "Gennaro!" Sal rushed from behind the counter to kiss the man on both cheeks. "How's your mama? Better?" He gestured to his sister, who was slicing mortadella. "Theresa, can't you see this man is starving? Give him something to eat before he faints on us."

He moved among his customers, handing out chunks of pecorino, asking after family, telling stories. It was the perfect place for me, where being quiet was an asset. But I noticed that Sal kept glancing expectantly toward the door and then away, slightly disappointed. I wondered whom he was waiting for.

At around two o'clock a bearded man came through the door, and I had the answer to my question. All the lines on Sal's face moved upward, and his look of expectation changed to one of pure pleasure. He struggled to control his expression, over-joyed to see the man but reluctant to show it. He pointed across the counter.

"We all call him Mr. Complainer," he said in a low voice. "Guy comes in every Sunday. Never stops complaining. According to him, we do nothing right. And still he keeps coming."

Mr. Complainer was tall and broad, probably in his early thirties, with lively brown eyes that reflected amusement, thick curly brown hair, and a scruffy beard. He was carelessly handsome, dressed in softly faded denims and a wrinkled linen shirt. Every eye in the shop was on him, and he seemed comfortable with that. "Who're you?" he said to me.

"Meet Wilhelmina," said Sal.

"Don't tell me you've finally hired help!"

"Your prayers have been answered."

"No, no, no." Mr. Complainer shook his head in a parody of woe. "It would take a lot more than one little woman to answer my prayers." He turned to address the other customers. "It's almost un-American, the way they run this place. Best damn cheese in the city, but you have to wait hours. So what does Sal Fontanari do?" He pointed at me. "He hires this unfortunate soul, who is obviously unaware what she's gotten herself into." Looking into my eyes, he added, "Take my advice and flee. Run as fast as you can. Go before it's too late!"

I struggled to come up with some clever comeback, but Sal was already speaking. "You," he said hotly, "have no soul. If it were up to you, Fontanari's would be turned into a factory."

The man was unrepentant. "Would it kill you to make the place a little more efficient?"

"As I keep telling you, my friend, plenty of other places would gladly sell you cheese."

Mr. Complainer turned to me again, and I had one of those moments when I wished I looked at least a bit like Genie. But I'm not sure it would have mattered; I was just an extra in this ongoing drama, and Mr. Complainer was deep into his part. "As you can see, the man's hopeless. But" — he gave a comically dramatic shrug — "you're a start. Who knows? Maybe you'll be able to do something with him."

Everyone in the store had stopped to watch the show, which was obviously giving both men pleasure. I had a vision of them enacting this familiar ritual week after week, year after year. Did this happen every weekend? Sal reached for a salami and tilted his head, silently asking if he wanted the usual. Mr. Complainer nodded almost imperceptibly, and as Sal started to cut, the man's mouth parted in a little sigh of satisfaction. Then Sal picked up a ball of mozzarella and the man shook his head violently. Sal smiled and put his hand into another bowl, coming up with a different ball. The man nodded.

"I just opened the summer Parmigiano." Mr. Complainer held out his hand, and we all watched him put the golden shard into his mouth. He nodded, just once, and Sal cut him a substantial wedge.

They had not stopped talking, although I wondered if the words even mattered. This was obviously an old routine, a ritual. "Sure," Sal was saying. "We could work faster, we could make more money. But would we have time for this conversation? We would not. What's the point of making piles of money to enjoy when you're not working? I'd much rather enjoy my work."

Mr. Complainer laughed. "Oh, Sal, you never let me down."

"My friend," Sal replied, "I hope I never will."

The man took his package and hesitated, his eyes running along the shelves, seeking something else to purchase, trying to delay the moment of departure. He apparently came up empty, because he gave a defeated little shrug and walked toward the door. People parted to let him through and out the door.

"Next!" said Sal. He picked up a small

91

wheel of cheese and held it out. "Stelvio! It just came in. Very rare. They only make it in the summer, when the cows go up the mountain to their summer pasture. Let me give you a taste; it's buttery but pungent. See?" His voice never stopped, a soothing ribbon of sound buoying us through the exhausting day. At six the crowd began to ebb, and by seven the last customer was walking out the door. Sal sat down on a stool and wiped his forehead.

"Saturdays are even busier," he said. "You coming back next week?"

"I don't know." I picked up the last piece of Stelvio and stuck it in my mouth. "I'm not sure I'm supposed to be working a second job. Jake might not like it. I'm not even sure it's allowed."

"Allowed?" his voice rose indignantly. "Allowed? This is America. The question is — did you enjoy yourself?"

Every muscle in my body ached and my hands were sore. But Sal had shown me the secret of real aceto balsamico, making me taste again and again until I could discern the flavor of each barrel the vinegar had passed through, from the mellow oak, to cherry, chestnut, mulberry, and finally the astringent prickle of juniper. Theresa had plied me with tiny cups of espresso made from beans roasted over wood. And at the end of the day, just as we were closing, Rosalie sliced a melon and handed me a bright-orange triangle. "Wilhelmina," she commanded, "taste!" I took a bite, stunned by the roar of cantaloupe juice inside my head.

"Yes," I said. They had made me feel that I belonged there. "Yes, I did."

"Then we'll see you next Saturday."

Seizing Opportunities

The steps were now covered with leaves, but in the autumn light the Timbers Mansion looked even lovelier than it had in the heat of summer. I loved Mondays, loved the feeling of the old house welcoming us back after a sleepy weekend. Walking into the lobby, I stopped to appreciate the smell of aged wood and furniture polish.

But when I got upstairs, I was startled to find a portly gentleman stretched across Jake's battered leather sofa, orange socks perched on the armrests. He was dressed in tweeds so ancient they seemed a part of him. Jake wasn't in yet, and I eyed the man warily, wondering how he'd wormed his way past security.

He just lay there, arms behind his head, openly studying me. He gestured to his jacket. "Peerless, is it not? I have been donning tweeds for eons. Each time my travels take me to London, I scurry off to the tailors of Savile Row. When you hit on something you like, cleave to it. That is my motto." He got up, stretching languidly, and held out his hand. "The new Sarah, I presume?" I liked his cologne, spice edged with smoke. "Come help me unpack."

"Oh, no, you don't." Jake had arrived. "Sammy's always trying to lure people into his lair, where they disappear for hours, doing his bidding. It's like falling down the rabbit hole. Defend yourself now or it'll be too late." Sherman bounded in, jumped up, and licked the man's face ecstatically. I felt like an idiot.

"You're Sammy!" How could I not have known?

"At your service." Sammy executed a funny little bow. He looked like an old-time professor, the generous face and oversize features framed by sparse sandy hair and punctuated by horn-rimmed glasses. It was impossible to tell how old he was, but older than Jake. I guessed sixty. Maybe.

"I have just journeyed back from a sojourn in Marrakech. Such a mysterious and sumptuous destination. Have you ever been?"

I shook my head.

"How unfortunate. It is the precise equivalent of clambering into a time machine and dialing back the clock." Sammy leaned over

95

and began to rummage through the battered paisley carpetbag at his feet. He emerged, triumphant, with a huge coil of sausage, which he wrapped jauntily around Jake's neck. "A small token of my appreciation," he said.

"How'd you get this merguez through customs?" Jake recoiled a bit. "Didn't the dogs sniff you out?"

"Moi?" Sammy asked, as Sherman nuzzled his hand. "I will have you know that those canines are my boon companions. Someday you must come journeying with me; I might divulge a few cherished secrets." He offered me a winning smile. "Help me unpack? You have my solemn word that you will not regret it."

"Sucker!" Jake called, restraining Sherman as I followed Sammy down the hall.

"Jake thinks highly of you," he confided as we walked toward his office. "He dispatched an email informing me of your triumph on the Sal Test. Highest marks. He feels that you are a most promising young lady."

"Really?" He'd never given me the smallest cue that he thought that, and a little arrow of pleasure went rushing through me.

"Indeed. He has asked me to keep an eye on you. And I can see that we are going to be fast friends." Sammy took my hand in his, drawing me into a cluttered office. I looked around at the jumble of objects stacked in precarious towers that threatened to topple at a touch. The rays of sunlight entering through the thick, bubbled glass had an ancient quality, as if they had come from some distant past. I remembered Sammy's description of Marrakech.

Sammy affectionately patted his possessions as if they were long-lost relatives. "Are you aware that this office was once the domain of James Beard?"

"One of the crazier callers mentioned that he'd worked here, but I didn't know it was true."

"Indeed. It was at the very commencement of his illustrious career. Long before he was known as the father of American cuisine." Sammy stopped to caress an antique metal object with a huge wheel on the top. "Is this your first encounter with a genuine duck press? The French Tourist Office sent it in gratitude for the Paris issue I produced in 2003." His fingers moved on to explore the hilt of a richly jeweled sword. "This is from the Maharaja of Jaipur." Sammy pointed to a photograph of a small turbaned man riding an elephant with elegant ears. "Rather extravagant thanks for an extremely small story. The jewels, sadly, are faux." He tapped another picture — himself rafting on the Nile.

"What are those?" My attention had been captured by the large, showy white blossoms cascading down the far wall. "Don't they have pots?"

"They live on air." He petted the orchids as if they were small birds. "Exquisite, no?" He picked up a bottle and began to gently spray the flowers. "They require no soil, but they do appreciate a gentle mist. Richard kindly cares for them in my absence."

Sammy made me feel as if I'd been reunited with a long-lost uncle, as if we'd always been connected. He led me to an ornately carved wooden chair ("I discovered this in Venice") and handed me the carpetbag. "Remove every object," he instructed, "and then we shall decide where to place them. But first we shall indulge in a cup of tea."

He turned on a hot plate and brewed Darjeeling in a beautiful copper pot, while I rummaged through the carpetbag, pulling out dried figs, enormous pistachios in pale-blond shells, and little squares of dark chocolate.

"I make it a rule to return from each voyage with a trinity of new foods." He handed me a fragile porcelain cup. "I learned that on my very first assignment. Sugar?" Picking up his own cup, he settled into a large leather club chair. "What a trip that was!" He took a sip, cleared his throat, and opened his mouth. But he apparently thought better of that story. "Perhaps later . . ."

He reached for the smallest bag I had extracted from his carpetbag. "Hold out your hand." I cupped my palms and he filled them with a shower of orange blossoms. They tickled, delicate as butterflies, and a sweet, slightly citric fragrance filled the room. "Do you know what this is?"

I didn't.

He held a blossom to his nose, inhaling gratefully. "This is osmanthus. It grows in southern China, where it is used in sweet-and-sour sauces and to concoct the most exquisite tea. It is impossible to procure in the United States, and it is my fondest hope that Maggie will be incapable of identifying it, thus unhinging her." He threw that out, a challenge and a question, as he watched my face. "Ah." He nodded with satisfaction. "I was certain that she was making your life wretched."

"How'd you know?"

"Have you been informed about Maggie and Jake?" His expression and tone were difficult to read.

"I know they once had a restaurant together. Maja, wasn't it?" I tried out tentatively.

"Yes, back in the dark ages, before you were born. They were a very odd couple. He was much as he is today — a smooth, handsome man to whom everything has always come too easily. But you would not have recognized Maggie. She was a splendid creature with a wild mane of black hair. She wore very short skirts and exaggerated makeup, and she was the first woman of my acquaintance who sported a tattoo."

"Maggie's got a tattoo?" I was mentally erasing the beatnik girl I'd imagined earlier.

"Three. One on her upper arm. One tiny one just above her ankle. And a very artful butterfly on her shoulder. This was long before every individual who toils behind the stove considered a tattoo de rigueur. But that was Maggie — tantalizing, provocative, rather flinty." He watched me readjusting my impressions of Maggie before continuing. "Maja was a defining moment in American cuisine. They were among the first to insist upon local products. Jake's friendship with Sal dates from that time. Maja's signature dish was stuffed squash blossoms, which relied upon Fontanari's fresh ricotta.

I believe Jake was at least partially responsible for the current fame of Fontanari's."

"That explains a lot; I wondered how they'd become friends. So what happened to the restaurant?"

Sammy took a sip of tea. "Success." His voice implied that this was obvious. "Jake authored his first cookbook and then became embroiled in one of those dreadful television shows. He commenced traveling, and young women trailed after him as if he were a rock star. Meanwhile, Maggie was left behind to tend the restaurant. She saw a picture of him with another woman. . . . The rest is rather trite; I am persuaded you will have little difficulty in imagining what happened next? She came to work at *Delicious!* and it was years before their next encounter."

"When he became the editor?"

"Indeed. Maggie arrived here in the mideighties, and it was another dozen years before Jake made an appearance. Even then, she was so choleric that she maintained a rigid silence for two entire years."

"God."

"Our Maggie serves revenge very cold."

"But she obviously got over it."

His smile was rueful. "That is entirely due to her ingenious coping mechanism."

101

"Yeah, she transfers her animosity to his assistants. Very convenient for him."

Sammy patted my knee in a there-there gesture. "Should you desire advice, I can offer some assistance. The delightful Diana emailed me with the information that you have the ability to identify almost any ingredient in a dish. Is this true?"

"I try."

"And that you nevertheless decline to participate in activities of the culinary persuasion."

"True. I don't cook." I wasn't sure I liked where this was going.

"Never learned?"

"I can cook. I just don't."

"A major miscalculation on your part." His tone was neutral. "You must have a reason?"

"Not one I want to talk about."

Sammy raised his eyebrows. "Goody. I adore a mystery." He stood up. "You had best scurry off now. Jake is nice, but not nearly as nice as he thinks he is. I have no desire to get in his bad books on the first day of my return."

"I should go, anyway." I stood up too. "Jake's taking me out for sushi, and I've got a lot to do before lunch."

Sammy's eyebrows went up. "Ah, the

traditional two-month mark. Be prepared."

"For what?"

Sammy gave me an enigmatic smile. "You shall see." He held the door open.

Jake's favorite restaurant was a serenely spare space on 8th Street that seemed more like a spa than a dining room. The staff greeted him with deep bows and bustled about, taking our coats and leading us to the front table so everyone could see that Jake Newberry was gracing them with his presence.

A beautiful older woman brought steaming towels and rustic ceramic cups of green tea. "Sumiko, we are in your hands," he told her, unwrapping his chopsticks and placing them on a smooth black stone. Then he looked at me. "Sal tells me you've been working at Fontanari's."

"Oh, only on weekends." I could feel my heart begin to race; was this a fireable offense? But that was stupid; why would he take me to a fancy lunch to tell me it wasn't working out? "Should I have asked?"

"What you do on your days off" — Jake seemed smoothly indifferent — "is entirely your own business. If you want to fill every waking hour with work, that's your prerogative. But I've been wondering why Sal calls you Willie."

"Rosalie disapproves of boys' names for girls. She calls me by my real name, Wilhelmina; Sal shortened it."

The waitress set a small glass bowl in front of each of us. Lacy little green fronds waved up through clear liquid; it reminded me of a forest stream in early spring, just after the ice has melted. I picked up a frond, and as I put it in my mouth, I experienced a moment of cool, pure freshness.

"What is it?" I asked Jake, enchanted.

"Mozuku, a special kind of seaweed from Okinawa. You don't think it's slimy?"

"Slippery, but I love the way it feels in my mouth."

"I knew I was right to hire you!"

My earlier worries slipped away with the first few tastes of the mozuku, and before long I was telling him about my almost daily conversations with Mrs. Cloverly. "I've been writing down the ridiculous recipes she comes up with." I spooned up more of the pliant seaweed. "They're so incredibly comical."

Sumiko returned with a slab of slate on which ten perfect pieces of sushi were artfully arranged. I watched Jake pick up a piece of nori-wrapped fluke, dip the fish into the soy sauce, and swallow, thinking how lucky he was to be able to afford sushi whenever he felt like it.

"You know, Sal Fontanari is very fond of you." The change of subject was so abrupt that it startled me. "He called after you took the Sal Test and said that the two of you were on the same wavelength. Did you know you're the first person outside the family he's ever allowed to work there?"

"Really?" No wonder Jane had been so surprised to see me behind the counter.

Jake nodded. "Really. And that's given me an idea." He ate a piece of tuna sushi, and I saw him shudder at the impact of the wasabi. "I've always wanted to run a story about Sal, but you know what he thinks about publicity. Every time I bring it up, he gives me a lecture about the fickleness of fame. Then he changes the subject. But I bet *you* could get him to change his mind. Tell him you want to write about Fontanari's."

"I'd love to!"

Jake wagged a finger at me. "Of course you would. Why else would you be here? That's the whole point of being my assistant."

"And Sal's a wonderful subject."

"No one better," he agreed, winking as if we were coconspirators.

That stopped me. I'd been so excited at finally being asked to write that I'd overlooked the main point. I stared down at my plate and dialed back the conversation, thinking about Sal. I knew I couldn't do it, couldn't even ask.

I looked directly at Jake; he wasn't going to like this. "I can't ask Sal to go against his principles." I hated the way I sounded. So prim.

Jake took a piece of tuna. "I thought you were ambitious. I don't think I'm asking too much." He flipped the fish expertly into the soy sauce, just a little dip, and put it in his mouth. "This is the first time an assistant's ever turned me down."

"I'm sorry." He had to lean in to hear me. "I just can't."

"Well, find another story, then." Jake was cold; I'd disappointed him.

"But what should I write about?"

Jake scanned the room for the waitress, made that little signing gesture, asking for the check. "That's entirely up to you. But the job won't be official until you write something for the book. And you're turning your back on a wonderful story. You'll never find anything half as good."

THANKSGIVING

Dear Genie,
Thanksgiving. Winter coming. Snow already. Hate the cold. Hate the short days. Hate the position Jake's put me in.

You'd write the story, wouldn't you? You'd charm Sal into saying yes. But I'm not you. Sal will never agree. And even if he did, how could I ever do him justice?

Still, I find myself watching everyone, storing away little tidbits, just in case, coming home at night and writing it all down. Yesterday I watched Mr. Complainer shifting in and out of line, calculating the odds, hoping Sal would be the one to serve him. All the regulars do it. It's like they think they'll get home and find some of his optimistic spirit wrapped in with the cheese. Rosalie, who misses nothing, caught me looking and misunderstood. She leaned over to

107

whisper, "I'm pretty sure he's single."

I can't even think about that right now. But I'll admit that being around Sal and Rosalie makes me feel lonely; they're such a solid couple, and they enjoy each other so much. I look at them and think how nice it would be to have a partner. And I do like Mr. Complainer: his energy, the humor in his eyes, the way he seems to get pleasure out of life. And he's the most physical person I've ever met. He's always putting his arm around Gennaro, as if he's afraid the guy's going to keel over. (Gennaro's so fragile, we all worry about him.) If there's a little kid in the shop, he'll reach down and lift him onto his shoulders so the kid can see over the crowd. He's not old, but it seems as if he's lived long enough that he's grown comfortable in his own skin. I like that. Still, he's got such a crush on Sal that he barely even sees me. The other day his number came up when it was my turn to serve the next customer. He's got an open face, and I could watch him struggling with himself, wondering if I'd be offended if he said he'd wait for Sal. In the end he gave me this big, sweet smile and asked for mozzarella.

"Ours or the imported?" It's a kind of

joke we have. He always buys Italian mozzarella, but I keep urging him to try Rosalie's. She makes it every day and it's really good.

He says ours isn't made of water-buffalo milk, like it is in Italy, so it's not the real thing. So I fish out a ball of the imported stuff, and as I wrap it I have a warm little feeling, knowing that we'll go through this ritual the next time I wait on him, and the time after that. And then I feel pathetic; this is what I'm looking forward to? But enough about him.

Aunt Melba wants me to go home for Thanksgiving. She even sent me a ticket. She said Dad would be so happy to see me walking in the door but that he'd never ask me himself. I know she means the best, but you can't be there and I'm not ready. So I'm giving thanks at Sammy's.

"Just the two of us," he said, which made me feel . . . special. I'm positive you'd love him too. Wish you were going to be with us.

xxb

I expected Sammy's apartment to be as cozy and cluttered as his office, but he was full of surprises. Perched on the thirty-fourth floor of a new Chelsea high-rise, the place was all sharp angles and cold glass, with glittering views of the Hudson River down below. It was snowing, and the fat white flakes swirling past the windows made me feel as if I were trapped inside a life-size paperweight.

Sammy greeted me dressed in a Chinese gown made of heavy gray silk and embroidered with dragons. He took my coat, led me to a downy chair upholstered in deep red, and handed me a glass with a stem so fragile I was afraid it would shatter in my hands. I took a sip of the cold white wine, holding the liquid on my tongue as it filled my mouth with the taste of butterscotch and sunshine.

"Old Meursault." Sammy almost crooned the words. "Life is too short for bad wine."

"How old are you?" Suddenly I worried that I'd offended him.

"I'm sixty-two," he said without a trace of embarrassment, "but age has no significance unless you have frittered your life away."

"And do you think you have?"

"I would not state it in that fashion." He drew the words out slowly. "Nobody has made merrier than I have. But I have always been persuaded that someday, when I grow up, I am destined for great things. And then I wonder when, exactly, I expect that will be."

"What would you rather be doing?" I had thought Sammy, of all people, was satisfied with himself.

"Aye, there's the rub." He beckoned me into the dining room and struck a match. Sammy had covered the entire center of the table with flowers and candles, and soon the room was suffused with shimmering light. I drew in my breath; the flames were reflected in the windows on three sides, which revealed a panorama of the river. The table stretched between the windows, so there was an illusion of sitting on air. The table itself was spare, a simple piece of polished wood holding pure white plates as thin as eggshells. "Now, sit down, sit down; the soufflé is ready, and if we fail to consume it this very instant, it will fall."

"No turkey?"

"My apologies if you are dismayed by my reluctance to hew to the standard menu. But I must admit that I have always considered the turkey a rather regrettable bird. I should have queried you in advance; are you very disappointed?"

"Not at all." How could I be? Sammy's gorgonzola soufflé was little more than intensely fragrant air, so ethereal it floated into my mouth, where it delivered a surprisingly powerful punch.

"Is your family devastated by your failure to join them for the festivities?"

"I'm not sure," I admitted. "It's the first time that I'm not going to be there, and I expected Aunt Melba to invite a million people. But it turns out that she didn't. She's making dinner at her place, just Dad and her."

"That has an intimate air. Are they very close?"

"Yes. They really enjoy each other." As I said it, I realized I'd used the same words to describe Sal and Rosalie's relationship in an email to Genie.

"But they are not a couple?"

"No!" The idea, somehow, was shocking. "Of course not. She's my mother's sister." Aunt Melba was simply there, next door, a fixture.

Sammy seemed surprised by my vehemence. "In times past, you know," he observed, "a man unfortunate enough to lose a young wife frequently married her sister. That way the children were not motherless."

"Practical," I allowed. "But unromantic." But why had neither of them ever married? Never even dated, as far as I could tell. I had a quick memory of the family trips we took and the way Dad and Aunt Melba always made a big deal of getting separate bedrooms. Too big a deal? Had I been missing something all these years? I was remembering the way Aunt Melba always finished Dad's sentences, recalling the affectionate smile on her face every time she looked at him, when Sammy got up again.

I rose too. "There's no way you're going to wait on me," I said, collecting the plates and following him into the kitchen.

Sammy had roasted calamari until the tentacles were crunchy little bits, the bodies tender as velvet. Then he bathed them in a smooth pool of aioli.

"So much better than turkey," I said as I forked up the last crisp tentacle. "What did you do before you worked at *Delicious!*?"

"I worked at many other magazines," he replied. "But the truth is that I have been at the book since the dark ages." He began to toss the salad, bitter greens in Champagne vinaigrette, but he stopped mid-toss. "Sammy before *Delicious!* is shrouded in the mists of time. I will have you know that I am an institution!"

The spare salad was perfect after the richness of the first two courses, and I ate in appreciative silence. Then Sammy served the simplest dessert — gently poached ripe pears bathed in a deep-chocolate–caramel sauce. "This is the best Thanksgiving dinner I've ever had." As I said it, I realized the meal was a lot like Sammy — unique.

"Surely you exaggerate." But he was beaming, and I was glad that such a small thing could make him happy. "This sauce, now — I learned to make it on the first voyage I ever took under the aegis of *Delicious!*"

As he spoke, I remembered how he'd started to tell this story when we first met, shocked to think it had been only a few weeks ago. Sammy had quickly become one of the best things about my life in New York.

"It was the seventies, a freelance assignment long before I was actually employed here. They sent me off with orders to unearth an unsung Tuscan hill town. I was astonished by my good fortune. Remy, the staff photographer — an exquisitely beautiful man — was with me. We bundled all his equipment into a rented Mercedes and tootled from one magnificent villa to the next, where we were seduced with gorgeous food and spectacular wines. The most memorable meal was lunch at a monastery where they raised all their own comestibles. In those days, that was almost unheard of — they even pressed oil from their own olives and churned cheese from the milk of their sheep. As we sat down to eat, one of the brothers decamped to the garden and returned with tomatoes; when we put them in our mouths, they still held the warmth of the air outside. The brothers produced wine from the grapes behind the monastery — rich old Sangiovese — and they grilled our lamb chops over cuttings from the vines. For dessert they presented us with this sauce over just-picked peaches."

Sammy stared into the candles, as if the scene were unfolding in their light. "The meal was the epitome of simplicity, but it made me feel as if, until that moment, I had never really tasted anything. Later we wound our way through the hills, singing arias from our favorite operas as we peregrinated from one tiny town to the next. Late in the afternoon we suddenly found ourselves embroiled in a traffic jam. I believe it was caused by a religious procession. We sat there for quite some time, and then Remy leapt from the car, crying, 'Let's go!' as he began to climb the hill. After a few kilometers we arrived at a sweet little *pensione* and engaged a room for the night. It was terribly romantic."

"What about the car?" Had they abandoned it in the middle of the road?

Sammy waved his hand; to him it was an unimportant detail. "When we returned in the morning, the car was precisely where we had left it; the traffic had simply deviated around it. Nobody was in the least put out." He stopped talking for a minute.

When he began to talk again, I was expecting him to reminisce about the good old days when Europe was an inexpensive playground for Americans. Or perhaps about the golden age of magazines, when editors sent reporters off on romantic excursions. But he surprised me again. "I got back into the car thinking how lucky I was to be aware of happiness. Most people don't recognize their own good fortune until it has departed. And then it is too late."

"What about Remy? What happened to him?"

"Our great romance ended when we returned to New York. I took a job with another magazine, but we remained friends. By the time I arrived at *Delicious!,* he had wearied of the metropolis and moved to Corfu, where he remains to this day, tanned and wrinkled. The last time I saw him he was clad entirely in white, redolent of coconut oil, and wearing far too many rings."

I laughed; I could see Remy so clearly.

116

"But you're such an amazing cook. Ever think about opening a restaurant?" I was chasing the last of the chocolate around my plate.

"I told you." He leaned across the table. "I am a very dilatory man. And I have wearied of myself. It is time that you sang for your supper. There is, for instance, the deep, dark mystery of why someone with your fine palate declines to cook."

The candles flickered, as if a breeze had wafted through the room. "I don't want to talk about that."

"Fair enough. All things come to he who waits." He wasn't offended, but he was not about to let me off the hook completely. "But in that case you have to tell me what you are writing. Jake always demands that his assistants write an article before he deigns to bestow a permanent job upon them."

I told him about the Fontanari idea and our uncomfortable lunch.

"You are surely aware that you had best find another story. Were I you, I would do so expeditiously. You may have noticed that all is not rosy in the magazine trade at the moment. Money is tight. Issues are thin. And, as I have already stated, Jake is not as nice as he thinks he is. He will not wait until eternity."

"But I don't have another story!"

"Then devise a way to do this one."

"I can't!" I'd expected more support from Sammy. "Sal would be furious."

He waved his hand. "Let us, for the moment, put the issue of Mr. Fontanari and his scruples aside. Tell me about the shop."

I began to speak, conjuring up the cast until they were all gathered at the table. I told him about Sal and how he talked all through the day, wanting his customers to love his food as much as he did. I told how he waited for Mr. Complainer to come in, about their call-and-response routine. I described the frail Gennaro, who came in daily for his mother's cheese. Sal's first love, Jane, was there, and his calm sister, Theresa. And, of course, Sal's compass, Rosalie, making sure he never lost his way.

There was a long silence when I finished, as if Sammy were politely waiting for them all to leave the room. "You seem to know exactly what to write!" He folded his hands across his lap. "You toddle on home now and put everything down on paper, exactly as you told it to me."

"But what about Sal?"

Sammy studied me, some unspoken thought flickering in his pale eyes. Then he pushed his chair back and left the table.

He returned carrying a dusty bottle of Armagnac. As he poured us each a glass, the rich, raisiny aroma rose into the air. *"Courage!"* He pronounced the word in French as he raised the snifter. "Trust yourself. You do not need Sal's permission. Risk his ire. If you write your story well, if you write it honestly, he will not take offense."

"You think?"

Sammy waved a large hand again. "Depart to your own domicile. Seize this opportunity while you have it; you never know what the future will bring. The difference between talking about it and doing it is doing it."

His words echoed in my head as I walked through the falling snow. The streets were eerily empty, the snow coming so fast it muffled sound and made my footprints disappear behind me. I got home and slogged up the stairs, leaving little mounds of snow melting in my wake.

I sat down, turned on my computer, and conjured up the crowded shop again. As they gathered around me — Sal and Rosalie, Theresa, Jane, Gennaro, and Mr. Complainer — their voices filled my head and I began to write, afraid to stop, afraid to think, afraid to jinx this. The words came to me in a furious storm, and by the time they ran out, the snow had stopped and the sun was rising. I had no idea if the story made sense, but I was afraid to lose my nerve. I dropped an email to Jake, attached the story, and punched "Send."

I was exhausted. Fontanari's was closed for the Thanksgiving weekend, which left three whole days for me to fret. By Sunday, I was so jumpy that I paced restlessly around my small apartment and finally went to bed, where I was unable to sleep. The prospect of facing Jake was so terrifying that on Monday morning I almost called in sick. Instead, I took a long shower, putting off the moment of reckoning, and stopped to buy Sherman a smoothie on my way in.

"You're late." Jake's voice was brusque. Sherman bounded over when he saw the Starbucks bag, jumping up for the smoothie he knew it contained. "You've been standing in line at Starbucks while I sat here wondering where you were?"

I poured the smoothie into Sherman's bowl. "Sorry I'm late."

"I've waited a long time for this story. But, Billie, I have to say" — he paused — "it was worth it."

"You like it!" I could feel my face begin to glow.

"It's wonderful." He also looked relieved. I couldn't tell if this was because he'd been apprehensive about my writing, anxious I wouldn't do Sal justice, or distressed about finding a new assistant. "I like your approach, the way you've made Fontanari's more than a cheese shop. And you've captured Sal, right down to his stupid, longwinded speeches. I hope he's prepared for the onslaught. They're going to get slammed. How'd you ever talk him into it?"

"I didn't." My voice was barely audible.

"What?" The word shot out of his mouth. "You've spent weeks taking notes, but you never bothered mentioning it to him? Billie, what were you thinking?"

"I wasn't sure I could do this. I meant to ask Sal before I started, but Thanksgiving night it just . . . happened. It came to me all at once."

Jake looked skeptical. "You wrote this in one night? The whole damn thing?"

I nodded.

"I suppose I have no choice but to believe you." He fiddled with the pages he'd printed out. "But you had no business doing this before clearing it with Sal. It's not like he's some stranger. There's absolutely no way I'd publish this without his permission."

It was your damn idea! I wanted to shout

121

at him. Instead, I asked, "Do you think he'll let us print it?"

"No." Jake's voice lacked sympathy. "I don't. It goes against all his principles. That's why I asked you to write it: I thought you were the one person who might be able to talk him into it. Frankly, I didn't expect the writing to be nearly this good, but I figured I could fix that. But I never, ever thought you'd just write the story without discussing it with him."

The pleasure of Jake's praise had evaporated, leaving nothing but shame and apprehension. I should have come up with a different story. "Can I let him see what I've written?"

Jake looked shocked. "Of course not! That would be completely unprofessional."

"I didn't know. . . ."

"You have to ask him." Jake pointed to the phone.

"Not like that," I pleaded. "I need to do it in person."

"That train left the station a while ago." His voice was hard. "You're just putting it off." Then his face softened. "Maybe you're right. Go now. Have you ever seen Sal angry?"

"No."

"I have." And now he allowed a little

sympathy to creep into his voice. "Not pretty."

I walked to Fontanari's, stretching out the time like a child who's been sent to her room. The snow had turned to slush, and the cold gray New York fog matched my mood. By the time I got to the shop, my toes were frozen, my fingers red, and I smelled of damp wool.

"Willie!" The pleasure in Sal's voice cut through me. "What're you doing here on a Monday? How was Thanksgiving?" He enfolded me in a hug and led me to Rosalie, who was making mozzarella in the back kitchen.

"Sal, I need to tell you something. . . ."

Beneath the milky fluorescent lights, I haltingly told my story. Rosalie kept kneading the balls of cheese, never looking up, but I watched Sal's face grow darker. "Oof," he said when I'd finished, dropping onto a stool. He looked as if he'd just been punched very hard in the stomach.

"There's nothing in it you won't like," I pleaded.

"You know how I feel about publicity! I've never let anyone write about us. Never. We do honest work here, and we don't do it so some pipsqueak will tell the world how

123

wonderful we are." His usually kind face was stern, distant. He sighed deeply and cupped his hands above his eyes as if the light had grown too bright. "I felt so close to you, almost like family. I thought you understood."

Anger would've been easier to take. "Forget it," I said, "forget the whole thing. I never should have sent it to Jake. But he won't publish it unless you say it's okay, so don't worry. It doesn't matter."

"No." Rosalie spoke at last, looking up from her work. "It does matter. What did Jake say about what you wrote?"

"That I made Fontanari's sound like a way of life." I was hoping this would make both of them understand all the love and admiration I'd put into the piece.

Sal wasn't having it. "That's what it is to me," he said flatly.

But Rosalie had heard me. "Wilhelmina sees us. And this is a big chance for her. We shouldn't steal it away."

Sal reached for his wife's hand. "If it were anybody else —"

"But it's not. And you know she would never hurt you." The look she shot me was fierce, as if daring me to prove her wrong.

"I wouldn't. You know that."

"Well, then," said Rosalie.

Sal stood slowly, as if his back hurt. "Let me think about it."

Jake put the piece in the March issue, lightning speed by publishing standards. But in real-world terms, that gave Sal almost three months to agonize over the article and its possible effect on the shop.

The story went online on a Friday night. The reaction was instant. And intense. On Saturday morning there was a long line down the block before we even opened. "All new customers," Sal groaned, peering out the window.

Mr. Complainer showed up at ten — a full day ahead of usual. "Hey, Sal," he called from the back of the crowded shop, "you still have time for us ordinary people now that you're famous?"

Sal threw me a what-did-I-tell-you look, and I went beet red, worried about what was coming next. But Sal gave it right back. "When'd you start reading food maga-zines?" he asked as Mr. Complainer ap-proached the counter. Impressed by the drama, the new customers made way.

"I don't read *Delicious!*," Mr. Complainer admitted. "But my friends all know I come here, and three of them sent me a link. I'm praying none of them recognized me. 'Mr.

Complainer'? Please tell me you don't really call me that."

I didn't even know his name; I was so used to calling him Mr. Complainer, I'd never thought how he'd feel when that showed up in print. It hadn't crossed my mind that he might read the article, and now, thinking of all the other things I'd written, I began to feel slightly sick. I'd mentioned that he had a man crush on Sal and treated the cheese like a communion wafer, refusing to accept it from any other hands. Now I saw that I might have hurt him.

"It's affectionate," said Sal hurriedly. "You know that. Weeks you don't come in, we miss you."

"But how'd the writer even know that? And who the hell was he, anyway? I don't remember anyone hanging around taking notes."

I hoped Sal wasn't going to out me; I didn't want Mr. Complainer to know I was the traitor. I didn't want anyone to know. To my relief, Sal said, "Some new kid at the magazine. They kept it pretty low-key. Even we didn't notice what was happening until it was too late."

"It's a good story," Mr. Complainer conceded, "except for that bit about me. He got almost everyone else right. I really liked what he said about you and Rosalie." Then he looked at me, as if he'd just noticed I was there. "Poor Wilhelmina." He was all sympathetic misunderstanding. "You didn't get a single line. How could the guy have missed you?"

"Guess I'm not very noticeable." I tugged at my apron and averted my eyes. He'd realized I was the least colorful character in the shop.

To my surprise he said, very quietly, "I think you undersell yourself."

Now I was really embarrassed. He was being kind, trying to make me feel better about being left out of a story I'd written myself. The irony was absurd, and I tried to come up with something to say, something to move the conversation in a different direction. Think! And then I had it.

"You mean the way you undersell Rosalie's mozzarella? I believe there was something in the article about Fontanari's excellent American mozzarella. Perhaps you'd like to try some?"

"No, thank you." He seemed as relieved as I was to be back on familiar ground. "I'd like a ball of *real* mozzarella di bufala. And just to show you my heart's in the right place, I will deign, this once, to accept it from your hands instead of Sal's."

"You sure about that? You may have to do penance by saying a dozen Hail Marys."

"I'll take that chance," he said.

All day, new customers came surging through the door, and Sal's mood went up and down like a boat riding the tide. At one point an uptown lady twitched her mink off a shoulder and trumpeted, "I don't see what's so great about this shop. I could have gone to Grace's Marketplace and saved the price of the taxi." To say Sal gave me one of his dark looks wouldn't even come close.

"See what you've done!"

"Don't worry." Rosalie came quietly up behind me in the late afternoon. "He's embarrassed, but this will pass."

I turned so I could see her face. "Embarrassed? About what?"

"I'll tell you." She brushed an invisible stray hair back into her bun. "The truth is that he's enjoying the attention. But Sal's not a man who can lie to himself, and this troubles him. If you'd asked if you could write about us, he would have told you no. But you didn't, and now he gets to have his cake and eat it too." She watched him hand a slice of cheese to a little girl on the other side of the counter. "I think that, deep down, he's afraid."

"Of what?"

"That it'll go to his head. That it'll change him." The look she directed at her husband held both love and faith. "But it won't. You can't change Sal. Nothing can. So you stop your worrying. This won't last, and in a week, maybe two, everything will go back the way it was before. You'll see. You take a break now, walk around the block, get out of here for a little while." She gave me a small push. "The air'll do you good."

I untied my apron, feeling a small ripple of disappointment eddy through the shop; the customers' wait would be longer now. But as I walked toward Chinatown, breathing in the scent of soy sauce, dried shrimp, and garlic, I gave myself to the raucous street, with its river of jostling people, and I could feel my shoulders relax as I slipped into the flow. Lured by the promise of cheap grease, I stared into the window of a dumpling shop, startled by the sight of a tall, thin woman in colorless clothing with chin-length brown hair and a wide mouth. She could have been anyone, but when she put her hand up to adjust her glasses, I realized she was me. I dropped my hand quickly, went into the small, steamy shop, and traded a dollar for five hot, juicy dumplings. My phone buzzed as I took the first bite. I looked down at the screen: Aunt Melba.

"Billie!" Her voice was high, a bit breathless, obviously elated. "We just read your story! We're so proud; your dad's bought up every copy of *Delicious!* in Santa Barbara. You've made Sal Fontanari sound like a cross between Santa Claus and the Dalai Lama; I can't wait to come to New York and meet him."

"Don't buy your tickets yet," I interjected quickly. "Right now the store's full of tourists, and he's pretty pissed."

"He can't be!" It was Dad on an extension. "You made the man sound like a saint." So they were together, in her house.

"You don't know Sal. He hates publicity, hates having strangers invade his little universe. He glares at me every time a new one comes through the door."

"Nothing lasts." Dad was using his lawyer voice. "He'll get over it. It's —"

"— only the first day," Aunt Melba chimed in, reminding me of how she always finished his sentences.

How odd, I thought: They were using the same words as Rosalie, but their meanings were so different. Rosalie lived in a rock-solid world, and she believed that everything settled back into familiar patterns. All it took was time. But we came from a land of

130

earthquakes, and my family knew how everything could shift in a single instant.

I left the shop, carrying my dumplings in a paper tray to the grassy area along Allen Street. Huddled on the bench, I could feel the cold green slats pressing into my thighs; it suited my mood. Reluctant to go back to Fontanari's, I ate the dumplings slowly, losing myself in the raw garlicky sting of the plump crescents.

"Hey, lady, can you spare a dumpling?" Mr. Complainer was standing in front of my bench. He looked wonderful, his brown hair tousled by the wind, his cheeks pink from the cold. I held up the tray with its lone remaining dumpling and he picked it up, practically inhaling it.

"I love these," he admitted, sitting down next to me. "A secret addiction we obviously share. Don't tell Sal; he wouldn't approve."

"Your secret's safe with me."

"Thank God. Sal'd start giving me the second-best Parm, and I'm not sure I could deal with that."

I laughed, wondering what he was doing here. He answered as if I'd spoken the thought. "I usually shop in Chinatown after Fontanari's. That place over there" — he pointed across the street — "makes the best

131

roast pork."

"So what do you do with all the stuff you buy?"

"What do you think I do with it? Cook. It's how I unwind, though it's gotten kind of serious. Last year I even went to Italy and took a two-week cooking class. It was great."

Funny how I'd thought of him as someone who came to see Sal, never considering his existence outside the store, never wondering what he did with all the pasta, olive oil, and cheese he purchased. It made me feel even worse about what I'd written.

Once again he seemed to read my mind. "It's so odd, the writer not mentioning you in the article. I hope you know you're the first outsider Sal's ever hired. It's quite a compliment. And you've lasted! What has it been, four months? I think that guy missed a pretty interesting story."

At this rate I was going to have to confess. I stood up quickly. "Gotta go. I've taken a longer break than I'm supposed to, and the shop's insane today. All those new customers."

"Yeah," he said, "that Bill what's-his-name has a lot to answer for. Guess I'll see you next week, Wilhelmina. With any luck the turmoil will have died down."

Walking back, I thought what an odd conversation it had been. I still didn't know his name, and neither of us had asked any of the usual questions: What do you do, where do you live, where did you go to school? Prying into people's personal lives always felt awkward to me, but he seemed like one of those easygoing people who could ask anyone anything. I guess he just didn't care to know.

When I got back to Fontanari's the line was longer, the tourists growing more irritable as evening came on. Sal's mood was still volatile, and I watched him warily.

"Next!" I called. A thin blonde, extravagantly made up, stared suspiciously at me. She nudged her companion. "I don't know who this girl is." She pointed to Theresa. "But that one must be the sister. And that one" — the finger moved on to Rosalie — "is the wife. Let's wait until one of the Fontanaris is free."

I glanced uneasily at Sal, hoping he hadn't heard, but he was putting his knife down and brushing off his hands. "Excuse me," he apologized to the customer he'd been serving. Then he came and draped an arm around my shoulder. "This is a family establishment," he said, making sure his

133

voice carried. Heads turned. He gave my shoulder a little squeeze. "And back here we are all Fontanaris." He winked at me and retreated to his corner of the counter. Rosalie crossed her arms over her chest and nodded, claiming me for her own.

THE MANIA OF THE MOMENT

As Rosalie had predicted, the tourists moved on to the next hot destination, and Fontanari's glided back into its familiar orbit. Weekend after weekend, Gennaro selected special cheeses for his mama. That summer Jane went upstate, where she unearthed her grandmother's recipe box, and she began showing up with long-forgotten dishes for Sal, Theresa, and Rosalie to taste. Mr. Complainer came too; now when I waited on him, I asked how he was planning to use the pecorino or the expensive imported San Marzano tomatoes he was purchasing.

"Any suggestions?" he'd ask, but I'd just shake my head and say, "You're the cook." I had no desire to broach the "I don't cook" conversation with him.

"Why won't you give him a chance?" Rosalie asked after witnessing one of these exchanges.

"He doesn't want one."

Rosalie's lips quivered, holding back her words, but she said nothing. She was convinced that I was missing an opportunity. I had thought, after the day of the dumpling, that there might be something there, but he never sought me out again.

It was okay; I was very busy. By the time I'd been at *Delicious!* for a year, running Jake's office had become an easy routine. During the weekdays I answered his phone, fielded reader requests, and bought endless smoothies for Sherman. I endured Maggie's meanness, and at least three times a week I listened to Mrs. Cloverly's increasingly convoluted complaints about the *Delicious!* Guarantee.

But I was also writing regularly. When Jake accepted the Fontanari's piece, the job became official, and he urged me to keep writing. I suggested shadowing Benny, and Jake agreed that the butcher would make a great story. In early April I spent a week with him. First we drove to Pennsylvania in his beat-up refrigerated van, visiting a gentleman farmer who raised free-range lambs on the most beautiful land I'd ever seen. The lovely animals were grazing across the hills, but when they saw us they came running. "Easter's coming," said Benny as they nuzzled our hands. He made a deal for a dozen lambs, and it made me sad to think that the next time I saw them they'd be nothing more than meat.

The next day we visited a young farmer in western Massachusetts. As we drove up the Taconic, Benny said, "Sean raises the best pigs you've ever tasted." Farmer Sean turned out to be a shy bearded guy, very handsome and not much older than me. We helped him load the pigs into his pickup and followed him to a small family-run slaughterhouse. I couldn't watch, or listen, and I was happy when our pig was in the van and we were on our way back to the city.

But in the shop I forgot my squeamishness, as Benny showed me how to break the animal into roasts, hams, loins, and chops, until we were down to the hooves and tail. At the very end we boned out the entire head, rolling up the crunchy ears, smooth snout, and tender tongue into a tasty little bundle.

Jake loved that piece, and in the summer he sent me off to Long Island Sound to spend a weekend with a chef who went fishing every morning so his customers could have the freshest catch. I learned to love what he called "trash fish," especially the mild little blowfish tails that he battered and deep-fried, turning them into something resembling ethereal fried chicken.

In the early fall, Thursday told me about the Northeast Organic Wheat Project; she was so enthusiastic about their stone-ground wheat that I made a pilgrimage to Trumansburg, New York, to find out what made it special. The farmers there were a serious group, convinced that native wheats were the answer to gluten intolerance. I followed them through the fields as they proudly showed off heritage wheats. "This here," said Farmer Greg, "is called 'Rural New Yorker.' It was developed for this climate back in the late 1800s by a plant breeder named Elbert Carman." Jake was jubilant when that article was picked up by every organic organization in the country.

Later that fall, I foraged for matsutake mushrooms in the Pacific Northwest with a guy who insisted on blindfolding me and driving me around in circles for an hour so I'd be unable to divulge his secret spots. Jake liked that one so much he promised to promote me the next time something opened up. But I wasn't holding my breath; nobody ever left *Delicious!*

Between my regular job, writing articles, and working at Fontanari's, I was too busy to lament my lack of a social life. Still, it wasn't a complete zero: The *Delicious!* people often gathered after work, and Sammy regularly invited me to fantastic dinners in his glass dining room.

I was feeling so much more anchored that when Dad called, begging me to come home for Thanksgiving, I actually considered it. "I know you needed to get away," he said, "and I've been trying not to bother you, trying to let you build a new life. But, Billie" — I could feel him swallowing his emotions — "it's been over a year since I've seen you. And I just miss you." I didn't say anything, and Dad spoke into the silence. "I know Genie won't be here. But do it for me. Please?"

How could I refuse?

"Thinking about going home without my sister makes me nervous," I confided to Diana. She and I had an easy friendship, unlike anything I'd known before. We went drinking once a week, and she often ditched Ned and his burgers so we could share a serious meal. One night, after the third glass of wine, I said, "Remember that night — God, it was more than a year ago — when we first went to dinner?"

"You mean Nowhere? When you gave me the beret?" She reached up and touched the hat; she wore it all the time.

"I was so nervous about that. I thought if you hated it, it'd be really awkward and you'd hate me too."

"Hate you? With that palate? Are you crazy? What I remember most about that night is how Tom kept trying to get us to identify his secret ingredients, and you nailed them every time. He was so impressed!"

"But it's so easy."

"I wish you wouldn't say that." Instantly, I felt awful; I kept forgetting that it wasn't that way for everyone. "It makes me feel worse. You're like one of those people who can hear a tune once, sit down at the piano, and just start playing it. It's so unfair. Speaking of which . . ."

I knew what was coming next: Diana had been trying to get me to give her the Cake Sisters recipes since the day I was hired.

"I tried making your gingerbread again last night, and I can't get it right."

"I can't give you the recipe. You know I promised my aunt I'd never give that one away," I said for at least the hundredth time. "I'm sorry. But think how great you'll feel when you finally get it."

"I *will* get it. Someday. But I know this is your revenge for all the awful things I said

140

to you that night. I still feel bad about that."

"Don't," I told her. "It was kind of a relief, because I knew you'd never say stuff like that to someone you didn't care about."

On the last day of October I woke to the shock of early snow; a freak snowstorm had blown in, covering the streets with a dense white blanket. I'd now strolled New York's sidewalks in every season, enough to know that etiquette proscribed eye contact. But the unexpected Halloween weather surprised us into friendliness, and I walked to work smiling at everyone I passed. By the time I reached the Timbers Mansion, my cheeks were red.

My phone was ringing when I got to my desk. Young Arthur's early, I thought, recognizing the number and noting the time. Mr. Pickwick called every Monday promptly at ten. I picked it up to hear his clipped speech. "I need Jake ASAP," he barked. "Put me through."

I transferred the call, thinking nothing of it, and sorted the morning mail. I printed out Jake's calendar for the day and brought it into his office.

He was sitting at his desk, holding the phone away from his ear as if it would scorch his skin. His face looked as if his bones had melted.

"Jake! What?" I thought he was having a heart attack, but he waved me away. Sherman lay belly-down beneath the desk, one paw across his nose. The air felt radioactive; I fled.

Seconds later I heard the phone slam into the cradle, and I tiptoed back and peeked in. Jake's face was gray. He was holding a piece of paper, watching it tremble with a kind of disbelief. "Call everyone into the . . ." His voice cracked. "Photo studio," he finally got out. "In an hour. The entire staff." Then he got up and closed the door, leaving me standing there, biting my nails, terrified about what was going to happen.

An hour later we filed into the studio, past a group of ominous-looking men in shiny suits. I was startled to find Young Arthur standing awkwardly among the cameras and the lights.

We stood in a loose semicircle, kitchen people on one side, editors on another. The art department huddled together, but Richard took one look at Jake's face and went to stand beside him.

Young Arthur cleared his throat, as if he needed to get our attention. "After much consideration . . ." You could tell he was hoping to sound apologetic. "We have

142

decided to close *Delicious!* The advertising environment is challenging just now, and we are going to concentrate our efforts on our other publications. I'm very sorry."

Most of us were too stunned to do more than stare at him with our mouths open. Everybody knew that the magazine business was having a hard time, but we hadn't known things were this bad. *Delicious!* was over one hundred years old, an American institution. When he finished talking, the only sound in the room was breathing.

Until Maggie burst into tears. I was shocked, but then I remembered that she'd been at *Delicious!* for almost thirty years. For the first time ever, I felt sorry for her. What would she do now? And then it hit me that Maggie was not alone: None of us had a job anymore. I looked at Richard, at Diana, at Jake; in the last two minutes, all of our lives had changed.

Jake went over to Maggie, patting her shoulder and handing her fancy cocktail napkins that had been laid out for a shoot, until she finally got herself under control. "How soon do we have to leave?" she asked, her face wet and swollen.

Young Arthur pulled at his shirt cuffs and stared at the floor. "I think that's immaterial," he mumbled. "You can be out of here very quickly."

"A couple of weeks?" The question came from Diana; I was sure she was already making a mental inventory of her kitchen.

"Oh, no." Young Arthur looked over at her. He seemed taken aback, and the tension in the room eased as we realized we were going to get a small reprieve. "It's the last day of October. Your passes will work today. And tomorrow until five P.M."

"Tomorrow?" Diana gasped. "You want us to get everything moved out by tomorrow night?"

"Yes." Young Arthur actually smiled. "You won't be taking much." He threaded his way through the cables. "I wish you all much luck," he offered when he got to the door. "Human Resources will be over shortly to answer any questions."

"Wait!" shouted Maggie.

He turned. "Yes?" He peered at her. "Maggie, isn't it?"

"I just want you to know," she threw at him, "that your father is rolling in his grave. This was his first magazine, the start of the Pickwick empire, and it was always his favorite."

"You may very well be right," he replied. "But my father, you know, is in that grave he's rolling around in." He walked out, leav-

144

ing a stunned silence in his wake.

We stumbled out of the studio in a collective daze, eager to flee that unhappy room. I went next door and found the kitchen in chaos. The cooks had been preparing to photograph a Southern feast, and every counter overflowed with food.

"My pork shoulders!" wailed Maggie. "I spent a week finding enough for this shoot. We've got fifty pounds of blue crabs and twenty-five pounds of sweetbreads too. I wonder what they're going to do with all that?"

"That's not your problem anymore," boomed one of the suited men who had accompanied Young Arthur into the building. Five pairs of cold eyes watched us, missing nothing. Lori was carefully wrapping a knife into cheesecloth. "Where do you think you're going with that?" one of them asked.

"It's my knife," she said defensively. "I got it when I graduated from culinary."

"Too bad." The goon wrenched it from her hand. "You had no business bringing personal equipment into this kitchen. The equipment all stays here; it's company property now." He flung the knife onto the counter, where it clattered violently before coming to rest.

"Time you got new knives anyway, Lori."

Paul tried to soothe her. "It's been a long time since you graduated."

"They're supposed to last a lifetime," she snapped.

Paul handed her a glass of wine from an open bottle sitting on the counter. It was eleven in the morning. "No point in leaving this for the Pickwicks."

One of the men glanced up at that, staring pointedly at the glass. Paul stared back, daring him to claim the wine as Pickwick property. The man's shoulders shifted uncomfortably inside his suit, but he blinked first. Paul ostentatiously took a giant gulp, sucking air noisily into his mouth like a professional wine taster. The goon gave him an ugly look, but he walked away, motioning for the others to follow.

Diana was silently emptying her shelves, packing up her cookbooks, rolling her secret spices into the vintage aprons she liked to wear, and I watched her, thinking, She's too calm. She didn't even seem angry. "What are you thinking?" I asked.

She kept methodically transferring spices, flour, and cans from the shelves to a box. "Plenty of other jobs out there for trained cooks."

I looked at her face, awed by her composure. Most of the cooks were crying as they

146

packed. The magazine business was changing, and jobs were hard to get; test kitchens like this were a thing of the past. Would they have to work freelance from now on? Goodbye, benefits. My stomach felt as if I had swallowed stones, and I found myself holding it with both hands as I went back to my office. Brown cardboard boxes had sprouted through the hallways, and I gave one a vicious kick and listened to the satisfying thud as it went end over end down the stairs.

Jake was in his office, hunched over his desk; Richard sat on the other side, looking grim. They waved me in.

Jake was forlorn. "Richard thinks I knew what was going on. He can't believe Young Arthur would do this without warning. He thinks I knew about it, that I've been working behind the scenes, trying to change their minds. Will you please tell him the truth?"

"Richard, if you'd seen Jake when the call came . . . I'll never forget the color of his face. He didn't see it coming."

"Those bastards!" Richard slammed his fist onto the desk as he got up. "Right before the holidays? Couldn't they have waited?"

"I feel like such a fool." Jake watched Richard leave. "How could I have been so blind? I knew that ads were down." He was making a visible effort to control himself. "I wish Sammy were here. It's unfortunate that he chose this particular moment to be traipsing around Turkey. We could use some of his lovable energy right about now. He'd calm everyone down. Did you call him?"

"I'll try." I called his hotel in Istanbul, but the clerk informed me that he was up in the mountains and could not be reached.

"I left a message," I told Jake, "but they didn't know when he'd be back."

"Damn!" Jake sounded bereft. "I just wish he were here; nothing gets him down." Then he folded his hands on the desk and looked up at me. "But that's not what I want to talk to you about."

It was only noon, but in the three hours since Young Arthur's call, Jake had aged; every one of his fifty-four years was now engraved across his face. I patted Sherman, thinking that after today I might never see him again. Or Richard. Or Sammy. I felt sick, and for a panicked moment I was afraid I was going to throw up on Jake's desk. I concentrated on swallowing the feeling.

"So do you want to?" Jake's voice seemed far away.

"Want to what?" I hadn't been listening.

Jake shook his head. "Focus, please. I was saying that Young Arthur wants to keep someone on to honor the Guarantee. He thinks cutting it off so suddenly would be bad for the company's image and would somehow hurt the other magazines. Totally irrational, if you want my opinion . . . Anyway, I told him if anyone was going to do it, you'd be the one."

"They'll keep paying me even though they've killed the book?" It sounded crazy. "How long can that possibly last?"

"He didn't say," Jake admitted, "and it's a good question. I don't imagine it'll be forever. But people hang on to their back issues, and Young Arthur wants to keep the readers happy. There was something about throwing the baby out with the bathwater, or maybe he has fantasies of bringing it back when the economy improves."

I don't know what he saw on my face, but something made him add, "You're a good writer, Billie, but you don't exactly have a huge body of work under your belt. Finding a new job is going to be a challenge in this economy, and it's always easier to find one when you have one. Freelancing is tough. What have you got to lose by staying on awhile? This entire staff is going to be out there looking for jobs. I'll do what I can for everyone, but it's not going to be easy."

I thought about all the editors, copy editors, and art people knocking on doors, begging for jobs. I wondered about Sammy. Then I thought about Paul, who had two kids, and the copy editor, who had three. How long did unemployment benefits last? I was suddenly exhausted by it all. I couldn't think. Jake watched me, waiting.

The silence stretched. "I'll take that as a yes." Jake's voice sounded firmer. He got up from his chair and paced around the room. "Now, can we get back to work? There's a lot to do."

The phone began to ring almost immediately. I hadn't thought about the press. *Delicious!* was a beloved institution, and the magazine's demise made news around the world. Reporters kept calling Jake, begging him to tell what he knew and when he had known it. When the reporters couldn't get him, they questioned me, and over the next day, I discovered that endings have their own odd thrill. In the mania of the moment, it's possible to forget what you are losing.

Most of us spent that first night in the office, drinking our way through the liquor closet. By morning the office had a rakish look, less grand old mansion than post-rush fraternity shambles. As we taped up the last of the boxes, Jake ordered coffee and the doughnuts filled with chocolate mousse that

Jacques Torres made especially for him. We were trying to sober up on sugar and caffeine when Maggie issued an unexpected invitation. "Come to my place tonight," she told everyone, "and we'll have a proper wake."

People's houses always surprise me, but in my wildest imagining I'd never have expected Maggie to live in a cozy old Brooklyn brownstone filled with rock posters from the eighties — Bruce Springsteen, Guns N' Roses, Talking Heads. I was staring up at a Cyndi Lauper poster when she staggered over.

"Girls just want to have fun." She could barely get the words out. "They're real, if you were wondering."

Jake gave her a sidelong glance. "How drunk are you?" He looked a little worried.

"Very," Maggie replied, "and I intend to stay that way for quite a while. Do you know how many years I worked at that damn place?"

"You know I'm there for you if you need me." His voice was low, and he put his arm around her. I averted my eyes; it was an oddly intimate moment.

"I'll be okay." She pushed him away and looked defiantly up at him. "I'm going to start a catering business."

Jake burst out laughing. "You? People would pay good money to keep you away from their parties."

"I am offended." She sniffed. "I may not be Jake Newberry, but I can certainly cook well enough to please the Park Avenue set."

"Oh, come on, Mags. I'm not casting aspersions on your cooking. But you in the service business? Think about it." Personally, I kind of liked the idea of Maggie kowtowing to women meaner than she was, but I kept the thought to myself. At the moment we were trying to be kind to one another.

"What about you?" Maggie challenged Valente. "What grand plans have you conceived?"

He looked embarrassed. He fiddled with his glass and admitted he'd already gotten calls from *New York* magazine, *Food & Wine*, and Williams-Sonoma; he was booked solid for the next two months. Richard confessed that he too had been fielding phone calls by the dozen. "And you, Diana." Maggie's voice had an edge of bitterness. "I suppose that dozens of fabulous opportunities have come your way as well?"

Diana's usually open face closed up. "I've been waiting for the right moment to tell you this." She was clearly uncomfortable, and she looked directly at me. "I actually got this job offer a while ago. Ned's going to work at a start-up in Palo Alto, and there's an opening in the test kitchen at *Sunset* magazine. I was confused about what to do, but Mr. Pickwick just made my mind up for me."

"What?" I was horrified to find that I was struggling to hold back tears. I should be happy for Diana; she had a job. But she was the one person I'd thought I'd get to keep.

I gathered an armload of dirty dishes and retreated to the kitchen. I filled the sink with scalding water, squirted in the soap, and plunged my hands into the wet heat.

"I'm sorry you're upset." Diana had quietly followed me. "You're my friend, and I should have told you. But I really didn't think I was going to go."

"No, it's great. Really. When I get over how much I'm going to miss you, I'll be glad you've got a job. But who's going to bug me about my clothes now?"

She threw her arms around me. "Don't think you're getting rid of me that easily."

I hugged back, drenching her in the process.

"I'm going to email so often you'll hardly know I'm gone," she promised. "And I'm not about to give up on that gingerbread recipe. . . ."

BOOK TWO

Dear Genie,

Watching Diana drive off felt so horrible. It wasn't like watching you go, but still . . . We said all that stuff about staying in touch, but everything's different from a distance. As you know.

Working at Fontanari's this weekend was as bad as being back home after everything happened — all that pity. Rosalie kept trying to play matchmaker, pushing me out front every time a single guy walked through the door. I could feel them all worrying about me, and it just made me edgy and irritable.

But the new job starts tomorrow, and I'm looking forward to that. How'd I get so lucky? Everyone else is out there pleading for work, and I get to hang out in a cozy mansion while I consider my next move. I'm sure I could get an editorial assistant position at some other magazine, but after *Delicious!,* it's all downhill. I don't want to just write, I want to write about food. I could always work at Fontanari's. But, much as I love them all, it doesn't feel like moving forward. I try to think what you'd do in my place.

xxb

My key still worked, but the mansion was dark as I climbed the stairs and so silent that even my quiet footsteps boomed through the empty building. When Jake said I'd be the one, I didn't quite get that I'd be the *only* one.

I could not have imagined these eerily empty halls, the thunderous silence, the vacant offices littered with trash. In the five days we'd been gone, most of the furniture had been moved out, but they'd left broken pieces, and here and there I'd come upon an upturned chair missing a leg or two. Piles of abandoned photographs lay in dejected heaps in every room, and in the halls big plastic dumpsters overflowed with old notebooks, broken staplers, and forgotten office supplies. Piles of unused boxes sat waiting to be filled. The air smelled like damp paper, and hanging over everything was an odd odor of decay.

Most of the office doors were open; criss-crossed yellow tape shouting CHECKED + EMPTY stretched across each threshold. It was dark, so dark. Sammy's door was closed, but tape with the word UNSANITIZED in huge letters had been posted there, as if vicious germs waited inside, poised to leap out and attack. I walked down the hallway, futilely flipping switches until it finally hit me: Someone had taken every accessible lightbulb.

They'd left a couple in my office, and it was a relief to watch the lights come stuttering on. But, beyond it, Jake's empty office loomed. I kept listening for Sherman, but of course he wasn't here.

How could I pretend this was a normal workday? Still, I began to open the mail I'd found spilled across the lobby floor.

"Dear *Delicious!,*" read the first one. "Is it true that you'll continue to honor your Guarantee? If so, I would like to point out that there was nothing wild about the 'wild mushrooms' in the turkey stuffing featured in your final issue. Shiitake, as you must surely know, are now widely cultivated. . . ."

And exactly what would you like me to do about that? I wondered crossly. It turned out that what Mrs. Bowman wanted was a refund because she felt tricked by our "false assertion."

A flash of rage surged through me. "Dear Mrs. Bowman, you could easily have gathered your own mushrooms and substituted them for the ones called for in the recipe." I stopped typing. What did I care? I deleted the words one by one.

"Dear Mrs. Bowman." I was typing more slowly. "I am so sorry that you were unhappy with our mushroom stuffing. If you will send us your receipts, we will cheerfully refund your money. We want our readers to have happy memories of a great magazine. All of us here at *Delicious!* wish you very happy holidays."

I sensed my phantom coworkers gathered around me, silently applauding. Then I picked up the next letter. I'd give everyone their money back. Why not?

Tomorrow, I thought, I'll buy lightbulbs. And some flowers. I'll bring in a teakettle. It's not so bad. . . .

A skittering sound came from the hall, and my heart began to race. I jumped up to peer fearfully into the corridor. Empty. Was that a mouse's tail disappearing around the corner? Or was it only my imagination? I sat down, trying to calm myself. I was being ridiculous, I knew that, but I needed a human voice to put this in perspective.

160

I thought about calling Aunt Melba, anticipating the conversation. She'd be sympathetic. She'd say, once again, how much Dad missed me. She'd suggest, again, that I quit the job and come home. No thanks.

As I was thinking that, my phone rang, and I looked down to see that it was Dad.

"Just checking in on you," he said. "This has to be hard. Things were going so well, and now this. I wanted to make sure you're still coming home for Thanksgiving."

"I wanted to talk to you about that. Would you mind terribly if I didn't come?"

"Yes." His voice was quiet. "I would mind terribly." He heaved a deep and audible sigh. "I miss you. I worry about you. I'd like to lay eyes on you. But I would understand."

"Really?"

"You think I don't know how you feel?" He sounded almost angry. "You think I don't understand why you ran away? I don't like it, but I understand it. And I know why you need to keep us at arm's length. If you think coming home right now will be too hard, well, you need to do what you think is best for yourself."

"Really?" I said again, a bit stunned by his generosity. "Thanks, Dad. I love you."

161

"I love you too. And I'll come — we'll come — as soon as you're ready. Say the word."

I hung up the phone and found that I was crying. "Stop it!" I lectured myself. "Just stop it!" I knew that what I needed was the familiar querulous voice of Mrs. Cloverly.

"Is something wrong, dear?" My call had startled her. When I explained that the magazine had closed, I heard a sad, watery little sigh. I knew how she felt; her world had just grown smaller.

"But the Guarantee will continue as before." I tried to sound jolly.

She sounded hopeful. "I can still call?"

"Absolutely." I was surprised by how much more cheerful she'd made me feel. "I'll be here every day."

But every day the gloomy building grew more neglected, and it was hard to keep my spirits up. I understood that Young Arthur wanted someone there to keep the building from seeming completely abandoned, but by the third Monday, the empty rooms with their yellow tape seemed even more forbidding, and Jake's dark office was a heavy, reproachful presence. The odd smell I'd noticed had grown stronger, and by Wednesday I was imagining whole families of mice rotting inside the walls. Walking down the hall, leaving for the long Thanksgiving weekend, my foot brushed one of the piles of forgotten photographs. It slithered toward me like a snake, and I went running down the stairs and out the door, slamming it behind me. I was relieved to have a few days away.

Dear Genie,
The Timbers Mansion has morphed into a nightmare, and I can't tell another soul how horrible it is. Dad and Aunt Melba would want me to come home, but what am I going to do in California? Go back to school? No, thanks; I don't think I could take it. Sal and Rosalie have offered me a full-time job, but that's not what I want to do with the rest of my life, and I couldn't bear to hurt them. You think I should stick it out, right? At least until I figure something else out? I know you do.

I spent Thanksgiving working at Fontanari's, and afterward we all went upstairs and ate turkey together. It made me think about Sammy. I remembered something he said the first time I had dinner at his house — that he was lucky to know when he was happy. I envied him, but now, looking back, it makes me feel so stupid because, in spite of everything, at that moment I was pretty happy too. It just went right by me. Next time I hope I'm smart enough to recognize happiness when I have it.

Miss you, miss you, miss you.

xxb

On the Monday after Thanksgiving, the Timbers Mansion smelled even worse. I climbed the stairs, juggling coffee in one hand and a bunch of roses in the other, burying my nose in the flowers. In the hallway I kept my eyes straight ahead, trying to avoid the broken furniture, the dumpsters, the tape across the doors. I put the roses in a vase, took a sip of coffee, and sank gratefully into my chair. Then I picked up the phone and called Mrs. Cloverly.

It was pathetic, really, that this crazy old lady in a trailer park had become such a necessary presence, but when I talked to her I could almost fool myself into thinking that nothing had changed. She'd spent the weekend cooking, and her three vile dishes kept us busy for an hour.

But when I hung up, the silence was so thick that I jumped when a board creaked in the hall.

It was not my imagination: Someone was

out there, walking toward me. I could feel the adrenaline pumping through my body. I stood up. At least they wouldn't catch me unawares.

The footsteps stopped outside my doorway and an apprehensive voice called, "Is somebody there?"

I knew that voice! I ran into the hall and threw my arms around Sammy.

"What on earth are *you* doing here?" he asked. "Are you attempting to terrify me into an early grave?"

"How the hell did you get in?"

"I will have you know that my key still works. And I was sternly admonished to retrieve my personal effects at the earliest possible opportunity."

"Then why didn't you come sooner?"

"For this?" He waved a hand, indicating the decrepit hallway in which we stood. "I was high up in the mountains when your missive reached me. I screamed. I wailed. I wept. I returned to Istanbul and began peregrinating through the city like a demented chicken, intending to change my tickets and embark on the next New York–bound conveyance. I was at the airline office when a thought struck: I was behaving like an ass. This was the last waltz, and nobody was about to question my expenses.

So I snatched up my tickets, rented a limousine, upgraded myself to the presidential suite, and made reservations in Istanbul's finest restaurants. Young Arthur be damned!" He looked me up and down and added frankly, "It seems that you should have done something similar, my dear. Whatever you have been up to has done you very little good."

I put my hand up to my hair, remembering that I hadn't bothered to comb it this morning. I wished I'd washed my face. I saw nobody during the week, and some mornings I was tempted to come to work in my pajamas. Still, it was humiliating to be caught like this. "Forget about me. What will you do?"

"Dear one, do not waste a moment fretting over me." He smoothed his tweed suit. "I was in this business before you were born. I know everyone. Now that I have returned, I shall have three offers before the week is out." He pulled me down the hall. "Come help me pack."

Sammy sniffed suspiciously and said, "What is that deplorable aroma?"

I shrugged it off. "Dead mice behind the walls, I think. Nobody comes to clean anymore."

"Hmmf." Sammy stood in front of his

166

closed door, staring angrily at the yellow tape. "Unsanitized?" He ripped it savagely off. "Unsanitized?" He fit the key into the lock. "What a barbaric notion." The door swung inward, creaking on its hinges, and I held my breath.

His lovely orchids were dead. They lay shriveled against the wall, mere skeletons now, their fronds groping blindly. But everything else had survived, and I picked up the beautiful copper teapot, happy to find it unharmed. Sammy snatched it from me, running his fingers across the patina as if it were a beloved pet. He looked again at the pathetic plants, then pulled them gently off the wall and deposited them in the garbage. "Ruby — Young Arthur's secretary, you know — has been leaving daily messages, insinuating that if I fail to clear out my office, everything will be forfeit to Pickwick. But you have yet to explain your own presence here. Wait." He held up a hand. "Allow me to conjecture. The Guarantee?"

"You're very perceptive."

"I take it Mrs. Cloverly continues to be your number-one customer?"

I couldn't help smiling. "Not anymore. The new crazies put her efforts to shame."

"Goody." Sammy sounded delighted. "Tell!"

"I'll do better than that." Suddenly feeling lighthearted, I went off to get the most absurd letter of the day.

Dear Sir or Madame:
Is it too much to expect that, despite the magazine's unfortunate, untimely, and in my opinion utterly unnecessary demise, you will continue to stand behind the *Delicious!* Guarantee? I certainly hope not, for I have a complaint of an extremely serious nature.

Each year I allow each member of my family to request one special cookie for Christmas. This year Aunt Emma has requested the Nutty Apricot Lace Cookies that you published in the seventies. I remembered them as crisp, chewy, and rather likable. Well, sir, I thought I had lost the recipe, but when I went to my file I had no trouble whatsoever locating it.

I did think that the recipe seemed to be missing some crucial ingredients. But I have enormous faith in your fine cooks, and I followed the recipe exactly as written. Let me assure you that I am being kind when I say that these were horrid little hockey pucks and that I wished with all my heart that the recipe had been lost.

Then I recalled the *Delicious!* Guarantee.

The ingredients were modest — oatmeal is not very dear — but it is the principle, you see. My receipts are enclosed. If you have an alternate but excellent recipe for something resembling a Nutty Apricot Lace Cookie, please enclose that along with the check. I don't like to disappoint Aunt Emma.

Faithfully yours,
Emmajane (Mrs. Gifford) Janson

Sammy laughed until he was wheezing. When he had finally sobered up, he gave me an incredulous look. "This is how you are currently employed? Responding to women who request refunds for antique recipes?"

"There's apparently no statute of limitations on the Guarantee."

He began to laugh again. "I will wager that Emmajane miscopied the recipe. Did you seek the original?"

"It wasn't in the database."

"And the recipe index?"

"Jake took his back issues with him." I hesitated a moment. "I'd have to go to the library to do that. And . . ." I gestured upward.

"You are loath to venture into that long-locked room. I quite comprehend. Have no

169

fear." He patted my arm. "I shall accompany you. Have you the key?"

"I bet it's in one of the drawers in Jake's desk. The desk is so big they didn't bother moving it out."

He linked an arm through mine, leading me into Jake's nearly empty office. "At one time the library was my favorite room in this entire edifice, but when Jake pronounced it off-limits, I quite forgot its existence. It has been eons . . . I would appreciate a last look."

The key was where I'd expected it to be. I snatched it up, and together we climbed the grand, dusty staircase. As we rose, the evil funk grew so strong that Sammy pulled out a handkerchief and held it to his nose. "No doubt it is the stinking corpse of the magazine, rotting around us. The smell! How do you bear it?"

"You get used to it."

He patted my hand and looked at me, eyes filled with pity. "Oh, my dear." His voice was soft. "Oh, my dear."

We walked through the sad shambles of what used to be the art department and stood before the scarred library door. It was a solid piece of wood, but when I put the key into the lock, it sighed softly as it swung inward on its hinges. We tiptoed into cool

170

darkness, the air scented with an ancient perfume that mingled paper, leather, and, oddly, apples. The Persian carpet was so soft that I felt as if I were floating into the long, high, book-lined room. The curtain-shrouded windows provided no illumination, and I fumbled for the light switch. As I turned it on, the room became infused with a soft golden light that fell across heaps of books lying on long oak tables, as if phantom readers had just put them down, planning to return at any moment.

Deep suede armchairs were scattered invitingly around the room; the Tiffany lamps above them gave off a jewel-like glow. A huge, ancient globe, taller than I am, stood in one corner, and in the other a giant dictionary perched regally on a wooden stand. "I had forgotten how beautiful this room is," Sammy whispered with a kind of reverence.

I walked to a desk in the middle of the room; it was fantastically decorated with inlaid wood, a midnight sky depicting the signs of the zodiac. The chair behind the desk was as tall as a throne, and when I sat down on the dark-blue velvet cushion, it seemed to enfold me in an embrace. I looked at the shelf next to the chair, unsurprised to find that it held back issues of *Delicious!*

While Sammy went off to explore, I settled into the chair, leafing through the back issues in search of Nutty Apricot Lace Cookies. If the recipe had been there, I would certainly have found it, but by the time I put down the December 1979 issue, I was positive that Mrs. Gifford's recipe came from some other magazine.

"Come here!" Sammy's voice was muffled, as if it was reaching me from a great distance. I stood up, but I could not see him. "I am in the nether regions of the library. Make haste!"

I followed the sound of his voice, but when I reached the back wall, Sammy was still nowhere to be seen. "Where are you?"

"Are you standing beside the very last shelf?" His voice was coming from behind the wall.

"Where are you?" I repeated.

"Go around to the end of the bookcase and give it a hearty shove." I walked to the edge of the shelf, put both hands in front of me, and pushed. It vibrated a bit, moved forward an inch, then rocked back into place.

"Do not be delicate. Harder!"

This time I put my whole body into it,

172

and the shelf rolled sideways, revealing a small doorway hidden in the wall. Sammy's head suddenly appeared, like a turtle from its shell. "Please join me." He was obviously thrilled that he'd surprised me, and he gave me a delighted grin before his face vanished.

The narrow doorway was about four feet high, and as I squeezed through I wondered how Sammy had managed it. I found him standing in a small dim room, the size of a child's bedroom, illuminated by a single lightbulb. Floor-to-ceiling shelves covered all four walls, and they were absolutely stuffed with papers. "What is this?" I whispered. "Did you know it was here?"

"I could not be more astonished." Sammy's face was filled with wonder. "I was poking through the shelves when I discovered an extremely rare travel guide from the 1860s. I dropped it — you know how maladroit I am — and when I bent to retrieve the book, I saw the wheels on the bottom of the bookcase. And" — he stopped dramatically — "where there are wheels, there must be a reason. So I pushed. Voilà! A secret chamber, replete with hidden treasure." He gestured toward the shelves. "Letters!" He pulled a file from the shelf. "Thousands of them, correspondence extending all the way back to the dawn of *Delicious!*"

"But what are they doing here? Why are they hidden?"

Sammy opened the file. "I have absolutely no notion." He took out a sheet, which crackled with age. "But I will hazard a guess that they were squirreled away years ago and simply forgotten. It is possible that no living soul knows of their existence."

"So weird."

"The mystery of *Delicious!*" Sammy sounded thrilled. "Is it not glorious? We have uncovered a secret; with any luck it will prove to be deeply sinister. However . . ." He held up the paper in his hand, and I could see that it was covered with clear, legible writing. "I am not very sanguine on that score. This one, it appears, was penned by a young girl, a mere child."

I looked over his shoulder as he began to read:

" 'November third, 1942, Dear Mr. Beard ___' "

"Why is she writing to James Beard?"

"I suppose it was because he was a regular contributor to *Delicious!* If you will allow me to continue, I am certain we will discover the reason for this letter." He cleared his throat and began to read again:

174

Dear Mr. Beard,

On the radio last spring, President Roosevelt said that each and every one of us here on the home front has a battle to fight: We must keep our spirits up. I am doing my best, but in my opinion Liver Gems are a lost cause, because they would take the spirit right out of anyone.

So when Mother says it is wrong for us to eat better than our brave men overseas, I tell her that I don't see how eating disgusting stuff helps them in the least. But, Mr. Beard, it is very hard to cook good food when you're only a beginner! When Mother decided it was her patriotic duty to work at the airplane factory, she should have warned me about recipes. You just can't trust them! Prudence Penny's are so revolting, I want to throw them right into the garbage.

Mrs. Davis from next door lent me one of her wartime recipe pamphlets, and I read about liver salmi, which sounded so romantic. But by the time I had cooked the liver for twenty minutes in hot water, cut it into little cubes, rolled them in flour, and sautéed them in fat, I'd made flour footprints all over the kitchen floor. The consommé and cream both hissed like angry cats when I added them. Then I was supposed to add stoned olives and taste for seasoning. I spit it right into the sink.

Mother looks so tired when she comes home, and I just couldn't give her salmi for supper. So I buried it in the backyard and made her some fried eggs. I know that waste is wrong, but I had no choice. Tomorrow I'm going to try again; I have my eye on the Peanut Butter and Lima Bean Loaf from a cookbook Mrs. Davis gave me, which she says is a "model of thrift."

That is why I am writing. Mr. Beard, I know you could do better. Don't you think it would be a good idea if you wrote a cookbook for people like me who are just learning to cook?

That could take a while, but in the meantime I have a question. We're baking cookies at school to send to the soldiers, and I refuse to waste my sugar rations on anything out of these silly books. So could you please, please, please send me a recipe I can trust?

I'll be checking the mailbox every day.

Sincerely yours,
Lulu Swan

"I wonder if he wrote back?"

"Judging by the date," Sammy was holding up the next letter, "he must have answered by return post."

November 15, 1942
Dear Mr. Beard,
I didn't know you were at Fort Dix, or that the editors had forwarded my letter, but if you don't mind my saying so, you would be much more useful to the war effort helping people like me. I'm not trying to flatter you, but Uncle Sam is wasting your talents. (Oh, yes, the answer to your question? I am twelve, but I will be thirteen soon.)

Thank you for the pamphlets from the Department of Agriculture. I had my doubts, but you're right: They surely beat Prudence Penny. Yesterday I took their advice and made green tomato mincemeat; they said it was a good way to use up the last tomatoes sitting on the vine.

I wish you could have seen the kitchen when I was done: It looked like a hurricane had blown right in the door! But I cleaned it all up, and when Mother came home the whole house smelled warm and spicy, Bing Crosby was singing "White Christmas" on the radio, I was wearing a clean apron, and she called me her "little homemaker."

What would you think about tomato mincemeat cookies? I bet no one else will think of that! Mr. Beard, if you'll help me figure out a recipe, I promise to never bother you again. Cross my heart.

Sincerely yours,
Lulu Swan

"Green tomato mincemeat does not strike me as particularly toothsome." Sammy put the letter back in the folder.

"Thrifty, though," I said. "And it was nice of him to send those pamphlets."

"He did more than that." Sammy held up another letter and then slowly lowered himself to the floor. "What is the point of remaining upright when being seated is so much more agreeable?" He patted the floor beside him and I sat down too.

November 29, 1942
Dear Mr. Beard,
Mother said it was "presumptuous" of me to change your recipe, but I knew you wouldn't mind, because I made it better. I added some nuts, just to give the cookies what Tommy Stroh calls "that old pizzazz." I gave them a new name too; I didn't think very much of Crybaby Cookies. They have become Magic Moments. So much better,

don't you think?

Mother likes to say that a fair exchange is no robbery, so I'm enclosing a pot holder as a thank-you. I made it myself. I was trying for the shape of a maple leaf, but it turned out more like a squirrel, so please pretend it's soft and fuzzy.

Your friend,
Lulu

P.S. Mother says I must ask if you are sincere when you say that you'd like to continue our correspondence. Are you? May I ask for more recipes?

Sammy was laughing softly. "Who on earth could say no to this child? Certainly not James Beard. And from what I have heard, he was extraordinarily generous to his fans." He was rooting through the file. "Here is another one!" He triumphantly held up a crinkled yellow sheet of paper.

December 8, 1942
Dear Mr. Beard,
Thank you for your letter. I read Mother the part where you said it's good when people change recipes to make them their own. She says that you are a very wise man.

Last week our whole school gathered in the auditorium for the cookie wrapping. First we popped gallons of corn to pack them in, and then we traded the cookies around so we could taste them all. Tommy said mine were the best, and although I don't want to sound conceited, he was right. I knew you'd send me a wonderful recipe!

Tommy and I put on a radio play to entertain everyone while they packed their cookies. It was about a girl who saves up money for a prom dress, but at the last minute she says, "It's only clothes," and buys war bonds instead. The play was a big success, and my whole school pledged to buy war bonds, which should have made me happy. But it gave me a queer feeling; it's easy to write propaganda when everyone agrees with you. Do you understand? I think I'd rather bake cookies; it feels more honest.

Your friend,
Lulu

Sammy looked down at me. "A girl after your own heart!" he said. "In my experience it is a rare female who can say, 'It's only clothes,' and mean it." His face grew pensive. "You know, my mother used to say

180

that when the war came, you discovered who you really were. Women changed. Children grew up overnight. I wonder what happened to this one." He opened the folder, thumbing through the pages until he found another letter from Lulu.

December 9, 1942
Dear Mr. Beard,
I'm sorry to write again so soon; Mother says I mustn't bombard you with letters. But I sent my Magic Moments off yesterday, and that made me think of you.

I hope the cookies will show Father that here on Lookout Avenue we are always thinking about him, always praying that he will land his plane safely. And I hope they'll remind him of our life here in Akron. Or maybe I should say what life used to be, before the war changed everything.

I haven't heard Mother laugh since she began building airplanes out at the Airdock. She always used to sing along with the radio, but yesterday she made me turn it off when "Cow Cow Boogie" came on; she said it gave her the jitters. She never used to get angry like other mothers either, but now every little thing upsets her. Today she yelled at me for cutting the bread too thick; she said it was wasteful. When I said it served the government right for making that stupid rule about not selling sliced bread anymore, she made me go to my room and think about all the soldiers who have no bread. I wish the war was over and Father was home and Mother back in the kitchen, singing with the radio. Is life ever going to be normal again?

Thank you for being my friend,
Lulu

I knew how it felt to wish life could go back to the way it used to be. Was it different during wartime, when it was happening to everyone at the same time? Was it easier when you didn't feel so alone?

"What do you remember about the war?" I asked Sammy.

"How decrepit do you think I am?" he snapped. "I will have you know that the war drew to a close long before I entered this world."

I could feel my face get hot. "Not to worry." Sammy patted my hand. "I brought that upon myself, nattering on about what Mother used to say about the war. But I believe those were the happiest years of her life."

"Wait, she was happy your father was gone?"

He leaned back against the wall. It was cozy in here, sitting on the floor in the murky light of the room, Sammy next to me and all that paper rustling around us. "On the contrary. But during the war she managed a gas station, and she adored everything about it — mucking about with the engines, changing oil, pumping fuel, washing windows. She was rather miserable when the war ended and she was obliged to resume the housewife's role; I remember her banging furiously around the kitchen, heaving pots and pans about. She said the house felt like a prison, closing in around her." Sammy stopped himself. "I am making my mother sound like a gorgon, which she was not. But she was not destined to do housework." He looked down at the folder, eager to end this conversation. "Let us hope for another letter."

December 18, 1942
Dear Mr. Beard,
The telegram man came today. I saw him walk up Lookout Avenue, through our little white gate and go under the grape arbor, and the whole time he was walking up the flagstone path to our door, my heart was pounding. When he rang the bell I didn't want to answer it.

Father is not dead, but the secretary of war regretted to inform us that he's missing in action. When I was finished crying, I went into the kitchen, splashed water on my face, and used up all my meat points for a hearty stew. Mother will need it to keep up her strength and her spirits.

She knew right away, the very minute she came in the door, that something was wrong. She saw the telegram in my hand. "Is he . . . ?" she asked. And when I shook my head no, she hugged me hard and went to wash her hands. I don't think she wanted me to see her cry.

Mother says we must prepare for the worst. But where does that get you? Besides, I do not believe for one minute that Father is dead. The world would feel lonelier without him, and it still feels the same. I know that one day he will get my Magic Moments.

I was going to send you some for Christmas, but Mother says that you have no use for cookies from a little girl in Akron who can hardly cook. (She always under-estimates me, but that is my cross to bear.) So I am sending you another pot holder. It comes with my very dearest wish that your holidays are happier than ours.

Your friend,
Lulu

"Are you crying?" asked Sammy.

"Of course not." I was grateful the room was so dark. Picturing Lulu alone in her kitchen had made something twist inside me. "Do you think her father ever got the cookies?" I asked. "I wonder if he survived."

Sammy held up the next piece of stationery. The handwriting was not Lulu Swan's.

"Aren't we going to find out what happened to her father?"

Sammy pointed to the shelves. "Thousands of letters are filed away up there, and I would wager good money that there are more from Lulu. That girl is not a quitter."

"But how're we ever going to find them?" I looked at the fat folders, with their acres of crumbling pages.

"You are a resourceful young woman," he said briskly. "I am certain that you will think of something." He was silent for a moment and then, as if the words were coming to him as he spoke, he said, " 'Dear James Beard' would make a lovely article. If there are enough letters, it could even be a book."

"You knew about the letters, didn't you?" It hit me that he'd lured me up here to provide me with a project.

"I beg your pardon?" Sammy looked so genuinely astonished that I knew I'd been wrong. "I am sorry to disabuse you of this remarkable notion, but I am flabbergasted by this find."

"Flabbergasted! What a wonderful word."

"Please consider writing the article. It is an excellent notion."

"I will. I'll think about it."

"Well, do not cogitate for a protracted period. The Timbers Mansion is worth a king's ransom, and in due course Young Arthur will attempt to sell it. The market is in momentary decline, but that will surely change. If you want to unearth Lulu's letters, you had best do so with celerity. And that, my dear, is the end of the speech." He unfolded himself from the floor. "I need to perambulate and get my blood flowing."

Sammy held out his hand and pulled me to my feet. We ducked through the door, pushed the bookcase back in place, and made our way through the golden light to the library door.

As it closed behind us, the stench of the building attacked us anew, stronger than before. But it didn't bother me much. Something had shifted. Lulu was in the library, sharing the Timbers Mansion. I was no longer alone.

LIBRARY LADIES

"What's wrong with you?" Sal grumbled the second time I gave a customer the wrong cheese. "Your head's somewhere else." Brow furrowed, he took my hand and led me into the back kitchen. "What's going on?"

"I was thinking about the war."

"Vietnam? Korea?"

"No, the big one. World War Two. Do you know what it was like during rationing?"

"Pop used to talk about how hard it had been. They couldn't get anything from Europe after the shipping lanes closed. Cheese wasn't rationed, but the only products they could get were made in America. Why do you ask?"

I'd been trying to imagine what it was like to live with the constant fear of death. The men you loved could die at any minute; they might, in fact, already be dead. How did Lulu bear that knowledge? How did anyone?

I was telling Sal about the letters when

Rosalie came charging into the back kitchen. "Theresa and I could use a little help out there," she said, tugging at my sleeve. "It's Sunday."

I looked at my watch: almost two o'clock, which was when Mr. Complainer always showed up. "C'mon, Rosalie, you know that man has zero interest in me."

"You never know," she said, herding me back into the shop. "Have you ever thought about contact lenses? Your eyes are so pretty."

Right on cue, Mr. Complainer walked through the door. Today, however, he was not alone.

"Oh, she's much too thin." Rosalie watched disapprovingly as he steered a blonde in a shearling coat toward the counter.

He pointed out various Fontanari landmarks: the towering wheels of Parmigiano, the chilies dangling from the ceiling, the cans of wood-roasted coffee on the shelves. She looked fascinated, laughing up at him, holding his arm. He introduced her to Jane, who took her hand and smiled indulgently, and I could almost hear her saying what a treat it was to see young lovers in the shop.

"That's a lot of makeup for a trip to the grocery store," Rosalie remarked.

"She's very pretty," I said.

"Too thin," Rosalie repeated, pushing me forward as their number came up. Mr. Complainer shot a disappointed glance toward the end of the counter.

"That" — he nodded toward Sal, who'd just started serving the guys from the local firehouse — "is the legendary Sal Fontanari, and since he's with his favorite customers, it's bound to take at least an hour. Meanwhile, we will be in the very capable hands of Wilhelmina. She's the first outsider Sal's ever permitted behind the counter of Fontanari's. We're all convinced she has magical powers. And this" — he turned to me — "is Amy, who hails from deepest New Jersey, where there are no shops like Fontanari's."

"Nice to meet you," said Amy primly. I hated her.

"What can I do for you?" I asked.

"We're having a party." Mr. Complainer took over.

"How many people?"

"Nine." He looked down at Amy. "Do I have that right? What do you think we should we get?"

"The usual," she said, making me long to tell her she would find nothing usual at Fontanari's. I bit my tongue. "Some Brie, maybe, and some Swiss. Nothing too strong.

A little salami — but not the kind with garlic."

"We have no garlic-free salami," I replied. As if such a thing even exists.

She glanced up at Mr. Complainer. "Boyd can't stand garlic, you know that."

Mr. Complainer looked pained.

"Bologna?" she suggested, pointing at the mortadella.

"We'll take half a pound." He gave me one of his nicest smiles, saying, "And maybe you could give Amy a taste of the fontina? That should be safe."

I handed a slice of our blandest cheese across the counter, and the blonde nibbled at a corner. "Oh," she purred, "that's so good."

I bet she was a cheerleader in high school.

"I told you that man was single," Rosalie whispered fiercely in my ear. "You should have listened to me." Her unspoken words — and now it's too late — lingered in the air.

"Some prosciutto?" Mr. Complainer was unaware of the drama taking place behind the counter. "Would you let her taste it?"

I took down the San Daniele, sheared off a paper-thin slice, and handed it across the counter. Amy gave it a dubious sniff. "It smells funny," she said. "What is it?"

191

"Italian ham," said Mr. Complainer. "Taste it."

She examined the meat as if it might be dangerous, carefully removed the strip of fat, and took the tiniest possible bite. "I prefer good old American ham," she pronounced.

He looked mortified, but he obediently followed her directions; the guests at this party would not be disturbed by unfamiliar flavors. "We do have to get some mozzarella," he said. "Betty loves it."

"You sure?" Amy sounded doubtful.

He was.

"Do you want the cow's milk mozzarella or the buffalo milk?" It was mean of me. I couldn't help myself.

Amy reacted exactly as I'd hoped. "Buffalo milk? Are you serious? Cheese made from buffalo milk?"

Mr. Complainer looked down at her, and I thought he seemed slightly impatient. "Real mozzarella, the kind in that caprese salad you're so fond of, is made from water-buffalo milk."

She shuddered visibly. "*Water* buffalo? Guess I won't be eating that again."

Across the room, Sal raised his eyebrows; Mr. Complainer had gone down a notch in his estimation. Rosalie was even more distressed. When they'd gone, she let out a little wail. "Did you hear what she said about the prosciutto?"

"I told you he wasn't interested in me." I gave her my best told-you-so look, but I did think it was strange. What was a guy who took cooking classes in Italy doing with a woman like her? She wasn't *that* pretty.

On Monday I arrived at the mansion in a better mood than usual and scrambled up the stairs, ignoring the dark hallway, trying to ignore the stench. Was it possible it had gotten even worse? I fled to my cubbyhole, determined to get my work out of the way as quickly as I could. I had decided to look for more letters from Lulu.

My first caller had attempted caramelizing sugar for the first time, with disastrous results. "Caramel always hisses, bubbles, and seizes before it settles down," I told her.

"Well, why didn't you say so?" she said irritably.

The second caller had tried to make a complicated rabbit-liver terrine into a vegetarian dish, and the third had sliced off the tip of her index finger on a mandoline. It went on like that, one time-consuming disaster after another, and it was hours before I could move on to recipe requests.

There were two for the Coffee Crunch Cake they used to make at Blum's in San Francisco, a recipe so popular I kept it on my desktop. Someone else wanted a fresh coconut cake she remembered from the fifties, and that was easy too. I forwarded the request for a reproduction of the 1965 Christmas cover to rights and permissions in the main office. But Julie Marr, in Rio Vista, California, had me stumped.

"My dad's ninetieth birthday is coming up," she wrote, "and he keeps talking about these great cookies he ate in the war. I wanted to surprise him with Anzac biscuits, but there are so many different recipes I don't know which to trust. Help!"

Anzac biscuits?

Google offered some assistance, informing me that the name was an acronym for "Australian and New Zealand Army Corps," but after that the online history grew cloudy. One source traced them back to the Scottish Highlands, another to the aborigines. I wondered if the library could help. I'd look up the biscuits, and then I'd look for Lulu.

As I climbed the stairs to the third floor, the stench grew steadily worse; this couldn't be normal. I'd have to call someone over at the main office. It had gotten so bad that I ran up the last few steps to the fourth floor

194

and sprinted toward the library, yearning for the cool apple scent. The room seemed to reach out and pull me in, and the soft chairs invited me to sit. As I moved deeper into the room, the quiet grew more profound. It was so peaceful that I could feel my heartbeat slow, as if I were breathing with the room, honoring its age.

The card catalogs, three huge old wooden files, stood near the fantastic desk. The first one wheezed as I pulled on the top handle, emitting a little puff of dust. Somewhere in the back of my mind was a dim memory of the card catalog at the Santa Barbara Public Library, the drawers filled with prim index cards of neatly typed Dewey decimal numbers. This was different; I looked down, startled, at a sea of colored ink. Flipping to "Anzac," I pulled up the first card and found myself staring down at angular writing scrawled with a red pen. "The first recipe for Anzac biscuits appeared in the *War Chest Cookery Book* (Sydney, 1917). That recipe, however, is for an entirely different biscuit than the one we know today. The first recipe for what we now consider an Anzac biscuit was the 'Anzac Crispie,' in the 9th edition of *St. Andrew's Cookery Book* (Dunedin, 1921)."

The card behind it had obviously been

written by someone else. The black ball-point writing was clear and rounded, each "t" neatly crossed, each dot centered just above the "i." "Anzac Day is a national day of remembrance commemorating the battle of Gallipoli. Anzac biscuits contain rolled oats, flour, desiccated coconut, sugar, butter, golden syrup, baking soda, and boiling water."

There was a third card, the elegant calligraphic script written in turquoise ink of such startling brightness that it seemed like a shout from the past. "Anzac biscuits are chameleons, coming in all shapes and sizes. There are no standard recipes, but during World War II, readers submitted dozens of variations. You'll find them in the letter files for 1943. And the excellent Australian *Commonsense Cookery Book* is always reliable."

What army of eccentric librarians had created these color-coded cards? I began to pull open drawers, looking for other colors and different handwriting, trying to determine how many there had been. But I found no green, no purple, no yellow. These strange cards came in only red, black, and blue. Who were these library ladies? When had they created this strange catalog?

The library shelves contained only books or magazines, so the recipes mentioned on the turquoise card must be among the letters in the secret room. I walked to the back of the library and slid the bookcase aside, half expecting to find the funny little doorway gone. But it was still there, and I squeezed through the narrow opening, waiting for my eyes to adjust to the darkness before reaching for the light switch.

The letters were arranged chronologically by year; 1943 took up an entire shelf, which was so high up I had to stand on tiptoe to read the labels. There were hundreds of folders, but I could see nothing labeled either "Anzac" or "Biscuit." Where were those reader recipes? I reached for the first folder on the shelf, which was strangely labeled "Aardvarks of America." Aardvarks? Are there aardvarks in America? I opened the file and removed the first letter.

Dear *Delicious!*,
I am responding to your latest contest: Here is my recipe for a wartime eggless mayonnaise. Peel and mash one small baked potato. Stir in a teaspoon of mustard, a pinch of salt, and a tablespoon of vinegar. Finally, slowly beat in 2 tablespoons of salad oil. Food will win the war!
Sincerely yours,
Julia J. Applebee

The next letter was also a response to the contest. This hopeful cook had submitted a recipe for a carrot roll with toasted oatmeal and cold mashed potatoes. The third submission was for sardine fritters . . . and so on. There were no aardvarks in the folder, just recipes for extremely peculiar wartime dishes. Perplexed, I put the folder back and reached for the next one.

This one was slimmer, but its name was as incomprehensible as the first. "Abracadabra" was typed neatly on its little plastic tab, and when I opened it I found that the letters were entries in another contest. The magazine had requested that readers submit their "magical substitutions" for ingredients that had become difficult to obtain. My favorite was from a woman suggesting twenty ways to serve sweet potatoes in place of pie.

Pulling down the next folder, and the next, I began trying to decipher the labels. "Big Cheese" contained letters to the editor in chief, and "Bitter" held nothing but complaints. Whoever had created these files had a wicked sense of humor, but she had organized them according to some mysterious system known only to herself. I felt she was daring me to figure it out.

I looked up at the shelves, studying the

labels. The letters from the prewar years were sparse, taking up only a few slim shelves, and there were no files after 1972. But between 1942 and 1946 there were dozens of shelves, containing what must have been tens of thousands of letters. I would never have time to read them all. I pulled down the "Aardvarks of America" file, riffling through the letters again, thinking that if I could figure out what aardvarks had to do with the contest, I might understand the system.

But what was an aardvark, anyway? I wasn't sure. I went out to the giant dictionary and learned that aardvarks are prehistoric creatures that live on termites and ought to be extinct. "In African folklore," the dictionary said, "the aardvark is admired because of its diligent quest for food." The contest in the "Aardvarks" folder had also been characterized by a diligent quest for food; was there something there?

I went back to the card file and studied the Anzac cards. Was Gallipoli a clue? Then my eye caught the name of the Australian cookbook: *The Commonsense Cookery Book.* This seemed promising, and I went back to the secret room and flipped through the "C" folders. "Cackle." "Char." "Colossus." "Comfort." And there it was: "Commonsense." I was so startled by the discovery that I dropped the file as I pulled it from the shelf, and it spilled its letters at my feet.

As I bent to scoop them up, my eye caught a sheaf of translucent papers in the middle of the pile, held together with a rusting paper clip. Turning the top one over, I saw that it was densely covered in a careful schoolgirl script. The Anzac biscuits went straight out of my head.

February 15, 1943
Dear Mr. Beard,
Mother calls it "magical thinking" when I say that Father will come back, but what I say is that hope can't hurt. She could use a little magic. She sits in Plant A all day long, drawing the schematics onto starched linen. She has to bend over the drafting table, and at night she's always pressing a hand to the place where her back hurts. She says it's hard work, but I think it's very romantic; a copy of her drawing goes onto every Corsair. I know it must have been a comfort to Father to have her drawing on his plane.

Yesterday was Valentine's Day, and I wanted to make something special to cheer Mother up. I found a recipe for cheese soufflé in the *Beacon Journal,* and

I knew Mother would like that — especially because it didn't use a single rationed ingredient.

I've always heard that soufflés are hard, but then I remembered what you said: "The only thing that will make a soufflé fall is if it knows you're afraid of it." I was determined not to let it get the best of me, and it worked! It came out all fat and puffy, and even though the recipe says it serves four, Mother and I ate the entire thing!

I've been trying to keep our spirits up, but it is very hard. May I tell you a secret? My homeroom teacher, Miss Dickson, is a horrid witch! I know it's not right to speak ill of adults, but everybody hates her. The awful thing, since Mr. Shoemaker went off to the war, is that I'll probably get her again next year. I'm not sure I can bear it.

Now, about you. In my opinion it's a very good thing that you're leaving the army. I'm sure cryptography is important, but I'm happy that Uncle Sam has come to his senses and sent you back to us. Maybe now you'll have time to write that book for new cooks.

Will you be very busy, now that you're a civilian? I hope I'll still be able to write. I think of you as my secret friend, and you cannot imagine what a comfort that is.

Your friend,
Lulu

Hope can't hurt. I turned the phrase over and over in my mind, wondering at what age optimism ends. Lulu's mother was right: Her daughter was a master of magical thinking. And not just because she had convinced herself — against all odds — that her father was still alive. She'd also turned a famous stranger into a magical friend. I tried to picture James Beard's enormous bulk, sitting at a desk, writing the letters. I so wished I could see what he had written back.

March 1, 1943
Dear Mr. Beard,
Yesterday felt like spring. Father used to call those days "a gift," and whenever one came along we'd start planning our garden. Even though he's not here, I got out the Burgess seed catalog, because I like reading the lovely names like Hearts of Gold carrots and Early Fortune cucumbers. But who would want to raise mangel-wurzels, kudzu, or kohl-rabi? They sound terrible!

Tommy came to walk me to school, and

I showed him the picture of the Climbing Trip-L-Crop tomatoes; the catalog says they grow sixteen feet tall and give three bushels of fruit! Tommy said that was more than I could possibly use, and I got so mad I decided to skip school and go to that little Italian grocery store in North Hill and ask for advice.

In the end Tommy came with me. Cappuzzelli's was filled with people drinking tiny cups of coffee, waving their hands, and speaking Italian, which moves twice as fast as English. The owner said his wife would be glad to give me some recipes, so we went upstairs to their apartment.

Mrs. Cappuzzelli is so tiny she looks like an elf, and when she opened the door we could barely see her in the whoosh of steam that came rushing out, smelling of tomatoes and garlic. She has long silvery hair tied up in a bun and smiling black eyes, and her apron wraps three times around her, like a little girl's.

She sat us down at a wooden table, sliced off slabs of bread from a big loaf, and rubbed them with olive oil and garlic. When I asked about recipes, she said that if I come back in September she'll show me how to make her tomato sauce (she called it "gravy").

It was a lovely day — at least until Mother came home. She sniffed around — she despises the smell of garlic — and wanted to know where I'd been. I could hardly tell her I'd skipped school, so I said there must have been garlic in the spaghetti at lunch. It was the best I could do on the spur of the moment, but if she finds out that they stopped serving spaghetti when the war started, I'll be in triple trouble.

I'm sending in my seed order soon. Do you have any suggestions for Victory Garden crops?

Your friend,
Lulu

No wonder the librarian had put this in a folder called "Commonsense." I looked down at the letter, reading the names of the vegetables. What on earth was a mangel-wurzel?

I stopped at the card file on my way out. And there it was, a card written in turquoise ink. "Mangel-wurzels, or sugar beets, did not become an important American crop until the Civil War. The Caribbean cane-sugar industry relied on slave labor, and abolitionists looking for an alternative began to grow beets instead. With the coming of the war, the industry accelerated to provide sugar for the northern states."

What an interesting piece of information, and how strange that the card was just sitting here, with no apparent connection to a book. I turned the card over, and on the back was another note: "There are some interesting letters on sugar substitutes in the reader-letter files from World War II. Look under 'Civil War.' "

I wondered if this had anything to do with Lulu. Probably not, but I wrote down "Civil War," thinking that tomorrow I'd look for the file. I flipped off the lights, went into the hall — and forgot all about sugar beets and Civil Wars. Something was terribly, horribly wrong.

In the Nightmare Kitchen

The smell. When I emerged from the fresh apple scent of the library, the odor of decay had become too powerful to ignore. Somewhere in the mansion, something much larger than a mouse was rotting. The stench grew more intense as I approached the staircase, and by the time I reached the third floor, the smell was so strong that I gagged and buried my nose in the crook of my elbow.

The dreadful odor was clearly coming from the kitchen; how had I not realized this before? I began making my way toward the door; the nearer I got, the stronger the smell grew, until it stopped me in my tracks. I held my breath, pinched my nose, turned back toward the stairs, and raced down to my office. I needed something to cover my nose and mouth.

Wrapping my scarf three times around my head, I climbed back to the kitchen and pushed the door tentatively open. What sprang out could not be called an odor; it was a living thing with tentacles that twined around me, wrapping me in a foul fog and spreading tendrils into my hair, around my neck, up into the delicate flesh of my nostrils. It was something evil, attacking and overwhelming me. I staggered back, coughing.

I bent over, hands cupped over my mouth and nose, and staggered into the miasma, groping for the lights. When the fluorescents crackled on, I straightened up and stood there, stunned and sickened by the sight.

No meat or produce belonging to Pickwick Publications had been allowed to leave the premises with the cooks. The goons had zealously done their job. They had protected the equipment. Then they had taken the furniture, turned out the lights, locked the door, and walked away from the rest of it. Left alone for five weeks, the kitchen had moldered into an enormous chemistry experiment. Rotten pork shoulders oozed across the kitchen counter, and crabs lay in stinking piles buzzing with flies. What had been heaps of organic greens had dissolved into slimy scum, leaking loathsome juices. It was a vision from hell.

I backed quickly toward the door, shaking

with disgust. An orange was sitting on the counter, the shape still round, the color still bright, and it looked so normal that I reached for it as I went by. I stifled a scream as it collapsed in on itself like a fetid water balloon and began to drip through my fingers. Nothing here had escaped unscathed.

I grabbed a towel, wiped my hands, and went running from the kitchen, slamming the door behind me and stumbling frantically down the stairs as if I were fleeing a fire. Thinking I might be leaving for the last time, I detoured down the hall for my coat before continuing my plunge toward fresh air.

Outside, I turned, looking back at the mansion, almost expecting to see rotting food oozing from the windows. But the grand old house stared stonily back. The air was cold and damp, and I stood shivering in the thin light of late afternoon, embarrassed by my panic. I punched Mr. Pickwick's number into my phone, and as I began to describe the scene to his secretary, my fingers could still feel the way that rotten orange had evaporated beneath them.

"I'll get a cleaning crew there as soon as possible." Ruby's voice was matter-of-fact — just another day at Pickwick Publications. "I'll try to get them to start tonight. But don't go back to the mansion until you hear from me."

It was a bleak, damp evening, the kind of cold that creeps beneath your skin and into your bones, making you feel you'll never be warm again. The sun had set, leaving dull pewter in its wake. I walked uptown in the growing dark, thinking I might find a friendly face at The Pig. Thursday would be there, and maybe even Jake.

To my surprise, I found Richard sitting at the bar. Thursday was standing on the other side, and as I watched she leaned intently toward him, looking into his eyes until their foreheads were almost touching, her ash-blond bangs mingling with his blue-black hair. So they were together! I wondered when that had happened.

She pulled back when she saw me, smiled, gestured to the stool next to Richard's, and plunked a plate of chicken-liver toasts onto the bar. She's famous for them, but looking at that gloriously decadent mush made my stomach lurch. I pushed it away. She raised her eyebrows.

"Are you all right?" Her eyes really were beautiful. "What's happened? If you've lost your appetite, something must be very wrong."

Richard put his hand on my arm. "You look like you've been walking with ghosts."

As I began to describe the scene, Richard pushed the plate farther down the bar. "Take any pictures?" he asked eagerly.

"God, no."

"You should have. It sounds amazing!"

"Please! I couldn't get out of there fast enough." I could feel the bile rising again.

"I have to see it." He shrugged into his jacket and grabbed the camera he always carried. "Come!" He pulled me off the stool. "We need to get there before the cleaning crew ruins everything."

He hustled me out the door, issuing one of those piercing whistles that bring taxis screeching to a halt. We were on our way downtown before I had managed to get my arms into my coat sleeves.

Back at the mansion, we raced up the stairs to the third floor, taking them three at a time. Richard gagged and covered his nose and mouth with his scarf. Then he opened the door.

His face was unreadable while he walked through the kitchen. He put the camera to his eye. "God," he sighed, "I've never seen anything like this. There must be tens of thousands of dollars' worth of rotting food here. Do you know what you'd have to do to replicate this?"

"You couldn't." And I couldn't bear to spend another minute there. "I'll be downstairs." I'm not sure he heard me go.

I waited a long time. The grandfather clock ticked loudly; even with the lightbulbs replaced, there was something spooky about the mansion at night, and I was glad when Richard returned, cradling his camera. "It was even more extraordinary than I'd hoped." He was walking back and forth, barely seeing me, and I knew that in his mind he was still upstairs in the kitchen, still envisioning the room. He seemed radiant, as if he had walked through an energy field, gathering electricity. I could almost smell the ozone.

"What are you going to do with the pictures?"

"I'm not sure." His voice was pensive. "I won't know what I've got until I develop them."

"Do you ever shoot digital?"

"I'm old school. I like watching the images struggle up through the developer. I like to get my hands on them, make physical changes. It's much more satisfying than working on a computer. You knew I started out as a photographer, didn't you?"

I looked at him, surprised. Richard seemed

so confident that I'd assumed creative director was his dream job, that he'd worked his way up to what he'd always wanted. I'd never thought to ask if he had other aspirations. "How did you end up working in magazines?" It was so odd, thinking of him yearning to do something else.

He gave me a bemused smile. "You have any idea how hard it is to make a living as an artist? I had to work my way through college, and then I got a magazine job to pay off my student loans. I was only going to do it for a little while. . . ." He gave me another lopsided grin. "I think Young Arthur actually did me a favor, pushing me out the door. And, thanks to you, I might have stumbled onto something here."

His hands were moving, framing the pictures he was seeing in his head. "I could never have imagined anything quite like that kitchen. That's why I knew I needed to see it. It was so disgusting that you wanted to puke — well, you know that — and at the same time so exotic, so beautiful."

"Beautiful?" I was incredulous. "You found that beautiful? It was a nightmare!"

"Not to me. It was like landing on another planet. I just hope I did it justice. I can't thank you enough."

I stared at him, regretful, even a bit

212

ashamed that I could not see the world as he did. Part of me wanted to run back and take a look before it was too late. But the need to escape was even stronger.

"My pleasure," I said.

UNDER MILKWEED

It took them two days to clean the kitchen, but it felt like forever. The whole time, the word "mangel-wurzel" kept popping into my head, like a tune you can't forget. It was such a ridiculous word, and I couldn't wait to find out if the next group of Lulu's letters would be filed under "Civil War."

As soon as Ruby called to tell me the kitchen had been "sanitized," I raced back to the Timbers Mansion. It was mid-afternoon, but I couldn't wait to test my theory.

The air smelled as fresh as clean laundry, and as I climbed the stairs I saw that they'd been swept, the banisters dusted. The ugly dumpsters still loitered in the empty halls, but most of the litter had been removed, taking with it the haunted feeling. I inhaled deeply.

I'd been planning to go right to the library, but when I dropped my coat in the office, the phone rang.

"Oh, Billie." Mrs. Cloverly's voice radiated relief. "I'm so happy to have found you! I've been calling and calling, and you never answer. Are you all right? I was afraid that something terrible had happened."

It was touching, really, and so I let her ramble on. She'd tried making homemade pasta, with predictable results; the recipe didn't work with powdered eggs.

When she finally finished complaining, I ran upstairs. Three days ago the idea had made some sense, but now the whole thing seemed so absurd that I was surprised when I found "Civil War," a fat file, neatly shelved between "Citrus Fruit" and "Clams."

The first letter was an impassioned ode to the rutabaga from a reader in Oshkosh. "During the Civil War," she had written, "people understood that it has remarkable sweetness when roasted. But why," she wanted to know, "are people intent on overlooking this versatile vegetable?"

"Maybe because it tastes terrible," I muttered, putting the letter aside. The next reader wrote in praise of sorghum as a sweetener, and a third had discovered six wonderful ways to sweeten food with apple juice. The letters were spare and sensible, testimonials from a frugal nation caught up in a great social experiment. Left behind, these women were fighting the only way they knew — converting their pots and pans into battleships and bullets, sacrificing their cooking fat for ammunition. And Lulu was right there, doing her bit.

March 16, 1943
Dear Mr. Beard,
The garlic got me. I thought Mother had forgotten all about me saying I'd eaten some at school, but wouldn't you know that she mentioned it to Miss Dickson on the night we presented the school play on the Civil War. (It was meant to be patriotic.)

"Spaghetti?" From across the auditorium, you could have heard Miss Dickson's voice rise to a screech in that horrid way it does. "Spaghetti? Surely you don't think Jennings Middle School would serve enemy food in our cafeteria?"

Mother's eyes narrowed and she gave me a look. Then she dug her fingers into my arm so hard that I had black-and-blues in the morning. "We'll discuss this later," she said. The "discussion" was very unpleasant. And that is all I am going to say on that subject.

Instead, I want to thank you for suggesting the bees. What a good idea! Mrs. Cappuzzelli keeps bees, and she's not afraid of them at all. If a tiny little old lady can face down a hive of bees, well, I guess I can too. Bees for victory; think of the sugar I will be saving!

Your friend,
Lulu

Enemy food? Spaghetti? It was a shocking idea. Everyone knows that Japanese American citizens were interned during the war, but I'd never heard about prejudice against Italian Americans. My first instinct was to call Sal, but, remembering how insulted Sammy had been when I asked about the war, I thought better of it.

Where was Sammy, anyway? He'd been so excited about Lulu, but ten days had passed since then and he hadn't come back. All his things were still in his office too. I called his apartment and then his cell, but all I got was "Kindly leave a message, and I shall return it with all possible dispatch. Please do not neglect to honor me with your telephone number."

I called Jake to see if he'd heard anything. "Don't worry about Sammy." He sounded distracted. "I bet he's stretched out on a tropical beach right this minute, discovering the next luxury destination."

"Yeah," I said, relieved. "I should have thought of that. How're you?"

"Not so hot," he admitted. "I still can't believe it's over. I think I might go away after the holidays."

"Sounds like a good idea. I'd be happy to watch Sherman while you're gone. I could even bring him in to work. It'd be like old times." I'd love having the big yellow dog with me at the mansion, and for a moment I thought Jake was going to say yes. But then he cleared his throat awkwardly and said, "Thanks, but there's no need. Talk soon."

Did his voice sound slightly strange? It was probably just me; everything felt off. I'd been calling Sammy's house every day, but there was never an answer. I couldn't believe that he would have gone away without a word to anyone. I called Richard, but he was as unconcerned as Jake. "Sammy can take care of himself. He's probably doing something for one of the big travel books. Want me to call around and find out?"

"Would you?" I knew I was being a pest, but it was only a couple of phone calls.

Feeling slightly better, I went back to Lulu's letters. I was still thinking about Sammy, still thinking how much more fun it would be if I were sharing this with him.

April 8, 1943

Dear Mr. Beard,

Thank you for telling me about Chef Boiardi and his efforts for the war. When I told Mother that Chef Boyardee was not only a real Italian from Piacenza, Italy, but that his factory's in Cleveland and it's making spaghetti for our soldiers, she felt ashamed about thinking of spaghetti as "enemy food." Someday I'll find the courage to tell Miss Dickson (not that I think it will make much difference).

Today our class went into the woods to observe the migration of the thrushes. We've been tracking their flight path, making maps as they return from South America. Looking up at the sky, I thought I'd like to be a bird: They have no checkpoints, no passports, no boundaries. No war. "Free as a bird" makes a lot more sense to me now.

It's been a wet spring, and the morels were everywhere. I showed Tommy the secret spots where Father and I always used to collect them, and before we knew it we had a huge pile. That's when Miss Dickson found us.

She began shrieking at us to put them down, saying they could be poison.

I know how to tell a false morel from a

real one, but of course she didn't believe me. "If your father were here, it would be a different matter," she said, which wasn't very kind. She knows Father is missing. She made us dump out all the morels, which seemed like a shocking waste. But at the last minute she relented and said I could keep mine since I was such an expert. I think she was hoping I'd eat them and die.

Tonight I'm going to make creamed morels for dinner. That will be a nice treat for Mother. But I'm planning to dry the rest and put them by. May I send you some? They'd be much more useful than a silly pot holder.

Your friend,
Lulu

P.S. While we were foraging for morels, we found a large crop of young milkweed shoots and they looked delicious. Can you eat milkweed?

I picked up the next letter, and the next, and then went through the entire file, but the "Civil War" file held no more letters from Lulu. I combed Lulu's words, looking for clues to the next letter. "Spaghetti" seemed like a good prospect. Or maybe "morels"? Then my eye caught the post-script, and I wrote that down too. "Can you eat milkweed?" Not a clue, perhaps, but I was curious. I decided to check with the library ladies.

They turned out to have a lot to say on the subject, but the pay dirt was on a blue card. "Milkweed," the librarian had written, "played an important part in World War II. There are some illuminating letters on the subject in the 'Foraging' file of 1943."

It seemed too good to be true: another direct instruction. I went back to the secret room, thinking it couldn't possibly be this easy. But there was, indeed, a fat file marked "Foraging," and when I opened it up, the illuminating letters were right on top.

September 18, 1943
Dear Mr. Beard,
School has started, and it's a terrible trial. I have Miss Dickson again, and I don't foresee any good coming of it. If only she'd decide that it's her patriotic duty to go work at the airplane factory! Teenagers all over Akron would rejoice.

Her latest project is what Tommy calls USS Dickson. Since we can't get kapok from Japan anymore, we've been collecting milkweed to make life jackets. A pound

221

of milkweed floss will keep a sailor afloat for ten hours, and Miss Dickson wants us to collect enough to make life jackets for an entire battleship!

Today I opened one of the pods and looked inside. I liked the recipes you sent me for milkweed shoots last spring — they taste just like asparagus — but now I'm wondering about the floss. Can you cook with it? Have you ever? Is it good?

Your friend,
Lulu

September 28, 1943
Dear Mr. Beard,
I've been called a liar twice today. And it's all your fault.

We're still collecting milkweed pods, but today I did what you said and put the immature ones into a separate bag to take home. I should have known Miss Dickson was keeping her eye on me, because when the bag was almost full, she pounced. She said I was a selfish, unpatriotic girl who was trying to sabotage her milkweed project. I told her that the immature pods are useless for life jackets and that I was keeping them to cook, but she didn't believe me. She called me a little liar and sent me to the principal's office.

I guess Principal Jones agreed, because he said nobody eats milkweed. Then he said he had the perfect punishment: I was going to have to prove what I said by cooking the floss and eating it. He took me down to the kitchen and handed me a pot. It's a good thing that I trust you.

At first I was afraid to take a bite, but Principal Jones was watching, so I shut my eyes and took a spoonful. You were right! It's so pleasant and chewy. I ate a second spoonful, and there must have been something about the look on my face, because Principal Jones picked up a spoon and tasted it too. "Miss Dickson owes you an apology," he said, as we sat down to share the rest. I told him you said that it tasted just like cheese when it's mixed with other foods, and he said that someday he would like to try that.

I took the rest of the pods home and cooked the floss with rice. It looked so much like cheese that Mother refused to believe me when I said that there was no cheese in the pot. "I don't know why you're lying, Lulu," she said, and made me go to my room. Sometimes I feel as if the war has kidnapped my mother; she's so differ-

223

ent than she used to be. I want the old one back.

Milkweed is delicious, but I'm through with it.

Your friend,

Lulu

I folded up the letter, wishing that Sammy were here; he'd love the story of Lulu and the milkweed floss.

October 10, 1943
Dear Mr. Beard,
I'm sorry to keep sharing all my problems with you, but Mother always believes the teachers, no matter how wrong they are. And I just have to tell someone.

Today Miss Dickson sent me to the principal's office. Again. She said the reason was rudeness and insubordination, but really she just can't stand it when somebody has an opinion that's different from hers! We were having a class on civics, talking about what makes America a great country. I said I thought one important reason is that we've all come from different places in the world and that we learn from one another.

She said I had an interesting point of view and asked me to elaborate. So I told about Mrs. Cappuzzelli and how she helped me with the tomatoes. When I was done, Miss Dickson asked if my mother knew I'd been "consorting with the enemy."

That made me so mad that I shouted a little, telling her that the Cappuzzellis are as American as she is. She started to shout back, going on about their "dark skin" and "barbaric" language. She said the government should have rounded them all up and put them in the camps like the Japanese so we wouldn't have to worry about them sneaking around behind our backs and sending messages home.

I told her that Mrs. Cappuzzelli wasn't sending messages to anyone, except for maybe her three sons in the army. And that did it. She said she'd heard enough.

She marched me off to the principal's office and told him that he should give me the paddle. My heart leapt, and I looked at it hanging behind his desk; it's very big. Principal Jones put his fingers together, as if he were about to do "Here is the church and here is the steeple," and stared at them for a long time. Then he turned around and picked up the paddle.

I felt as if I was going to cry, but I was determined not do it in front of Miss Dickson. Her mean little mouth smiled, and she told him she thought ten strokes would be the proper penalty for such a grave infraction. I gasped, and even Mr. Jones seemed a bit shocked.

He said we should get it over with, so I stood up. Then he told Miss Dickson that he doesn't believe in humiliating students by allowing anyone to witness their punishment. She looked so disappointed, but he just stood there, waiting for her to leave.

When she was gone, he told me to sit down. There was the strangest expression on his face, as if he wanted to say something but knew he shouldn't. We sat there, looking at each other for the longest time. Then he put the paddle down and told me I had to learn to control my temper.

Now I have to stay after school every day this week, cleaning the blackboards in all the classrooms. It's very inconvenient; sometimes I think I'd rather have had the paddle.

Your friend,
Lulu

I picked up the next letter, and the next, but as I worked my way through the folder, I reluctantly accepted the fact that there were no more letters here from Lulu.

Where would the next batch be? I went

back, looking for the secret word. Nothing leapt out at me. I had decided to try "floss," "civics," and "patriotic," when my phone began to vibrate. Probably Aunt Melba, who'd been calling constantly, wanting me to come home for Christmas. She kept telling me how much Dad missed me, how much they both did, and I just wasn't ready to have that conversation again. But it wasn't Aunt Melba.

"You find out where Sammy is?" I said to Richard.

"Sorry." He sounded chagrined. "I forgot. I'll ask around. But that's not why I'm here."

"Here? In the mansion?"

"My key still works. I just got the pictures back, and I came to show you. Where the hell are you?"

"In the library."

"The library?" The way he said the word, I might have said I was on the moon. "I've never been in there."

"You'll love it. Come on up. I'll meet you at the door."

Minutes later Richard stood on the threshold, silently surveying the room. "It's more beautiful than I'd imagined," he said, but I could tell he wasn't really paying much attention. He was focused on the photographs

227

in his portfolio, and he went to the desk and began to carefully lay them out.

He had captured a gorgeous but alien world, both terrifying and seductive in its strangeness. In Richard's kitchen, the rotten food had become abstract forms, a landscape of destruction both alluring and dangerous. His pictures combined the eerily erotic quality of a Georgia O'Keeffe orchid with the weird ordinariness of a Diane Arbus freak. You wanted to turn away. And at the same time you wanted to jump into the frame and walk around in that mysterious terrain. No wonder this was what he had always wanted to do; I stood staring at Richard's photographs, amazed by his ability to see all this. "They're gorgeous. And terrible too." I stood looking for a long time, mesmerized by his images.

Then I held out my hand and led him to the great wooden card catalog; I wanted to give him something in return. "Open any drawer."

Richard didn't ask why. It was one of the things I liked best about him. He just pulled open the nearest drawer, and his long, deft fingers flicked through the cards until he came to one that interested him. " 'Bottarga,' " he read, " 'the dried roe of mullet or tuna, is a southern Mediterranean delicacy that is often called "poor man's caviar." Generally neglected by modern cookbooks; letters are your best resource. You will find inspiration in the letters of Elizabeth David (who is especially good after a few glasses of wine) and the great (but often inaccurate) Waverley Root.' " Richard returned the turquoise card to the file. "Where are the letters filed?"

As we walked the length of the room, past all the wooden tables, I was very conscious of his hand in mine, conscious of his little lurch of surprise when I rolled the bookcase aside to reveal the tiny door in the wall. Without a word, he doubled over and disappeared inside. I heard a sharp intake of breath.

I squeezed in next to him and turned on the light. Richard reached out and stroked the nearest shelf as if it were a living creature.

"They're letters? All of them?" He pointed to the folder I'd left lying on the ground. "You were reading that one? What's it about?"

"Milkweed." I tried to make my voice indifferent, not quite knowing if I should tell him about Lulu. But it was, of course, too late. He had picked up the folder and was already reading as he slid gracefully to the ground.

I watched him in the deep quiet of the room, listened to the sound of his breathing. Emotions flitted across his face — laughter, outrage, pity. Finally he looked up. "Are there more?"

"I'm hoping to find enough to turn them into an article. It was Sammy's idea; he thought it might even be a little book."

"You should!" His voice held a sharp note of anger. "Not many people know what happened to Italian Americans during the war." I could see a muscle working in his throat. "Did you know that I'm Italian?"

"Phillips? It's not exactly an Italian name."

"They changed it at Ellis Island. DiPellicci was too big a mouthful for the immigration people, so they chopped it off. But changing their names wasn't enough. Everybody talks about the internment of the Japanese — it was terrible — but in some parts of the country, being Italian was just as bad. I don't think people on the East Coast were affected, but my nonna lived in San Francisco, and she has terrible stories about what happened to them. Roosevelt signed an executive order allowing the military to arrest suspected enemy aliens, and her father was thrown in jail. They wanted to intern Italians, and it seemed like it was going to happen. It didn't, but my nonna couldn't go more than five miles from her house, and they couldn't go out after dark. There was a curfew. It was a crazy time. She had two brothers in the army, but it didn't matter; one day some men just came and kicked them out of the house."

"Kicked them out?" I was incredulous.

"They weren't the only ones." He didn't even try to hide his bitterness. "Her whole neighborhood was evacuated. Ten thousand people in California lost their homes."

I couldn't think of anything to say.

"Nonna says her mother couldn't believe that the country she loved so much would do that to her." Richard gazed up at the shelves around us, and I wondered what he was seeing. "You can look it up. Joe DiMaggio was a national hero, but while he was in the army they wouldn't let his father, who'd been a fisherman all his life, go out on San Francisco Bay. They considered him a security risk."

"What about your grandmother? What did she do?"

"Nonna's father was in jail, and her mother didn't want to leave without him. But then the mayor of San Francisco — his name was Rossi — was accused of giving a Fascist salute, and she got scared. She borrowed money, came to New York, and moved in with friends here. Nonna still doesn't like to talk about it — she's ashamed."

"What happened to her father?"

Richard gave an angry laugh. "The madness ended before the year was out. Fiorello La Guardia had more guts than Rossi, and he made an enormous fuss. On Columbus Day the attorney general went to Carnegie Hall and announced that Italians would no longer be classified as enemies. But it didn't do my great-grandfather much good; he was on the West Coast and they kept him in jail until the war in Europe ended." He took a ragged breath and with obvious effort changed the subject. "How old is Lulu?"

I wanted to ask a million questions, but Richard clearly didn't want to talk about it anymore. "She would have been thirteen when she wrote this. I'm hoping she kept writing to Beard throughout the war."

"But you haven't found his letters? How great would it be if you found his replies! Then you'd really have a book." He seemed relieved that I'd let the subject of his family drop.

"But why would they be here?"

Richard stretched out, settling his body against the wall. "Why are all these letters here? What was the point of hiding them? Does Sammy have any ideas?"

"I think he was as surprised as I was. But he's obviously not very interested; he hasn't been back since the day we found this secret room."

"What about Maggie? She spent half her life at *Delicious!* You should ask her."

"No way! As far as I'm concerned, the only good thing about the magazine closing is that I never, ever have to see Maggie again."

"She's not so bad. Let's take her to The Pig and see what she knows about your three librarians."

"You call her." I had no desire to see Maggie. "Count me out."

"Oh, come on." There was a challenge in his voice. "I never figured you for a wimp."

Dancing Horse

By the time I got to The Pig, Maggie was sitting at the bar with Richard, sipping a Manhattan, and Thursday was setting a plate of deviled eggs in front of them. Thursday was wearing a Madonna-like smile. Was it seeing Richard that made her so happy?

"You look no worse for wear." Maggie was giving me the once-over. "I thought you might have the half-starved look of so many out-of-work people."

"You mean like you?" The old enmity had come roaring back, and she was no longer one of my bosses.

She gave a shout of laughter. "Well, you're right, it's been a rotten time. I've been catering, which is just another way of saying that I've been in hell."

"That bad?" Richard took a bite of an egg.

"Worse." Maggie upended her glass and took a huge swig of her drink. "Last night I did Christmas cocktails on upper Fifth Avenue, and I was honestly afraid I'd kill the hostess before the evening was over. I had no idea how spoiled I'd gotten at *Delicious!* She made me go up to her apartment six times in the two weeks before the event to 'rehearse the hors d'oeuvres.' If she wasn't filthy rich I'd swear she just wanted free food."

"You're missing the point." Richard was still nibbling on the edges of the deviled egg, reluctant to commit to it. "It's not about the money. She wanted to show you who was in charge."

"You're right." Maggie scowled at the memory and downed the better part of an egg in a single bite. "I should never have gone into this business. She demanded changes in all the recipes. Every damn one! And she made them all worse."

"No." Richard sounded amused. "She made them hers."

"In my home" — Maggie made her voice very high, a bad parody of Julia Child — "we serve only prime beef; you will have to show me the butcher's bill. Are those ordinary apples you're using? Please! I'll have nothing but heirlooms in my kitchen. And I always insist that the caterer make the puff pastry right in front of me, where I can see it. Why should I pay all this money to serve frozen products any fool can buy in the supermarket?"

"You put up with this?" I was stunned. "You?"

She looked embarrassed. "I need the money. I'm not sure that my business is going to make it. Still, when she said that the only acceptable caviar was beluga from the Black Sea, I told her to find another caterer. Serving the eggs of the last beluga sturgeon on the planet isn't something I want on my conscience."

"Brava!" Richard clapped his hands.

"That" — Maggie put up a hand and halted him in mid-clap — "turned out to be a serious mistake. Because after I'd gone through the sustainability rap, her eyes started shining and she said, 'We simply must redo the menu! Everything we serve will be local and sustainable.' "

Maggie being cowed by a Fifth Avenue matron? I loved it.

"So!" She turned on me. "While I've been killing myself for the cocktail crowd, it seems you've been eating bonbons in bed. You look like you've put on weight."

"I'm glad adversity hasn't changed you."

She gave another crack of laughter and pulled the cherry from the bottom of her glass. "I think being out of Jake's shadow will be very good for you."

"Won't it be good for you too?"

"If you're asking if Jake bankrolled my business, the answer is yes." She gave a wry smile. "I think he's still feeling guilty about the restaurant we had back in the eighties; we could have had an empire by now if he hadn't been such a jerk. But maybe I shouldn't have taken the money from him."

"Being nice to people must be quite a strain." I was surprised by how much I was enjoying myself. I looked at Maggie, wondering if this was how Lulu felt around Miss Dickson.

"It *is* a strain." Maggie said it without a hint of embarrassment. "But what are you doing these days?"

"That" — Richard saw an opportunity and rushed in to grab it — "is what we want to talk to you about. Billie's still at the book, honoring the Guarantee —"

"You're kidding!" Maggie's voice was sharp now. "Young Arthur closes *Delicious!* but keeps you? No wonder Pickwick's in so much trouble."

"Well, thank you very much."

"Oh, don't get your knickers in a twist. I didn't mean anything by it."

"— and," Richard continued, as if he had

not been interrupted, "she went up to the library. We were wondering what you know about the *Delicious!* librarians."

"Sorry." She drained her Manhattan. "Can't help you there. The last one was gone by the time I arrived."

"But you must have heard stuff." Richard rose as Thursday beckoned us to one of the elegantly rickety antiques that passed for tables at The Pig. "Knew people who knew them? Can you remember anything? Anything at all?"

Maggie furrowed her brow as she settled into her seat. She looked down at the platter of tiny Kumamoto oysters Thursday had set in the middle of the table; she picked one up, tilted her head back, and allowed the sweet cucumber-flavored mollusk to slip down her throat. Thursday stood listening as she opened a bottle of wine. "You know, in Mrs. Van Allen's day, the magazine was nothing like the place you knew. It was kind of a ladies' seminary. A few selected males of the Sammy persuasion were permitted to join the staff, but it was mostly us girls. The HR person from Pickwick told me they once sent a hunk of a man over to try out as an assistant, and Mrs. V. called, asking what they were thinking. 'The girls and I,' she said, 'wouldn't like that at all.' She made them wear white gloves every day." Maggie paused to down another oyster. "The white-glove days were ending when I arrived, but a few of the old girls were still there. God, were they high on that library! Whenever they talked about it, their eyes would light up. According to them, when the magazine lost its last librarian, it lost its soul."

Maggie had eaten most of the oysters, and now she moved on to the salad, one of Thursday's more inspired creations. She'd shredded kale into confetti and tossed it with sweet little currants and richly toasted pine nuts. Mixed with lemon juice and oil, and laced with grated Parmesan, it was an incredible concoction. Maggie put a forkful in her mouth and paused to appreciate it.

"So did they tell you anything about the last librarian?" prompted Richard.

"Bertie?" said Maggie. "It was hard to know what was true. They were all in love with the legend of Bertie."

"What do you mean, legend?"

"Apparently there was nothing Bertie didn't know about food. Nothing. You could ask any question and instantly get the right answer. If you wanted a recipe for, say, bouillabaisse, you'd learn that in Marseille they always used rascasse, grondin, and conger, but in Bagnolles, just down the road, they didn't consider it authentic unless it contained lotte. Bertie could give you a recipe without looking it up and could also tell you how the recipes in Waverley Root, Elizabeth David, and Julia Child differed. Every time I went looking for a source, one of the old biddies would roll her eyes and say, 'Oh, if only Bertie were here. Bertie would know the answer.' "

"But you never actually met her?"

"To be honest, I never believed that Bertie was real. I thought it was some phantom they'd dreamed up to make the rest of us feel stupid."

"Do you have any idea when she left?"

Maggie had powered through her salad, talking with her mouth full. She was eating as if she hadn't eaten in weeks, and when Thursday arrived with plates of airy gnocchi, her eyes lit up. "Exactly what I wanted!" she cried, scooping one up. "No idea."

"Come on, Mags!" said Richard. "Try a little harder. When did you get there?"

"Mid-eighties. And I figure Bertie had to have been gone at least ten years by then. It would have taken them that long to create the myth. I haven't thought about the library in ages, but I remember some fantastic story about Bertie sneaking in late at night to work on a mystery project."

"What?" Richard and I shouted together, and Maggie put down her fork and opened her eyes very wide. "Wait. What are you two up to? Why do you want to know this stuff?"

"Just curious," I started to say as Richard simultaneously blurted out, "Billie's found —" before my glare stopped him cold.

"Found what?" Maggie was looking at me intently.

"The amazing card file in the library," I tried.

Maggie's smile softened her face, and I saw how lovely she must have once been. I thought about the butterfly tattoo on her shoulder. "I'd almost forgotten about that." She had a dreamy look. "I used to love going in there to leaf through those cards. All those colors!"

"Which one is Bertie?" I asked. "Do you know?"

"Isn't it obvious? The blue one, of course."

"Perfect!" There was laughter in Richard's voice. "Of course. That color used to be called peacock blue, until the Sheaffer ink people stupidly renamed it turquoise."

"How do you know that?" Maggie was staring at him skeptically.

"I'll have you know I'm a proud member of the fountainpennetwork.com," he said.

"Art directors!" she scoffed.

I cleared my throat. "Could we get back to Bertie? How old was she when she worked there? Was she married? Was she a certified librarian?"

Maggie waved her hand. "Haven't a clue. For all I know Bertie was a dancing horse who ran away from the circus. I don't know a thing — except that during Bertie's last days at *Delicious!,* she was sneaking in and out at midnight. Whenever the library was mentioned, Mrs. V. would smile knowingly and say that one day the whole world would be grateful to Bertie."

"Do you have any idea why?" asked Richard, but Maggie had had enough. "I'm tired of this." Her voice was cross. "Damn *Delicious!,* damn Bertie, and damn Pickwick Publications. They fired us, and as far as I'm concerned they can go to hell — and take their legends with them." She picked up her wineglass and took a long drink. When she put it down, her face was as blank as if a shutter had been lowered. She was closed for the night.

FEAST OF THE SEVEN FISHES

Hi, Genie.

Not going to complain. Things are definitely better since we found the Lulu letters. I can't think back to the time before New York — not yet. But this time last year I was fretting about the Fontanari story, terrified about what Sal's reaction would be when it was finally printed. And that turned out okay.

So what if I have a ridiculous job and no clue about my future?

So what if Sammy's disappeared and nobody knows where he is?

So what if the one good friend I've made has left the state, never to return? (Although she wasn't lying when she said she'd write every day.)

Even Mr. Complainer seems to have vanished; he hasn't been to Fontanari's for the last two Sundays, and I admit that I miss him. Leave it to me to miss

243

the chance when I had it. If I had it.

Did I say I wasn't going to complain? Sorry.

It's Christmas. I'm working at Fontanari's every day, and the place is packed. I'm spending New Year's Eve at Rosalie and Sal's. My resolution is to get contact lenses, if only to shut Rosalie up. Things could be worse.

At this rate, next year will be even better, right?

I love you.

xxb

Tina Fey had told some *New York Times* reporter that she was gifting Fontanari olive oil to all her friends, and the line that greeted me when I got to the shop stretched down the block. Sal was convinced that was why Mr. Complainer had abandoned us: He'd finally moved on to a more efficient shop. "You want a store filled with cops and complainers," he said morosely. "Now we've lost Mr. Complainer. Who's next?"

"He wouldn't go somewhere else," I said, somehow knowing it was true. Then I remembered the blonde he'd been with the last time, and I wondered if he was embarrassed. Had he caught Sal's look of disappointment? I hoped not; Sundays seemed longer without him.

New Year's Eve was always the busiest day of the year, and when we closed the door at seven, customers were still trying to push in, desperate for one last item that would make their party perfect. Sal was such an easy touch, until Rosalie finally put her foot down.

"This is our night," she said, firmly locking the door. "We've got resolutions to make! Coming, Theresa?" She herded us all up the stairs.

Sal and Rosalie were the only people I'd met in New York who occupied a real house. The shop was on the ground floor, the bedrooms on the top, but in between was one enormous room. Part kitchen, part living room, part dining room, it was filled with sisters, aunts, grandchildren, and cousins, all talking, gesticulating, kissing. More people kept arriving, trying to find room on the long table to set yet another platter.

Sal tipped his wineglass toward the table. "We do the traditional seven fishes on New Year's instead of Christmas." He handed me a glass of wine. "What does your family do for New Year's Eve?"

"Nothing much." Dad, Aunt Melba, and I always tried to stay up to watch the ball drop in Times Square, but I don't remember ever making it. Genie always had a date.

Sal frowned. "But what about the resolutions?" He took me around the room, introducing me to a bewildering number of relatives until his daughter, Toni, came to my rescue.

"Dad! Stop! Billie doesn't need to know how every one of these people is related to us." Grabbing my hand, she pulled me to a sofa. "You think this is bad?" She sat down next to me. "Imagine what it was like when I brought boyfriends home. I married the only date I ever had who could talk my father to a standstill."

I nodded, which was all she expected from me; in this maelstrom of words, silence was acceptable, and I was content to watch and listen. Sal clinked a spoon against a glass, and Toni pulled me to the table and sat down next to me. When Sal sat on my other side, my night was made; sitting between them, I felt anchored, safe.

Rosalie stayed on her feet, setting down platter after platter of food. The meal began with pickled squid, oyster shooters, marinated anchovies, and scungilli salad. Then Rosalie set an enormous bowl of pasta con le vongole in front of Sal, who ladled it out, talking the entire time. The pasta was followed by huge platters of scampi, which we passed around. It was almost eleven when Rosalie set three enormous stuffed turbots on the table, and it was near midnight when she appeared with a plate of warm sugar-dusted sfinge.

"So our first taste of the New Year will be sweet," Sal whispered in my ear. He grabbed my left hand and Toni grabbed my right, and we were linked around the table, joined together, all of us, facing whatever the coming year might bring. Sal leaned over to whisper, "Italian families always welcome the New Year like this." He gave my hand a squeeze and shouted, "Ten!"

I thought about Richard and wondered if he was with his family, holding hands and counting down the seconds to the future. Sal shouted, "Nine!," and I joined in, shouting, "Eight! Seven! Six!" along with them.

As the seconds ticked away, I looked around the table. It was comforting to think of them sitting here, year in, year out, playing out this ritual. I thought again of Richard. Was he with his grandmother, the one who was still so bitter about the war? There was another thought, right behind that, nagging at me.

"Five!" we shouted. "Four!"

If Richard's nonna was alive, then why not Lulu?

"Three!"

How old would she be? I began to do the calculations. She was twelve in 1942 . . .

"Two!"

. . . so she was born in 1930. That would make her . . .

"Happy New Year!"

Next to me, Toni blew her party horn. Lulu would be only eighty-one. She might still be alive.

Like a song you can't forget, the words "enemy food" repeated themselves over and over in my head. They even took on a rhythm, that old song "Mother-in-Law," so that before long I was humming them. I could hardly wait to get back to the library and find out if that was the next clue.

January second fell on Monday, so I didn't have long to wait. When I got to the mansion, the mail was filled with tales of holiday disasters: dry turkeys, exploded hams, melting icing. I flicked quickly through the emails and letters. Calamity could wait.

In the library, I found a single card titled "Enemy Food," wedged between "Egyptian Cuisine" and "Escargots." I picked it up and peered at the peacock-blue ink. "During the

Second World War, there was such a deep prejudice against all things Italian that, in some parts of the United States, spaghetti, lasagna, and all forms of pasta were considered 'enemy food.' There are some very interesting letters on the subject filed under 'Italian Recipes,' 1943."

Pleased that my intuition had been correct, I went into the secret room, pulled down "Italian Recipes," sat with my back against the wall, and opened the file.

October 14, 1943
Dear Mr. Beard,
I picked my ripe pumpkins this morning, and after school Tommy helped me carry them to Mrs. Cappuzzelli. She's been promising to show me how she makes her special ravioli. We were just starting to take the seeds out when Marco came in, saw the ravioli dough, and started waving his arms around, shouting, "American food, Mama! American food! Mussolini eats pasta, and I won't eat what he eats." I'd like to introduce him to Miss Dickson.

Mrs. C. never said a word, but when Marco finally left, slamming the kitchen door behind him, she looked so worried. I don't think it has anything to do with food; she's afraid he's going to try to prove that he's a "real American" by lying about his age and joining the army.

I tried to think of something to cheer her up, but you'll never guess what did the trick: I asked if she had ever eaten pumpkin leaves. She thought that was just about the funniest thing she'd ever heard and laughed so hard she began to cry. "Not for people, only for pigs," she kept saying as she wiped her eyes.

I don't see what's so funny. We eat beet greens, don't we, and turnip leaves? Why not pumpkin leaves? Mrs. C. said she would never eat a pumpkin leaf, but she's going to show me how to cook the blossoms. Don't you just love the idea of cooking flowers? I imagine them bursting into bloom, right in the pan. But I'm not about to give up on pumpkin leaves; I bet you can eat them too.

Your friend, always,
Lulu

P.S. It's been so warm here it seems like summer might go on forever. Father loved Indian summer, and I like to think the sun is shining down on him, wherever he may be. Mother says we'll get a presumed-dead letter soon, but she's always expecting the worst, and where does that get you?

I tried to imagine what Lulu would look like as an old woman, but in my head she remained stubbornly thirteen. How did you locate someone when you didn't know her married name, where she lived, or what she had been doing for the past seventy years?

Maybe she had married Tommy. That might be a place to start. I could search for her father's army records. Maybe I could even find an old Akron phone book.

November 2, 1943
Dear Mr. Beard,
Thank you for asking, but, I'm sorry to say, things are no better. Miss Dickson just hates me — and I cannot find it in my heart to turn the other cheek. When she starts in on me, I always lose my temper, and I expect that I am going to get to know Principal Jones very well this year.

Yesterday she put up a poster that says, "Remember Pearl Harbor. Purl harder." Then she made us all go down to the woodworking shop to make knitting needles. We are knitting scarves for the soldiers. If you ask me, they're not going to want these lumpy, itchy old things, but I

251

wouldn't dare say so. When Tommy said that knitting was for girls, she sent him to the principal's office. I don't know if he got the paddle, but he came back with a red face and started knitting like crazy. He's very good at it. I am not; Miss Dickson held my scarf up so everyone could see it. "Pity the poor soldier who gets this one," she said, and for once we were in agreement.

Thank you for the pumpkin-leaf recipe. I knew you would have one! I did exactly what you said, took all the strings out of the leaves, washed them really well, and cut them into skinny strips. Then I cooked them with a little bit of onion until they were very soft. I added a cut-up tomato too.

Mother made an awful face, but when I told her they didn't cost one penny and were very nutritious (I made that part up, but I'm sure it must be true), she ate them up. She packed them into her lunch pail this morning, and when I looked surprised she said the women in her Corsair group have started a thrift contest. The one who makes the best lunches using the least ration points this winter will win a whole ham for Easter.

Mother's sure to win, because I'm going

to help. Tomorrow we're making her a raw pumpkin salad. We'll grate some pumpkin and squeeze lemon juice over it, then mix in some onions, tomatoes, and herbs. Mother suggests that we drizzle a little bit of my honey on top. Not one ration point — and think how pretty it will be. Isn't it nice that Mother's taking an interest in food again?

Your friend,
Lulu

The Goodyear Aircraft Corporation! There might be some record of Mrs. Swan's employment at the Airdock.

December 4, 1943
Dear Mr. Beard,
Last night we listened to Mr. Murrow on the radio. Did you hear his broadcast? He went along on a bombing raid to Berlin, and some of the planes that went with him didn't make it back. It was an awful thing to hear. I looked over at Mother and her face was white. Then I remembered that she might have built the very airplanes they were flying. Did you know that the Corsair has the biggest, most powerful engine and the largest propeller of any fighter in history?

Afterward I tried to cheer Mother up by telling her a story I read in the newspaper. The pilots make ice cream by putting the ingredients in a can and putting the can in the back of the plane, where there's no heat. The vibrations churn the cream, and the cold temperatures freeze it. I think it's so clever, but all Mother would say was that she doubted they'd do anything so frivolous when they are fighting the enemy.

Sometimes I think she doesn't remember Father at all, which is very sad, because that is just the sort of thing he would do. I can see him stepping out of the airplane with his can of ice cream under his arm, saying, "Cheated death again. Grab a spoon; we're going to celebrate!"

I hope we have something to celebrate soon.

Your friend,
Lulu

A Terrible Symphony

I found the Murrow broadcast online. It was called "Orchestrated Hell," and after I had listened to it twice, I went to the computer and ordered five books on World War II. Imagining a still-living Lulu changed everything; what had once been ancient history had come charging into the present.

The end of 1943 was terrible. The British were bombing Berlin, but the cost was enormous. The war was spreading across the globe, and no matter where you landed, something dreadful was going on. In the Pacific, the Americans were slogging through the Gilbert Islands and raiding Rangoon. The British were having awful adventures in Italy, and the Americans were on their way to join them. Just after Christmas, Eisenhower took on Operation Overlord, which would become the Normandy invasion.

How could they bear it? Soldiers left for

years, some without ever coming home. No Internet, no Skype, and the letters were all censored. When someone died, it could be months before the family even found out. It seemed like another world, like the dark ages, as if the people who lived in it were a different, tougher race.

That night I dreamed of bodies falling from the sky. Even in my sleep I recognized the images from 9/11 — that man with his leg bent, boots out before him, as he plunged from the glass tower. It made everything seem more immediate. Lulu's war had become my own.

But the next morning I realized there was something more. It was not only Lulu who worried me. I pictured the glass building and saw that it wasn't the World Trade Center; it was where Sammy lived. Where was he? If he'd been off doing holiday research, he should be back by now. I kept calling his apartment, but there was still no answer. It had been five weeks since anyone had heard from him.

I went into the bathroom and splashed cold water on my face, trying to wash the dream away. When I got to the mansion, I sat down at my desk and dialed Sammy's number. No answer. This wasn't right; he'd been gone too long. I was starting to feel truly alarmed when the phone rang. It was Mrs. Cloverly, at her most querulous.

"I made that red salad that was on the cover some time back, thinking it would be perfect for Christmas. Well, it was no such thing! It was vile, absolutely vile!"

"Happy New Year to you too, Mrs. Cloverly," I replied.

"Oh." She seemed surprised by her own rudeness. "I hope your holidays were very pleasant, dear." And then, as if she had been sitting by the phone for weeks, clutching this complaint to her chest, she rushed on. "My holiday was ruined by that despicable salad!"

I was starting to apologize when Richard texted that he was on his way up. "What a coincidence, Mrs. Cloverly. The man who invented that particular dish will be here any minute. Perhaps you'd like to discuss the recipe with him?"

"Oh, no, dear," she said quickly. "A man? I couldn't do that! In fact, I must be on my way."

"So odd," I said to Richard when he appeared. "The idea of talking to a man seemed to terrify her. I wonder why."

"Probably been a long time since her husband died, and she hasn't talked to one of us in years."

"She must be so lonely! I imagine her as a very old lady who's outlived all her friends." As I spoke, I suddenly remembered Lulu. "I need to thank you." I waved him into the chair.

Richard sat down as I told him about the Fontanaris and how sharing the traditional dinner with that big Italian family had made me think of his grandmother.

"You're right." He was looking past me, seeing something on the wall behind me that I could not. "If my nonna's still alive, there's no reason why Lulu couldn't be. But I have no idea how you could possibly find her. Do you?"

"No," I admitted. "But speaking of finding people: I'm worried about Sammy. I keep calling but there's no answer. It's been more than a month since he was here. It's not like him."

"You know Sammy." Richard looked slightly embarrassed, obviously remembering that he'd promised to make some calls. "I'm sorry," he said, "with the holidays and all, I forgot. But I'm sure he's lying on a beach somewhere, acquiring a beautiful tan. Or he's someplace exotic, riding a camel. He's going to think it's hilarious that you've been anxious about him."

"I hope you're right." I was not convinced.

"But you didn't come here to talk about Sammy."

"No. I just wanted to look at the library again. I thought I might take some pictures. Do you mind?"

"Not at all." I was glad to have company. "And you're going to like the next clue."

"And that would be . . . ?"

"I'm pretty sure it's 'ice cream.' "

There were dozens of cards for ice cream, but none were written in bright-turquoise ink. I must have looked so disappointed that Richard said, "You could still be right. Maybe it's filed under another word for ice cream?"

I brightened. "Father could be in France. Maybe it's under 'crème glacée.' "

But it wasn't.

"How about Italy? Try 'gelato,' " Richard suggested. But it wasn't there either.

I wasn't ready to give up. "Is there some kind of unique Akron ice cream?" I wondered aloud, still convinced I had the right clue.

"Let's see." Richard took out his phone and tapped in a few words. "There's a place called Strickland's Frozen Custard that's apparently been an Akron institution since 1936."

And that was it. The "Frozen Custard"

card was written in bright-blue ink, and Bertie didn't beat around the bush. "What goes best with ice cream? Cookies, of course. You'll find a very interesting note on the subject in a reader letter from 1943. Look for the file labeled 'Exotica.' "

December 15, 1943
Dear Mr. Beard,
When your cookies arrived, Mother said that she could not accept them, but then she read your note. She said to tell you that the Goodyear girls all send their thanks. We named them Ration Frees, and everyone at the factory thinks they're swell.

I've been thinking and thinking how to thank you, and for a while I was in despair. But then I came up with a good plan. You sent us the Perfect War Cookie. Now I'm sending you the Perfect After-the-War Cookie; it exists only in my imagination, but it uses all the ingredients I miss most.

I've named my cookies Snowballs, but not because that's what they look like. It's the way they make you feel. You know how it is when a snowball is flying toward you on an icy-cold night? The stars are glittering, and the snow is twinkling, but you're wrapped up in mittens and boots,

260

so you're toasty warm. It's surprise and comfort, all at the same time; that's how I want them to taste. Do you know what I mean? Here's the recipe: It has chocolate, maraschino cherries, marshmallows, and pecans in a very buttery batter. I know they'll be delicious.

I wish I could bake a batch for Father. As soon as the war's over, I will. I'll make a batch for you too. In the meantime, I wish you a very happy Christmas. Now that you've joined the United Seamen's Service, I'm hoping to receive a letter from every exotic place you visit. Puerto Rico! Brazil! Panama! Even the names sound delicious. Here's hoping that next year is filled with many good things for all of us.

Your friend,
Lulu

She'd written the recipe out on an index card, the penmanship even more careful than usual. Richard studied it for a moment, his lips moving over the list of ingredients. "These sound pretty great."

"They do not! They sound disgusting. Think about it — chocolate, cherries, marshmallows, pecans — it's just too much."

"I never knew you were such a food snob."

Richard hit me lightly on the shoulder. "Cookies are supposed to be kid food; what's happened to your inner child?"

"My inner child's obviously got more sense than yours." Were we really having this ridiculous argument?

Richard pocketed the index card. "I'm going to prove you wrong. I'm going to make Lulu's Snowballs and make you eat your words."

"Don't forget to bring that recipe card back!" I replaced the letter in the folder and returned it to the shelf.

"I'll guard it with my life." Hoisting his camera, Richard went off to take his pictures.

I didn't believe he'd really bake the cookies, but the next day he was back, cookies in hand. "What do you think?" He held out a chunky orb.

I took a bite. "I was right: It's a bunch of ingredients stuck in a batter and locked in mortal combat. Kind of exhausting."

"Maybe it's a guy thing," he replied. "I like them fine, but Thursday's with you. She actually spit hers out."

"Wait," I said, "you've just given me an idea. If guys like them so much, let's take some over to Sammy's."

262

"But he's away," Richard pointed out.

"He's got to come back soon. They'd make a nice welcome-home gift."

Richard looked at me thoughtfully. "You're really worried, aren't you? You want to check in on him?"

"Nobody's even gotten a postcard. I think there's something wrong. But I don't want to go alone. Humor me?" I pleaded.

Richard was laughing at me, but I didn't care. I had a bad feeling about Sammy.

"Okay." He was giving in. "Meet me at The Pig at ten, and we'll go over together. Maybe Thursday will come too."

In the end, Jake joined us, which turned out to be a good thing. Sammy's building was one of those places where visitors had to be announced, and when he didn't answer the intercom, the doorman crossed his arms and refused to let us in. You couldn't blame him; it was late and we were a motley group. Then he recognized Jake, did a comical double take, and fell all over himself apologizing.

We left the doorman downstairs, looking slightly worried, and took the elevator up to Sammy's floor. I rang the bell. Nothing. Jake leaned on it, hard, and we began to bang and shout. Richard stood a little apart, arms crossed over his chest. "I told you he wasn't

263

here," he was saying, when the door opened a crack.

It was no more than a grudging sliver, but Sammy's nose emerged. "Stop it at once! Are you intent on rousing my neighbors?" He refused to open the door any farther.

"We brought you a present —" I began, but Sammy cut me off.

"Why are you attempting an invasion?"

Jake lunged at the door, shouldering it open, and Sammy shuffled back. He blinked at us, pale and mole-like in rumpled cotton pajamas. Then he began to growl. "What are you doing here? Are you inebriated? Depart! Go away. Vanish. The hour is late. What do you mean by rousting me out of bed in this fashion?"

"We wanted to show you what Lulu is up to." Richard held up the plate of cookies.

"Who?" Sammy's lips jutted forward.

"Lulu," I reminded him. "That little girl in the library? Remember?"

"Oh, yes." He said it so vaguely that I wasn't at all sure he did. His looks were shocking; in the weeks since I'd seen him, he'd turned into a frail old man.

We were still standing in the doorway, but now Jake moved in, sweeping Sammy aside. When Sammy put up no resistance, the rest of us followed in his wake.

264

The place was a mess. The elegant living room was littered with spilled bottles, dirty glasses, and crumpled newspapers. Empty boxes of candy littered the coffee table. It smelled like unwashed clothes, and a dusty film lay over every surface. There was something almost obscene about it.

We walked in to the kitchen, expecting more of the same, but it was as spare as an operating room. When I pulled open the refrigerator door, I found nothing but an empty bottle of Champagne and a shriveled lemon.

"What have you been eating?" I demanded.

"Oh" — Sammy's voice was vague — "these days my appetite is rarely tempted."

"What have you been doing?" asked Richard.

"Sleeping, mostly." Sammy yawned. "I feel as if I have years of sleep to catch up on."

"When was the last time you left the apartment?" This was from Jake.

"What is this, the Inquisition?" Sammy crossed his arms. "None of your damn business." He had tossed himself into a kitchen chair. "I returned from Istanbul with the sense that a great adventure lay before me. I had met a wonderful new man, and the world looked like my oyster. Fool that I am,

I anticipated that seeking a new job would prove a positive pleasure."

He ran his hands through his hair, making it stand up until it was framing his face like a pale, fuzzy halo. "What I encountered was utter indifference. Was I disheartened? Not at all. For my next act I polished my résumé and went on 'informational interviews,' merely to remind the world of my existence. I believe I called on every publishing establishment in the metropolis, conversed with dozens of editors, took dozens more to lunch. Another exercise in futility: My services were no longer required — by anyone." His face was bleak.

"My options dwindled, and finally I had exhausted them all. The days were growing short. My spirits were declining. And one fine day I returned to discover Andre clearing out his side of the closet. His explanation was all 'home for the holidays,' but we both knew he would never return. It was over."

"When was that?" asked Jake.

"I don't know." Sammy ran his hands through his hair. "A few weeks ago? A month? After Andre left, I lost all track of time. I cannot conceive of any way that my life can possibly improve."

I recognized that feeling of bleak despair,

and I went over and gave him a hug. He didn't push me away, but he sat stiffly inside the circle of my arms.

How do you bring someone back to life when he's beyond caring? It won't last, I wanted to tell him. You'll feel better. But the words wouldn't come, and I stood there, feeling stupidly inadequate, wishing I knew what to say.

But I did have a plan. I took Richard's arm and drew him into the living room. He listened solemnly and then began to laugh. "Great idea! We can definitely do that."

Jake was asking so many questions that Sammy didn't notice when Thursday and Richard quietly disappeared. When they returned, their arms were filled with groceries from the twenty-four-hour market on the corner.

"I'm making you dinner," Thursday said, pulling out a carton of eggs, a wedge of cheese, and enough produce to make the kitchen resemble a farmers' market on a busy Saturday morning.

"Why on earth would I desire dinner at this time of the night?" Sammy asked crossly.

"Because you haven't been eating." She tied on an apron and reached for a small bowl. "And we're not going to have your death by starvation on our collective conscience." She turned on the oven.

"I can consume the cookies," he said petulantly.

"No." She began to crack eggs. "I'm going to make you a lovely cheese soufflé."

"That bowl is too small," shrieked Sammy as the eggs spilled onto the counter. She was an even better actress than I'd hoped. "You have been hitting the whiskey," he accused. "And rather heavily, it seems."

Richard was quite the actor too. He pretended to be so drunk that, as he grated cheese, he created a mini snowstorm, sending flakes flying around the kitchen.

"You are both intoxicated." Sammy watched another egg ooze onto the counter. "Stop, stop, stop, you are making a fine mess. Remove yourselves from my kitchen." He seized the whisk from Thursday's hand and pushed her out of the way. My plan had worked! He opened the cupboard and extracted a shining copper bowl. "This is how you make a soufflé." With a few elegant twists of his wrist, he separated the yolks from the whites. "The only thing that makes a soufflé fall," he was talking almost to himself, "is if it knows that you are afraid of it.

"Jake," he ordered, "convey Richard to

another room before that entire pound of Parmesan lands on the floor. Inebriates should never be permitted in the kitchen."

He began buttering the soufflé dish, washing lettuce, making vinaigrette. The aroma of melting cheese mingled with butter and wafted through the kitchen. It was joined by the high, clean scent of freshly squeezed lemons. Sammy's face had lost its look of despair, and he was moving with grace and determination.

"Billie." His voice was all crisp command now. "Set the table. Use the sterling. Open a bottle of wine. I believe you will find an '82 Ducru in there somewhere. I was reserving it for a special occasion. This might as well be it. Meanwhile, I believe I shall permit myself a shave."

The soufflé came out high and golden. Each crisp leaf of lettuce glistened with the faintest sheen of oil. It was after midnight. The food was perfect, the wine like velvet in our mouths. I caught Richard and Thursday exchanging a high five.

"And now," said Sammy, "I shall have that cookie, if you do not mind." Richard passed him the plate. "What are they called?"

"Snowballs." I said the name softly, gratefully.

Sammy took a bite. "Excellent," he said, taking another. "And very aptly named."

DRIPPING PUDDING

"Show me!"

I jumped; I kept forgetting how many people still had keys to the mansion.

"I have startled you!" Sammy sounded chagrined. "That was certainly not my intention."

The frightened hedgehog we'd cornered in his apartment the night before had vanished; Sammy was back. Dressed in his customary tweeds, he gave off his familiar scent of spice and smoke, and exuded general well-being. He'd even had his hair cut.

"You've come to collect your things?"

"All in good time. I am consumed with curiosity about the letters." He executed one of the old-fashioned little bows that would have seemed absurd from anybody else and offered me his arm. "Will you join me in the library?"

"Aren't we being formal," I said as we

headed for the stairs.

Sammy stood at the library door for a long moment, just taking it in. Then he moved slowly forward, refamiliarizing himself with the room. It reminded me of the first time we met and how joyfully he'd greeted his possessions after his long trip to Morocco. Then he headed for the secret room.

I stopped him.

"I want to show you something first." I led him to the card file, and he stood staring suspiciously at the ungainly wooden cabinet. "What am I supposed to do? Say 'abracadabra'?"

"Open any drawer. Look something up."

"What?"

"Anything. What's your favorite food?"

"Yorkshire pudding!" He obediently opened the "XYZ" drawer, leaning in for a closer look, sniffing the air as if this were a stove and he had to determine if a sauce was ready. He flicked through the cards, pulled one up, and began to read the bright-blue writing.

" 'The first recorded recipe for Yorkshire pudding appeared in 1737 in *The Whole Duty of a Woman,* where it was known as "A dripping pudding." Ten years later, in *The Art of Cookery Made Plain and Easy,* Hannah Glasse renamed it Yorkshire pudding;

nobody knows why. (The usually reliable Mrs. Beeton, incidentally, got the recipe wrong.) James Beard calls Yorkshire pudding "a gift from England" but remains skeptical about most American recipes, which he calls "inedible, to say nothing of being indigestible." ' "

Sammy studied the card, his face suffused with a kind of wistful nostalgia. "Dear me. How could I possibly have forgotten the legend of Bertie? How the old dears used to talk about her! I always regretted not having known her, but she was already history by the time I arrived. Remarkable, is it not, how vivid the ink remains after all these years? Such flamboyance!"

"You knew about Bertie?"

"Indeed. One of the more formidable characters to have graced the halls of the Timbers Mansion."

"We guessed that Bertie was the blue librarian. But there's no clue on this card."

"Clue? I fail to comprehend your meaning." Sammy looked at me, head cocked to one side.

Explanations seemed too complicated. Instead, I pulled up the ice-cream card and handed it to him. "Bertie's created a kind of treasure hunt. To find Lulu's letters, you have to read the last letter in the file and look for the most unusual words. After a while you get the hang of it. Then you come out to the card catalog. If you've guessed right, Bertie tells you exactly where to find the next letters."

"So." Sammy read the ice-cream card. " 'What goes best with ice cream? Cookies, of course. You'll find a very interesting note on the subject in a reader letter from 1943. Look for the file labeled "Exotica." ' " He returned it to the card catalog and began to walk toward the secret room. "If I comprehend correctly, Bertie is informing us that Lulu's subsequent missive will be found among the reader letters of 1943 in a file labeled 'Exotica'?"

"Exactly!"

Sammy had lost weight during his exile, which made it easier for him to wriggle through the small door. He eased himself onto the floor as I went to the 1943 shelf, pulled the "Exotica" folder, and handed it to him. He read for a moment in the dense silence of the room, and when he began to read out loud, his voice was almost reverent. " 'You know how it is when a snowball is flying toward you on an icy-cold night? The stars are glittering, and the snow is twinkling, but you're wrapped up in mittens and boots, so you're toasty warm. It's

surprise and comfort, all at the same time.' "
He looked up at me. "What a lovely child."
He replaced the letter and picked up another.

"There's another letter in that folder?"
How had I missed it?

Then I remembered the argument Richard and I'd had about the cookies. He'd taken off with the recipe card and I'd simply put the folder away. Now I leaned over Sammy's shoulder to see what I'd missed.

January 26, 1944
Dear Mr. Beard,
Yesterday, when I went to the Cappuzzellis', I could tell right away that something was wrong. Mrs. C. looked so distressed. "He's gone," she said.

It was Marco. He didn't even leave a note. She's sure that he's joined the army, even though Mr. C. went to all the recruiting stations and could find no trace of him. I said he probably changed his name. Mrs. C. said he would never, but I say if he can lie about his age, he can certainly lie about his name.

She put her arm around me and said, "They have taken all four: Mario, Massimo, Mauro, and Marco. But at least I have a daughter here at home," and I liked the feeling. "I'll show you how to make my meatballs," she said, getting out her meat grinder. She put them into what she calls "Sunday gravy," and even packed some up for me to take home so I can make meatball sandwiches for Mother's lunch.

Maybe that will cheer her up when the men at the factory are mean. Mother says it's because they believe a woman's place is in the home, but if you want my opinion, I think they're ashamed they're not over there fighting for our freedom. And even though she never says so, I know that Mother worries that one day the Germans will attack the Airdock, and we'll lose each other forever.

And now for some good news: Mother is ahead of everyone except Estelle Dixon in the contest — and we still have two months to go!

Your friend,
Lulu

"Tell me about this contest."

"I think you need to read all the letters, right from the beginning." I got up and began to collect folders, pulling them from the shelf in chronological order. I handed him the pile and sat down, reading over his shoulder in the dim light.

When he closed the final folder, Sammy said, "Lulu's mother does not resemble the women with whom my mother was acquainted during the war." He had the folders cradled in his lap, unconsciously stroking them as if a cat were curled up there. "She appears so much less sanguine. It is almost as if she herself had gone off to war, without ever leaving home."

"I think it's because she was in Akron." I'd been giving this some thought. "The whole city threw itself into the war effort. Before the war, sixty people worked at Goodyear Aircraft; by the time it ended, there were almost forty thousand employed. And that was just one of the war factories; Firestone was building machine guns, Goodrich was making rubber rafts and life preservers, and a local company called Sun Rubber went into the gas-mask business. I think all those people felt that they were part of the battle, that they were saving the country."

"I see you have been very fruitfully occupied."

"You're the one who told me it would make a good article, or maybe even a book. I thought you might be right. But if you really want to know the truth, being here would have driven me completely crazy if not for Lulu."

"Ah." Sammy looked at me, concern etched across his face. "I see that I have not been alone in my anguish. What a pity that we were unable to offer each other consolation. It is high time that changed."

I had no idea what he meant by that. Sammy got to his feet. "Let us go in search of supper. There is a thing I want to discuss with you. And I find I have a powerful desire for Yorkshire pudding."

Yorkshire pudding isn't exactly the food trend of the moment, and we ended up in one of the last red-velvet restaurants in New York. I hadn't been in a place like that since my sixth birthday, when Dad took Genie and me to the House of Prime Rib. This place was even older; it looked like a Victorian brothel, complete with "serving wenches." Sammy settled comfortably into an outsize chair as the waitress brought huge hot popovers, cold butter, and great slabs of steak. By the second bottle of wine, we had abandoned ourselves to that ridiculous room, gnawing on bones and licking our fingers as if the war had just ended and we were making up for lost time. We finished with wonderfully old-fashioned chocolate éclairs.

There was something strangely sensual about this moment, and even though I was sharing it with a man more than twice my age who preferred members of his own sex, I couldn't shake the feeling that this was a seduction scene.

When we were done, Sammy leaned back in his chair and said, "That was quite a drama your little group performed last night."

"The drunk-in-the-kitchen act?" I thought we'd gotten away with it. "That was my idea. I figured no cook could stand watching someone bumble around his kitchen, making a mess and ruining a meal. Thursday agreed; she said if you were too depressed to do anything about it, we were going to have to take drastic measures. She even bet Richard ten bucks you'd snatch the whisk out of her hand by the fourth egg."

"Did she prevail?"

"You barely lasted to three."

"How foolish of Richard to wager against Thursday!" Sammy took the last sip of wine. "Her most treasured belief is that any problem can be solved with the right recipe. It is what one finds so particularly attractive about her: She will not rest until she has located it."

He cocked his head then, searching my

face. "May I speak frankly?"

I was suddenly wary. People only ask that when they're about to tell you something you'd rather not hear. When I didn't answer, he jumped right in. "Have you always been so slovenly?"

It was the last thing I'd expected, and the question caught me so off guard that I forgot to act offended. "Um, probably. When I was little, everybody was so busy staring at my sister that it never seemed to matter how I looked. She was born beautiful, just like our mom. I take after my father's side. Nobody ever looked twice at me."

"Your sister?" Sammy leaned forward. "How is it that you never speak of her? Have you quarreled?"

"Of course not!" I spoke with more vehemence than I'd intended. "It would be hard to fight with Genie; she's kind of a perfect person, nothing at all like me. She's good at everything: In high school she was senior-class president, on the debate team, junior tennis champion of Santa Barbara, and she always got straight A's. She's an artist too; she can draw anything. She should have been the world's most horrible big sister, but she was even good at that."

Was that pity I saw on Sammy's face?

"Why are you looking at me like that?"

His face went slack, as if he'd drawn a curtain across his emotions. "I am going to hazard a guess" — he was speaking cautiously — "that this paragon of a sister you have kept hidden from your friends has something to do with the extremely unattractive façade that you present to the outside world. But, dear girl, it is time that this nonsense stopped."

"You think I try to look bad?" To my horror, my voice cracked. "You think I do it on purpose? I've spent my whole life wishing I looked like my sister! But I don't!"

At my outburst, Sammy's face came alive. "You are welcome to tell yourself anything you like." He took a deep breath. "That is your prerogative. As it is mine to disbelieve you." He leaned across the table and took my hand. In his glasses I could see my own reflection, and for a moment I hated the drab hair, thick eyeglasses, and tattered gray sweater with its constellation of small holes.

"It seems to me," he continued, "that this façade is a barrier you have erected to keep the world at bay. Of course, it is none of my business."

"You're right." I said it as coldly as I could. "It is none of your business."

He raised a sandy eyebrow. "And yet you

281

considered it your business to come barging into my house in the middle of the night. . . ."

He did have a point.

"I was appreciative of your efforts," he continued, "as you should be of mine. What are friends for? Last night you forced me to face the facts."

"And just what are those facts?" I glared across the table.

He looked unblinkingly back as he raised a closed fist and slowly unfurled his thumb. "One. *Delicious!* was an extraordinary voyage, but it has come to its conclusion. Two" — he raised his index finger — "nobody is going to employ me; I have grown too long in the tooth. And three" — the middle finger joined the others — "I have achieved financial security, but unless I resolve the question of my future, I am very likely to achieve my own end. Last night, after your group departed, I gathered my wits and conceived a grand plan. And it involves you."

"Me?"

"I have come to a crossroads, and I am at a loss to know which way to turn. At the moment, I require a project, and you would be doing me a great favor if you would allow me to assist you." He offered me a tentative smile; I realized this was costing him something. "It will not be forever. The pundits are predicting that the market will change with the weather. And the instant the economy recovers, Young Arthur is sure to summon his realtors. This being January, that gives us three paltry months, which is precious little time to locate the entirety of Lulu's letters."

Was he kidding? I'd be thrilled to have company in that dreary old mansion. Who was helping whom here? But Sammy wasn't finished. "We" — he reached for my hand and held on, prepared to ward off any protests — "are going to make a mutual improvement pact."

"We are?" I thought he was joking.

"Loneliness is pernicious, and your diet sounds absurd; from what I have been told, you have been surviving on cheap Chinese takeout. We will commence by dining together on a regular basis." He was serious! "A nourishing diet will do wonders for your disposition. And a bit of company will improve mine."

"Have you forgotten that I don't cook?"

"Nonsense!" He batted this away like an inconsequential fly. "This pose you affect of refusing to cook has become as tiresome as your aggressively unkempt appearance.

Both verge on the offensive. You are an eminently capable young woman. But, in the meantime, it will be my pleasure to become your personal chef."

"And what do I have to do in exchange?"

"Given a few nugatory changes, you might be rendered quite appealing." He stared thoughtfully at my hair. "I have been thinking that you might lighten your locks. A bit of color would have a salubrious effect."

"You're the only person in the world who uses the words 'nugatory' and 'salubrious.' "

"Thank you." He inclined his head and then pointed to my eyes. "Contact lenses, perhaps? And an improved wardrobe might have a salutary effect on your morale."

It was ridiculous. He seemed to see himself as my fairy godfather, and I saw no point in arguing. His increasingly archaic vocabulary was a sure sign that he was getting drunk, and I crossed my fingers beneath the table and agreed to everything, convinced that by morning he would have forgotten the whole thing.

ANZIO

Dear Genie,

My heart goes out to Sammy; I can't imagine how it must feel to be as old as he is, and as lost. When they closed *Delicious!* I lost a job, but for him it was like walking off a cliff. He was going along, enjoying his life, thinking things would never change, and then — boom! He found himself hurtling through thin air, unable to find anything to hold on to.

Now he's found me, but I'm afraid I'm going to be another disappointment. He seems to have before-and-after fantasies, where Billie the nerd ends up as some kind of goddess. What's he going to do when that doesn't happen? My only hope is that we can find enough of Lulu's letters to write a book. It would make him so happy.

And I'll admit that having him at the mansion has changed everything. Reading the letters with him is like discovering a strange new planet where the men are all gone and the women make do. Their lives were changing every day. Now I wake up every morning, eager to get to work.

I'm glad I told him about you too. I hardly ever do that — I think Diana's the only other one — but if we're going to be true friends, he needs to know you're out there. Always were, always will be.

xxb

Now that Sammy was at the mansion, looking for Lulu's letters was fun. It wasn't easy; the clues seemed to have become more elusive. I was convinced the next one would be "meatballs," and when that didn't work we spent a week researching dozens of variations — "polpette," "kofte," "frikadeller," "albondigas," "bouletten," "bola bola" — before giving up. Next we tried "contests." There are a stunning number of food competitions in America, but after researching everything from old-fashioned pie eating to Rocky Mountain oyster tournaments and cow-pie flipping trials, we reluctantly accepted that we were getting nowhere. Then I tried "gravy"; one card sent us searching pointlessly through Italian cookbooks, another directed us to eighteenth-century French recipes, and a third had us reading about the history of the tomato, before we finally admitted defeat. I couldn't help feeling that Bertie was deliberately sending us off on wild-goose chases; two weeks later, we were back to square one.

We reread the letters. "Perhaps we should investigate that institution where Beard was working," Sammy suggested.

"The 'National Seamen's Service'?" I went to the card file. "Nothing."

"Try 'Seamen,' " he said. "Or 'Service'?"

I kept flipping disconsolately through the cards. "Nothing."

" 'United States Seamen's Service'?" he suggested.

My fingers stopped moving, and I pulled up a card. "Not 'United States.' 'United Seamen's.' " I handed it to Sammy.

" 'Although merchant seamen came under constant attack, they were not considered servicemen. But the government found these traveling sailors to be a vital source of information and created an international string of clubs to provide them with food, drink, and a decent place to stay. Anyone with an interest in the Second World War will find the letters on the subject of this

287

unique department of the War Shipping Administration fascinating; they can be found in the 1944 files.' "

I was through the door the minute he'd finished reading the last sentence.

March 16, 1944
Dear Mr. Beard,
Father has been found! He says he's a cat, he survived a crash, and he's got eight lives to go. He can't tell us the details, but we know that he's in the hospital in Sicily, and he says he will be flying again very soon. He writes almost every day now, as if he's trying to make up for lost time. Mother seems different too; yesterday I heard her singing "Paper Doll" in the shower.

The Cappuzzellis have had a letter too. Marco did lie about his age, and now he's headed overseas. Mr. C. wants to wire his commander, but Mrs. C. just moans and says, What's the point? By the time he got home he'd be almost eighteen, and he'd join up again.

A few days ago I asked Mrs. C. what they eat in the springtime in Sicily. She told me about the wild vegetables they gather on the hillsides. That reminded me about the milkweed shoots last spring, so yesterday I went back to forage for them. I had forgotten how delicious they are.

I made Mother a nice little milkweed salad for her lunch. That should show up Estelle Dixon! She's still ahead of us, but there are a few more weeks until Easter, and I'm not giving up. I will be sorry when the contest is over; making these thrifty lunches with Mother has been such fun.

About the onions: You were absolutely right. I sliced two very thin, sprinkled them with salt and pepper, and covered them with vinegar. Then I left them to sit in the refrigerator for a few hours; Mother said they make her sandwiches taste so much better.

Your friend,
Lulu

"Why are you looking so glum?" Sammy was jubilant. "Father is in fine fettle. Mother is warbling in the shower. And our Lulu is out in the countryside, collecting milkweed shoots. What misfortune are you anticipating?"

"Look at the date." I pointed to the top of the letter.

"March 1944. Where is the difficulty?"

"You know those books I've been reading? If he's in Sicily, he's going to be part of the

Anzio campaign; the landing was called Operation Shingle. It started badly and got worse. The Allies dropped more bombs there than anywhere else on the continent. And it didn't help much. The Germans had set up antiaircraft guns, and, despite the air support, the soldiers were just sitting ducks. By March they'd been bogged down there for two months. The generals were fighting among themselves — reading about it makes you so mad! — and sending men off on crazy sorties, where they got separated from the army. It was terrible."

Sammy shuddered. "I believe there was a film called *Anzio.* Dreadfully realistic. As I recall, I had nightmares for weeks. But by late March, D-Day was just around the corner. I would conjecture that all the pilots were sent to Normandy to cover the landing."

"They weren't." I'd been doing my homework. "Eisenhower wanted to create a diversion in Italy, and he kept them there."

"Anything must have been better than Normandy," Sammy murmured. "Now, where do you suppose we will encounter her next letter?"

"Who sang 'Paper Doll'?"

Sammy thought for a minute and then began to laugh. "What a perspicacious young woman you are! It was the Mills Brothers. An ideal clue."

We raced to the card catalog, and when there was not a single blue card for "mill," "miller," or "millstone," we were both incredulous. "It seemed so perfect!" I fumed as we retreated to the secret room.

We spent the rest of the day following clues that led nowhere. "Cat," "onion," "vinegar" — all useless.

"I believe that will do for today," said Sammy. "I find that I am being bombarded by images of Anzio." He did look very pale. "I simply cannot erase it from my mind. Tomorrow is another day."

He turned to go, and we were already at the library door when I realized I'd forgotten my purse.

"I left it in the secret room." I went back to retrieve it.

"The brave young soldier," Sammy called after me, "risks life and limb to rescue a fallen comrade at Anzio."

"I think you've just christened the secret room," I said when I re-emerged.

Sammy gave a forced little chuckle, but he still seemed anxious.

"Laugh if you want." I cradled my purse as I walked down the stairs. I meant to keep talking so he'd stop seeing the war images in his head. "But this brave young soldier actually has been plotting a kind of rescue. Rosalie's birthday's on Sunday, and when I asked Sal what they were doing, he looked at me like I was crazy. 'We don't make a big deal of birthdays,' he said."

"I take it that you do not approve?"

"I don't. Rosalie works so hard." I'd wanted to throw a big party, but then I thought better of it; Rosalie would spend the entire evening making sure everyone else was having a good time. "I was thinking she'd like a romantic lunch, just the two of them. They almost never get to spend time alone."

"I trust you have enlisted Thursday?" The color was coming back into his cheeks.

"Yeah, she loved the idea and came up with this great little menu. And Richard's going to decorate The Pig's private dining room."

"I shall contribute a bottle of Dom Perignon," said Sammy grandly, and I hoped that I'd managed to make him forget about war.

"How're you going to get Sal out of that shop?" Thursday asked at our final planning meeting.

"I have my ways," I said, wondering

292

exactly what they were.

I was still worrying about it early Sunday morning as I stopped to buy a bunch of roses on my way to the shop. It was a start.

"Are those for Rosalie?" asked Sal. "She'll be pleased."

This was the moment. "I was thinking . . ." I began haltingly. "This is the slowest time of the year. . . ."

It took a little while for me to get it all out, but when I was finally done, Sal stared at me as if I were an alien creature. "Leave the shop to you and Theresa?" His tone suggested that he would be more likely to leave a couple of orangutans in charge. "Abandon my customers? What will they think?"

"You were gone for hours when you took me on the Sal Test," I said. "What's the difference?"

He looked at me incredulously. "That was work! I was doing it for Jake. I wasn't just going off to have a good time. Besides, Rosalie was here."

"They'll think," said Theresa, who had come in quietly with Rosalie, "that you've decided, for once in your life, to act like a normal human being and put your wife before your customers." I'd been so busy trying to persuade Sal, I hadn't noticed them entering the shop. Rosalie was putting bread on the shelves and filling the cases, acting as if all this had nothing to do with her. But she didn't object, which seemed like a hopeful sign.

I don't know what tipped the balance, but when Kim Wong arrived to present Rosalie with the chocolate invitation that she'd created for the occasion, Sal threw up his hands. "I give up," he said. "You win. Rosie, go get your coat. Looks like we're taking the day off."

Still, he was spewing instructions as he walked out of the shop. "Don't forget that Gennaro's mama likes the spring Parmigiano, not the summer. Don't give Jane cold mozzarella; she'll throw it in your face. And Mr. Abruzzo prefers the bresaola to the speck —"

"You think you're the only one who knows how to run the shop?" Theresa pushed him through the door. As it closed behind him, she was saying, "No, don't answer that. Please." But when she turned around, I saw that she was apprehensive. "I've never been in the store without Sal or Rosalie," she admitted.

At first everything was fine. "They're celebrating her birthday!" Gennaro clapped his pale hands together and looked prayerfully toward the ceiling. "*Benissimo! Mama*

294

will be so pleased." Jane actually compli-
mented me on the mozzarella. And, as
predicted, on this cold February day, the
shop was less frantic than usual.

But then, for the first time in two months,
Mr. Complainer walked through the door.
"Oh, no!" To my horror, I said it out loud.

"Nice to see you too."

"I didn't mean it like that." I carved off a
chunk of pecorino and handed it across the
counter, a peace offering. Awful Amy, I
noted happily, was absent. "It's just that
Sal's going to be devastated that he missed
you."

"He's not here? He's always here." He ran
both hands through his curls. "Is something
wrong? Is he sick?"

"He's fine. Fine. It's Rosalie's birthday,
and he took her out to lunch."

"You mean," Theresa chimed in, "you
made him take her to lunch."

"Really?" asked Mr. Complainer. "Good
for you!" His smile held so much warmth, I
could feel my cheeks begin to flush.

"Nobody can make Sal do anything," I
said.

"I think you're being modest." He was
beaming his approval.

"She is," Theresa agreed.

"I did plan a little lunch," I admitted,

surprising myself by hoping he'd keep looking at me like that. "And Sal wasn't exactly
thrilled. Why did you have to show up and
make matters worse? He's never going to
forgive me; he's been looking for you every
Sunday."

"Really?" Mr. Complainer laughed with
open delight. "You're not just saying that?"

"No. He really misses you."

He clearly had no idea how much Sal
liked him. I handed another piece of cheese
across the counter. "He's convinced you've
been going down the street, where the line's
shorter."

"That's crazy!" Mr. Complainer seemed
incredibly pleased. "I would never . . . He
should know that. I treasure my Sundays
with Sal."

"So how come you haven't been in?"

"I'm teaching up in Cambridge. This is
the first time I've been in the city in almost
two months."

A professor? He was a professor? But
teaching one semester didn't necessarily
make him that. Writers sometimes taught.
Aunt Melba had once spent a semester at
Cranbrook. And I supposed all kinds of
other people moonlighted at universities. I
wanted to ask what he taught, but it wasn't
the Fontanari way; Sal said it was fine if the

customers wanted to tell us about themselves, but it wasn't our place to ask. But I could say this: "So we can tell Sal you'll be back?"

"As soon as I'm done with the gig, I'll be back to — how did that writer put it? — 'worship at the Fontanari altar.' "

He'd remembered my words!

"In the meantime, though, I need a care package to get me through the next two months. Nothing tastes like Fontanari's."

Parmigiano, pecorino, prosciutto — he wanted it all. I was starting to pack up the order when he stopped me. "And, Wilhelmina, I think I'd better have three balls of mozzarella."

"The real thing?"

"Of course I want the real thing!" I was reaching for the imported mozzarella di bufala when he stopped me. "Why would I want week-old Italian stuff when I could have the cheese Rosalie made this morning? Don't you know anything?"

I stared at him incredulously. "That" — I scooped the cheese out of the vat — "is going to make Rosalie's day."

"Please tell her I wish her a very happy birthday."

"I'll do that." He turned to go and then hesitated, searching the shelves as if to make sure he hadn't forgotten anything. Then I realized he was doing what he always did with Sal: trying to delay his departure. When he got to the door, I screwed up my courage and called after him, "Don't you be a stranger."

Sal wasn't the only one who'd missed him.

Sal and Rosalie returned with pink cheeks, and as Rosalie pulled out her phone to show me how Richard had made a tablecloth of bay leaves, covering the entire table with them, Sal demanded a blow-by-blow account from Theresa.

When she got to Mr. Complainer, he groaned. "Wouldn't you know it? The first time I leave, the guy decides to show up. Just like him. Is he coming back?"

"Ask Willie," Theresa replied, wiggling her hips a little. "They had quite the conversation."

Rosalie snapped her phone shut. "Was that woman with him?"

"No. And he wanted *your* mozzarella."

Sal took off his cap, then put it back on, settling it more comfortably on his head. "He bought Rosie's mozzarella?" He put his arm around his wife. "Now we've surely lost him for good."

"For a while, anyway," I said. "A couple

of months. He's teaching somewhere out of town."

"Away from the city? Poor guy!" Sal could not believe anyone would voluntarily leave New York. "Wonder what he teaches that could make him stay away so long."

"You don't know?" I was surprised.

"It never came up." Sal drew himself up. "We stick to what's important."

Rosalie glanced toward the door, as if the phantom Mr. Complainer might still be standing there. "Two months is a long time. Come to dinner tonight, okay?"

"Rosalie cooked her own birthday dinner," I told Sammy the next morning. "And it was great. Of course. She made Jewish artichokes — which were so crisp they crackled when you put them in your mouth — lasagna, porchetta, and a puntarelle salad. Her oldest nephew was there, and she made him sit next to me. He took one look, bolted his food, and then bolted toward the door."

Sammy laughed.

"I wish she'd stop matchmaking. I don't want a boyfriend!"

"Of course not." He looked straight into my eyes. "Why would you desire romance? Your life is replete exactly as it is."

"Your point is taken," I said. "But here's the thing: He was giving his lame excuses, and Rosalie said, 'I made ice cream!' as if that could keep him there, and the creep actually asked if he could take it to go. She gave a defeated little shrug and began to pack it up. I suddenly thought about Lulu's father coming down the steps of the plane, ice cream under his arm, saying, 'Cheated death again.' "

"I am persuaded that there is a reason you feel compelled to share this with me."

"The first sentence of Lulu's last letter was 'Father has been found!' Maybe that's the clue."

"What is the clue?"

"Father!"

"We should look in the catalog for 'father'?"

"No, not 'father.' " In my excitement I could barely talk. "Father is a Swan. I'll bet anything the next clue is 'Swan.' "

A smile was spreading across Sammy's face. "That is precisely the sort of clue Bertie would relish."

We ran up the stairs and pulled open the "S" drawer with an enormous sense of anticipation. Sammy riffled through the cards.

"Just one? And it's red?" My face must

have been comical.

"Surely there must be another answer." Sammy sounded glum. "Bend your mind to this. Is there an alternate word for swan?"

I thought for a moment. Then I had it. "Father's a Swan, but Lulu's not."

Sammy looked at me as if I had lost my mind.

"She's a young Swan."

"The ugly duckling!" Sammy immediately got my point. "What an extremely sharp-witted young woman you are!" He went to the "D" file and triumphantly pulled up a blue card. "Wild game was much prized as a source of meat during wartime rationing. Among the reader letters of 1944 you will find some fascinating advice on the care of young ducklings from the inimitable James Beard."

Our race to the secret room — Anzio, as Sammy had begun to call it — sent books tumbling to the floor. I went right to the 1944 shelf and searched through the folders, looking for "Ducklings." The file was very fat. "There must be a lot of letters here!" Excited now, I pulled it off the shelf and sat next to Sammy on the floor.

April 18, 1944
Dear Mr. Beard,

Mother won the contest! I've been racking my brain for ham recipes; so far I've made ham salads, ham and molasses loaves, and bean soup with ham. Yesterday I made ham turnovers for all the women in the Corsair group; Mother says they were a big hit. But I'm starting to understand what they mean about two people, a ham, and eternity. If you have any interesting recipes for ham, please send them my way.

The air-raid warden came by last night to check our emergency supplies. He said we were the only house in the whole neighborhood that had every single supply we were supposed to: fifty feet of garden hose with a spray nozzle, one hundred pounds of sand, two three-gallon metal buckets filled with water, a shovel, a hoe, an ax, and a ladder. We even have the leather gloves and dark glasses!

Tommy thinks the Germans are going to try invading us before we invade them, and he says we should sleep with our shoes on. He's not the only jumpy one. There are blackouts every night, and now that we know the big invasion is near, nobody's sleeping very well.

Please write to me, Mr. Beard. Some-times I think that everyone in Akron is going crazy.

Your friend,
Lulu

June 5, 1944
Dear Mr. Beard,
Rome has fallen! We've just finished listening to Mr. Roosevelt tell about the liberation of the city, and I'm so happy. I know I'm being selfish, but I hope Father is still in Italy and not part of the big invasion being planned. We all know it will start any day now and that the men will be in terrible danger. Sometimes I lie in bed, wondering how anyone could be brave enough to run right into enemy fire. I'd like to think I could do it, but in my heart I know I couldn't. I wish I had more courage.

Did you hear President Roosevelt's speech? I wrote some of it down. "Italians have come by the millions into the United States. They have been welcomed, they have prospered, they have become good citizens, community and governmental leaders. They are not Italian Americans. They are Americans — Americans of Italian descent."

I looked over at Mother as he was speaking, and her mouth was in a straight, tight line. She hates to be in the wrong, but I

303

hope that will be the end of her calling Mrs. C. the enemy.

School is almost out, and it makes me feel like dancing. Middle school is over, I'm going on to North High, and I'll never have to hear Miss Dickson's voice again. I'll be joining the U.S. Crop Corps soon, and I know that being a Victory Farm volunteer is going to make this a very fine summer.

Your friend,
Lulu

June 27, 1944
Dear Mr. Beard,
Yesterday was the first day of vacation, and it started off so well. Now it seems like we're winning the war, and it makes us all feel better, more optimistic.

I have a whole week until Crop Corps starts, a week that belongs entirely to me. Mrs. C. promised to teach me how to make orecchiette (it means little ears), and we were just starting to knead the dough when we saw the telegram man climbing up the stairs. Mrs. C. put her apron over her head and began to wail, and Mr. C. came upstairs to see what was happening. When he saw the telegram man, he started shaking his head and saying, "Go away, go away, go to a different house."

We sat there watching through the screen door as he came toward us. It took him forever — each step seemed to last an hour — and I kept hoping he would never get there. As long as he didn't knock on the door, everyone was still alive.

But then he was there, and Mr. C. was taking the telegram from his hand. "Which one?" said Mrs. C., so quiet I could hardly hear her. When Mr. C. said, "Marco," she screamed and crumpled to the floor. He would have been eighteen in ten days.

The telegram was short and so cold. The secretary of war deeply regretted to inform them that their son was killed in action and extended his sympathy for their great loss. Then the telegram said that they couldn't even return the body, if it was recovered, because of "conditions," and if more information was received they would be informed. Mr. C. went over to Mrs. C. and held her in his arms, and they just stood there, holding each other, crying. I didn't know what to do, so I crept out of the room, closing the door softly behind me. Suddenly I felt like a stranger.

Mr. Beard, life can change so quickly; one minute you're happy, the next minute you're not. I'm afraid that Mrs. C. will never want to see me again, because she'll think I bring bad luck. Every time I'm there, she'll be waiting for the telegram man.

I thought I'd be happy this summer in the Crop Corps. But now I know that just feeling we're going to win the war isn't enough. None of us will be happy until the whole horrid thing is finally over.

Your friend,
Lulu

"Is something the matter?" Sammy's voice was alarmed. I could feel him hesitating. I tried to wipe the tears away, but they kept coming, and for a long time neither of us moved. He handed me the big white linen handkerchief he always carries and patted my back. My throat was raw and my shirt was soaked, but I just kept crying.

Finally I lifted my head and looked at Sammy. "Dare I conjecture," he was speaking slowly, "that you have not plummeted into this slough of despond merely because of Lulu?" He swallowed hard. "Is it your sister?"

I could feel myself go soft inside, could feel the words filling my mouth, eager to come out. Sammy slid over and wrapped his arms around me. He put his lips to my

ear; his breath was warm as he whispered,
"Tell me. Tell me."

CAKE SISTERS

Where to begin? I closed my eyes and took myself back. And then I told Sammy my story. All of it.

The year I was ten, Dad's birthday fell on a Saturday. The three of us got up late and had our weekly pancake contest, seeing who could flip one the highest. As usual, it turned the pristine kitchen into an enormous mess. But today Dad looked at the batter-covered counters with the dirty pans and sticky plates and said, "Forget the dishes; it's my birthday. We're going to the beach."

It felt like a holiday, like Christmas or Thanksgiving, and I skipped up the stairs to get my bathing suit. Genie followed more slowly. "It's embarrassing" — she pulled the towels reluctantly off the rack — "going to the beach with your father." She was almost twelve.

It was a hot, clear day, and Genie stretched out on the sand while Dad and I went body-surfing. The water was soft against our skin, and Dad waved at Genie, urging her to join us. But she had her sketch pad out. Dad squinted slightly, his wet hair black and seal-like in the water, looking back at her. "She looks more like your mother every day." I followed his gaze; from here Genie could have been a woman, her bikini stretched taut across her hips, her legs long and golden against the white sand.

"Was Mom that beautiful?" In the old pictures you couldn't tell, and I had no memory of Mom. People said how sad that was, but I had Dad and Aunt Melba. And I had Genie.

"She was." Dad splashed toward me. He studied my pale skin, brown eyes, and straight hair as if seeing me for the first time. He outlined my face, his fingers gentle on my cheeks. I dove into a wave; when I surfaced, he was still looking at the place where I'd gone down. "I know you won't believe this," he said, "but one day you're going to be beautiful too. More beautiful than Genie."

"Thanks," I said, "but nobody's more beautiful than Genie." Why would he say something so absurd? I dove down again,

opening my eyes to find a school of jellyfish
floating through the murky underwater
greenness. From a cautious distance I
watched them suspended in the water like
delicate parachutes, thinking that beauty
was only part of it. Genie was good at
everything and so outgoing that our teachers never could believe we were related. I
surfaced and looked over at the beach.
Genie was lying on the sand, her eyes shut
now.

We went home sun-drunk and drowsy,
trailing sand through the hall and up the
stairs. I went off to shower, and as I toweled
myself dry I stared into the mirror, trying to
see myself as Dad did. I wanted to believe
him, but a sturdy ten-year-old in glasses was
looking back at me. Boring. Ordinary. She
had no waist, no hips, and hair so short she
might have been a boy. I put on a white
cotton dress and slipped into sandals. In
the next room Genie was singing a Randy
Newman song, and the lyrics drifted toward
me: "Got some whiskey from the barman,
Got some cocaine from a friend, I just had
to keep on movin', Till I was back in your
arms again." She had a nice voice, and I
hummed along as I waited for Aunt Melba
to signal us that she was ready.

When she called, Genie ran down the hall

to Dad's room. "Quick!" she said. "Aunt Melba's oven's on fire. We have to go help!" Still pulling a shirt over his head, Dad raced down the stairs, with Genie and me sneaking quietly behind him. When he disappeared behind the hedge next door, we heard thirty people shout, "Surprise!" We squeezed through just in time to see the little tremor of shock run up his back.

"Why didn't you warn me?" he asked Aunt Melba; he was looking down at his rumpled cotton shirt, torn jeans, and bare feet. Dad didn't like surprises. I thought about the gingerbread, wishing we'd made something that seemed more like a birthday cake.

"C'mon, Bob," she said, stroking his arm, "you didn't think I would ignore your fortieth birthday?" Then she began to apologize. "I know Barb would've made paella or roasted a whole pig. Something exotic. But I did my best."

"You did great," Dad assured her, making a visible effort to adjust his attitude. He leaned down to kiss her cheek, and it hit me for the first time that Mom must have been a lot taller than her sister. I was already as tall as Aunt Melba, and Genie had a couple of inches on her.

It was a wonderful party. We ate grilled

steaks, Aunt Melba's perfect hash browns — crisp on the outside and almost melted inside — and salad with blue-cheese dressing. She served daiquiris to the grown-ups, pouring them out of her own colorful ceramic pitchers, and the party grew a little raucous. As dark began to fall, she took a torch and lit the candles in the paper lanterns she had strung through the trees circling her yard. It was beautiful, and as I looked around I thought how hard Aunt Melba tried to do things right. But it was a lot like Genie and me: No matter what she did, Aunt Melba thought Mom would have done it better. Then I remembered the cake, and a little wave of anxiety rippled through me. Dad was going to hate it. It couldn't possibly live up to Mom's.

When it was time to sing, Aunt Melba called us all inside. I could tell the guests had been hoping for something decadent — or at least chocolate — because there was a moment of disappointed silence when Genie and I carried the gingerbread into the long living room. I glanced at Aunt Melba, who seemed both terrified and excited, and then at Dad, who had the oddest expression on his face. I'd never seen that look before, and I knew, with absolute certainty, that we'd made a mistake. When

"Happy Birthday" ended, he blew out the candles and Aunt Melba cut the cake. Dad took a bite, sitting so still I felt slightly sick. There was a kind of electricity in the room — everyone could feel it — and then Dad reached out to us, gathering Genie on one side and me on the other, hugging until it hurt.

"My girls," he said. "Thank you." But it was Aunt Melba he was looking at, over our heads. It was a solemn moment, almost scary. Then Dad smiled and said, "You know what? This is even better than your mother's gingerbread."

The room had been alive with tension, but now it broke and everybody started talking all at once, giddy with relief. "What a cake!" said one of Dad's law partners, while another asked for seconds. Three women clamored for the recipe.

"It's got fresh ginger —" Genie began, but Aunt Melba stopped her.

"That recipe's a secret," Aunt Melba said, hustling us into the kitchen, with Dad close behind.

"Why?" asked Genie.

"You never know. You shouldn't give your recipes away. You might want to go into business."

Dad put up his hands, as if he was trying

to end this conversation. But it was too late. "Why would anyone want to buy a cake made by kids?" asked Genie.

"Because it's made by kids." Aunt Melba was looking into my eyes, and when she spoke, she was talking to me. "A cake is just a cake, but a cake made by kids is something special. Especially a kid as talented as you. I bet you could make a lot of money."

"You don't mean it," Dad said.

"Yes." She looked at Dad's face. "I do. If your housekeeper doesn't want them messing up the kitchen, they're welcome to use mine."

To everyone's surprise (except Aunt Melba's), Cake Sisters took off. Aunt Melba kept scrapbooks of it all. The first clipping was an embarrassing one from the *Santa Barbara News-Press,* which went on about how young and adorable we were and how we'd recreated our late mother's gingerbread to start our business. It made me cringe. The next one was better, a spread from the *Los Angeles Times* about an improbably tall angel-food cake we'd named for Mom. The reporter also admired the Melba, a small dark devil's-food concoction filled with cherry-studded chocolate ganache.

As you turned the pages of the scrapbook,

the cakes became increasingly elaborate. In our second year Genie dreamed up the Giant Hostess Cupcake Cake, and I worked out the most amazing recipe. That was a huge success; *Food & Wine* magazine called it "incredible edible pop art." The next year Genie came up with Melting Cakes and I figured out how to create them. But the wedding cakes were what really made us famous. There were dozens in the scrapbook, each one unique. For a few years, every Santa Barbara bride considered a Cake Sisters creation her natural birthright, and we were very busy.

Aunt Melba threw herself into our project; she even went to New York to take a course in sugar arts.

"I thought it would be a lot like ceramics," she told me, showing off some fantastic sugar flowers she'd made, "and I was right. I had so much fun; there's nothing quite as wonderful as imagining something in your head and then making it come true."

"I wish I could do that," I said wistfully.

Startled, Aunt Melba asked, "But doesn't it feel like that when you invent a cake?"

"No. That's so easy. I taste it in my mind and then all I have to do is find the flavors. I'd much rather be able to draw like Genie."

She gave me a long, searching look, but

315

all she said was, "I hope you don't have to wait as long as I did to find out you're wrong about what you think you want."

I expected to close the bakery when Genie went to college, but as I watched her dressing for her senior prom (she was going with the class president, Eli Pierce), she said offhandedly, "How would you feel about keeping Cake Sisters open next year? I could really use the money."

She pirouetted in front of the mirror, pleased with her reflection. "Should I wear these?" She held up a choker of baroque pearls that had once belonged to Mom, bent her head, and pulled the hair off her neck. "Help me put them on?" She smelled like lilacs, brown sugar, and nutmeg.

"How would it work?" I kept my voice flat and turned my head so she couldn't see my face. I'd been dreading the thought of life without Genie. "The bakery, I mean. You'll be up in Berkeley."

"It's not like I'm leaving for the ends of the earth." She gave the mirror a final satisfied glance. Downstairs, Eli rang the bell. "I could come home on weekends."

I didn't think she'd do it, but I was wrong: Genie came home so often, it was as if she'd never even left. Aunt Melba was surprisingly cross about it. "It's not natural," she grumbled halfway through Genie's freshman year. "Kids are supposed to go away to college and stay there. It would be nice if she gave you a little breathing room."

"But I like having her here." I was loyal. "And you know she needs the money. She likes nice things."

Aunt Melba sniffed. "That sports car! And all those clothes. She'll be sorry; by the time you're thirty her money will be gone and you'll just be getting yours. You're going to be happy you had your dad invest yours in that trust. By then it should have doubled at the very least."

"So I'll be rich and she can borrow from me."

Aunt Melba looked disgusted.

She was still grumpy a few months later, as I began to receive college acceptance letters. She urged me to choose Reed or Stanford — anywhere but Berkeley.

"Why?" I asked, unable to understand why she didn't want me to follow in Genie's footsteps.

Her answer was not what I'd expected. "I know what it's like, having a big sister like Genie. Barb was always better at everything. I got good grades, but hers were perfect. She beat me at every game we ever played. I was pretty enough, but she was gorgeous.

And in the end?" The words were catching in her throat. "She got your father."

She didn't mention it again until the weekend I left for school. We'd decided to close the bakery, since Genie and I would both be up north now. Aunt Melba helped me pack up the equipment, seeming slightly dejected as we stacked cake pans in a box. "If you were going to school around here," she said, "you could keep the bakery open. You don't need Genie; cooking's your gift, not hers."

"But without her it would be no fun."

Aunt Melba took the big roll of duct tape, closed the flaps of the box, and firmly taped it shut.

When I got to Berkeley, I was glad I'd ignored Aunt Melba's advice. I loved having Genie there, was grateful when she forged a path for me. She told me what classes to take and what clubs to join. She took me to parties, introduced me to her friends, and occasionally fixed me up with a discarded boyfriend (although they were so disappointed to get second-best that it never worked).

In the spring of my junior year, I was sitting on Telegraph Ave., drinking iced green tea with a boy I'd been dating from my

English class, when a shadow fell across our table. My date looked up, and for just a moment I saw Genie through his eyes. She was wearing a short, tight black skirt, a pale-pink T-shirt, and silver sandals, her hair curling loosely around her face. He was nice enough, and we had decent sex, but we'd fallen together mostly because we were the two nerdiest kids in the class. Now I heard him gulp and watched him put his hand up to shade his eyes.

"This is Owen," I said.

Genie glanced at him briefly, sat down, and took a sip of my tea. "Aunt Melba called." She took another sip. "Beverly Jackson's getting married on June fifth, and she wants us to make her cake."

"But we closed the bakery."

"Aunt Melba told her. But you know Beverly. Stupid rich and always gets her way. She called me."

"No problem," I said. "Go to plan B."

"Yes problem," replied Genie. She was twirling her hair around her fingers, and I saw Owen's eyes follow her hand. "I did."

"What's plan B?" he wanted to know.

Genie gave him her quicksilver smile. "When we don't want to do a job, we demand an absurd amount of money. I mean, no kidding, crazy. An amount so huge, no sane person could possibly say yes."

"I'm assuming that Beverly said yes?" He looked straight at her. "You obviously didn't ask enough."

"Thirty grand?" She gave him back his own cool look.

Owen choked on his iced tea.

"No way!" I said.

"Way." She was still tugging at her hair. "She said she doesn't plan to have a second wedding, and she couldn't care less what this one costs. So I told her we'd get back to her. What do you think?"

"It's an awful lot of money. . . ." There was no way we could possibly live up to it.

"That's what I thought." Genie unfurled a radiant smile, and I realized she had misunderstood me. She sprang up, threw a quick "Nice meeting you" in Owen's direction, and floated off. I stared after her in dismay.

Owen exhaled, as if he hadn't breathed the entire time she'd been there. "That's your sister?" He watched the rosy rectangle of her shirt recede into the distance. I shrugged; I was used to it.

How could a cake be worth thirty thousand dollars? That night I stayed up late, trying to reach Genie. I wanted to tell her we had to back out, but she'd obviously expected that: Her phone went right to voice mail.

In the morning I walked across Sproul Plaza to the apartment Genie shared with three roommates. She opened the door wearing nothing but underwear and a T-shirt. Little red lines were running through her eyes, and there was mascara on her cheeks. From behind her came loud snoring, and I saw a half-naked guy sleeping on the lumpy sofa, surrounded by empty bottles and overflowing ashtrays. "Sorry." She followed my eyes. "Hard night."

"I'll make some coffee." I stepped through the debris. "But we can't do this cake. I'm sorry, but thirty grand is insane."

Genie went into the bathroom and began brushing her teeth. "It's for three hundred people." Her mouth was full of toothbrush, and the words were thick. She rinsed. "I looked up the big guys — Ron Ben-Israel and Sylvia Weinstock — to see what they're charging. They get that kind of money for special orders all the time."

"Have you seen their cakes?" I had to shout over the coffee grinder. "We're not them. They really know what they're doing. We're just two sisters from Santa Barbara who like to bake."

"If it doesn't bother Beverly," she went

into her bedroom and called through the closed the door, "why should it bother you?"

I didn't have an answer. "It just feels wrong" was all I could come up with. "Embarrassing."

"Not to me." She emerged from the bedroom in a lavender silk robe, looking suddenly wide awake. The smell of coffee filled the air, erasing the smell of beer. "Put a lot of milk in mine," she added, "and sugar. I need the energy." I sniffed at the milk — not quite gone — and poured it into her cup. I stirred in three teaspoons of sugar and handed it over. She took a huge sip and sighed. "Better." She took another sip. "Graduation's in May, which will give us three weeks after to go home and concentrate on the cake. Think about it, Billie; we won't have to work this summer! I can take time off before starting law school."

"Why don't you start now? Do you even sleep anymore?"

"Not much." She took another sip of coffee. "I'm not about to blow my GPA at the very last minute."

"You've already gotten into Yale Law. Would one random A-minus really matter?"

Genie gave me a scathing look. "Don't change the subject; we were talking about the cake. I've had an idea."

She went over to her desk and began rummaging around for a sketchbook. She took a deep draft of coffee and began to draw. As I watched her pencil skip lightly across the page, I wondered, again, why she was going to law school. To be even more like Mom? Beneath her fingers, an edible landscape was taking shape, hundreds of individual cupcakes, each topped with a different flower. As I watched, she layered the little cupcakes until they formed a perfect eighteenth-century garden.

"Start thinking about flavors," she said. "Rosewater, lavender, orange blossom . . . You'll figure it out."

"Are you sure we can pull this off?" I asked.

"Of course!" She gave me her most persuasive smile. "It's going to be fantastic!"

Genie graduated and we went home to Santa Barbara. For the next three weeks we lived and breathed that cake. Genie and Aunt Melba fiddled with designs, while I experimented with rosewater, orange oil, and saffron, trying to figure out the precise flavor of each tiny cupcake. One morning I brewed an infusion of saffron and stirred it into the flour, milk, and eggs, watching as the color captured the batter, turning it a vivid gold. I stuck my finger in and licked. Too strong? Mesmerized by the spreading color, I called, "Somebody come taste this."

Aunt Melba's finger dipped into the batter and disappeared into her mouth. "You're a genius. It tastes even better than it looks." She dipped again.

"Where's Genie?"

"In the bathroom. She says she's not feeling so well."

"She's been working harder than either of us." Why did I feel the need to defend her?

"She always works hard." Aunt Melba dipped her finger in again and licked it thoughtfully. "This is fabulous."

"What's fabulous?" asked Genie, coming into the kitchen. I held out the spoon and she took a tentative lick. I noticed that her cheeks were flushed.

"You okay?"

"Fine," she said. "I'm fine."

As the wedding grew closer, our days grew longer. Aunt Melba and I would quit, exhausted, at midnight, but Genie seemed tireless. She'd gotten us into this. We'd come down in the morning to find the kitchen filled with the fanciful flowers she'd produced while we were sleeping.

On the morning of the wedding, we stacked twenty-one hundred tiny cupcakes, each topped with a handmade flower, and the cake into Aunt Melba's van, and I navigated the long, curving, tree-lined driveway that led to the Jackson estate. There was a steep curve at the front of the house, and I slowed to a crawl, admiring the enormous tent stretching along the far side of the property. An army of florists, caterers, and musicians was busily transforming the tent into a wedding wonderland.

It was warm for early June, and we didn't want to risk a meltdown. We stashed the cupcakes in the air-conditioned kitchen: We would construct our landscape slowly, tier by tier, inside the tent.

"I'll be the mule." Genie seemed tired and edgy.

"Fine," I agreed, beginning to lay the groundwork as she ferried cupcakes from the kitchen.

It took all afternoon, but as the garden came together, I saw that Genie had been right: The masses of flowered cupcakes were even more beautiful than her drawing had been. It was breathtaking, like a painting by Monet, and a few people gathered beneath the tent to watch.

By the time we were ready to add the final touches, the crowd had grown. The hairdressers switched off their blow-dryers, and in the sudden silence we could hear the musicians tuning up. Then the music stopped, flutes and violins going quiet as the players came to join us. There was a clatter of silver when the caterers put down the sterling spoons they'd been polishing. The bartenders came too, leaving ice cubes melting in the sun. I could hear the bridesmaids giggle nervously as I climbed onto a ladder, and when Genie handed up the first tier, there was a small whoosh, the crowd holding its collective breath. As I lowered it gently into place, a sigh rippled through the tent. The lights were bright, and as Genie handed me one tier after another, I felt triumphant, an artist completing a masterpiece.

We had come to the final tier, the one where the tiny bride stands beside her tiny groom underneath a miniature arbor. I offered to trade places, so Genie could complete the cake; it was, after all, her invention. But she shook me off. "I'll go get the last tier. I need to use the bathroom," she called over her shoulder, "and you're already up on the ladder." She disappeared into the house.

When she emerged, we all turned to watch her cross the driveway, her eyes focused on the two little figures on the cake cradled in her arms. She never saw the Jaguar come barreling around the curve. I doubt she heard the squeal as Beverly's brother slammed on the brakes and rubber shimmied over tar. Then Genie was up in the air, the cake above her, pinned against the sky. And then they were both falling, the motion so slow it seemed she would never reach the ground.

"Did she survive?" Sammy startled me. His voice seemed to be coming from very far away.

I shook my head slowly.

"So what you are telling me is that this sibling to whom you occasionally allude has been deceased for almost two years?"

I nodded. "But I'm the one who should have died. That car was meant for *me.*" My voice cracked on the last word. "Genie should have been up on the ladder. It was my fault."

Sammy gripped my shoulder, hard. "No, Billie." He sounded sympathetic, but I heard something else as well. Steel. "It was not your fault. It was a tragic accident."

"Don't you see? Aunt Melba thought up Cake Sisters so I could have something I was better at than Genie! She did it for me."

I expected him to argue, the way Dad and Aunt Melba had, insisting I had no reason to feel guilty. But Sammy simply sat there, silently rubbing my back, letting me cry. After a few minutes I could feel my muscles relax beneath his hands as the scene began to fade.

"What moved you to tell me now?"

I thought it was something in Lulu's letter, that feeling that everybody was looking at her differently now, thinking she had brought bad luck. It was exactly how I'd felt since the day that Genie died. I'd run away from everyone who knew the whole awful story — and kept it from everyone who didn't. I couldn't admit, even to myself, that Genie was really dead. I couldn't bear the knowledge that when people looked at me, they'd be looking past my shoulder, watching for the telegram man with his tragic news.

Sammy waited patiently as I marshaled the words. Then, tired of all the hiding, I let them go. "When Lulu said, 'Life can change so quickly; one minute you're happy, the next minute you're not,' it all came back. Because that was the minute when everything changed for me."

"Billie, Billie, Billie." Sammy's hands dug into my shoulders. "How can you be so blind? Change works both ways. You must accept those moments, experience them, and let them go. Because if you allow yourself to get stuck in that minute, nothing will ever change."

"What are you saying?"

"I am telling you that if things can change for the worse, the opposite is also true. But only if you open yourself to the possibilities. As Lulu did. It is what one finds so appealing about her."

It was too much to think about. I felt wrung out by the emotions of the afternoon. I didn't want to talk about myself or my sister anymore. "Are there any more letters?" I asked.

Sammy sighed, and I knew that he was reluctant to let this moment go. He wanted to go on talking, but he didn't push it. "Just one," he said, peering into the folder. He put his arm around me, drawing me closer, and I leaned in so we could read together.

July 15, 1944
Dear Mr. Beard,
You were right; cooking for Mrs. C. did make me feel better. I made the panettone that she taught me at Christmas, because I thought she'd like to serve it after the funeral.

The funeral was beautiful. They held it at St. Anthony of Padua Church, and, listening to the singing, I remembered what Mrs. C. had told me. When the church was built, all the Italian families chipped in, and she went around the neighborhood with a little red wagon, collecting food for the builders.

When the service was over, we all went back to the apartment. People were crying and laughing, all at the same time, so different from the way it was in our house when Grandmother died. Mrs. C. told everyone I'd made the panettone, and then she kissed me. Before I left, I told her that I'd been afraid that she wouldn't want to see me again, and she gave me a little slap and called me pazzesca — crazy. She said in bad times it's the people we love who can help us. Then she gave me a big hug and said that Marco wasn't coming back but we still have his memory and she was grateful that we have each other. It made me feel like I had become part of her family, and I went home feeling so much better.

Your friend,
Lulu

April Fool

Sammy and I now shared a secret language, and whenever something bad occurred — the rain refused to stop, a pot boiled over, someone nabbed the taxi that was clearly meant for us — he'd look at me and mouth, *"Pazzesca!"* It was a little thing, but it made me feel safe, cozily anchored in the world. We had each other. I think that's why I finally stopped stalling and got contact lenses.

I didn't see much difference, but Sammy was elated. "If you would also consent to a new coiffure, you might eventually join the human race."

"Don't push your luck," I warned.

"Pazzesca!" he said, and I burst out laughing.

This new easiness helped us weather a bad time in the library: Lulu had vanished.

At first we'd been convinced the secret word was "panettone," and we followed it for a full week, researching the background of the bread and sifting through regional variations and each of the ingredients, before admitting defeat. Bertie had become more devious, and we were trying hard to read her mind.

"What about a parallel word?" I suggested. "Maybe 'coffee cake'?"

But that was fruitless too. We spent another week researching Christmas breads: "kugelhopf," "la pompe des rois," "julekage." By the time we'd reached the unpronounceable "joululimppu," we were both ready to admit we'd been following a false trail.

And time was running out. The weather was getting warmer, and I could see tiny green buds on the trees peeking over the walls of St. Patrick's Old Cathedral when I walked to Fontanari's. One day in mid-March I ran my palm across the rough brick wall, thinking how Lulu had described the Mass at St. Anthony of Padua. It gave me an idea.

"What are the most important saints?" I asked Rosalie when I got to the shop.

"You look different. Have you gotten religion?"

"No, only contact lenses."

"Didn't I tell you? See how much better

you look!" She gave me an impulsive hug. "Maybe you could get your hair cut now?"

"Saints," I said. "Tell me about saints."

"Everybody has their favorite." She frowned slightly but dropped the subject of my appearance. "When I'm in trouble, I pray to St. Anthony; he's always seemed like the most sympathetic. But Sal's partial to St. Jude — you know, the patron saint of lost causes."

"Not so!" Sal was filling the case, turning each cheese until he was certain its most attractive side was facing the customers. "St. Bartholomew's the one for me; he's the patron saint of cheese-makers. But, Willie, you can't go looking for clues among the saints; there are way too many."

He was right about that. When the religious angle led us nowhere, we tried "little red wagon," and then, in desperation, "grandmother."

As April approached we were right back where we'd started; Bertie had definitely become more devious. For the next two weeks we went over and over the letters, unable to figure out the next clue.

The weatherman predicted a fierce rainstorm on April 1, which exactly suited my mood. I was eager for thunder and lightning, but in the end it was just a paltry burst of rain that thudded down for a couple of hours before passing out to sea. In its wake came beautiful dry weather, and the next day, when Sammy came bounding into the mansion, jubilant over the unexpected sunshine, I growled at him. "What are you so cheerful about? It's April, and it's been six weeks since we found a letter."

"I propose," he replied, "that we contemplate the possibility that we have arrived at the termination of this project."

"No!" I was positive he was wrong. "The last letter we found was dated July of 1944. The war lasted another whole year. She must have gone on writing to him."

"Perhaps she no longer sent the letters to *Delicious!* Or perhaps Bertie grew fatigued with the project. Possibilities abound. I, for one, require a respite. Will you indulge me for a day?"

"How?" I glanced at the calendar, wary of our shrinking window of time.

"Ask me no questions. We shall embark upon on a lunchtime expedition."

At noon he led me north on Washington Street, detoured west on Little West 12th Street, and turned up Tenth Avenue. "Where are we going?" I kept asking, but he refused to say anything until we arrived at a small boutique tucked beneath the High Line. I

334

shrank back, but Sammy took my arm and led me through the door.

"Is Hermione available?" he asked the woman behind the desk. In answer, a slight young woman with a mass of black curls came whirling toward us, throwing herself ecstatically into Sammy's arms. "Where've you been?" she cried, hugging him.

I relaxed a bit. With her round cheeks, red lips, and wild hair, she looked nothing like the frigidly elegant saleswomen who patrolled the uptown shops. She put her hands on her hips and said to Sammy, "When I left you in Marrakech, you promised to stay in touch. And how long ago was that?"

"Far too long," he admitted, drawing me toward them. "This is my friend Billie, who has been contemplating a makeover. Do you think you might be of assistance?"

Hermione studied me frankly, her eyes traveling from head to toe. "Do you mind?" She reached out to touch me. "Hard to tell what's underneath those baggy clothes." Patting me down like one of those TSA guards at the airport, she cried, "You're so thin!" She directed Sammy to a chair. "Sit! We're going to amaze you. What fun!" She tugged me through the shop, loading her arms with flimsy skirts, skinny slacks, and sweaters in Easter-egg colors.

"I'm just trying to get a preliminary idea." She nudged me toward the dressing room. "I want to see what colors work for you." As we passed a rack of pants, I grabbed a pair. Hermione peered at the tag and gave a little snort. "Twelve?" She snatched them from my hands. "You're kidding, right?" She replaced them with a six.

I stared dubiously at the scrap of cloth. "There's no way these are going to fit." I was still protesting as I pulled the zipper up.

"Perfect!" Her voice was smug. "I'm guessing you buy most of your clothes in thrift shops."

Was it that obvious? "I'm pretty hopeless when it comes to fashion," I admitted.

She handed me a purple silk blouse. "Try this. I know women who'd kill for your body. And I bet you don't even belong to a gym."

It was so strange, having her hand me clothes and scrutinize me as if I weren't there. I felt like a life-size doll. She handed me another blouse. "Put this one on. Green's a difficult color." She stood back, eyeing me critically. "But obviously not for you; that's great. Let's try this." A red sweater. A yellow one. "Is there any color that doesn't look good on you? And you've been running around in this." She scooped the drab oatmeal sweater from the floor and then, as an afterthought, confiscated my khakis as well. I made a little squeak of protest, but she stopped me from retrieving them. "Embrace the change! Wait! I've just had a thought. I've got something that's going to be perfect."

Carrying my old clothes, she left me alone to look in the mirror for the first time. There was a waist I'd never noticed, and in these pants I actually had hips. I turned sideways; had my body changed?

"Try this." Hermione was back, holding out a gossamer dress of rainbow chiffon so airy I thought of fireflies on a moonlit night; the colors winked and changed with each motion. I put it on: The bodice clung tightly to my breasts and waist, but the full skirt was like a tutu, the fabric brushing my legs seductively. It was the girliest garment I'd ever seen, let alone worn. I loved it.

"Go show Sammy."

I looked at the price tag. "Oh, I don't think so —"

"Show him!" She pushed me out of the dressing room.

Sammy was sitting out front, but his eyes were carefully trained on a magazine. The dress gave me courage, and suddenly I wanted to be more than a doll for Hermione's amusement. I grabbed a gray jacket, cut as severely as a man's, and put it on over the dress. Hermione's head jerked up. "Oh, my God!" she said. "That's perfect! What made you think of that?" She towed me back to the dressing room and made me look into the mirror. "And you said you had no fashion sense!"

The combination was great: The severity of the jacket underlined the fragility of the dress. Hermione was gathering up all the clothes I'd tried on. "Forget these. I want you to go out there and look around. Grab everything you like; don't worry about size or how you'll wear it. Just bring me everything that speaks to you. Anything at all."

Bewildered, I prowled the store for things that appealed to me. I could feel the fabric of the dress brushing against my legs and I began to move by instinct, not editing at all, picking up anything that caught my eye. On the first foray I grabbed a few simply cut but colorful clothes and went back to the dressing room, ignoring Hermione as I layered a short red skirt over a pair of orange leggings with a pearly T-shirt. I added a pair of red sneakers. She stood watching, arms crossed, saying nothing.

Next I tried tight black pants with a soft

white linen shirt whose billowing sleeves and lace cuffs covered my wrists. I pulled on a long black Victorian vest and twirled, liking the effect. Hermione smiled. When I'd put on a man's black shirt with the black pants, I added a red suede jacket so soft it seemed made of air.

"Fabulous!" said Hermione. "Those colors are so good on you!"

"I was just playing," I said apologetically. "I'd never actually have the guts to wear this jacket."

"Why not? You look incredible. You've got the perfect body for clothes like that. Go show Sammy."

"You're kidding, right?"

"No! Please believe me: You've got a good eye and a certain style that's all your own. You just never knew it. Go show Sammy," she repeated, pushing me out of the dressing room.

"She's insane!" I said when I saw him. "Utterly out of her mind. She thinks this ridiculous outfit looks good."

"It does not look good." Sammy was walking around me, taking it all in. "It looks fascinating and oddly elegant. It looks *pazzesca*!"

"You're serious?" I touched the soft jacket. It was unlike anything I'd ever worn before, and yet it felt right. Comfortable. As if it belonged to me. I wondered what Genie would have said if she'd seen me dressed like this. But I knew the answer: Genie would have refused to let me leave the house. She would have barred the door and told me not to be an idiot. Then I wondered about Aunt Melba; what would she think of this outfit?

I went back to the dressing room and put on the long white cotton shirt and the Victorian vest. I looked at myself in the mirror, liking what I saw, and went back into the store.

Sammy turned to Hermione. "Pack it up, please. We shall take all of it. As for those . . ." She was holding my old clothes. "Burn them!"

"But I can't afford all this!"

"Am I remembering incorrectly? Did your father not create a trust for you with the proceeds from Cake Sisters?"

"But I can't touch it till I'm thirty!"

"You have merely to request a small advance from your father." Sammy reached out to touch the lace cuff. "I am persuaded that he would be very pleased to oblige." He turned back to Hermione. "Pack it up, please," he said again, grandly. "And have it delivered to my abode. My friend here is sadly lacking in amenities. No doorman."

He held an arm out to me. "Shall we? I will be extremely pleased to be the escort of so elegant a creature. You make me feel like a fortunate man. I anticipate a favorable outcome to this day, and I have every expectation that we shall finally find the missing missives from Lulu."

But what we found, when we got back to the mansion, was a message from Ruby. She wanted me to call her immediately.

"Oh, Billie," she said, a spark of excitement in her usually placid voice, "Mr. Pickwick just met with his real estate agents, and they're on their way over. He's going to sell the mansion!"

I'd been anticipating this moment for the past five months, but, still, it took my breath away. "You okay?" she asked, and I realized I'd been staring mutely at the wall, silently clutching the phone.

"Yeah, fine." My mind was racing. How much time did we have?

Slightly dazed, I stumbled down to Sammy's office. "She said they'd be here any minute."

His face turned ashen. "Their arrival is imminent?" He gave a helpless little gesture, taking in the copper teapot, the rugs, the duck press, and the sword. "How unfortu-

341

nate that they should catch us unawares. I had anticipated a bit more warning. This affords me a conspicuous lack of time in which to remove my personal effects. What shall we do? It is obvious that I must make myself scarce."

"Did you keep those 'unsanitized' tapes? We'll put them back up and lock your door. I'll say I don't have the key."

We closed the door and Sammy turned the key, pocketing it as I crisscrossed the door with long strips of the yellow tape. Sammy watched me struggle to make it stick. "I am desolated to abandon you. But I shall scurry off. Do not, under any circumstances, allow those people access to the library. Recall that the key went astray long ago. If fortune favors us, their chosen locksmith will operate with the normal sloth of the New York tradesman. That will buy us a bit of time."

"Where're you going?"

"I shall pay a visit to the Fales Library. Despite this regrettable development, I continue to feel fortunate. Fales, as you know, contains America's largest antique-cookbook collection."

"NYU? I thought that library at Radcliffe had the great cookbook collection."

"Old news. Fales has eclipsed Radcliffe,

and they specialize in New York City. It seems propitious; perhaps somebody there will have knowledge of Bertie."

"Propitious!" His vocabulary could still make me laugh.

Sammy had barely left the building when the bell rang. A patrician couple strolled into the lobby, gazing appreciatively around. "Joan-Mary Whitfield," said the woman, stripping off brown kid gloves and holding out a smooth white hand with beautifully manicured nails. The camel-hair coat slung carelessly across her shoulders echoed the color of her hair, which was blown into a rippling pageboy. She'd tossed a silk scarf artfully around her neck, prominently displaying the "Hermès" written on the colorful horseshoe print. Her boots were made of the softest leather, the kind that melts beneath a single drop of snow. I wondered if she had always been pretty or if she was one of those women who become more attractive in middle age.

"And this" — she indicated the man — "is my colleague Christopher Van Patten."

"Chris," he corrected, holding out a hand as beautifully maintained as hers. Tall and well built, he looked accustomed to dominating a room. I noticed him appraising my new clothes, and I thought that Sammy had been right; this man in the custom-made suit was eyeing me with respect. I liked that. His eyes moved past me to rest on the chandelier over the stairway. "This is a great pleasure." His voice was self-consciously deep, as if he'd worked with a voice coach to get that deep bass sound. "I've walked past the Timbers Mansion so often, wondering what it would be like inside."

Joan-Mary moved farther into the lobby. "Would you be good enough to give us a tour?" In contrast to her partner's, her voice was small and whispery.

"Don't you want to wait for Mitch?"

The woman made a face. "Given his prices, you'd expect him to show up on time." She glanced my way, then explained, "We've asked an architectural historian to help appraise the building." The bell rang, right on cue. "That must be him."

I went to the door, surprised to find a familiar figure standing on the steps. For a minute I just stood there, smiling. What was he doing here?

"It's not him," I called over my shoulder.

There stood Mr. Complainer, in worn blue jeans, sneakers, and an old peacoat. He had a knapsack slung across his back, his hair hadn't been cut in a while, and his beard was thick, giving him the appearance of a sailor who's come ashore for the first time in months. He seemed happy to see me, but if he was surprised he hid it well. It made me wonder if Rosalie had sent him as a belated April Fool's joke. "How'd you get here?" I asked.

"Walked." He made no move to come in, and I saw that he was now wearing a slightly baffled expression. Maybe she hadn't sent him? Then he said, "You look very different when you're not wearing an apron. Wait — you are different. You aren't wearing glasses!"

"I got contact lenses." Apparently he thought I always dressed like this, and the idea pleased me. To Sammy I was a caterpillar who'd metamorphosed into a butterfly, but to Mr. Complainer this was the way I was out in the real world. He was contemplating me with open admiration, and it made me feel confident, even a little giddy.

Behind me, Joan-Mary called impatiently, "I hear you out there, Mitchell Hammond. Don't keep us waiting."

"It's not your historian," I repeated, just as Mr. Complainer was saying, "I'll be right in."

I jumped. "You?" It came out like an accusation. "That's what you were teaching in

Cambridge?"

He gave an awkward nod and put out his hand. "Mitch Hammond, Architectural History 346. My brilliant powers of deduction tell me that when you're not playing SuperCheeseGirl you turn into Billie Breslin, girl reporter. I should've guessed it, but I'm a bit slow. Wilhelmina: Billie — it all makes sense."

I took his hand, as uncomfortable as he was. We were both remembering what I'd written about him. But he gave me a solid shake, and I could feel him putting whatever he'd felt about the article behind him. It had been a while.

From inside, Joan-Mary called again, "Mitch!" She sounded more urgent now.

"We'd better go in," he said. "After you."

"There you are!" Joan-Mary kissed him once on each cheek, and Chris shook his hand. "Can we please get started? We've got a lot to do." She looked at the staircase. "No elevator?"

Conscious of Mr. Complainer standing behind me, I replied, "No. I'm sorry," and then wondered why I was apologizing.

"Thank God," he said.

"But it would make the building more valuable," Joan-Mary pointed out.

"It would ruin the building," he said

curtly. "Like that Federal mansion you destroyed last year."

"You can't blame me. The clients didn't want to climb stairs."

Chris pulled out a small leather notebook and wrote something in precise, square handwriting. "If we're going for a professional sale, they might want to put an elevator in."

"Please don't say that!" Mr. Complainer took a turn around the lobby. "It would ruin this room."

"This argument" — Joan-Mary was staring at the banister — "is premature. Let's see what we've got before we make any drastic decisions. Lovely carving."

"Right." The two men followed her up the stairs. As we went from floor to floor, they were extremely businesslike, and Mitch seemed determined to put as much distance as possible between us. I remembered the blonde he'd brought to Fontanari's and wondered if she'd been with him in Cambridge.

Joan-Mary rattled Sammy's doorknob, asked about the key, and Chris made a note.

Did the fireplaces work? I told them that I knew Jake's did but wasn't sure about the others. Another note.

"Beautiful proportions," Joan-Mary said

when we walked through the photo studio. "Think what a spectacular dining room this would make!"

When we got to the kitchen, Joan-Mary looked around for a long minute. I couldn't tell what that meant, and all she said was, "We'll need to spend some time in here, but there's no point in wasting yours. Let's go upstairs." She headed back to the stairway. "What's up there?"

"It used to be the art department," I told her.

She nodded, but when we reached the door to the art department, they each took a small, shocked step backward. I thought they were reacting to the fluorescent lights and scuffed metal furniture until Mitch said, "It's criminal!" in a voice so angry I knew it was something more. He walked into the center of the room. "They knocked down all the walls! Originally this would have been a series of small rooms. Servants' quarters." He pointed toward the library door. "But I can't figure out what that is. The door could be original, but it doesn't belong up here." He eyed me for the first time. "What's in there?"

"I've never been inside." I hoped my face didn't look as warm as it felt. "It's supposed to be the library, but they locked it years before I got here."

Chris strolled up to the door, tried the handle, then did it again, harder. "Definitely locked." He made another note. "There's this door and that one down on the second floor." He and Joan-Mary both looked expectantly at Mitch, who pointedly turned away.

"Aren't we going to get the lecture?" she asked.

He reddened a bit and shook his head.

Joan-Mary glanced at me. "He's blushing because he knows that ordinarily we'd simply call a locksmith. But Mitch goes ballistic if you let anyone else touch 'his' buildings."

"Go ahead," he said. "It's perfectly fine with me if you want to let some clumsy oaf come in and destroy all the details. Why would you want to know anything about the history of this building? It's just unimportant little trifles like when the locks were put in, when repairs were made, who was living here, what their lives were like. Why would you want to know any of that?"

"You can tell those things from the locks?" I was intrigued.

Mitch leaned back against the wall. "If you know what you're looking for. Nails, locks, scratches, repairs — they're kind of

349

like fingerprints."

"You make it sound like a crime scene."

"Not a crime scene: an opportunity." He turned to Joan-Mary. "These things tell you the story of a building. Why would you risk destroying that?"

"So we *are* going to get the lecture." She regarded him almost coyly.

Mitch raised his hands and took a step forward. "No lecture. But what exactly is your problem with letting me unlock those doors?"

Another coy look. And that whispery voice. "You know you charge twice what any ordinary locksmith does."

"You get what you pay for."

"I wonder if I'm glad you came back early from — where were you?" Joan-Mary gave him a sidelong glance.

She was obviously enjoying this, and I was reminded of the call-and-response routine Mr. Complainer did with Sal. Was Mitch like this with everyone? He seemed intent on wringing every bit of juice from ordinary life.

"Cambridge."

"I'm afraid that your colleague's early return from his sabbatical is going to turn out to be rather expensive for me."

"But so much more interesting. Besides,

you're not the one who's paying."

She nodded. "Okay, you go prowl around and do whatever it is that you do. Chris and I have to go down to the basement and see what we've got in the way of infrastructure."

"I'll come back tomorrow, if that's all right with you." Mitch made his way to the staircase. "I didn't bring my tools. And I want to do a little research before I begin."

Watching him leave, I had mixed feelings. I got the sense that he found it as uncomfortable as I did, seeing me outside of Fontanari's, and that he was making his escape. But I was relieved too: What if he'd opened Sammy's office on the spot? I'd been racking my brain, trying to think up plausible stories, and now we'd been given a reprieve. Sammy and I could come back tonight and clear it out.

"I hope he doesn't find anything too interesting." Joan-Mary seemed to be talking to herself.

"What do you mean?" I was curious.

"If he discovers that someone famous once owned this house, or if it was the site of some important battle, it could become a nuisance."

"Unlikely," said Chris. "We'd know."

"I hope you're right." Joan-Mary turned back to me. "We'll probably be here for a while, assessing the state of the furnace and the electrical capacity of the building. Please don't allow us to waste any more of your time."

For the next couple of hours I heard them moving around the building, and occasionally I'd hear a scrap of a sentence. It sounded as if they despaired of the heating and electrical equipment, and they were very concerned about how they were going to replace the cracked panes in the antique windows.

They were arguing as they approached my door. He thought it should be sold for professional use, while she insisted that they should try to sell it to the ambassador of some wealthy nation.

"It's such a lovely home," she kept saying.

"Joan-Mary," he replied, "beneath the gruff exterior of a businesswoman beats the heart of a romantic." She laughed; it was a lovely, musical sound, and when they came through the door her cheeks were flushed.

"Do you think the building will sell?" I asked.

Joan-Mary looked at me, her mouth slightly open. "Are you serious? How often do you think an intact Federal mansion comes on the market in the heart of Manhattan? There are Federal row houses, but true mansions are extremely rare. The few that exist have been carved into apartments, or tragically renovated. This one could certainly use an upgrade, but it's been remarkably preserved. It will definitely sell."

"Quickly?" I pressed.

"That," Chris answered, "will depend on many factors. Not the least being price."

"But for the moment," Joan-Mary was speaking again, "as soon as Mitch finishes whatever it is that he's going to do, I'm going to recommend that Mr. Pickwick have the building staged. I'm sorry to say you'll find it rather disruptive."

Chris made a little face at Joan-Mary, as if he was conceding a point. "If we want people to consider it as a home, I suppose we'll need to encourage them to recognize the possibilities."

Joan-Mary was pulling on her gloves. "Anyone with eyes," she said, "could see that this building was made for memories." She gave a little wave. "Thanks. We'll be seeing you soon."

I had come to love the Timbers Mansion, and I liked Joan-Mary for liking it too. It made me happy to think of the old building getting spruced up and turned back into a home. Maybe some child would find the secret room. What had Joan-Mary said? That it was "made for memories." The words resonated, and I suddenly thought of Lulu's last letter. "We still have his memory," Mrs. Cappuzzelli had said. On a mad impulse, I ran up to the library and looked up the word.

Bertie must have known how difficult this clue was. She didn't beat about the bush. There were only six words on the card, written out in her bold turquoise handwriting. "Memories. See reader letters, 1944, the 'Farming' file."

August 21, 1944
Dear Mr. Beard,
Why didn't you tell me how tiring farm work was? I had no idea. At night I'm so fatigued I don't even have the energy to make dinner, and Mother's taken over the cooking. I'm sorry to say that her heart isn't in it; she's grown very fond of frozen baked beans. She says they must be good for us, and since they aren't rationed we can have as much as we want. But who wants the horrid things? Besides, most nights I'm too worn out to eat.

My favorite chore is milking. It frightened me at first, but now I find it comforting. I like to lay my head on the cow's furry flank. And I like that little nudge they give at the end, like they're grateful to be relieved of the burden.

My least favorite job is the raspberries; they're nasty things that scratch your arms. The bees fight you for them too, so I was happy yesterday when we finished and moved into the corn. Farmer Loudon thinks girls make the best detasselers. It's very dirty work, but at least you don't have to stoop. We walk up and down the rows in teams, talking while we take the tassels off the stalks.

I've learned so much this summer. But what I have mostly learned is that I don't want to be a farmer. From now on, a garden is quite enough, thank you very much. Mother says that is a relief; she doesn't want a farmer for a daughter.

I must go. The bus comes at six A.M., and right now that seems only minutes away.

Your friend,
Lulu

"Detasseling?" Sammy was surrounded by the billows of steam rising from the wok in front of him, but even so I could tell how pleased he was that his intuition had been right: It had been a lucky day. "Have you the foggiest notion what that might be?" Emerging from the clouds, he pointed a metal spatula at me. "Do be careful with that letter. It has no business in the kitchen."

According to Wikipedia, detasseling is a way to cross-breed two varieties of corn by removing the pollen-producing flowers from the tops of the corn plants. "Apparently," I said, carefully folding the letter and putting it back into its envelope, "during the war, the corn farmers all hoped for rural helpers, because they knew how to do it."

"It sounds positively medieval." He motioned for me to pick up the white ironstone platter on the counter, and I held it as he piled on the rosy steamed shrimp. The thoroughly urban Sammy wore a look of distaste. "No doubt detasseling tasks are now performed by machines." He waved me toward the dining room. "Make haste; the shrimp grow cold."

"Nope. Even today, with genetically engineered corn, they still do some detasseling by hand."

"I am impressed." He pulled out a chair for me. "I expect that this knowledge will one day serve you well."

"And I expect it's the next clue." It was not lost on me that Sammy had made my favorite dinner, the shrimp curled, translucent as pearls, inside their fragile shells. He'd used the good china too. Something was up, but as he refused to say what, I told him about Mr. Complainer appearing at the mansion.

"Am I remembering correctly that he not was due to return for another month or so?" asked Sammy.

"Apparently he was substituting for a colleague who returned early." Joan-Mary had mentioned that. "But I wish I'd known he had such an interesting profession. He never seemed to consider the cost when he came to Fontanari's, and when he told me he'd spent a couple weeks taking cooking classes in Italy, I just pegged him as a rich guy."

"I too" — Sammy stood up — "was struck by a bolt from the blue." He paused dramatically. "I found Bertie."

"Shut up!" I dropped the last shrimp, splashing soy sauce, vinegar, chilies, and ginger onto the lace cuffs.

"Indeed." Sammy looked triumphant. "I will admit that it was utterly serendipitous. The librarian I succeeded in unearthing at NYU was very pretty but positively useless. I was turning away, dejected, when she said, 'Maybe Bonnie Slotnick could help you.' "

"Bonnie who?"

"Bonnie Slotnick is the proprietress of a vintage cookbook store in the Village. As it was only a few blocks distant, I could not see that I had much to lose, so I wandered her way."

"Bertie's real name is Bonnie?" I was confused.

"Billie!" Sammy frowned at me. "Surely you did not expect it to be that easy?"

"But you said you found her."

"Bonnie is a lovely woman with an impressive knowledge of cookbooks, but she is definitely not Bertie."

"But she knows her?"

"No, she does not. She listened very politely to what I had to say and then spent some time delivering a diatribe against Pickwick Publications and their iniquity in murdering her favorite magazine. I was beginning to consider this a lost cause when she came sputtering to a conclusion, saying that she had an idea. She dialed a number and conversed for quite some time. When she finally hung up, she said, 'Anne Milton is on her way over.' "

First Bonnie, now Anne. "What about Bertie?"

"I shall arrive there in due time." I banged the table with the palm of my hand in frustration. The silverware jumped. Sammy lifted an eyebrow. "Twenty minutes later, a rather grand dame strolled into Bonnie's emporium. Remarkable-looking: quite tall, with sapphire eyes, and a thick head of absolutely superb white hair. I must add that she was wearing the most exquisitely tailored suit it has ever been my privilege to behold, in an extraordinary shade of blue."

"That's exactly how I imagined Bertie!"

"It was not Bertie! Anne is a retired professor of literature. And her closest friend was a librarian at —"

"*Delicious!* Was she Bertie?"

"Well . . ." Sammy obviously wanted to draw the story out. "Yes and no. Her friend was indeed Bertie. And Bertie was employed at *Delicious!* But it was not our Bertie."

"What do you mean, not our Bertie?"

"Her friend was Bertram Arnold Joseph Ancram."

"Bertie's a man?"

"Indeed. Of the masculine persuasion. I could not have been more astounded."

"Do you think Maggie knew?"

"Oh, Maggie." He waved a hand. "Always up to mischief. But to bestow the benefit of the doubt, it is eminently possible that she had no more knowledge of this fact than did I myself. Bertie departed before either of us made an appearance at *Delicious!* We were merely acquainted with the myth of Bertie."

"I bet she knew," I said darkly.

"It is of no moment. What does matter is that Miss Milton was entirely cognizant of the secret room."

"She knew about Anzio? Did Bertie build it?"

"I felt that it would be unsportsmanlike to allow her to narrate her tale in your absence. She will join us for dinner tomorrow evening, when all will be revealed."

He let her get away? "I'm not sure I can bear the suspense. It's a long time till tomorrow night."

"The time will fly; there is so much to do. I must vacate my office before morning.

And I intend to make a midnight raid on Anzio. Anne had some very good suggestions."

"She knew about Lulu?"

"She seems to know everything. She asked if we had noted Bertie's fondness for puzzles and puns. When I related how long it had taken us to unravel the mystery of the ugly duckling, she regarded me with what I can only describe as pity. Then she inquired if we had fiddled with the letters in the other names."

"We should have thought of that!"

"I gave it a whirl. 'Lulu,' with its paucity of letters, offers rather poor possibilities, but when I began diverting myself with 'Swan,' I was absolutely enraged. How could I have overlooked this? There is an absolutely obvious word. Bertie would have been powerless to resist it."

"What?"

"As far as I can tell, there is only one anagram for Swan. But it is a doozy."

"A doozy?"

"Awns, for your information, are those rather beautiful arrow-like spikes on top of wheat plants. They are the bristles on all cereals — barley, rye — a myriad of possibilities. They are . . ." He stopped himself. "Oh, my word!"

"They're tassels!"

The moon was nearly full, and in the milky darkness the library seemed even more enchanted than usual. I looked around, already nostalgic, knowing our days here were numbered.

Sammy reached for my hand, and we moved slowly, breathing together, to the card file. The "Awn" card referred us to the various cereals, and we went through the cereal cards one by one, carefully reading Bertie's notes. At "Wild Wheat," we hit pay dirt.

As I read, "The awns of wild-wheat spikelets are self-cultivating," I could imagine Bertie writing the card, delighted by his own cleverness. "During World War II, many young people were forced to be equally self-sufficient. There is no better proof of their resourcefulness than a letter filed under 'Wheat,' 1944."

The file, when we found it, was distressingly thin, and I opened it with a sense of foreboding.

October 1, 1944
Dear Mr. Beard,
The telegram came yesterday. "The secretary of war desires me to express his

deepest regret that your husband, James Swan, has been reported missing in action since September 14, in France. If further details or other information is received, you will be promptly notified."

Oh, Mr. Beard, we did not even know that Father had been deployed to France! Since Paris is liberated, he must be somewhere in the south. But I know, in my heart, that he's not dead; if he were, the world would feel emptier. But it feels the same way it did yesterday, and the day before, and I am absolutely sure that he is out there somewhere, still alive. I just pray that he's not badly wounded. I'm consoled by the fact that the weather there is pleasant now. I hope he's in a lovely little village where they grow their own food and keep their own bees, being protected by good people.

Mr. Beard, Mother and I will be very grateful if you will add your prayers to ours.

Your friend,
Lulu

"I knew it wasn't going to be good!" I'd been reading up on the end of the war; late in the summer of '44, over the objections of Churchill, Eisenhower began to move troops from Italy to the south of France. "The operation was called Dragoon," I told Sammy. "It was like another D-Day, although it never received much attention. The English thought the resources would be better used in Italy or the Balkans, but Eisenhower was insistent. He wanted to open the ports of Marseille and Toulon."

"Was it successful?"

"Yes, but also expensive: Seventeen thousand Allied troops were killed or wounded."

"And Father was among them," Sammy mused, "for the second time. He does appear to get himself shot down with remarkable frequency." Sammy said it slowly, as if an idea was coming to him as he spoke. "Perhaps he was doing it on purpose, so he could collect information behind enemy lines? Did it ever occur to you that he might have been a spy?"

"Oh, please." This seemed like a stretch. "What occurs to me is that Bertie always leaves us hanging. Where is Father? Will he be rescued? Tune in next time to find out. I wish he'd known we'd be racing the clock; he might have made this easier. What now?"

"Rather obvious, don't you think?" Sammy was beginning to get up from the floor, and I could see how tired he was. "You must surely have noted the frequency with which Lulu employed Beard's name in this letter. Now would be the moment to investigate anagrams for 'Beard.' "

"Not tonight," I said. "We've got to get all your stuff out of your office."

It was very late by the time we had boxed everything up and lugged it back to his apartment. Too exhausted to go home, I collapsed onto his sofa, pulled a cashmere throw over myself, and fell into a restless sleep. I think I was having a dream about the Timbers Mansion when I suddenly woke up, looked around for a sheet of paper, and began writing anagrams of "James Beard."

"Mad bee jars." "Be dear jams." "Jade's Amber." "Rad bee jams." As I stared at the words, the clue became obvious. I went back to the sofa and slept without dreaming.

I woke again to the smell of coffee and the scent of oranges. I went into the kitchen and Sammy handed me a cup of coffee. "Honey!" I said, feeling very clever.

"You know I loathe the stuff," he replied. "So I assume that you are not requesting a bit of sweetener for your coffee. I take your meaning; you are not the only one who devoted the night to anagrams."

I felt the pride slip off my face.

Sammy patted my arm. "Never mind. It is merely great minds thinking alike. Honey is definitely the clue. Drink your coffee quickly; if you are to have the opportunity to investigate this theory, you must depart with alacrity."

"I should change." I looked down at the wrinkled blouse I'd slept in, the cuffs spattered with soy sauce. "Where did you put my new clothes?"

Sammy looked at me with obvious impatience. "This is no time to fret over fashion!" But he went and got the package. "I am beginning to regret your metamorphosis. Hurry! You must arrive at the mansion ahead of that fellow."

I went into the bathroom and took the quickest shower of my life. I put on the red skirt with the pink T-shirt and orange leggings, glanced at myself in the mirror, and hurried out. "Don't worry." I kissed Sammy on the cheek. "I'll take a cab."

It was one of those hopeful early-April mornings, and after I got out of the cab I had to stand for a moment, taking in the fresh air and watching cloud reflections drift across the windows.

"I'm going to tell on you." I jumped sky-high. Mr. Complainer's voice seemed to come out of nowhere. I hadn't noticed him sitting on the top step.

"What?"

"I'm going to tell Sal you take a taxi to work. You know he won't approve; he thinks taxis are strictly for tourists." He put a hand up to shade his eyes. "Interesting outfit."

"Glad you like it."

"And interesting reaction."

"What do you mean?"

"How long have you been working at Fontanari's? A year and a half? And this is the first time you've ever given me a straightforward response to something that's not about Sal or salami."

"Really?" That couldn't be right.

Mr. Complainer kept talking, and I saw this was something he'd thought about. "Remember that time I came and found you on Allen Street?" I did remember, although I'd had no idea he'd been looking for me.

"You mean when I was eating dumplings?"

"Yeah. I sat down and we talked about the shop. Then I ventured something more personal and you immediately jumped up and said, 'Gotta go.' You made it very clear that our relationship was strictly confined to cheese."

"Oh." Brilliant response, but it was all I could think of.

"And" — he stood up, brushing off the seat of his pants — "now that I know you're the one who wrote that article, I get it. You made what you think of me pretty clear."

His face didn't match his words; it was open, almost hopeful, and it gave me confidence. I took a step up so I was looking directly at him and said, before I could change my mind, "That was a long time ago. Wanna start over?"

He took a step backward; had I said too much? Then he held out his hand. "Hi. I'm Mitch Hammond."

"Billie Breslin." I took it. "And what I want to know is, what are you doing, sitting on my steps at eight-thirty in the morning?"

"Listening to the building. I told Joan-Mary I'd meet her here at ten, but I came early, thinking I'd sit outside and kind of get a feel for the place."

"Listening to the building?"

"Yes. Buildings will talk to you — if you let them. There's something very odd about the Timbers Mansion; I've been trying to research it and I keep coming up blank. That's never happened before. There's always something. Tell me if I'm out of line here, but I was hoping you'd let me take a crack at the library door before Joan-Mary gets here. I'd like to get started. You think you could take me up?"

"Why not?"

I unlocked the door and we went inside.

368

As I led him up the stairs, I was conscious of his eyes on me as we climbed. But when I turned back, I saw that he wasn't watching me. "They told me the Timbers Mansion was a jewel," he said, looking around appreciatively, "but I had no idea it would be like this." He ran a hand lovingly along the banister. "This is superb work. And it's never been painted. This must have been a real suburban palace."

"Suburban?"

"Manhattan started as a little colony down at the very tip of the island. When rich people wanted to give their children healthy country air, they moved uptown."

"This was uptown?"

"It was when this house was built. God, I hope it doesn't go to some rich asshole with no respect for history. It ought to be properly restored."

I began to understand why Joan-Mary had hired him. His passion for the building was palpable, and he kept pointing out details I'd missed. "Look up at the ceiling. . . ." Following his finger, I saw the band of tooth-like moldings where it met the wall. "It's a classic Federal feature. I noticed it outside; it's echoed at the roofline."

When we reached the fourth floor he winced, as if the pain he felt was physical.

He went over to the dormer windows and ran his hands across the glass, as if he could heal them with a touch. "What they've done here . . ." He shook his head. "As I said yesterday, they've ripped down the walls. It's so wrong. Originally this would have been a number of small unheated rooms for the servants."

"Cold in the winter."

"Very. If it turns out that the library is original to the building, it's going to be very strange. Why would someone put a library up here?"

He was scowling as I led him to the door, and for a moment he stood taking it in. Then he knelt down in front of the lock, prodding it gently with the tips of his fingers. The lock was coated with thick black paint and seemed quite ordinary. He laid down a cloth and began to take things out of his tool kit. "Tell me what you know about this room."

"Not much. It was locked when I got here, and they told me it had been that way for years."

I wondered if he could tell, from the condition of the lock, how recently the door had been opened. He turned back to the lock and resumed moving his fingers softly across the surface. "I'm trying to figure out how many coats of paint are on this thing. I'll take out the lock and remove the paint, but I want to get as much information as I can before I begin. It never pays to move too quickly." He glanced up at me as he said this, and I wondered if I was about to get the lecture.

"Little details tell you a lot, but when people don't know what they're looking for, they usually destroy them. Maybe we'll find something hiding underneath this paint." He picked up a small brush, dipped it into some kind of solvent, and swept it across the heads of the screws before gently fitting a screwdriver into the slot and very slowly starting to turn. He seemed to have a delicate touch, and the screws released with a little sigh, wriggling in his hands as he carefully examined each one.

"Bronze." He sounded triumphant. "The screws are solid bronze. And I bet when I get this doorplate off, it will be too."

He worked silently for a few minutes, and I leaned against the wall, watching the muscles move beneath his shirt as he carefully removed the plate. Absorbed in his work, he obviously forgot I was there, and I thought how different he seemed here than at Fontanari's. There he was a visitor, a sponge eager to learn what he could, and eager to please. Here he was totally in charge. His motions were crisp, efficient, assured. He knew exactly what he was doing, and I discovered that there is nothing more attractive than competence in action.

He examined the back of the plate, nodding as if it had confirmed his thoughts, then set it down on a cloth and began to coax the lock out of the ancient wood. "Aren't you a beauty," he breathed as it slid into his hands. "Solid bronze. Here, feel." He tossed me the lock.

"It's heavy!" I nearly dropped it. The outside was shrouded in paint, but the secret parts, the ones that had been hidden inside the door, gave off a dull metallic gleam.

He nodded. "I'll tell you this: That lock was not here when the house was built."

"How do you know that?"

"See this?" He was pointing to some initials stamped into the side.

" 'BLW,' " I read.

"It stands for Branford Lock Works, an old New Haven company that was not known by that name until after the Civil War."

"And the house was built before then?"

"Without a doubt. My guess is early 1830s, the last gasp of the Federal style.

That remains to be seen, but the lock has to be a later addition; I won't know how much later until I can get the paint off and see the pattern underneath."

"Why would they put a new lock on the door?"

"Why would anyone? To keep people out. Back then, locks were the only way to ensure privacy, and wealthy people tended to change them as the technology improved. The lock business was very big and extremely competitive, and locksmiths were always trying to make new and more-efficient models. There was obviously something important kept in this room."

"Like what?"

"Could have been anything. If it was an office, you'd assume the owner wanted to ensure that nobody was snooping through his papers. If it has always been a library, it must have contained valuable books. Putting in a new lock every few years would be reasonably inexpensive insurance. The room will tell us, if we give it enough time."

He startled me by reaching for my hand and pulling me down to his level. His breath was warm, and for a moment his face filled my entire vision. Then he turned to peer through the circle the lock had left in the door, and I felt, rather than heard, his sharp intake of breath.

He gently guided my shoulders so that I was in front of him, looking through the place where the lock had been. "Tell me what you see."

The room was in shadow, and I could just make out the library tables piled high with books, the lamps, the cozy chairs. From here the room seemed like a distant diorama; I felt as if it were reaching through the keyhole, yearning to gather me in. I was aware of the pressure of Mitch's hands on my shoulders. "A very beautiful library."

"No." His soft voice warmed the inside of my ear. "Don't look into the room yet. Focus where the lock used to be. Do you see the carved initials?" I squinted, and then, yes, I did see them, an ornate "F" and an even more ornate "A," carved in old-fashioned script.

"Somebody signed this room. Somebody was so proud of something here that he wanted to leave his mark. But he — I'm assuming it was a man — did it in a place where no one was ever likely to see it. That's strange. I've seen that only once before."

I turned to look at him. His entire face had grown more animated. He pulled me up. "Let's go inside. I want to poke around before anybody else arrives. After you."

He pushed the door open, but he did not go right in. He just stood on the threshold, sniffing the air.

"I always love that apple smell —" I clapped my hand to my mouth.

But Mitch wasn't paying attention to me. He was taking deep, appreciative breaths, inhaling the air. "Apples. Leather. Paper. I'd like to bottle the scent of old libraries."

"The aroma of history."

"Hardly." He tapped my shoulder. "The smell of history was more like chamber pots, used linen, and unwashed bodies. Old New York was a pretty stinky place; it lagged way behind other cities in providing clean water to its citizens. The Croton Reservoir didn't open until 1842. It's possible that the past smelled good, at least out in the country, but before the advent of indoor plumbing this city would have been filled with a throng of rank odors. That's what I like so much about old libraries — they smell the way we'd like to imagine the past."

I felt a little stab of disappointment. I knew it was silly, but I couldn't help feeling that I'd been subtly rebuffed. He took a step into the library, and I followed.

Mitch stopped in the middle of the room, turning slowly, as if he were listening for voices. In the quiet, I thought I heard them too: an oyster vendor hawking his wares, the town crier announcing the news, carriage horses clopping by outside. I thought I could detect the scent of wood smoke, and a shiver went through me.

"Cold?" He broke the spell. "I was expecting it to be colder in here. When a room's been shut up for as long as this one has, it's always cold. It can take weeks before a room warms up. But it's not cold in here. Very strange."

He had turned away as he talked, so I couldn't read his face. Was he suspecting something?

"Was this always a library?" I threw it out more as distraction than a question.

"I don't know yet." He was prowling around, examining the lamps, the globe, the desk with its inlaid-wood zodiac signs. He touched every piece of furniture he passed, very lightly, as if he were receiving information through his fingertips. "The entire layout of this building is odd, but I can't understand why they would have put a library up here with the servants' quarters. There had to be a reason." He was talking more to himself than to me. "There's a story here, a secret. That's a serious lock, clearly intended to deter the curious. I'll know more when I've gotten the paint off."

"Are you going to restore it?"

"Depends on what Joan-Mary has in mind. The client may not want to spend the money. As she said, I'm expensive."

"True." Joan-Mary had come in so quietly that she spoke before we were aware of her presence. Now I saw her standing in the library doorway, her face alight with astonishment. She let out a small, happy sigh. "What a beautiful room. So much more than I'd hoped for." She glanced at Mitch. "Good thing we called you."

He went to the door, took her hand, and led her into the room, an oddly proprietary gesture, as if he'd claimed the library and she was a visitor. "I am very grateful that you didn't let a locksmith at that door. The lock's already talking to me."

She laughed, brushing her hair out of her face. "And what does it have to say?"

"At the moment it's covered with more than a century of paint, so the voice is a little muffled. But it's a Branford, which means that it can't be original to the mansion. The Squires lock company didn't become Branford Lock Works until at least thirty years after this house was built. And that in turn" — he looked at her, all seriousness — "might tell us why they put this room up here, whether it has always been a library, and, most important, why they locked it. What the hell were they hiding? This room has some secrets, and I'm going to enjoy finding out what they are."

"How long will you need?" Joan-Mary's question made me wonder if he was paid by the hour.

"It all depends. I'll start with this lock. I'm guessing it's an Eastlake model, which would put it in the 1880s, or about fifty years after the house was likely built. Then I'll want to wander around, get a feel for the place, see if there's any minor restoration that might impact a sale. I'll let you know."

"Fine. I've got showings scheduled all day, but call me when you have an idea of the scope of this project. I've got some gardeners coming this afternoon to clean up the yard. And we'll probably need to stage the place."

"Keep your decorators out of this room, okay?"

She turned a withering look on him. "Why would I let them in here? This library's perfect exactly as it is."

"And give me a day or so before you loose your stagers on the rest of the mansion?"

"I know, I know." She began pulling on her gloves. "You don't want them messing up your crime scene."

I was walking out the door with her when I felt a hand on my shoulder. "Billie? Would you mind if I asked you a few questions?"

I stopped, feeling strangely anxious. "What do you want to know?"

"Just what you remember people saying about the library."

"Nobody ever talked about it in the time I was here. Sorry." Was that what he really wanted to know? He was watching me, saying nothing, and I noticed that his brown eyes were flecked with gold. I was the one to break the silence. "Are you looking for anything in particular?"

He squeezed my shoulder, and I thought what an extremely physical person he was. I remembered how he'd been at Fontanari's, a large man who used up all the available air. "An interesting woman." He stared at me, mouth quivering a little. "Isn't every man?"

I flushed. "That's not what I meant."

He touched my cheek briefly, but I could feel his fingers burn my skin long after he took them away. "I know. To be honest, I'm not completely sure what I'm after. But a room like this, one that hasn't been repainted and redecorated a thousand times, has a lot to reveal. The floors in the rest of the house have been replaced, but these . . ." He crouched and ran his long fingers across one of the boards. "Give me your hand." He pulled me down until we were both crouching, then he laid my hand against the wood, which was surprisingly soft and satiny. "It's been sanded by time. No splinters here. By almost two centuries of feet marching across it. You can't imitate that, although people certainly try."

He stood up, pulling me with him again, and we walked to the windows. Mitch pulled the curtains aside. "See the glass?" The uneven panes were like amber, thick and wavy with thousands of tiny bubbles trapped inside. "All the windows in the house are Palladian, but I'll bet these are the only ones with original panes. See how watery the light is? Modern glass transmits light in an entirely different way."

I reached out and touched the glass, which was smooth beneath my fingers. Outside, in the garden, the forsythia was just beginning to bloom. Mitch said, "If I can figure out why the library's up here, it will help me evaluate the rest of the house. There may be secret panels, hidden rooms."

My heart did a little somersault. "And what about a ghost?"

"Oh, that would be too much to hope for.

Do you know the going rate for haunted houses?" He walked me to the door. "Get out of here and let me work. But come and check on me from time to time. Just in case I discover that ghost."

Mitch was in the library all day, and I was torn. Part of me wished he would leave so I could look up "honey," but part of me liked knowing he was there. Every now and then he'd stick his head into my office to share a little detail. "Look at this!" It apparently did not occur to him that I might not be as thrilled as he was by an antique lock, but his enthusiasm was infectious. "I was right. It's an Eastlake."

He held out the lock so I could see the vaguely Asian motif.

"Branford invented it, but it was widely copied. But the interesting thing is that this lock replaced a more serious one. Three of them, in fact. Between the time this house was built and the Eastlake was installed, something important was kept in that room."

"Joan-Mary's right," I told him. "You do consider this a crime scene. Any idea what that might have been?"

Mitch turned toward the hall but said over his shoulder, "I have a hunch, but I'll keep

381

it to myself until I know more."

Now I wished he would leave. I had to search for Lulu's letter, and Mitch's diligence was reminding me that our time was running out.

Mitch wasn't the only one poking around the place; Joan-Mary's gardeners had arrived, and I could hear them outside all afternoon, laying sod, planting shrubs, and loudly complaining about the difficulty of the job.

"Another oyster shell!" I heard. "What the hell?" I went into Jake's office and looked out the window; at the far end of the garden, against the back fence, a huge pile of shells was growing. "What the hell are they doing here?" one of the gardeners asked. "It's not like this part of Manhattan was ever landfill."

"They were just trying to make our work harder," grumbled his colleague, dumping out another load of shells.

To my relief, the gardeners left promptly at five. Mitch was not far behind them. "Nice working with you," he said. "See you soon."

That was it? I felt let down, but at least his abrupt departure gave me time to run upstairs and look up "honey."

There were dozens of entries in the card

catalog, but only two were in turquoise. "The sadly underappreciated bees of Ohio," Bertie had written on the first card, "produce some of the world's finest honey. A rare and mysterious product, Mad Bee Jars were highly prized by connoisseurs. Notes on this extraordinary American comestible can be found among the letters on beekeeping."

The second card said only this: "See also 'Jade's Amber' a closely related product." Looking in the "J" drawer, I found the entry, and as I read the bold turquoise writing, I could picture Bertie chortling at his own cleverness. "Honey," he had written, "was widely used as a sugar substitute during World War II, causing the creation of a spate of new apiaries. Among them was a small concern in Akron, Jade's Amber, whose young proprietor kept bees throughout the war. She offered some extremely interesting recipes, which can be found among the reader letters on beekeeping. Sadly, the apiary was shuttered at war's end. See also 'Mad Bee Jars.' "

"Beekeeping." Of course. The file was quite fat.

October 18, 1944

Dear Mr. Beard,

Still no word about Father. Mother and I are remaining hopeful, but it's very hard. Mother tries to be cheerful, for my sake, I realize, but sometimes when she doesn't know I'm watching, I can see how sad she is.

Yesterday the principal called me down to his office. It made me nervous, but my homeroom teacher, Mrs. Bridgeman, gave me such an encouraging smile that I decided nothing too terrible was about to happen.

It turned out he'd been talking with Principal Jones, who told him about the milkweed floss. Then he asked all about my bee hives; he's been trying to keep bees but he says that they frighten him. I think he might have said it just to put me at ease, but we talked for a while, and then, to my surprise, he asked if I would consider giving cooking classes.

Would I! My first class will be next week. I asked what he wanted me to teach, but all he would say is, "You're the teacher, Lulu." So, dear wonderful Mr. Beard, if you have any ideas, I'd be very grateful.

Your friend,
Lulu

October 29, 1944
Dear Mr. Beard,
Thank you for all those ideas. You were absolutely right: A class on pumpkins was a fine way to begin. When I said I was doing a Halloween class on pumpkins, everybody was expecting plain old pumpkin pie. Were they ever surprised! First I showed them how to toast the seeds. We did do pie, of course, using my own honey, but then I brought out the pumpkin leaves and said that we were going to cook those too. Everybody looked a little doubtful, and nobody wanted a taste until Mrs. Bridgeman took a bite. She said it was delicious, and after that a few more people were brave enough to try them. Rosie Mullaney even said she liked them. Still, I'm sad to say that pumpkin leaves are not destined to become an Akron staple.

Mrs. Bridgeman asked if I knew of any other ways to use pumpkin, and I told her about Mrs. Cappuzzelli's ravioli. And guess what? Next week Mrs. C. is going to come in and show us how to make them. I wish Marco could see his mama teaching Americans to make the food he had no use for.

Your friend,
Lulu

November 8, 1944

Dear Mr. Beard,

I feel as if I am slowly losing Father. Sometimes, when I'm lying in bed, trying to remember his face, the only image I have is the photograph on the mantel. I know it's superstitious, but so long as I can hold him in my mind, I believe he will be safe.

Will this war ever end? The Western Union man is so busy that we call him the Angel of Death. Last week we heard that Susie Rivera's father was shot down in Leyte. Three of Rosie Mullaney's brothers have been killed in the South Pacific. And Tommy's oldest brother, Joe, lost a leg at Aachen and is being shipped home.

I'm guessing that you won't be eating turkey this year — or ever again. I laugh every time I think about you and the four thousand pounds of turkey you cooked for the servicemen in Miami. But we won't be eating turkey either; the one I raised got so big Mother suggested giving him to the Cappuzzellis. She said that a chicken would do for us, and their family is so large. Sometimes Mother surprises me.

I'm so glad to know you're coming back

to New York soon. Maybe when the war is over we will finally meet.

Your friend,
Lulu

December 12, 1944
Dear Mr. Beard,
The cooking classes are going very well. Tommy's been helping me. I think he needs an excuse to get out of the house now that his brother has come back. Joe has turned into an angry, bitter man, but it's hard to blame him. Even though his leg is gone, it still hurts him quite a lot. They call it "phantom pain," and he may have it all his life. It seems so unfair. I hate this war.

Next week we'll do cookies. Even though it's more impossible than ever to get the ingredients for Snowballs, we're going to start with those. By this time next year, the war may be over, and rationing will be behind us. Hope can't hurt.

Your friend,
Lulu

December 29, 1944
Dear Mr. Beard,
I was anticipating a miserable Christmas, but you just never know how life is going

to turn out. Mrs. Bridgeman invited Mother and me to Christmas dinner. She said that with Mr. Bridgeman in the South Pacific, we'd be doing her a favor. We pooled our ration stamps and bought a real roast. I brought some of my canned beans and carrots, and I baked a Liberation Cake. As I was frosting it, I remembered Father telling us how the soldiers call stale bread "make-believe cake." I hope that, wherever he is, he has real cake for Christmas.

We found another surprise waiting at Mrs. Bridgeman's house: Mr. Jones. Even though he's no longer my principal, it made me feel queer to have him sitting across the dinner table. But afterward we stood by the fire for a while, singing carols, and for just a moment it felt so jolly that I forgot about the war. Then I came back to reality with a guilty jerk. That was when Mr. Jones leaned over and whispered in my ear. He said that being sad wouldn't bring Father back, that no matter where he was, he'd want me to be happy.

How did he know what I was feeling? But since then I've given his words careful consideration, and I've decided that he's right. From now on I'm resolved to set a good example for Mother. I know Father would want that.

I hope you had a happy Christmas too.

Your friend,

Lulu

That was the last letter in the "Beekeeping" file, and I began to search for clues to the next letters, thinking over what Anne Milton had said about Bertie. Anne Milton! I'd forgotten all about dinner. I stuffed the letters into my bag and made a dash for the door.

MAD BEE JARS

"You are extremely tardy!" Sammy sounded miffed, but his face was relieved. "Anne Milton has been tarrying for a full fifteen minutes."

"But look what I've found. . . ." I pulled the letters from my bag and waved them in his face.

He pushed them away. "Not now, not now." Sammy hurried toward the dining room at something very close to a run, Chinese robes flapping about him. "I fear that the chicken will be dry."

Following him, I stopped in the dining room doorway, stunned by the transformation. Sammy had filled the starkly modern room with masses of cherry blossoms. He'd covered the table with his grandmother's heavy damask cloth, which rippled smoothly to the floor, and covered that with an astonishing quantity of ornate sterling pieces. He'd set candelabra all around the room, creating an effect of old-fashioned luxury.

The most radiant old woman I'd ever seen was standing by the window. Thin and ramrod straight, Anne Milton was wearing a suit of dusty-rose wool, with a white satin blouse. "Isn't this lovely?" She took my hand and gave a small gurgle of appreciative laughter that made her seem momentarily young. "It is such a treat not to be eating alone, as I so often do these days. I never miss Bertram quite so much as when I'm at the table."

"Sit down, sit down." Sammy made the introductions as he poured pale Raveneau Chablis into fragile crystal glasses until the fresh scent of the wine filled the room. He picked up a knife and began to carve the bird, slicing into crisply burnished skin.

"I hope I'm not being rude. . . ." I was just so curious.

Anne flashed me a sympathetic smile. "Not at all, dear. I understand your impatience. You'll want to know how I met Bertie."

She settled into her chair, picked up a spoon, and turned it over, running a finger across the lily-of-the-valley pattern. "It was on V-J Day. I was at Barnard College then, and when the news came, we girls all rushed into the street and started walking to Times Square. It was as if the whole city were trying to get there, pulled by some impulse to be together. Were there bells ringing? I think so, but maybe it just felt that way.

"We could hardly believe that the war was really over and the boys were going to come home, and . . . well, you've seen the pictures. You know how it is when your feet have been asleep and suddenly the blood comes rushing back? You start sensing parts of your body that you had forgotten were there. It was like that. Everything felt good and clean and possible. If you hadn't lost anyone, you felt blessed. And if you had, for that moment at least the sacrifice seemed noble; after all, we had saved the world."

Sammy passed the vegetables, and Anne stopped to lift a few fat spears of asparagus off the platter.

"We walked all the way downtown, and when we got to Times Square there was such a throng that I became separated from my friends. I was looking frantically around for them, jostled by all those laughing, happy people, and the strangest thing happened: I turned and found that I was staring at myself. At my twin."

I had been entranced by her soft, musical voice and the graceful movements of her elegant hands, but now I remembered what, and whom, she was talking about. "I had no idea who he was, and for a minute I thought I had lost my mind from the sheer joy of the moment. It was so improbable to be in Times Square, in that enormous crowd, and be looking at my double. We were even the same height. He seemed as startled as I was, and then he pulled me toward him and kissed me. Not a passionate kiss — a European kiss, one on each cheek. And then he took my hand and we walked down the street together. It felt like the most natural thing in the world. We had not said a single word — but I knew then that we would be together for the rest of our lives."

"You were married?" In my mind I was picturing a man who looked exactly like Anne walking up the aisle in a stark white church, his hand clutching hers.

"Oh, no," she said this hurriedly, clearly not wanting to give the wrong impression. The picture faded, and I waited to see what would replace it. "Well, I would have married him." Her voice moved lower. "I was in love with him, you see. Bertie loved me too, but not in that way. He was not a woman's man, if you take my meaning."

She said this without a trace of embarrassment. If Anne had ever been disappointed or angry, those feelings were long gone. I glanced quickly at Sammy as I readjusted the picture: Anne looking on while the man she loved stared longingly at a masculine stranger off in the distance.

"But why did he hide the letters?" I blurted out.

Sammy's hand came down on the table. Silverware clattered. "Cease these interruptions! Permit Anne to relate her story. We do not yet know that it was Bertie who hid them."

"He'd gone to library school," Anne continued, "and so the army trained him in cryptography in New Jersey. That was where he briefly met Mr. Beard, who impressed him enormously. Like Mr. Beard, Bertie desperately wanted to serve overseas, and he was quite bitter about being sent to Virginia. He always thought that, much as he tried to hide it, the government suspected that he was homosexual, and that was why they refused to send him to the front. In any case, when they finally released him, he came straight to New York. He had just arrived when I met him."

"Was he working at *Delicious!*?"

"No, not then. When we met he was the librarian at a private school, but it was the wrong job for him. He was in his thirties, and he had no talent for children. When he learned that *Delicious!* was looking for a librarian, he immediately applied for the job."

I looked at Anne, mentally removed forty years, and made her into a man. Bertie would have been very handsome — tall and straight, with those blue eyes, light hair, and rosy cheeks. He would, I realized with a start, have looked a lot like Jake. He must have caused quite a stir among the white-gloved ladies of *Delicious!*

"Who did he replace?" I asked.

"The woman who wrote in black — I never knew her name. He said she had an ordinary mind, but she was the best they could do during the war. She did do one thing he approved of. . . ." She stopped to slice off a sliver of chicken. "This is delicious. Not trusting the wartime mail service, she made a copy of every letter before forwarding it on. The magazine had a Verifax machine — they were new at the time — and she was very proud of that. For safety's sake, she kept the originals at the library, rather than run the risk of having them get lost."

Across the table, Sammy gave me a significant look. "Did she continue making copies after the war ended?"

"Yes, by then it had become second nature to her. But Bertie put a stop to that; he said that copying the letters during the war was a sensible precaution but that copying them afterward was an invasion of privacy."

"Did he have knowledge of any other librarians?" Sammy asked, and I put my hand out, irritated, trying to stop him. What did it matter? But Anne's answer was brief.

"Bertie never knew the woman who wrote in red, but he admired her. Apparently she died quite suddenly. It seems to be a coincidental hazard of the job: Bertie also died unexpectedly. He was killed in a bicycle accident in 1972, when still quite a young man. Not yet sixty. It was mere chance that he had managed to hide the last of the letters before passing on."

"But why? Why did he hide them?" I couldn't wait any longer to ask.

"That" — she gave a small snort — "is open to conjecture. I don't suppose we'll ever know the truth. What he said was that it was for their own protection."

"From what?"

Anne toyed with her fork as she looked down at the table, weighing her words. "From Old Mr. Pickwick. He wanted to destroy all of Mr. Beard's letters."

"But why?" Sammy and I said it simultaneously.

Anne Milton sighed. "This happened in the early fifties. Consider what was taking place in this country at the time." She stared at us, urging us to work it out for ourselves, and I saw that she must have been very comfortable in the classroom. "It was a terrible time, you know — the McCarthy era, a time of witch hunts and suspicion. People all over this country were behaving badly. And Old Mr. Pickwick had very little love for Mr. Beard."

"But Pickwick hired him!" The passion of Sammy's outburst told me that he was one step ahead of me.

"He fired him too. Or didn't you know that?"

"Pickwick fired Beard?" asked Sammy. "They certainly leave that out of the legend of *Delicious!* What happened?"

"Who knows the real story? I only know what Bertie told me, and I can't be sure it's true. According to him, Mr. Pickwick was having lunch at the Plaza when Mr. Beard came in with a group of friends. After imbibing copious amounts of wine, they grew rather boisterous. Pickwick was an abstemious soul, and he stomped back to the office, shouting that he would not have such a person representing his magazine.

Then he called Beard in and told him to pack his things and go."

I had never heard that. "Are you sure?"

"No. I can only tell you what Bertie told me. It may have happened differently; perhaps it was Beard who quit. What I do know is that, after Mr. Beard had gone, Mr. Pickwick ordered the editors to empty out his desk and destroy all his papers. He did not want a single scrap of paper left behind, no evidence that the man had ever been employed by the magazine."

"I see." There was both sadness and resignation in Sammy's voice. "It was because he was gay."

"Bertie certainly thought so."

What did she mean by that? That she thought otherwise? "I don't understand."

"Oh, Billie." Sammy sighed and looked at Anne. "Sometimes I forget how young you are. Just think about it."

Anne reached out and patted my hand. "I think it is hard for your generation to understand how different things were back then. McCarthy created paranoia, accused everyone of being a Communist. We forget that he didn't just go after people because of their politics; he was a hateful man, and he had it in for homosexuals too. It was called the Lavender Scare, and people were hounded out of their jobs. The truth is, I have no idea if that had anything to do with Pickwick firing Mr. Beard; I always thought that Bertie was oversensitive on that score. But it's certainly true that Mr. Beard's proclivities were well known, even though he didn't publicly acknowledge his sexual orientation until quite a bit later. Mr. Pickwick was very conservative, and I don't imagine that he appreciated having a prominent homosexual representing his magazine. We will probably never know what his reasons were, but we know that he wanted Beard expunged from the record. From that day forward, Beard didn't mention *Delicious!*, and *Delicious!* didn't mention him. It was all very Orwellian."

"They certainly mentioned him later on!" Sammy was indignant.

"I gather," Anne said quietly, "that was not until the elder Mr. Pickwick had passed on."

"But you don't think that's why Bertie hid the letters, do you? You think there's something else," I conjectured.

To my surprise, she blushed. "What a very perceptive young woman you are." She suddenly looked younger. "You're right; I once suspected that Bertie might have another reason."

Sammy had grown uncharacteristically quiet, and I followed his lead. Whatever was on Anne's mind was making her skittish. We barely breathed.

"I don't like to talk about it, because it's so . . . well, so improbable," she began hesitantly. "Maybe I just made it up because Bertie told so many stories about his stint as a cryptographer. But . . ." She looked down, fiddling with her napkin, folding and unfolding it. Finally she tucked it into a very careful triangle and set it deliberately next to her plate. "Mr. Beard was also a trained cryptographer, and I always wondered if there wasn't something hidden in those letters, some kind of code, that Bertie recognized." Now she raised both her eyes and her voice. "It's silly, childish even. I'm probably wrong. But Bertie was so determined to protect the letters that I couldn't help thinking that they might contain more than a correspondence between a young girl and a famous cook. He kept saying that the letters were valuable historical documents, that they were not Mr. Pickwick's to destroy. On the other hand . . ." She stopped for a second, considering. "I am also aware that he went out of his way to plant that suspicion in my head, to make the whole thing more important, more mysterious, than

400

perhaps it really was. That would have been like him; as you will have noticed, he had a great flair for the dramatic."

"Whatever the reason" — I couldn't keep myself from saying this — "I don't understand why he didn't just take the letters home. If you ask me, he went to a lot of unnecessary trouble."

"I could not agree more." Anne said this with asperity. "That is exactly what I suggested. But Bertie would have none of it. He was not, he said, a thief."

"But Pickwick didn't want the letters!"

"Precisely." Her annoyance was still palpable after all these years. "He refused to 'steal' the letters, and he would not destroy them, so he spent several ridiculous weeks wringing his hands. He lived in constant fear that someone would discover that the letters were still there."

"Poor fellow." Sammy was apparently feeling much more sympathetic than either Anne or I. "How long did this go on?"

"After a few weeks of dithering pointlessly about, Bertie stumbled upon the solution. Literally: He found the hidden room that was, by his lights, the perfect place for the fugitive letters."

"How did he find it?" asked Sammy.

"In much the same manner that you did.

But there was a difference: Bertie was absolutely unsurprised. He had always suspected that the Timbers Mansion might once have been a station on the Underground Railroad, and now he had his evidence."

"The Underground Railroad!" Sammy sounded as surprised as I felt. "It fits. The Timbers Mansion must have been built sometime during the 1830s."

"He was so happy when he found it," Anne continued, as if Sammy had not spoken. "He had found the ideal solution to his problem. He had confirmed an old suspicion about the Timbers Mansion. And he had enhanced his reputation at the magazine. 'They think I am a magician,' he told me with great glee. 'They think I can disappear at will.'"

"Do you mean to say," I asked as the implication of this sank in, "that he never told anyone else about the secret room?"

"Not to my knowledge."

"But what about the rest of the letters? There are thousands of them. I can understand why Bertie wanted to protect Beard's letters, but what was the point of putting the others in there too?"

"Oh," she tossed this off casually, as if this was of no importance, "that happened much later." She began to calculate. "Nearly twenty years, I'd guess."

"The plot thickens." Sammy stood up and pushed back his chair. "But before you commence the conclusion of your tale, allow me to fetch the denouement of dinner."

He went into the kitchen, reappearing with an antique Chinese bowl laden with strawberries and a crystal cruet filled with thick, ancient balsamic vinegar. He put a plate of dainty, paper-thin langues de chat in front of Anne, who picked one up and took a delicate bite before continuing.

"We now jump to 1970. Picture the time. Mrs. Van Allen was the editor then, a dragon of a woman who never referred to her employees by anything other than their surnames. She required all females to wear hats, nylons, and white gloves when they appeared in her office. She was appalled by what was happening in America: She considered the antiwar movement an abomination, decried the loss of civility, shuddered at the mere thought of a hippie, and thought that everyone with long hair ought to be locked up."

As she drew a picture of the time — sixties' slogans and protest songs — Anne conjured up an entire era, and I saw what a fine lecturer she must have been. I imagined

Mrs. Van Allen looking out the windows, wincing as protesters marched past the Timbers Mansion with their signs. "Bertie thought she was a horrid old biddy, but he was a master at concealing his feelings, and she never had the faintest notion. Had she known that he was what she called 'a fairy,' she would have been appalled. When the elder Mr. Pickwick passed on, she came running to Bertie, lips trembling, afraid it was the end of an era. He consoled her, but he was privately elated; his hope was that the young Mr. Pickwick would bring in new blood. But when Mr. Pickwick hired an appraiser to take stock of the library, Bertie became anxious himself. The books, he knew, were safe, but he fretted about the letters."

In the candlelight, Sammy caught my eye; we had been fearing much the same thing. Anne intercepted the look but misconstrued it. "You have to understand" — she leaned forward — "at the time, few people were interested in food or food history, and I'm sure he was correct in thinking that the letters would have been considered worthless. Bertie was convinced the day would come when Americans would take an interest in their food heritage. 'It would be criminal to lose them,' he kept saying. He'd already hidden the Beard letters, and now he thought how easy it would be to move the other letters into the secret room as well."

"Was this in the early seventies?" I'd noticed that the letters seemed to stop there.

"Yes! It was the year he died. I could look up the exact date in my diary, if that would be helpful, because I helped him."

I pictured them sneaking around in the dark of night, but when I described this vision, Anne laughed. "Very romantic!" Her eyes twinkled. "But very far from the truth. You see, by then Bertie had been at *Delicious!* for twenty-five years, and the library was his private domain. We simply came in over the weekend. It was great fun. I remember the moment when we put the last folder on the shelf and I left the hidden room for the last time. As we pushed the bookcase back into place, Bertie began speculating about who would find the letters and when that would be. A cloud crossed his face, and when I asked what was wrong, he was so upset that for a minute he could not speak."

I knew exactly what was bothering him. "He was afraid that nobody would ever find the letters!"

Anne nodded. "He'd gone to all that trouble, and he suddenly saw what an enormous chance he was taking." She looked across the table and gave me a radiant smile. "What a great pity that he can't be here. You are, quite literally, his dream come true."

I Love to Eat

Dear Genie,

I know that when I hit the "Send" button, all these words go to an inbox that hasn't been opened in one year, nine months, and thirty days. But I miss you so much, and somehow writing helps.

The thing is, I can't stop thinking about Anne and Bertie and their strange, sad love story. And you're the one I want to talk it over with. It seems like such a waste, all that passion just sitting there, no use to anyone. She threw herself into her work; he amused himself by creating an elaborate treasure hunt.

In some funny way it reminds me of Maggie and Jake: They were no good together, but neither of them has found anyone else. They must be pretty lonely. Then I wonder about Dad and Aunt Melba . . . and I don't even know where to go with that. Remember all those

407

family trips we took, how careful they always were about having separate rooms? But they're together all the time, she finishes his sentences, and yet I've never even seen them holding hands. Have you? Were they sneaking around behind our backs? Or are they just good friends? Do they even know what they are anymore?

And then there's my Mr. Complainer. I find myself listening for his feet on the stairs, find myself wishing he'd come in. Am I crazy? When he's not there, I wish he were. And when he is, I wish he'd touch me. How did this happen? Is he right — did I really put him off all that time at Fontanari's? Looking back, it seems I did change the subject every time he asked something personal. Maybe I'm the one who's changed?

But then I remember the horrible blonde he brought into the shop, and I wonder: Are they still together? Even if they're not, I can't be his type. Am I making an ass of myself?

Oh, Genie, couldn't you be alive, just for a day? You always had all the answers. I know I need to let you go. But not quite yet. Not yet. Please.

xxb

P.S. I've decided to get my hair cut. New contacts, new clothes . . . why not a new 'do? I'll probably choose someplace awful and come out looking like a freak. That would be just like me.

I punched "Send" and watched the words vanish. Then I defiantly surveyed my new wardrobe; there wasn't one thing here Genie would approve of. Today, I thought, was the day for the red suede jacket. I kept everything else simple: black pants, a black T-shirt, plain black flats. I stared at myself in the mirror, realizing I needed something else, just a tiny punctuation. I pulled on a pair of thin red socks, gave myself one last look, and headed to the mansion.

All morning I listened for Mitch, but when the doorbell finally rang it was Joan-Mary, with two young, handsome, skinny men in tow. Their voices were squeaky with admiration for the Timbers Mansion. "I know exactly what to do here," said the blond one, who seemed to be in charge. "By the time we're done, people will kill to get this place. You'll have ten offers the first day."

"You promise?" Joan-Mary looked pleased. "I'll leave you to it, then." She turned her attention to me. "Eric and Alex will just reconnoiter today, but I'm sorry to say that tomorrow will be different. They'll be bumping furniture up and down the stairs. I'm afraid it's going to be rather disruptive, and, if I were you, I'd stay out of their way."

"But shouldn't somebody be here?"

"You'll have to let them in. And lock up when they leave. But there's absolutely no reason for you to stay while they're working. You won't get a single thing done."

"So I can tell HR you're giving me tomorrow off?"

"Do." I'd been joking, but she didn't catch the humor. She took her leave, and I immediately called Sammy.

"I'm alone here with a couple of decorators. They're going to stage the mansion. But now that Mitch has unlocked the library, I guess I can walk right in. Where do you think I should look? I was wondering if 'pumpkins' might be the next clue."

He considered that in silence while I climbed the stairs. "Insufficiently subtle," he finally decided.

"What about 'Liberation Cake'?'

"Not impossible. But we are nearing the end of the game, and Bertram seems to have increased the complexity. I am persuaded that the temptation to meddle with 'bread' would have proved overwhelming. Such a

410

tempting anagram for 'Beard.' "

"Maybe French bread?" I suggested. "Since he was in France? Should I try *'pain'*?"

"Far too simplistic. 'Baguette,' perhaps?"

"I'll try," I said skeptically, going to the card catalog and opening the "B" drawer. "Oh, my God, are you channeling Bertie now?" I asked. "Here it is! This is what he wrote: 'During World War Two, American soldiers in the European Theater of Operations had their first taste of true French bread. There are some interesting letters on the subject in the "Boulangerie" file of 1945.' "

I imagined Sammy's pleased expression. "Elementary, my dear. I suggest that you hastily locate the letters and repair to your office with the file. It would be foolish to attract untoward attention to the library."

"Right." I ended the call, found the file, and took it down to my office, waving cheerily at Eric and Alex as I passed them on the stairs.

March 26, 1945
Dear Mr. Beard,
Please be very, very careful; the thought of you being in Europe frightens me very much. Even though I know that you are

411

excited about going there, about being back in Paris once the city is liberated, it just seems so scary. I know that you have important work to do, but I was happier when I thought about you being in South America.

When I get very frightened, I think about you walking into one of those little French bakeries, and then walking down the street with one of those long, crisp loaves of bread under your arm, and it makes me feel happier.

Please take very good care of yourself, Mr. Beard. I will be thinking about you.

Your friend,
Lulu

April 12, 1945

Dear Mr. Beard,

I gave Mrs. C. the recipes you sent from Naples, and she said after the war is over we will make mozzarella in carrozza together. Everybody is always talking about what we're going to do after the war is over.

Have you been reading about the concentration camps? Now that I know about places like Auschwitz, I can't stop worrying that Father ended up a prisoner of war. The newspaper said they were forced to dig trenches and break up rocks on a starvation diet, and when they grew too weak to work they were sent to a gas chamber and asphyxiated. I'm afraid that if he was taken prisoner, we might never know the truth about what happened to him. Mother and I do not discuss this, but we don't have to. I know she's thinking exactly the same thing.

Please send me some cheerful news.

Your friend,
Lulu

April 13, 1945
Dear Mr. Beard,
President Roosevelt is gone. It is such a shock. He's the only president I can re-member, and I just can't imagine some-body else in the White House. I'm sure President Truman is a good man, but even the words feel peculiar in my mouth. A world without President Roosevelt seems like a strange and scary place.

Mr. Jones was at the house when we got the news, and he put his arms around Mother and me and we all just stood there, trying to comfort one another. Isn't it sad that the president died before the war was over? Everyone says the end won't be long now.

413

In class Mrs. Bridgeman read the telegram Mrs. Roosevelt sent to her boys. "The president slept away this afternoon. He did his job to the end as he would want to do. Bless you all and all our love." Slept away — isn't that a lovely way to put it?

And so we will all do our jobs and wait for the war to be over and life to return to the way it used to be. It's been such a long time; I can hardly remember what that was like.

Your friend,
Lulu

I was staring at the letter, thinking how sad it was that Roosevelt died before the war ended; three weeks later, it was over in Europe. When I looked up, I saw that Eric was standing in my door.

"We're done for today," he said. "We'd like to come back tomorrow at nine-thirty. That okay with you?"

"Fine. See you tomorrow."

I waited until he left, then picked up the next letter in the file. The phone rang before I could read it. Sammy. "I find that I have an uncontrollable craving for Thursday's gnocchi. Would you be good enough to join me at The Pig?"

"Now? I haven't read all the letters!"

"Bundle them up and fetch them along. We can peruse them after dinner. It will be something to anticipate. Hurry, now; I find that I am extremely peckish." Giving me no chance to argue, he abruptly hung up.

The Pig was so crowded that I was halfway across the dining room before I realized that Sammy was not alone. Richard, Jake, and Maggie were all sitting around the table, while Thursday stood near Richard, her hand on his shoulder. As I approached, they all, embarrassingly, turned to watch.

Was it a surprise party? Why were they all here?

Jake stood up. "Look at you!" He pulled out a chair. "I wish you'd gotten the fashion bug sooner. This is quite an improvement on those dreary clothes you used to wear."

"Great jacket." Richard reached out and ran a finger down the soft suede.

I was feeling pretty good until Maggie said. "Were you the victim of one of those magazine makeovers? If you ask me, everybody always looks better before."

"Give it a rest," chided Thursday. She looked me up and down. "The contact lenses are an improvement. But if you're going to dress like that, you really ought to do something about your hair."

Her frankness always disarmed me. "I know. I know. But I don't have a clue where to go."

"To Eva, of course." Thursday pointed to a woman with brightly hennaed hair, sitting at the bar. "She's the best."

"Can we please eat now?" Maggie held up her empty plate. "I don't know about the rest of you, but I'm finding this a major bore."

"Uh-oh." Thursday moved toward the kitchen. "Better feed the beast."

Maggie watched as Thursday walked across the restaurant, eyes narrowing when she stopped to talk to Eva. "Can we move on, please, to the reason for this gathering? We're here to welcome the prodigal editor home. Remind me, Jake, how long you've been gone?"

"It's been three months since the great Sammy intervention." Jake clinked his glass against Sammy's. "I left the next day."

"And you have only just returned?" said Sammy. "That was quite the voyage."

"True." Jake raised his arms, gathering us all in. "What a racket! I had no idea. I went halfway around the world, and it didn't cost me a penny; the entire thing was paid for by the tourist offices of the countries that I visited. After Sherman died —"

"Sherman died?" I was horrified. "Why didn't you tell me?"

Jake reached both hands across the table to take mine in his. "Billie, I'm so sorry. I should have said something, but I couldn't talk about it. It felt like I was losing everything I cared about at once. First the magazine and then Sherman."

I thought back to the conversation we'd had when I offered to take care of Sherman. "Is that why you were so strange? Sherman was already dead, wasn't he?"

"I'd just come back from the vet," he said. "I knew if I talked about it, I'd start crying. I'm sorry. I know you loved him too."

I raised my glass. "Here's to Sherman: I hope there are smoothies in heaven."

"With him gone, there was nothing holding me here. I've always wanted to go to Madrid Fusion, and that was pretty amazing; all the molecular guys were there. Ferran made a soup that started cold and became increasingly hot as you swallowed it. Then he turned carrots into pure air. This Japanese guy was cooking straw."

"Straw?" Sammy sounded incredulous.

"Yeah, he smoked it. It tasted terrific. While I was there, I got an invitation to the Hokitika Wildfoods Festival in New Zealand. It really *was* wild. They were featuring live huhu grubs, worm truffles, and possum pie. One of Redzepi's cooks was there from Noma, doing demos, and he did a recipe that used all 159 kinds of horseradish they have in Denmark."

The waiter set a platter of oysters onto the table. "New Zealand has the most amazing oysters — big, with that coppery taste of belons — but also kind of crisp. Taiwan was next, and then Singapore."

"What made you deign to return?" Maggie, of course.

He grinned at her. "The other day I got a call asking if I wanted to do a stint on *Top Chef Masters,* and I thought it might be fun."

"Must be nice to be Jake Newberry." You couldn't blame Maggie for being bitter. "I can cook circles around you, but nobody's invited me on any swell jaunts. You think it's got anything to do with the fact that I'm a woman?"

"You think it's got anything to do with your wicked tongue?" A shadow crossed Jake's face, and he held up his hands. "Sorry, that was mean. I shouldn't have said it."

"No," said Maggie. "You shouldn't have." She took an oyster, squeezed a lemon, tilted back her head, and swallowed.

We ate oysters in an embarrassed silence until Sammy turned to Richard. "And you, sir, have you unearthed any new disasters to capture with your camera?"

Richard picked up an oyster, jockeying for time. "Actually, I have. The guys at the fire-house on Great Jones Street have been letting me go with them. I don't shoot them working, but I take pictures after the fires are out. I like what's left, the drama at the end. I'm calling the series 'Material Memory,' and I think it's going to be my next show."

Endings, I thought. Destruction. He could even find beauty in that. I wished again that I could see the world through his eyes, if only for a moment.

Thursday arrived with the gnocchi, and we drank more wine. By the time she brought out a suckling piglet, peace had been restored, and the voices wove themselves around me, comforting as a cocoon. I looked around the table, thinking how lucky I was to have these people in my life.

At ten-thirty, Sammy stood up and made a great show of yawning. "I must toddle off now." He gave me a significant look.

I obediently got to my feet. "Me too," I said. "I've got an early appointment."

"And a later one too." Thursday slipped a

piece of paper into my hand. "Here's Eva's address. I figured you could go on your lunch hour, so I told her to expect you at noon."

We took the letters back to Sammy's and settled on the sofa, where we could read them together.

August 23, 1945
Dear Mr. Beard,
V-J Day was so exciting! We were all so happy that the war was finally over! I can hardly believe that everything went so wrong so fast.

I'd been working with the Crop Corps, but when we heard the news, everybody put down their tools and headed into town, as if we'd made some secret plan. There were people standing on every rooftop, and toilet paper was strung everywhere, like a crazy Christmas in August. It felt like a party. When it started to get dark, we all headed home, but there were huge traffic jams and it took forever. Horns were honking and people were dancing, and the crowded bus felt like another party. Still, I wished it would move faster; I was afraid Mother would be home worrying about me. But when I got there, she was sitting in the kitchen, crying in the dark.

At first I thought that the telegram man had been there, but it wasn't that. Mother said that when the announcement came, everyone in the factory shouted with joy. But then the public-announcement system went on again, and the voice said, "Take everything with you. We're locking the doors." None of the women understood.

Mother asked the supervisor, who reminded her that they'd all signed pledges promising to give up their jobs when the boys came back. "But they aren't back!" I said. Mother said it doesn't matter — they've built too many airplanes, and now that the war's over they're no longer needed. The government's canceling all the contracts and the company's laying all the women off. When there are jobs again, they'll go to returning soldiers.

Mr. Beard, I'm so confused. I know it's right for the brave men who've served our country to get their jobs back. But what about the women? Don't they deserve a chance too? Women like Mother kept everything running; don't they count now that the war's over? Mother lost Father, and now she's losing her job. It doesn't seem fair.

I know that if Father were coming home,

he'd expect to go back to the bank. If that were the case, and if I were being honest, I guess I wouldn't be thinking about the woman who's been doing his job for the past few years. But now I do wonder about her and what she's going to do. Maybe her husband isn't coming home either; maybe she needs the job.

Mother tells me not to worry; she says we have enough money to see us through, at least for a while. But if Mother doesn't find work soon, I think we'll have to sell our house. I don't mind so much, but it seems hard on Mother, losing everything all at once.

I thought that when the war was over times would be better. Father is still only presumed dead, but I'm sorry to say I've given up hope. I feel as if there's a huge gulf separating me from all the lucky people in the world; they have so much to look forward to.

> Your friend,
> Lulu

"That's exactly how I felt when Genie died," I told Sammy. "Like nothing good was ever going to happen to me again."

"I understand." He said it with such compassion that I knew he really did. "That was my experience over Christmas. I felt I had made a false turn and was now doomed to the dark side of the street. Despair is a terrible ailment." There was a short silence, and then Sammy cleared his throat. "Is there another letter?"

"Four," I said.

He took my hand. "Not another word until we have read them all."

December 9, 1945
Dear Mr. Beard,
We've had no news from the government, and I'm beginning to wish they'd declare Father dead. Is that a terrible thing for me to say? I know it's horrid, and I don't think very highly of myself, but my main concern is Mother. All this uncertainty is hard on her. Yesterday, while we were washing the dishes, Bing Crosby came on the radio, singing "White Christmas," and Mother stood at the sink and just burst into tears. It made me remember the last Christmas before the war, when Father came home with the radio; it was a present from his boss. When he turned it on, "Chattanooga Choo Choo" was playing, and he bowed to Mother and said, "Madam, may I have this dance?" Then he twirled her around the kitchen until they were both laughing

so hard they ran out of breath and had to stop. I know we're just two little people in Ohio and that they have many things to worry about in Washington, but it's mean of them to keep us in the dark.

Mother's still looking for a job, but with all the returning soldiers she's had no luck. She comes home so discouraged every night, and although she tries to keep it from me, I know she's terribly worried about money. The other night I invited Mr. Jones to dinner, and when Mother saw that I was planning on stuffed pork chops, her mouth got tight and she said that just because rationing was over it didn't mean we can afford meat. Still, she put on a nice dress and even some lipstick before he came, so I don't think she was very upset.

Your friend,
Lulu

January 6, 1946
Dear Mr. Beard,
I hope you don't mind; I took the chocolates you sent from Paris to the Cappuzzellis' when we went for Christmas dinner. At first Mrs. C. didn't want to take them — she said you meant them for me — but I told her they'd taste much better if we all shared. Good chocolate's still impossible

to get here, and they were such a treat!

Mrs. C. invited Tommy too, but he had to stay home with his family; it's their first Christmas together since before the war. She also invited Mr. Jones. "So sad, a bachelor man, all alone at the holidays," she said. Then she patted my cheek and added that she didn't think he'd be alone long.

After dinner, we all went to midnight Mass at St. Anthony of Padua Church. Mother doesn't have a great regard for Catholics, and I was surprised when she agreed. But the church was beautiful, all marble and lit by candles, and Mother closed her eyes as she listened to the choir. In that moment her face was peaceful, the way it used to be before Father left. I said a little prayer then, just for him.

So it was an almost-happy Christmas after all. I hope yours was too.

Your friend,
Lulu

February 4, 1946
Dear Mr. Beard,
We've sold our house. It happened so fast! Mother decided that, with housing so short, selling would be the patriotic thing to do. She put a notice in the paper, and

the next morning there were lines of people at the door.

Next week we'll move out of Elizabeth Park Valley into a little apartment over in North Hill. We were very lucky to find a place to rent, even a small, dark one, and I try not to let Mother see how unhappy I am. But the rent is low, and the kitchen has modern appliances (although I'm not sure how I feel about that new electric stove). Mr. Jones says I'm welcome to use his kitchen anytime I like.

I know that, come spring, I'll miss my garden. Tommy says I can plant one at his house, but that would mean putting up with Joe, who just gets meaner all the time. And I'm not so sure Mrs. Stroh would like it; now that we're poor, she's not nearly as nice to me.

I like knowing you're back in New York. Maybe someday we'll finally meet? Then again, maybe we'd better not. What if we found out we didn't like each other after all?

Your friend,
Lulu

August 1946
Dear Mr. Beard,
Television! You're going to be on television!

I can hardly wait. Mr. Jones has a television, which is a lucky thing, because Mother would never allow me to go to a bar, even to watch you. She and Tommy and I — and as many of the Cappuzzellis as can fit into Mr. Jones's living room — are going over to watch *I Love to Eat.* Isn't it strange? I feel as if we're finally about to meet.

I'll write the minute the broadcast is over.

Your friend,
Lulu

"That was the last one," said Sammy. "Does that mean that Lulu failed to keep her promise to pen a post-broadcast missive?"

"Maybe it's somewhere else."

"How very disappointing! I wonder if Anne has any knowledge of what happened next," Sammy mused as he escorted me to the door. "First thing in the morning I shall call to inquire. And I promise to inform you without delay."

I had barely arrived at the mansion the next morning before Sammy called to say that Anne could not recall a letter about the broadcast. "However," he said gleefully, "she informed me that there is at least one more letter. Lulu wrote it after her meeting

427

with the great man."

"She *met* him?"

"Apparently, although it was considerably later; Anne says there was an interlude of several years."

"Did Anne know if Father had turned up? Did Mother find a job?"

"I regret to inform you that Anne has no recollection of the contents of the letter. And," he sounded slightly worried, "she also broached the subject of ownership. She thinks it would be prudent to investigate to whom the letters belong."

"They're historical documents. Why would they belong to someone?"

"Anne informs me that everything belongs to someone. She suggested that we consult a lawyer at the earliest possible opportunity. There could be important implications."

"I'll call Dad," I said, although I couldn't see how it would matter; the copyright had to have run out. "But I can't do it right now. The decorators have arrived." The bell was ringing, and I had an appointment to keep.

SOME PICKLES

At noon I was standing at the door of the salon, my hand on the door where *Eva, Eva, Eva* was written in swirling letters on the glass. A woman with thick blond hair came out, and as I stepped aside to let her pass, I scrutinized her. The waves that fell to her shoulders made no attempt to look natural, and her wide black brows and chunky glasses gave her a kind of sassy confidence that thumbed its nose at nature. She wasn't pretty, but she caught your eye and kept it.

Now she caught me staring. "Is it that bad?"

"No. It's gorgeous. Really."

"I don't know." She sounded unsure. "I look so different from the way I did when I walked in. . . ."

"I wonder if she'll do as well with me?"

"Only one way to find out." The stranger held the door open. "It's not like a tat or getting pierced or something. It's a minor

429

commitment. It grows out."

Three hours later, I was certain that everyone was looking at me the way I had looked at that girl. Eva had cut my hair short, shooing away my protests as she feathered it around my face. "You have such beautiful cheekbones," she murmured as she clipped. "You want to emphasize them. And those eyes . . ." She'd performed some kind of complicated, time-consuming procedure involving foils, cotton, and brushes, but when she was done, my hair had turned into a fluffy halo, a riot of golds and bronzes winking and glittering in the light. I reached up, loving the smooth silky feel beneath my fingers.

"Let me do your makeup." I tried to rise from the chair, but Eva gently pushed me back. "It'll be my gift. I can't bear to see you wasting those eyes."

"They're so boring." I stared into the mirror. Even without the heavy glasses, they were just plain brown.

"Wait." She whirled the chair around so I could watch. It didn't take long, but when she was done, my eyes had become a smoky bourbon. They were huge now, and she had painted my mouth a subtle pink, emphasizing how generous it is. I stood up and stared at the stranger in the mirror, at her streaked hair and elegant clothes.

I decided that it wasn't pretty that I felt, but confident. If I saw this girl walking down the street, I'd think she was cool, that she led a fascinating life. She looked nothing like the real me. But maybe most people were crouching behind a façade. Maybe inside the sleek Joan-Mary was a frightened little person. Was that why Sammy had adopted his uniform of tweeds? Did they give him courage? Maybe that was why he talked the way he did. Maybe everyone was scared.

The sun was high when I left the salon, making the sidewalks sparkle. I walked slowly, savoring the warmth, catching my reflection in the windows I passed, still not quite a believer. I could feel people's eyes on me — the tall black man bouncing on the balls of his feet as we waited for the light, the construction workers leaning on their jackhammers, the pair of teenage girls who looked up from their texting — and it felt strange to be so visible. I'd thought that I would hate it, but I was wrong. It felt good to be part of this bright spring day.

I got back to the mansion to find the formerly spare lobby sporting long drapes on the windows and a Turkish rug on the floor. A pair of matching sofas upholstered in red velvet faced the grandfather clock, which was surrounded by framed art and tasteful plants. The overall effect was so appealingly old-fashioned that you half-expected Edith Wharton to come waltzing down the graceful staircase.

I walked upstairs to find an even more remarkable transformation. The offices had been turned back into bedrooms, and my office, which remained untouched, now seemed sadly out of place. I found Alex kneeling by a high, canopied four-poster in Jake's office, tacking down a rug. He grinned sheepishly. "I think we might have gone a little overboard." He hammered in another tack. "Is it too much? This is the first time we've worked for Joan-Mary, and we're trying to make a good impression. Wait until you see the dining room!"

He led me proudly up the stairs to the old photo studio, which now contained the largest table I'd ever seen. "Seats thirty-six," he said proudly. "Forty in a pinch. I've been dying to find a room large enough for it. Think what a wonderful embassy this would make — that huge kitchen's perfect for catering." He gave me a small apologetic smile. "But it's taking longer than we expected, and I'm afraid we haven't started up on four."

"I'm in no hurry."

"Don't worry, we shouldn't be more than a couple of hours. We'll save upstairs for tomorrow. We're not planning to do much up there; I want to turn the open space into a child's playroom, which won't take much more than an antique rocking horse and an old cradle. The library, of course, is gorgeous exactly the way it is."

While I waited for the decorators to finish, I called Dad. He listened quietly, but when he spoke, it was as if he were talking to a client. "The physical letters belong to Pickwick Publications. No question about that. But that doesn't mean they can publish them; they don't own the copyright."

"You mean because the letters were written to Beard? So the copyright belongs to his estate?"

"No. Lulu wrote the letters, so the copyright remains with her. You would need her permission to publish."

"We're not sure she's alive."

"In that case, the rights revert to her heirs."

"What about the letters Beard wrote to her?"

"Do you have any reason to believe she has them?"

"Of course she does!" I was positive about

that. "She would have kept them."

"You may be right. But although she owns the physical letters —"

"I know, I know. The copyright belongs to the Beard estate. I wish I'd mentioned this to you before; I never thought we'd have to worry about the copyright on something so old."

Dad didn't seem worried. "I wouldn't be too concerned. Once you find them, I imagine that the heirs will be thrilled by what you've found. The Beard estate as well. It's a charming story."

I hung up and spent a long time considering this new problem. Even if we never found the last letter, we now had enough letters to make a wonderful article; I was sure I could find a place to publish it. But I couldn't do that until I located Lulu or her heirs. Where to begin . . .

I called Sammy and told him what Dad had said.

"This is worrisome," he replied.

"I know. We don't even know where to start looking for Lulu."

"Not that." His voice was testy. "I have no doubt that we shall find a solution to that particular problem. What worries me is that you have not uttered a single word about your session with Eva. Is the result absolutely odious?"

"I don't think so," I said. "But you'll have to see for yourself."

"I am longing to do that. Unfortunately, I shall have to postpone that pleasure until tomorrow. Anne Milton has invited me to dine with her."

He said it hesitantly, letting me know that he was afraid my feelings would be hurt. But I was relieved; I needed time to get used to the haircut. "It's better that way," I confessed. "I'm so nervous about the way I look that I called Sal and Rosalie and told them I couldn't work this weekend. You know what it's like there; all the regulars will want to discuss it."

"Very wise," he said. And then, obviously struck by a thought, he added mournfully, "But I suppose that tonight you will be depending upon Mr. Ming for sustenance. I must confess that I find your reliance upon mediocre Chinese food utterly deplorable!"

It was a shock to wake up the next morning and find yesterday's stranger in the mirror. I made faces at her, smiling, frowning, turning this way and that, trying to decide if I liked her. "It's not a tattoo." I said it out loud. "Not permanent."

Mitch would probably show up today, and

I found myself reaching for the chiffon dress Hermione had forced on me. In the end I pulled the severe gray jacket over the frothy material, rolling up the sleeves. I added a pair of leggings and simple black ballet shoes. I picked up my bag, scrambled for my keys, and went outside, feeling alternately abashed and buoyant. But it was spring, the air was sweet, and I walked all the way to the mansion.

I found Mitch sitting on the top step. "Glad to see you don't take a cab every day." He stood up. "Wow! You cut your hair!"

I hoped he didn't think I'd done it for him. I could feel myself begin to blush.

"Looks good." He moved on; apparently it didn't strike him as such a big deal. "I promised Joan-Mary I'd come see what her stagers have done. She gave me a key, but I didn't want to frighten you." He needed no excuse for his presence, and it made me smile; had he wanted to see me? "She's never used them before, and if it's a disaster she wants to be prepared."

I opened the door, turned on the lights, and let him into the refurbished lobby. I couldn't tell anything from his expression. He walked slowly around, pulling back the drapes, testing the sofas, peering at the

436

plants. He went up to the grandfather clock and put his head against the cabinet, listening to the whir of the wheels.

"Alex was afraid they'd overdone it," I offered.

"I'd say so." I still couldn't tell if he approved. "I can't wait to see what they've done upstairs."

"Be my guest." I scooped up the mail and headed for the stairs. "I've got work to do."

He followed me up, notebook in hand, and as I went to my office I heard him moving in and out of the rooms along the hall. He was very thorough, and it was a few hours before he reached my end of the corridor, moving purposefully through my workspace into Jake's office.

After a few minutes, I went in and found him standing in front of the fireplace, inspecting the mantel.

"What're you looking at?"

He pointed to a deep fissure running across the front. "This should be replaced. It's the kind of detail that makes people begin to worry about the cracks they can't see. I could repair it in a few hours." He added it to what appeared to be a long list, then shoved the notebook into his shirt pocket and turned to me. "Are you hungry? I think it's warm enough to eat outside.

Let's go see."

The gardeners had raked the yard and put down sod; the decorators had added a little stone table. The spring sun was shining hesitantly through the clouds, and forsythia glowed around the perimeter of the yard, making the air seem warmer. "Definitely picnic weather," he said. "Where do you usually order from?" We were still debating take-out options when Sammy showed up, carrying a large wicker basket.

"I could not allow another minute to pass without seeing you!" He set the basket dramatically down on the table. He scrutinized me for a moment and then said, in a low voice only I could hear, "I have underrated Thursday, I had my doubts about relying upon her judgment, but I see my worries were in vain. I heartily approve." He held out a hand to Mitch, saying in a louder voice, "I am Sammy Stone."

"Mitch Hammond." I wondered if Sammy had come to inspect me or Mitch. Both, I thought.

"Pleased to meet you." Sammy was now appraising Mitch. "Billie mentioned your participation in this project." He pointed to the basket. "If you would care to partake of our repast, we would be delighted." He began to pull out covered dishes and set them on the table.

"Is there enough?"

Sammy gave him a withering look, unwrapping cold chicken, fragrant with lemon and garlic, hard-boiled eggs, and jars of homemade pickles. He'd brought a pitcher of fresh lemonade and brownies for dessert.

"My lucky day." Mitch picked up a chicken leg. "In more ways than one." He winked at me.

"Have a pickle." Sammy held out the mason jar. "Kirbys. I brined them myself." He gestured toward the mansion. "I understand that you have breached the locks. What dark secrets have you unearthed?"

"A rather remarkable library. After lunch I'll give you a tour, if you like."

"Thank you very much, but that will not be necessary. I was on the premises long before the room was declared off-limits. I do not suppose that it has undergone a transformation in the intervening years." He shaded his eyes against the sun and looked toward the garden wall. "On the other hand, that strange heap over there does pique my curiosity. Whatever can it be?"

"I've been wondering that myself," said Mitch.

I put down my chicken thigh. "Oyster

shells," I told them. "The gardeners complained that every time they stuck a shovel in the dirt, they turned up more shells."

"Interesting." Mitch eyed the heap appraisingly. "New York Harbor was once lined with oysters. You could walk out at low tide and gather them by the bushel. The poor lived on them."

"But the Timbers family wasn't poor." I bit into one of Sammy's pickles, and the flavor filled my mouth. "Why would they have a yard filled with oyster shells? It makes no sense."

"Another piece of the puzzle. Okay if I take this?" Mitch held up a chicken thigh. "It's what I like best about my work. As you gather information, you're coaxing a building to reveal its secrets. In the end it always fits together. You just have to find the pattern."

Sammy and Mitch talked about old buildings for a while, and I sat listening, thinking it was a subject they both loved. After half an hour or so, Mitch stood up and began to stack the plates. He grabbed a brownie and tossed it in the air. "I'll take this for later, okay? Thanks for lunch; when I took this job, I had no idea I'd get so lucky."

Sammy watched him amble off. "So that is your Mr. Complainer." As I helped him repack the wicker basket, he mused, "Although he seems like a perfectly pleasant fellow, he presents an extremely unwelcome complication. He is far too curious for my taste, and I do not like the notion of seeking Lulu's last letter while he is on the premises. How long is he expected to remain?"

"Nobody has said."

"I fear your presence here may slow his progress."

"What are you talking about?"

Sammy did not dignify that with an answer. "Your young man does not strike me as a fool, and I do not imagine that Anzio will escape his attention for very long. And then where will we be?"

"You worry too much," I said. "And I have to get back to work. There was a mountain of mail this morning."

It was true. In the five months since *Delicious!* had closed, the volume of mail had increased threefold. It was as if the readers were trying to wish their beloved magazine back into existence.

Today's most promising project was a reader looking for Talamanca peppercorns from Ecuador. "In the May 2008 issue," she wrote, "you said that these were the best peppercorns in the world. And you were

441

right! They are wonderfully fragrant and spicier than any other peppercorn I have ever used. They make Tellicherry seem laughable. I have been ordering them from the source you suggested, but yesterday, when I tried to reorder, I was told that they are no longer in stock. Help! I am like an addict in need of a fix. Please tell me where I can replenish my supply."

It was the perfect distraction; an hour later I was talking to a passionate pepper importer who had a great deal to say about the fragrance and flavor of his particular pepper. I was so deep in conversation that I was startled to look up and find Mitch standing in the doorway. How long had he been there?

"Did you know," I told him when the pepper importer finally hung up, "that peppercorns represent twenty-five percent of the world trade in spices?"

"Fascinating. But not nearly as fascinating as what I've just found."

A flash of adrenaline lurched through me. Anzio! Already! "How'd you find it?"

He looked amused. "The basement is always the first place you explore in an old house."

"The basement?" I was so confused, I didn't have to feign surprise. The word came out oddly, all the emphasis on the first syllable.

"Yes, the *base*ment. In many Federal houses, the basement isn't completely subterranean. The first floor, or parlor floor, had the formal rooms, where guests were received. The bedrooms were upstairs, on the second and third floors, and if there was an office, or a library, it was generally up there too. The servants' rooms were always on the top floor. So what's missing from this picture?"

"The kitchen!" I was so relieved.

"Exactly. Come see."

I followed him into the hall, and he talked as we walked. "In houses like this, they usually put the kitchen belowground so it would be cool in the summer and warm in winter. I went downstairs to try to find the old kitchen, and I found the original hearth."

"But Joan-Mary and Chris spent a lot of time down there."

"I'm sure they did; wait until you see the furnace! They must have been so preoccupied with the infrastructure that they missed everything else. Can't blame them; it's from the dark ages. It can't possibly be code, but it's probably been grandfathered." He opened the door to the basement and led me down some rickety stairs. "Be careful here. They're rotten in some places. Hold on to me and put your feet where mine were."

I put my hands on his waist, stepped cautiously, kept close. The basement had windows all around, but they were so grimy that even on this bright day we were plunged into murky gloom. We reached the bottom and waded into dancing dust that enveloped us in an ancient, musty smell.

A huge contraption towered over us like an enormous metallic spider, its attenuated legs impeding our progress. Mitch took my hand to lead me behind the furnace. "This thing must be at least a hundred years old," he said, pounding on one of the long, rusted pipes with his free hand. "Watch your head."

We ducked beneath the labyrinth of pipes, slowly making our way to the back wall. I was so aware of my hand in his that when he let it go I felt a little jolt of disappointment.

"There!" Mitch pointed proudly to an enclosed fireplace. It didn't look like much to me, but it was dark. I went closer to inspect it, running my hands across the rough brick surface.

"See?" he exulted, coming up behind me. "It's not just a hearth, it's the original beehive oven, built right into the wall. That's very rare: Almost all the old ovens were demolished when cast-iron stoves came in. I think it may be the only one in the city. Joan-Mary's not going to be pleased."

"Why not? Won't she be thrilled?"

"It creates a complication." I stared at the old oven, remembering Joan-Mary's worry that Mitch would find something too interesting. Apparently he had. "When the Landmarks Preservation Commission gets wind of it, they may want to landmark the interior of the building." He was right behind me now, speaking in my ear.

"But wouldn't that make the mansion more valuable?" I did not turn around.

I could feel him shake his head. "Probably the opposite. At the moment, anyone who buys the mansion can do whatever they damn please. Even," he added darkly, "tear down the walls, the way Pickwick did up on the fourth floor. But if the interior gets landmarked, every change will have to be approved by the commission."

"What about the library? Wouldn't that be worth landmarking?"

"A library" — I was aware of his breath on my neck, and little shivers ran up my arms — "even a very beautiful one, isn't all that rare, and I'm not compelled to go running to the commission about it."

Wait until you find Anzio, I thought. Wait until you discover it's more than a beautiful old library. Wait until you find out it was a stop on the Underground Railroad. I had no doubt he would find the hidden room; the only question was when.

He put his hands on my shoulders, and I felt the shock down to my toes. He leaned in, whispering in my ear, "Let's just say that Joan-Mary may regret having hired me." Very slowly, he turned me so that we were standing face-to-face. He was speaking so low that I had to lean in to him to hear. "I, on the other hand" — his hand was gently caressing my cheek — "am very pleased she did."

His breath smelled like fruit, like oranges and cherries. I realized I'd been waiting for this moment since I'd first seen him sitting on the steps. I looked at his hands, thinking of Rosalie as I noticed that he wore no rings. How had she known? Then he put his arms around me, and as he began to kiss me, I inhaled the clean, slightly salty tang of his body. His beard was very soft. I tried to think of the last time I'd been kissed. It was so long ago — in another lifetime, the one in which Genie was still alive. Finally I stopped thinking altogether and simply kissed him back.

I'd forgotten what it was like to live in your senses and let time stop. When he let me go, I felt breathless and slightly dizzy, and as I came slowly back into my body and the room, I remembered where I was. I opened my eyes and looked up at him, this lovely man with the wild brown curls. His eyes met mine with so much hope.

"Don't you ever hide your feelings?" I asked.

He put one hand on each side of my face, and for a long moment we looked at each other. He didn't blink. "Fear doesn't get you very far," he said. "At least in my experience."

I thought how much confidence it took to walk through the world with your heart on your sleeve. Hope can't hurt. And then I thought how lucky I was to be here, to be experiencing this. Things can change in a single moment.

I thought of Lulu then, and I reached out and touched the stove again, just to ground myself. I ran my fingers across the rough surface of the old hearth, and through my heightened senses I was aware of every sound, every scent.

Maybe it was being with Mitch that made me really look at that hearth and think about the generations of women who had stood here over the centuries, cooking food for the family upstairs — and, for a little while, at least, for the fugitives hidden away on the fourth floor.

For the first time it struck me that the hidden room was very far away. Who had carried the food up and the chamber pots down? Was it the servants? Did someone in the family sneak up the stairs in the dark of night, ferrying food to the secret guests? With that thought came another one: I knew where to find the final clue. Had known, in fact, for quite a while.

"What?" Mitch had felt the tremor run through me. "What just happened?"

"I had an idea." I buried my face in his chest. I loved the way he smelled. "It's something I should have thought of a long time ago."

BETWEEN TRIBOROUGH BRIDGE AND UNION SQUARE

Flushed and confused, I was happy to find a message from Mrs. Cloverly waiting in my office.

"It was that chocolate ice cream," she said plaintively. "The recipe promised that it would be the richest I'd ever tasted. . . ."

I remembered tasting it for Diana, remembered the Fontanari cream I'd insisted she use when she was working out the recipe. As Mrs. Cloverly talked on, I sent Diana an email, imagining her laughter as she read Mrs. Cloverly's bizarre combination of carob powder, instant coffee, and skim milk. "She hasn't changed a bit," I wrote. "The ice cream was simply vile."

As I typed, I could hear Mitch moving about the mansion. I thought he'd enjoy Mrs. Cloverly, and I followed the sound until I found him, upstairs in the photo studio. He was tapping on walls and thumping on floors, but when I told him the stories, he roared with delight. "Oh, I'd love to meet her," he said, and then, as if this were something we'd discussed, asked casually, "Where should we have dinner tonight?"

It took a lot for me to say, "I can't have dinner with you tonight."

He looked more surprised than disappointed. "You've had a better offer in the last half hour?"

"No, but I have a previous commitment." It wasn't a complete lie. Mitch was going to find the secret room, and he was going to find it soon. I had to get there first. His talk about the Landmarks Commission had made me uneasy; once he knew about it, everyone else would too. This wasn't something I could put off.

He seemed to accept that. "Rain check?" he asked.

"Rain check," I agreed.

"Tomorrow, then?"

"Tomorrow," I promised.

He leaned down and kissed me, once on each cheek. "I'll dream about you." And he began to gather up his tools.

It was almost eight by then, and I went around behind him, turning out the lights. The moon was full, and it gave the furniture a silvery glow and filled the Timbers Mansion with a sense of peace. Walking through the lovely rooms, I felt for the first time that the library belonged here. The house was reclaiming its spirit, and the library, which had stood aloof and apart for so many years, was turning back into what it was always meant to be: the heart of this home.

I went to the card catalog, kneeling to reach the bottom drawer of the old wooden cabinet. I turned the cards, one by one, until I came to "Underground Railroad," right where I'd expected it to be.

To a casual reader, Bertie's words would have been meaningless. "The Underground Railroad," he had written, "operated for one brief, hopeful moment in history. Strangers reached out to one another, offering aid and the promise of a better life." I imagined them as he must have, this improbable pair, the older man helping the young girl survive her war. "These encounters," Bertie continued, "were mostly fleeting — ships passing quickly in the night. But sometimes the perilous undertaking forged lasting ties, and lives were irrevocably changed." I stopped for a moment, savoring the final line. "Recipes from that time were rarely written down. Most were passed from one person to the next in a long oral tradition. The 'New York' archives of 1948, however, contain one extraordinary exception."

I went into the secret room, making a point of pulling the bookcase back into place and closing the door behind me. This felt like a solemn moment. I had not thought of looking in the "New York" section, but the file was exactly where Bertie had put it so many years ago, a slim folder filed between "Triborough Bridge" and "Union Square." I opened the "Underground Railroad" folder, knowing that Bertie had been the last one to touch it, shivering as I extracted the single envelope.

Easter Sunday, March 28, 1948
Dear Mr. Beard,
It sounded so romantic when you suggested meeting at Macy's butcher shop. But when the time finally came, I wished we'd chosen a more conventional place. How would you know me? What if I was a disappointment? What if you saw me and walked away? For one terrible moment as I was crossing Herald Square, I wished I'd let Mother come with me, and by the time I walked through the door I was shaking with nerves.

I saw you right away, but your back was to me, and I just stood there, trying to decide whether to run away. Then you turned around. Until that moment, I thought that when people spoke of someone's face "lighting up," it was merely a figure of speech.

Oh, Mr. Beard, I have every moment stored away, and when things get sad here in Akron I'll think about how we baked together in your little kitchen. I had the strangest feeling that we'd done it all before, that I knew what you were going to say before you said it. Even before we took them out of the oven, I knew my Snowballs were going to be too sweet. You're right — it is a child's cookie and I am grown now. The recipe will have to change.

Dinner at your house! I still cannot believe that Mother agreed that eighteen is old enough to drink a glass of wine. I don't think I'll ever forget the taste of that Burgundy, or the way it felt in my mouth, almost heavy, so different from water.

I believed that was the best day of my life — but only because Saturday had not yet come. I remember every single thing we did, from breakfast at Rumplemeyer's — surely that is the world's best hot chocolate — to riding down Fifth Avenue on the top of the double-decker bus.

When I told Tommy about all the odd

foods we saw in the Chinatown stores — dried shrimp and turtles and great long octopuses — he thought I was making it up. But when I told him about that poor frog hopping down the sidewalk, trying to make his escape, he laughed until tears ran down his face. I wish he could have been with us at the funny little "Chinese tea parlor," because he would have enjoyed the way they bring the food around on trays and let you point at the dishes you want. He would have appreciated the simplicity of that — and the way they calculate the bill by counting the empty plates.

But I'm glad that he wasn't with us at Le Pavillon. He would never have understood that meal or how much it meant to me. For the few hours that we were at the table, I felt as if I'd become a different person.

Maybe it was the way Mr. Soulé made me feel when I walked into that beautiful room, as if he'd been waiting especially for me. I remember every morsel, from the sole in its silken sauce to the chicken with black truffles. Isn't it odd that it took a luxurious meal like that to make me understand what Mrs. Cappuzzelli has been trying to teach me all along? A great meal is an experience that nourishes more than your body.

The feeling stayed with me. The next morning, when Mother, Mr. Jones, and I were walking through those strange, crowded downtown streets, where people were sticking their hands into pickle barrels, pointing to smoked fish, and eating sliced herring, I saw the scene in a whole new way. They weren't buying food: They were finding their way home.

We walked through Little Italy and Greenwich Village, and I tried to imagine myself in a foreign country. And while I was imagining, Father came back to me so strongly. I could smell the aftershave he used to wear, and once I was sure I heard his voice behind me. It wasn't him, of course, but it made me feel sure again that Father is not dead.

That feeling used to make me so unhappy, but now that Mother has Mr. Jones, and I'm going off to Wellesley College, I'm not angry anymore. I'm certain that Father is alive, and, wherever he is, I hope that he is happy.

Mr. Beard, I don't know if I'll ever see you again. I hope so. But if that is not to be, I hope we'll continue to be friends.

You've given me so much.

> Many, many thanks
> from your friend,
> Lulu

P.S. When I gave Mrs. Cappuzzelli the aged Parmesan, she acted as if her hands were filled with diamonds. Then she made some fettuccine — rolling it out so thin you could see right through it — and we sat down and ate it with nothing but butter and grated cheese. It will always be my favorite kind of pasta.

P.P.S. You were absolutely right about Mrs. Stroh; Tommy and I have been going out for three years, but I think she smiled at me — really smiled — for the first time when I gave her that leberkäse from Schaller & Weber.

That was it. Lulu was gone. Would I ever hear that voice again? I sat for a long time, holding the letter in my lap, trying to imagine this new Lulu. I conjured up the picture in my mind and let it age, watching her face growing lined, her hair turning white, until she was an old lady. I half-closed my eyes, almost dozing as I pictured her. Then a chair crashed in the library, and the sound shot through me, an arrow of adrenaline. What was that?

Only my imagination. It was late, and I was alone in an empty old building, walled up in this tiny room. The blood rushing in my ears was so loud, I could barely hear anything else. And then I did hear it, a slow sound, like an animal bumping clumsily about in the library. I cringed back against the wall, trying to figure out what to do. There was nowhere to go. My skin went hot, then cold, and I could feel the goose bumps come up on my arms. The sounds were coming closer. It was not my imagination.

But no one except Sammy knew about the secret room; I was safe in here. Had I left my purse in the library? My coat? Pulse racing, I looked down at the floor, relieved when I saw the purse at my side and the jacket beneath it. I was safe! They'd take whatever it was that they'd come for and leave. I could stay in here all night if I had to, hidden away.

But the sounds had become methodical; whatever was out there was searching for something. Bumps turned into thumps and then deliberate knocks against the wall. They were coming closer. Terrified, I rose very slowly, dizzily reaching for the string on the swinging bulb. It went out, and I huddled in the thick darkness, heart banging against my ribs.

Be logical, I told myself, stay calm, try to think who it might be. Sammy wouldn't be searching like that, and Mitch had to be safely home in bed. Had Anne Milton told somebody about the room? The knocks were nearer, so close I could feel them echoing through my body. I heard books being moved, and now the creature out there had reached the wall behind me. There was a scraping noise as the shelf moved, and then footsteps approached the door. I crouched in the dark, petrified as the first crack of light appeared. It grew slowly wider, and then a terrible scream began to bounce off the walls, so loud that I covered my ears.

It must have been a full ten seconds before I realized that the scream was coming out of my own mouth.

At first I registered only size: The man was huge. Then my eyes focused and the apparition turned into . . . Mitch?

He bent and gathered me into his arms. "Shh, shh, shh," he crooned, smoothing my hair away from my face. "It's all right, it's only me." He rocked me against his solid body, and as my terror subsided, my muscles began to ache from the adrenaline that had gone shooting through them.

"What are you doing here?"

Mitch looked down at me. "I might ask the same of you." He settled against the wall and pulled me toward him, so that my back was resting against his chest and his arms were cradling me. "I thought you had an important commitment. What're you doing here so late? And how could you have found this hidden room when you'd never been inside the library?"

"You first." Relief was thrumming through my body. I relaxed against him, finally feeling safe.

"When you refused to have dinner with me, I felt kind of rejected. I was worried I'd read you wrong. I walked home, and when I got there I was so restless I didn't know what to do with myself, so I decided to come back and try finding the secret room; I knew it had to be here." He paused, then said, "I certainly wasn't expecting to find you. I think you scared me as much as I scared you."

"Good." I leaned into him. "Serves you right for nosing around. But how'd you know about Anzio?"

"Anzio?"

"It's what Sammy and I call this room. Long story."

"Mine too." I felt a muscle jump in his arm.

"So you were saying . . ."

"There were so many strange things about the library, and as I found one anomaly after another, I was sure they would add up to the Underground Railroad."

He'd gotten it so much faster than I had. "What strange things?"

"For one thing, the library being up here on the fourth floor; it made no sense. Then there were those carved initials inside the lock. I've only seen that once before, in a hidden room designed by an abolitionist architect. When I discovered there'd been three locks on the door, I was almost positive. And then I saw the oyster shells. . . ."

"What do they have to do with it?"

"The most famous stop on New York's Underground Railroad was Thomas Downing's Oyster House at the corner of Wall and Broad Street. Apparently, when Mr. Downing rowed out to collect oysters, he also collected runaway slaves and stowed them in his basement. It made everything fall into place, and I began to think the Timbers Mansion was more than just a stop on the Underground Railroad. I thought it must have been another house built specially to help the abolitionist cause. That would explain a lot."

"Like what?"

"For starters, why we couldn't find any documentation about the building of the Timbers Mansion. There were fierce riots over abolition for many years, even in the north, and if you were going to build a house to harbor runaway slaves, you'd want to keep it secret. I went online looking for documentation."

"Find anything?"

"Not at first. The Timbers family was extremely private, and they left very little in the way of letters or diaries. But I stumbled onto something else, almost by accident."

"What?"

"A notice in the social pages of the *Boston Daily Advertiser* in 1824. It wasn't much — just 'Mr. and Mrs. Charles Timbers attended a ball given by Mrs. Timbers's sister in their honor, blah, blah, blah.' But there was a guest list, so I researched all the guests. You never know when you'll hit pay dirt. And I did. Mr. and Mrs. David Lee Child were at that party. He was a lawyer; she was Lydia Maria Child. Ring any bells?"

"Never heard of her."

"But you've undoubtedly heard her most famous poem. Everyone has. 'Over the River and Through the Woods'? She was not only

461

a poet, though; she was also a prominent abolitionist and a founder of the Female Anti-Slavery Society. It wasn't much, but, with everything else, it made me feel pretty sure that there would be a secret room here. So I made copies of all the documentation and —" He stopped, looking down at me. "What?"

I'd just remembered that Sammy and I hadn't copied Lulu's letters. We kept putting it off, wanting to find them all first. Now it might be too late.

"Nothing important. Go on."

"There is nothing else. I was going to start searching tomorrow, but I was so restless, I thought, what the hell, no time like the present. I thought I'd surprise you with my marvelous find. And then" — his eyes twinkled — "you'd have to have dinner with me."

"You almost scared me to death."

"I'm sorry. That was not part of my plan. How long have you known about this room? And why didn't you tell me?" He glanced at the shelves above us, as if noticing them for the first time. "And what the hell is in here that's so damn important you had to blow me off?"

I told him about Sammy's discovery of the room four months ago, and when I got to Lulu's letters he began to ask questions. How many were there? Were Beard's letters here too? When I explained to him that Sammy and I had wanted to locate the last letter before he found the secret room, he understood.

"Of course. You were afraid I'd go running to the Landmarks people and you'd lose your last chance. And, I'm sorry to say, you're not wrong. I have no choice. Have you found it?"

I handed him the letter. The paper rustled as he read, and when he was done he looked up and recited, " 'They weren't buying food: They were finding their way home.' It's lovely, Billie. . . . And so are you."

Then he reached out and gathered me to him, and we were kissing. This time it was nothing like the gentle kisses of the afternoon. He kissed me roughly, hungrily, and I could feel my lips begin to swell as my body arched toward him. The floor was hard beneath me, his entire weight pressing me down, and I felt relief and joy in equal measure. All the voices in my head quieted, and I allowed myself to drift along on pure sensation.

When he let me go, I felt drained and pliant, ready for whatever happened next. Mitch whispered, "Wait, wait." He removed first his jacket and then mine, fluffing them into a little nest.

"I've got a better idea." I disentangled myself, went into the library, gathered all the chair cushions, and dropped them on the floor of the secret room.

Mitch sank onto the pillows, pulling me down on top of him as he began to kiss me, this time with infinite gentleness, running his hands softly across my breasts, my ribs, my hips. "If only I had a few rose petals," he murmured.

We didn't need them. We took our clothes off slowly, watching each other as we did. He was beautifully made — large but graceful — and my own body felt lithe and light. I hadn't been with a man in nearly two years, and I was surprised that I was not embarrassed.

"You're perfect," he said, running his hands down my body.

"I'm not."

"Shh," he whispered, barely audible. "Come here." His body was so warm, his skin so soft, and as my flesh met his, I felt, for the first time since I could remember, that I was exactly where I wanted to be.

"Don't go to sleep," I begged later, and he gathered me to him and murmured into my hair, "Wouldn't dream of it. I have so many questions. What will you do now that you've found the last letter?"

I rolled over onto my back, staring up at the ceiling. I could feel the files in the room, gathered around me like old friends. I wanted this night to never end. I wanted to stay here forever, feeling his arm beneath my neck and his leg across my thigh. I felt anchored.

"I've found the last letter," I said. "But now I have to find Lulu."

Member of the Club

Someone was shaking me, forcing me to surface reluctantly from my dream. "Let me sleep," I murmured, pushing the hands away, trying to remain submerged.

But the voice was in my ear, soft, insistent. "Billie, wake up; it's morning."

I opened my eyes and saw the files of Anzio above me. My heart did a little leap as I awoke and remembered where I was. Then I looked at Mitch, watchful. What now?

As if he knew what I was thinking, he reached out and lightly tousled my hair. "We okay?" I rubbed my head against him like a cat, and he drew me to him, murmuring, "First mornings can be so awkward, and I don't want to blow this."

"But what about the blonde?" I had no idea I was going to say that until the words were out of my mouth. I hadn't even known that I was thinking it.

"What blonde?" He was wearing a bewildered expression.

"Your girlfriend."

"I don't have a girlfriend. At least, not at the moment."

"So you broke up with her when you were up in Cambridge?"

The mystified look hadn't left his face. "I honestly don't know who you're talking about. I haven't had a serious relationship in a while."

"What about that beautiful blonde you brought into Fontanari's?"

"Amy?"

"Yes, Amy."

"You think she's beautiful?" He was laughing now.

"Everybody in the shop thought she was gorgeous." I gave his chest a little thump.

Mitch caught my hands and pinned them behind me, pulling me forward until our chests were touching. "I think I'm insulted." He kissed me, very hard. "How could you possibly think I'd be with someone like Amy? Did you hear her? As I recall, she refused anything with garlic, complained that prosciutto smelled funny, and was horrified to discover that mozzarella's made with water-buffalo milk. I was so embarrassed."

467

"So why were you throwing a party with her?"

"It was my parents' fiftieth anniversary. I had to come home for it, although if I'd known my idiot sister-in-law was going to insist on shopping with me, I would have stayed away. I'm beyond offended that you could think I'd have any interest in a woman like that."

"Sorry." But I was singing inside. Then his watch caught my eye and I sat up: It was after eight. "Mitch! We've got to get out of here! Eric and Alex are coming to stage the art department."

"Don't they know it's Saturday?" He pulled me back down, and I felt his laugh, a low rumble in his chest. "Joan-Mary's undoubtedly coming too. Realtors never rest, and she'll want to see the oven. I bet she's already on her way." But he didn't move, just lay there, lazily running his hands down my arms, my spine, across my breasts.

I strained away, reaching for the string on the lightbulb. "They'll be here any minute!" I began looking around, trying to find my clothes. "Hurry! We've got to get out of here before anyone else arrives."

"Or" — he ignored my frantic mood — "we could just hide in here all day. They'd never find us. I can imagine worse fates."

His arms reached for me, but I kept my muscles tense, and he gradually released his hold. He sighed almost imperceptibly and hitched himself up to look at me. I watched his face grow serious. "You do know I'm going to have to tell her about the hidden room?"

I punched him lightly in the shoulder. "That's why I'm in such a hurry! The Landmarks Commission too, right?"

"I have no choice."

"So get up and help me. I've got to get Lulu's letters out of here! We haven't copied them yet. . . ." I jammed my legs into the leggings, pulled on the chiffon dress, and reached behind me for the zipper.

"Let me help." Mitch was watching me, a smile flickering across his face. Still lying down, he reached for the zipper.

"Get up!" I started to gather files from the shelves, dumping them onto our makeshift bed. "Hurry!" I was trying to remember which files held the letters. "Could you please get dressed?"

"It's okay! It won't be the end of the world. It's not like you'll never get in here again." But he obligingly began to get dressed as I tried to visualize each file, muttering, " 'Commonsense,' 'Exotica,' 'Farming,' 'Beekeeping'. . . ." Why hadn't we copied them as we read? Or at least kept them in one place?

We made eight trips to my office, and each time I expected to hear the front door opening. But we were on our final trip before Joan-Mary called a "Hello?" from the lobby. Mitch executed an abrupt U-turn and ambled unhurriedly up the stairs. I heard him go into the library, hoping he'd find some safe place to stash the folders in his hands. I dashed to my office, heaved my folders into a drawer, and slid into my chair. Flushed and breathing hard, I ran my fingers through my hair, trying to smooth it down.

Chic as usual, Joan-Mary entered my office, unfurling an aqua scarf from her neck. "What are you doing here on Saturday?" Even now, her breathy voice surprised me.

"I took the day off from my other job," I improvised quickly, "so I could come in to catch up. Taking the afternoon off the other day put me behind."

"How conscientious!" Joan-Mary came closer to the desk, regarding me with curiosity. "You had your hair cut. It's wonderful. Who did it?"

"I went to a place called Eva."

"On Bond Street? I've heard of her. She's very good."

"Thanks. Have you heard about the oven?"

"Yes." She grimaced. "And wouldn't you know it's the only one in the city? I'm told it's historically significant."

"That's great!"

"Oh, yes, just fabulous."

"Thought I heard your voice." Mitch strolled into my office, looking rumpled and adorable.

"You're here too?" she said. "Doesn't anyone believe in weekends anymore?"

To my relief, Mitch ignored her remark. "Forget about the oven. I've found something far more interesting."

"When did you have time to find something interesting? Are you spending your nights here now?"

"I had a hunch and came over early to check it out."

"Wonderful." She raised her eyebrows. "What have you found? A secret room, perhaps, hidden behind a panel?"

"How'd you know?"

Her eyes flew to his face, startled. "I was kidding."

He gave her one of his mischievous smiles. "I'm not."

"Where?" Her face now combined fascination and irritation. The left side of her brain was busily spinning a plan to work this to her advantage, while her right brain was thrilling to the notion of a secret room.

"Behind a false wall at the back of the library." Mitch didn't try to hide his excitement. "I'm pretty sure the mansion was a stop on the Underground Railroad. But here's the interesting thing: The secret room's not a later addition. It's original; members of the Timbers family were abolitionists. They designed the library specifically for that purpose; that's why it's so oddly situated."

"Oh, dear." Joan-Mary sat down abruptly; the right brain was losing. "I wasn't expecting this. I suppose you have to call the Landmarks folks?" Her eyes were pleading, but when he nodded, she accepted reality. "Will you hold off until I talk to Mr. Pickwick? I want to walk him through this, make him understand the implications."

"No problem. It is, after all, the weekend." He handed her a sheet of paper. "I've made a list of recommendations. And there's a preliminary appraisal too."

She stood up, all business now, folding the papers into her purse and pulling out her phone. She began to punch in numbers. "Do nothing till you hear from me. I'm going to try to tell him in person." She walked

472

out, and as her voice disappeared down the hall, we could hear her asking Young Arthur if he could see her in the next half hour.

"She didn't even ask to see the secret room!" Her lack of curiosity shocked me.

"She's in crisis mode." Mitch shrugged into his jacket. "Trying to save the sale. I should go as well." Suddenly he too was all business. "I left your folders on the first table in the library. You can't miss them." His tone didn't change, but now his eyes caught mine. "We still have that rain check?"

"Not tonight. Sammy and I have to copy the letters. We can't do it with all these people running in and out, and I don't think we can risk putting it off. We'll have to do it tonight."

He studied me for a moment, and I knew he was trying to decide whether this was my attempt to put some distance between us. Then he reached out very deliberately and put his hand on my arm. We both could feel the jolt of electricity that passed between us. "Does this frighten you? I certainly didn't expect it, and it scares me too. But those are the things that always turn out to be worth doing. So I'm not about to let this go. I wish I could cook for you tomorrow, but I promised to go visit my parents in New Jersey. So we'll have to wait

473

till Monday."

"You're cooking?" I asked, trying to lighten the mood. I wondered if he'd read me right, seen something I wasn't prepared to admit, even to myself. It would be so much easier to end it here, before it had a chance to hurt. If I was honest, the thought of a relationship filled me with terror.

"I'm a good cook. You'll see. Come right after work. I'll text you the address; it's not far from Fontanari's." He didn't linger over the kiss and left quickly — afraid, I thought, to give me time to change my mind.

I had so much to do. I should call Sammy. But for the longest time I did nothing, just sat at my desk, thinking about last night, wondering about the future. I think I might have dreamed the entire day away if I had not been interrupted by the sound of footsteps in the hall. Pulling myself together, I went to investigate. To my surprise, I found Young Arthur.

I hadn't seen him since the day he'd closed the magazine, and he obviously didn't recognize me. He made a strange little startled motion, and I realized that he had not, of course, expected to find anyone working on a weekend. "I'm Billie Breslin," I said quickly, "the one who's here for the

Delicious! Guarantee."

"Oh, yes," he said absently. "I'd forgotten." It occurred to me that he might not even know that it was Saturday. "You've heard about our hidden assets?" He was wearing some kind of cologne that made the back of my throat prickle.

I nodded. "Pretty exciting."

"Some might consider it so." He walked into my office and stood looking speculatively around him, and when he spoke it was more to himself than to me. "But from my perspective, it makes things rather complicated. The realtor tells me a fast sale is almost impossible now; nobody wants to be burdened with a lot of red tape. I thought I'd just come see this bit of history for myself."

Young Arthur ambled into Jake's old office, peering around as if he'd never seen it before. He sat down briefly on the big four-poster and gave a little bounce, like a kid testing a mattress. He got up and ran his finger across the long crack on the mantel, and I remembered what Mitch had said. Then he went over to the window and gazed down at the garden, where the forsythia was now a riot of yellow. Abruptly, he turned and walked out. I thought he'd forgotten I was there. I could hear him climb ponderously up the stairs, hear him move into the library. He didn't linger; five minutes later, when I heard his descending footsteps, I finally punched Sammy's number into my phone.

My mind wandered as I read him the last letter, the night coming back to me in staccato flashes, a tumble of remembered sensations. Mitch's arms around me, his voice in my ear, and the way our bodies fit together.

"Read it once more."

I jerked back to the present, focusing on the words this time. Lulu, I thought, had acquired a mature generosity she hadn't had before. " 'Wherever he is, I hope that he is happy,' " I repeated. "Do you think she really believes that he's alive?"

But Sammy had heard something else. "He took her to Le Pavillon!" His voice was dreamy and very far away. "I always longed to go there."

"Was it famous?"

On the other end of the phone, there was a tiny hiss of horror. "Famous?" His voice broke. "My dear, it was much more than that: It was important. It was perhaps the premier restaurant of the last century. In 1939, the French government dispatched Henri Soulé to New York with orders to establish a restaurant on the grounds of the World's Fair. They offered him carte blanche; his only mission was to demonstrate the superiority of true French cuisine. Soulé marshaled a band of superb chefs, conveyed them to New York, and created an enormous sensation. His success was so complete that the government sent them back the subsequent summer. Then disaster struck: The war started while they were on this continent. Stuck in New York, the entire crew launched an establishment of their own. Imagine how Lulu must have felt, walking into the most celebrated restaurant in the universe."

"She didn't seem overwhelmed."

"Soulé obviously looked upon her with approbation. He was famous for that; he scrutinized each customer, singling out favored patrons as 'members of the club.' His criteria were inscrutable; he never elucidated how he knew whom to lionize. It had nothing to do with either fame or fortune; it was just what he called 'a feeling.' "

Le Pavillon was Sammy's kind of place.

"Lulu obviously found favor with the great man; what would I not give to learn how her life turned out."

"Well, we do know some things. We know

that Mother and Mr. Jones got together."

"Predictable." He was dismissive. "I anticipated that some time ago. Is it fair to conjecture that Lulu married Tommy?"

"I doubt it. People don't usually end up with their high school boyfriends."

"You may be right." Sammy's voice sharpened. "May I ask where you found the letter?"

I told him. "What an ignoramus I am!" he cried. "We have been speculating about the Underground Railroad for months."

"Mitch figured it out too," I said, telling how he'd come barging in.

"How terrifying! You must have been petrified — alone in Anzio under enemy attack."

"It wasn't fun!"

"Are you quite certain of that?" There was a knowing tone in his voice.

I felt a little glow of happiness. This time it wasn't the memory of Mitch: It was the fact that Sammy knew me so well.

Well enough to ask no further questions. "We had best scan the letters with alacrity. Shall I come now?"

"I don't think we'd better risk it. The stagers are coming back today. Maybe Young Arthur too. And I have no idea when Joan-Mary might decide to return to take a look at Anzio and the oven."

"Given the hullabaloo surrounding the mansion, it would be unwise to risk a daytime foray. Shall we make it a late-night mission?"

"Great minds think alike."

"Excellent." His voice became brisk. "Shall we say ten P.M., at the mansion?"

"Aren't we being formal."

"My dear girl, would you have it any other way?"

"One thirty-six A.M." Sammy laid the copy of Lulu's last letter carefully into the box. It just fit. "Have you received another message?"

"He must have gone to bed." Mitch had been texting little messages all night, informing me of the unspeakable things he was doing to Amy.

"I like your young man." Sammy closed the two boxes we had filled and began gathering up the folders. "Let us return the originals to their proper place."

We carried the folders back to Anzio, pushing them onto the shelves. When we were done, we stood in the doorway, taking in our surroundings. The tiny room stared back at us, bland and silent, its single bulb hanging motionless. Sammy sighed. "We will probably never see this again." I took out my phone and snapped a picture, trying to memorize the dense, almost physical feel-

480

ing of quiet and the pleasantly musty smell. Sammy reached for my hand. "We have been happy here," he said simply.

Outside, it had begun to drizzle, and we hailed a taxi, the cab shooting through rain-slicked streets. We slid along watery reds and greens, the changing lights captured in the canvas of wet tar. It was very still, the sidewalks empty, with only the occasional cab nosing south. "New York seems such an oasis in the middle of the night." Sammy had his face pressed against the window. "For this moment, we alone possess the city."

The doorman came out, umbrella raised, to help unload the boxes. I started to climb back into the cab, but Sammy stopped me. "Stay." He handed the driver a fistful of bills. "Please? Solitude is not my preference. Not tonight."

I was relieved. I didn't want to be alone either, and I trailed Sammy through his elegant lobby, thinking gratefully of silk pillows and velvet quilts. I had no idea what tomorrow would bring, but for tonight I was grateful to find shelter here.

Sammy made me breakfast the next morning; while I ate, he called Anne to suggest she contact Young Arthur first thing Monday morning. "If you inform him of the valuable letters secreted in the library and offer to catalog them, gratis, you may be able to rescue them from a terrible fate." They were still strategizing when I left. I went home, grateful I'd told Sal and Rosalie that I wouldn't be in. So much had happened during the last week, and the day stretched before me, blissfully empty.

"You sound happy." Dad always called on Sunday. "Did something happen?"

"Not really." Was it that obvious? "It's just spring. The weather's been beautiful. Everybody in the city's happy." I wasn't ready to talk about any of the past few days' events. Not yet. I got on the subway and rode all the way out to Flushing, losing myself in a neighborhood so foreign I might have been in Hong Kong or Seoul. I wandered for hours, going in and out of exotic malls. When I got home I took a long hot shower, ordered a major Ming feast, washed it down with half a bottle of wine, and went to bed early.

In the morning I looked longingly at the chiffon dress, wishing I hadn't been wearing it the other night; it made me feel so good. But I didn't want Mitch to think I wore it every day, so I pulled on the orange leggings, the short red skirt, and the T-shirt that looked like mother-of-pearl. I glanced in the mirror — did I look okay? — and then treated myself to a cab. I was feeling oddly fragile, worrying about what the day would bring, nervous about tonight's dinner with Mitch. Sure enough, just as the cab pulled up to the mansion, my phone began to ring and I saw that it was Mitch's number. Was he calling to cancel?

"Have a nice time at your parents'?" I asked.

"I can't tell you how much I'd rather have been with you. But that's not why I'm calling. I'm calling to admit that you were right to blow me off and copy your letters the other night. Pickwick apparently spent yesterday camped out at the Timbers Mansion, and now he's decided not to sell. He's on his way over, as we speak, with his personal decorator."

"How do you know?"

"He asked me to meet them there. Joan-Mary suggested that my services might be useful."

"Poor Joan-Mary; she's worked so hard. She must be furious."

"It comes with the territory. It's a tough business. And it wasn't all for nothing; he'll recommend her to his rich friends."

"I'm beginning to see why she considered

Anzio and the oven a nuisance."

"As far as I'm concerned . . ." He paused for a fraction of a second, and I could feel him weighing the wisdom of whatever he was about to say. He chanced it. "The way I see it, this was the universe's way of throwing us together. If Pickwick Publications hadn't put the house on the market, you and I would have spent the rest of our lives sniping at each other at Fontanari's."

I had to admire the way he went for it. "Yeah, I might never have known there was more to you than a great big complainer."

"I think that's my cue to hang up."

Ruby was right behind him, calling to warn me that Young Arthur was on his way. "Mr. Pickwick says he's going to restore the building to its former glory, whatever that means." I could hear her settling into her chair, preparing for a good gossip. "You should have heard him; he sounded almost normal."

"He's turning the Timbers Mansion into a museum?"

"Not a chance. He's turning it into corporate headquarters. Thinks it will be classy. He keeps comparing it to Gracie Mansion. And listen to this: He's renaming the place Pickwick House."

"He can't do that; it's always been the

Timbers Mansion."

"According to him, the Pickwicks have been there longer than the Timbers family ever was and they should have renamed it a long time ago. Anyway, some historian just called — she sounded like an old lady — to say there are some kind of valuable letters hidden in the library. Sounds dicey to me, but she apparently knew one of the librarians in the deep dark past. Odd, isn't it, that she called today of all days? She wants to catalog them, and the lawyers think there might be a tax advantage."

Anne had lost no time; she was worried that they might throw the letters away before she could get to them.

"So," Ruby continued, "be prepared. He's meeting the historian there. And he's got some other weirdos coming too. That decorator he's so in love with, who thinks she's God's gift to the universe. His architect and an architectural historian, whatever that is."

Ruby was still talking when the downstairs door opened. From the sound of the voices, there were three of them, but by the time they came up the stairs, reinforcements had arrived. As they came down the hall, I went to the door, trying to see who was there. Anne gave me a surreptitious wave behind Young Arthur's back. Mitch did too. The

485

man with the shock of pure white hair over a startlingly young face must be the architect. The aloof young black woman had to be the decorator, and the harried-looking girl at her side, scribbling furiously on a pad, her assistant.

Young Arthur spotted me in the doorway. He seemed as surprised to see me as he had on Saturday. He'd obviously forgotten that I worked there. "What about her?" he asked the black woman, jabbing a thumb in my direction.

"I can't have anyone in the Timbers Mansion while I'm working." Ruby was right; she did have a lordly manner. She turned to the assistant. "She'll have to be moved. Call Ruby and have her arrange it with someone in HR." As the entourage swept on to Jake's office, Anne carefully avoided eye contact, but Mitch wiggled his eyebrows at me, and I covered my mouth, trying not to laugh.

In the next room, Mitch and the architect conferred while Young Arthur told the decorator how he wanted his office to be furnished. As I listened to him going on about desks, sofas, and bookcases, it hit me that *Delicious!* would disappear with the Timbers Mansion. Work uptown in the corporate offices? I'd been wondering how I would know when it was time to go. When

486

Young Arthur and his entourage left the premises, I picked up the phone, called the main number at Pickwick Publications, and asked for Human Resources. I was done.

The woman I spoke with seemed flustered. "So you're giving two weeks' notice?"

"No. I'd like today to be my last." Sal had always said he'd hire me full-time at Fontanari's.

"You're the only one in the building, as I understand it," she said, and the hesitation in her voice made me realize that she didn't know what to do. "I'm going to have to put you on hold."

It was at least five minutes before she came back on the line. "We're sending someone right down," she told me. "He'll do an exit interview and answer any questions you might have. He'll be there within the hour."

"You have created a dilemma," said Sammy when I described the conversation. I could almost see him rubbing his hands with delight. "There are no instructions in the rule book to cover this particular situation. Naturally they want to ensure that you do not abscond with company property. Some flunky will take possession of your computer and formally escort you from the premises. You have precious little time. Do not waste another moment conversing with me."

"What do I have to do?"

Sammy was unusually succinct. "Erase your electronic footprints. Delete your emails. And be certain to copy every telephone number and email address that may prove useful in the future."

"Like what?"

"It would be wise to ascertain that we have a means of communicating with all our former colleagues. There are certainly some numbers you neglected to put into your cell." A note of exasperation crept into his voice. "You have merely to peruse your Rolodex. The worthwhile numbers will immediately make themselves known. Cease this dawdling!"

Next I texted Dad and Aunt Melba.

"About time you left that miserable job!" Aunt Melba's reply was almost instant.

Dad's came right behind it. "Melba's right. Come on home!"

"No," I texted back. "I'm going to Akron. I have to find Lulu. At least, I have to try."

"How exciting," was Aunt Melba's immediate response. "I have a feeling you're going to find her. I'm so curious what she'll be like."

Dad's response, typically, was more measured. "Do your best. But please don't expect too much. A lot of years have passed, and you don't have much to go on. If there's anything I can do to help . . ."

Finally I called Mrs. Cloverly, to tell her I would no longer be fulfilling the *Delicious!* Guarantee. Unfortunately, she was so intent on telling me about some vile English-muffin recipe the magazine had run back in the sixties that I wasn't sure she'd understood.

"But why would you bother making home-made English muffins?" I asked, giving in.

"Isn't that obvious, dear? They cost far less than store-bought. And since somebody was kind enough to give me English-muffin molds for my birthday, I could hardly let them go to waste."

"People must consider you quite the cook."

I smiled as I said it, but the joke flew right over her head. "People were always giving me cooking utensils." She was in dead earnest. "Mostly I took them back — who needs all that nonsense? — and I built up quite a credit at the Cleveland Cookshop. Unfortunately, I still had it when they closed. Very annoying, I must say. But that's neither here nor there. We were discussing muffins. I just wish you could taste them."

"Well," I said, thinking that this might be one way to make her understand that I was leaving *Delicious!,* "that's not impossible. Now that I don't have a job, I'm planning a trip to Akron."

"Cleveland is so close! You must come visit." Was she willfully refusing to hear me? "In fact, you could stay with me. Why pay for a hotel?"

I hastily declined her invitation; I had always imagined her house as a double-wide in a trailer park, stuffed with a large collection of miniature ceramic birds. "At least come to tea," she urged, giving me her address. "I promise not to make you eat these vile muffins."

I promised. Then I hung up and began to empty my desk. By the time the man from HR showed up, I was deleting the last files on my computer.

"Got everything?" He was younger than I'd expected, tired-looking, in a badly fitting suit.

I pointed to the small cardboard box. "Not much to get. I haven't exactly made this home."

He pulled out a form and began to ask perfunctory questions about why I was leaving the job. When he was finished, he nervously jingled the change in his pocket.

"I'm supposed to escort you out the door."

"Do you mind waiting a minute? I'd like to take a last look."

He gave his lips an anxious lick. "I'm not sure I'm supposed to let you."

"Oh, come on. I'll only be a couple minutes."

He seemed troubled, but at last he nodded. "I'll wait downstairs. Don't take too long."

I walked up the stairs, remembering that first morning when Jake and Sherman had stood waiting for me on the landing, mourning again the passing of that lovely dog. He'd been my first friend at *Delicious!* In the old photo studio, I had a memory of Maggie sending me off on that wild-anchovy chase. Passing through the kitchen, I could almost hear Diana's voice. "Gingerbread Girl . . . Maggie thinks you're wasting our time. But what you're really wasting is your talent."

Her words stayed with me as I climbed the stairs again, and they were still with me as I walked through the empty art department.

Then I was at the library. The reassuring apple scent engulfed me, and I flashed on the first time Sammy and I had come through this door. We were unaware that the room was crowded with ghosts who were about to propel us into the present and force us to face the future.

I flicked the switch and watched the soft golden light spread across the shelves. Savoring the deep calm, I sat down on a soft suede armchair and picked up one of the books piled onto the long library tables. I got up and went to the card catalog, laid my cheek on the rough wooden surface, and pulled a drawer open just to hear its deep, almost human sigh. I gazed at the colors, grateful to the benign librarians who had nurtured my friendship with Sammy. I hoped Anne would be able to rescue them from whatever lonely fate the Pickwicks had planned.

I moved on to the zodiac desk, thinking of the day Richard had spread his photographs across its fantastic surface. Seeing his pictures for the first time, I'd been awed by his ability to find beauty buried in the grotesque. But, more than that, Richard had made me understand that sight is not a gift but an act of will.

I made a final pilgrimage to Anzio, turned on the lightbulb, and looked up at all those crumbling files. I remembered how safe I'd felt waking up here with Mitch, and then an avalanche of memories came tumbling down. Sammy telling me about his mother's war. Richard's fury about his nonna and how she'd lost her house. The Murrow broadcast, "Orchestrated Hell." And the day I introduced Sammy to Genie . . . and began to let her go.

"Thanks, Lulu." I said it out loud, feeling foolish. And then I said it again. "Thanks for everything." I ducked out of Anzio, slid the bookcase back against the wall, and left the Timbers Mansion for the last time.

■ ■ ■ ■

BOOK THREE

■ ■ ■ ■

APPETITES

Mitch's place wasn't far from mine, but it was in an oddly hidden pocket of the city where the Lower East Side collided with Chinatown, and I'd never been there before.

"Take the F to East Broadway," he'd texted. I emerged from the subway to find myself on a wide, heavily trafficked street dense with trucks careening off the Manhattan Bridge. On one side of the street, children played in the park; on the other side, pedestrians pushed past one another, hurrying home, trying to beat the dark. Grocery stores with crisp roast ducks hanging in the windows stood next to coffee boutiques and shops filled with pungent barrels of exotic pickles.

"Text me when you get to the paint store," he'd said. "I'm next door. I'll come down and let you in."

I'd expected something old and gracious, but this building was shiny-new. Mitch was waiting near the lobby door. He hustled me inside, put his arms around me, nuzzled my neck. "I'm glad you're here. I was afraid you'd change your mind, but you're actually early." Arms still around me, he led me into a tiny self-service elevator.

"I quit my job!"

"I thought you would," he replied evenly. I glanced at him, disappointed; I'd expected more of a reaction.

He seemed to sense my mood. "You said you had to go find Lulu." He rubbed his soft beard against my cheek. "How could you do that and keep the job? Push two."

When the elevator door slid open, we were right inside his apartment, which gave me an immediate impression of space and light. Then I saw that it was not an apartment but a long, spare, high-ceilinged loft with windows on both ends stretching from floor to ceiling. Cabinets made of a soft butterscotch-colored wood ran down one entire wall. The other wall was white, which made the red sofa against it very bright and the geometric coffee table very black. In the middle of the room, there was a table made of the same butterscotch wood, a rectangular white island with two sinks, and a large old-fashioned high-backed black-and-white enamel stove with two ovens, four burners, and a grill.

I walked to the windows on the east end and looked down at the park across the street. A man was pushing two children on the swings, sending them higher and higher. Mitch took my hand. "Come." He led me to the other side of the loft. As we got closer, I could see that the floor ended in a spiral stairway. The window at this end stretched down another story, all the way to the ground. In the late-afternoon light, the space was spectacular, all air and sunlight, open to the garden just outside. I could make out grass and trees, and something in the middle. A bench, maybe?

"It's not what I expected."

"You thought I'd have an old house, right?" Mitch kicked off his shoes, and I saw that his socks were unmatched; one turquoise, the other purple. I smiled. "Well, I used to. I bought a run-down old Victorian in Brooklyn right out of college, when you could get them in Fort Greene for practically nothing. I worked on it for years. It was an Eastlake, actually."

"Like the lock?" I was glad I'd remembered.

"Yes! The house was always nagging at me about some detail that needed fixing, and somehow I kept doing more and more.

Then a client saw it and fell in love. Made me an offer I couldn't refuse. He wanted everything — not only the furniture but the art and the plates. Everything. I wasn't looking to sell, but . . ." He ran his hand up my arm. "At first I was kind of depressed, but then I realized that he'd offered me a kind of freedom. You have no idea what a relief it is to come home and do nothing. C'mon, I'll take you downstairs."

I followed him down the spiral staircase. The wall behind it was painted deep green and filled with framed pictures and drawings. Most were of buildings, although here and there a photograph showed a large family skiing or boating. In one picture they were sitting outdoors at a picnic table. In another they were all standing in front of Notre Dame in Paris. I went closer to look at the most recent photograph; the father resembled Mitch so much that I had the strange impression of looking thirty years into the future.

"Big family," I said.

"Yeah." There was something guarded in his voice, an I-don't-want-to-talk-about-it quality, and he tugged on my hand, pulling me down to the bottom of the stairs. The bedroom was half the length of the loft, but the enormous window made it feel open, spacious. I stopped to stare into the garden, and he came and wrapped his arms around me, nestling my back against his chest. "It's so beautiful. Like being outside."

He tightened his arms. "At night I lie here and look at the stars. Sometimes I wish there was a fireplace, but you can't have everything."

The bedroom was very different from the stark modern loft upstairs. Everywhere I looked, my eye fell on an unusual object. An antique wooden angel, obviously rescued from a church, hung over our heads, blowing a trumpet. A metal MEN WORKING AHEAD sign stood below the stairway, the ludicrously proportioned man pointing upward with a fat finger. And two worn marble pillars — holding up nothing — flanked the doorway to what I assumed must be the bathroom.

The bed facing the window was a high platform covered with a worn Indian star quilt, the colors gently faded. Mitch plunked himself onto the bed and reached beneath it. "And now for the major attraction." A small prickle of fear ran down my back. Was this going to be something weird? He pulled out a drawer. A light came on, and I felt a rush of cool air.

"You have refrigerated drawers in your bed?"

Mitch gave me a grin you'd get from a kid caught with his hand in the cookie jar. "It's such a drag to go all the way upstairs when you're hit with a midnight craving for ice cream."

"That may be the most decadent thing I've ever seen."

"You" — he drew me down onto the bed — "have clearly led a very sheltered life. You have a lot to learn about decadence."

"And you're going to teach me?"

"I intend to try."

Neither of us said anything for quite a while.

I woke with the moon shining through the huge window. Mitch had pushed back the star quilt, and the sheets felt smooth beneath my legs. I turned my head; he was watching me.

"I hope dinner's not ruined." He reached out and ran his hand across my face, touching my forehead, my cheeks, my chin.

"No worries." I stretched, languidly content. "We can always eat ice cream."

"Absolutely not. I invited you for dinner. And dinner you shall have."

"I'm not hungry." My appetite had vanished so completely that I couldn't remember how hunger felt or imagine ever experiencing it again.

"Well, *I* am starving." He began to climb out of bed, and I reached for him, unwilling to let him leave. He bent to kiss me and I tugged him down again. "Don't go." His body, when he twined his legs with mine, felt like liquid mercury.

The next thing I remember him saying is, "Now I'm really starving." He got up and pulled on a pair of shorts. "I need sustenance. You stay here; I'll bring you dinner in bed."

He padded up the stairs, and after a few minutes I heard the hiss of meat hitting a grill; the scent of charring beef wafted down the stairs. I sniffed, thinking he must have put the potatoes in to bake before I arrived; I could smell the sweet earthy scent of the crisped skins. I heard a bottle being uncorked and then the sound of liquid hitting glass.

Mitch came downstairs, bringing with him the clean scent of the vinegar he'd been mixing into the salad. He handed me a wineglass, its deep crystal bowl filled with a dark, almost black liquid.

"I bought these glasses for the old house. This is the last remaining pair." He took a sip. "But this wine deserves them. Hugh

Johnson calls Hermitage 'the manliest wine of France.' "

I leaned into the glass, inhaling the intoxicating scent, all violets and leather. I could feel him watching me as I took the first sip, rolling the rich wine around in my mouth.

He went back upstairs then and returned carrying a wooden platter perched precariously on top of a teak salad bowl. On the platter were the baked potatoes and an enormous steak.

"One of Benny's?"

"Sal's got me well trained." He began to carve. "I wouldn't dare buy meat anywhere else." He picked up a thin slice and fed it to me. The meat was rare and tender, with a metallic tang, and I thought it was impossible to imagine a sexier meal. We didn't eat much.

I woke up again to find Mitch lying next to me with a bowl of ice cream balanced on his chest. "My idea of heaven," he said. "Coffee ice cream and a beautiful woman in the middle of the night. What more could a man want?" When he kissed me, I tasted coffee and sugar, and when he touched me, his fingers were still cold. "In the morning" — he rolled onto my side of the bed — "we'll take a bath."

"You have a tub big enough for both of us?"

"It's one of those old porcelain monsters with lion-foot legs. I took it from my parents' house when they had their bathroom redone. They were going to throw it out." He said this as if he'd prevented a terrible crime from taking place.

"They don't like old things?"

"Not really. They believe in constant upgrades. They'd especially like to upgrade me."

"But you resist?"

"Always have. I'm the youngest of four brothers, and my parents had already done a great job with Bruce, Bill, and Bryan. They're all architects like Dad. They expected me to go into the family business. But I lacked the most important requirement."

"And that is . . . ?"

"The desire to make your mark upon the earth. You need that if you're going to be an architect. I, on the other hand, believe in preserving what's already here."

"So you were the black sheep in the family?"

I said it lightly, but I could feel his body stiffen.

"Huge disappointment. But it was almost

505

like they always knew I would be. Mother's name is Betty, and my father's Boyd."

"And your brothers all have 'B' names."

"You got it. I'm an 'M' in a 'B' family. They named me Bernard Mitchell, but nobody's ever called me anything but Mitch. Thank God! I'd hate to be Bernie, but as far as my family's concerned, I've always been a little off."

It did not seem the moment to point out that he was with another "B."

"They all work for Boyd Hammond Associates. They all live within fifty miles of one another. And they all married thin blond women who look so much like Amy I can hardly tell them apart."

"Amy is married to . . ."

"Bryan. Valerie and Karen are just like her. Enough about me. Your turn."

I could feel my muscles tense. I didn't want to talk about Genie; it was too soon. But I didn't have to go there, because he continued, "What I really want to know is how you ended up at Fontanari's. I never could figure that one out."

It was the perfect question; I was relieved. I told him about the Sal Test, which made him laugh until he was wiping his eyes. "They did that to Jake's assistants for eight years? That's insane! But I can just imagine

Sal's face when he let someone get away. I bet it ruined his day."

"Are you crazy? It would have ruined his week, at the very least."

"You're right." He reached out and stroked my hair. "Has he seen your haircut?"

"It's only been four days!"

"So what? He's going to be jealous that I saw you first."

"No. He's not." It was the closest I'd come to acknowledging that this was — might be? — a relationship, and that wasn't lost on Mitch. He pulled me in to his chest so we were nestled like spoons.

"You mean," he was whispering into my ear now, "that he'll be happy to see us together?"

I didn't say anything, but he felt my head nod against him, and he moved closer until it was hard to tell where my body ended and his began. I fell asleep again. We were cautiously revealing ourselves to each other, and my last conscious thought was this: I'm happy.

The next time I opened my eyes, light was creeping into the room, the rising sun reflecting off distant skyscrapers. I closed them quickly, afraid of morning, worried that once we left the safety of the bed, we'd lose the hard-won closeness of the night.

But Mitch leapt up, stretching luxuriously, his entire body radiating joy. "I'll draw us a bath." He disappeared between the absurd marble columns, and I could hear him humming as water splashed into the tub.

When I followed him, I saw that the tub was huge, the lion feet planted right in front of the window. In the daylight I could see an old moss-covered stone fountain in the middle of the garden. "I bought that in Florence." Mitch turned off the taps, and water stopped hissing into the tub. He tossed in a handful of salts, sending the scent of orange and clove soaring through the room. It was not the sort of thing I imagined he'd have bought himself, and I wondered about the woman who'd left them here.

"These were Emma's." It was if he'd read my mind. "She's been gone for quite a while."

I lowered myself into the water. It was hot, fragrant, wonderful. I could feel my hair begin to frizz a bit in the steam, and I ducked under the water. When I surfaced, he was walking out the door. "Aren't you coming in?"

"Don't go anywhere." He had turned so I could see the lovely line of his back as he wrapped a towel around his waist and his neat, tight butt. "I'll be back."

While he was gone, I luxuriated in the warm water, my body still thrumming with happiness. The sun was up now, and tiny birds were hopping in and out of the fountain, fighting for position, occasionally looking in at me.

Mitch returned with a copper skillet heaped with pancakes. "I am" — he cut off a wedge, dipped it into a dark pool of maple syrup, and leaned in to feed it to me — "the world's greatest pancake maker."

"My dad thinks he's the pancake king," I said.

"Nope," corrected Mitch. The thin little cake was feather-light, crisp on the edges, delicate beneath its glossy maple coat. He stuffed half a pancake into his own mouth. "Great, aren't they?" He wolfed down another. "Falling in love always makes me hungry." Mitch was sitting on the floor, working his way through the pancakes as I sat in the tub, inhaling the scent of oranges, clove, butter, and maple syrup.

"Do you fall in love a lot?"

"Oh, yeah, all the time." His voice was light, but when he spoke again, it had lost that quality. "Actually, just twice. The first was a high school romance that lasted halfway through college. God, we were into

509

each other! I really thought I couldn't live without Heidi. When she found someone else, I was devastated, and it was a long time until I let myself feel that way again."

"What happened that time?"

"Emma and I lived together for four years, and it was very pleasant. She's wonderful, and we were great friends. Still are, in fact. She's an art historian, and everybody thought we were perfect for each other. But I wanted . . ." He met my eyes. "More."

I didn't exactly respond. "I guess love makes me lose my appetite," I said, before I ducked beneath the water, embarrassed. Afraid. It was going so fast.

When I came up, he was still watching me. "You guess?" He ran the last of the pancakes through the syrup on the plate. "Don't you know?"

"No." I wasn't sure I should say this. "It's just that I've never lost my appetite before."

Mitch kept his eyes on me, waiting for something. When I remained silent, he shrugged, went out, and came back carrying another pancake-filled skillet. Setting it on the floor, he removed the towel and climbed into the tub, lowering himself until the water swelled almost to the rim. He gave a contented sigh and reached down for the flapjacks. He ate slowly, straight from the skillet, savoring each bite while the water sloshed gently around us. When he was finished, he reached out of the bathtub and, with infinite care, set the skillet on the floor.

"How long is 'quite a while'?" I asked.

"You mean when did Emma leave? Almost two years ago." He gave me a lopsided grin. "But don't feel sorry for me. I haven't been completely alone."

"Thanks for sharing." I splashed water at him.

"I'm guessing that you've been alone for a long time?" With his hair plastered to his head and his wet beard, he seemed somehow smaller, more vulnerable, and when he smiled, his mouth took up more of his face. "Tell me what was it like, growing up in Santa Barbara."

I looked down into the water and saw myself, such a shy kid, tagging behind my smart, beautiful, popular sister. An image floated up, some clueless grown-up telling Dad how lucky he was that Genie was such a beauty. I could see Dad's worried eyes on me, feel his hand as he smoothed the hair out of my eyes. I glanced up; Mitch was watching me.

"I think something terrible happened that you have a hard time talking about." He leaned into the porcelain embrace of the tub. "You can tell me."

I closed my eyes and began. I told him first about Mom dying when I was a baby, about growing up with my big sister, my sweet father, and the aunt next door. I told him about Genie, how gorgeous she was, how perfect. "She was so beautiful that people stopped her on the street, just so they could look at her violet eyes. And she was good at everything: She had a 4.0 average, she was a great athlete, and there was nothing she couldn't draw. She was on her way to Yale Law. Everybody loved her."

"Must have been hard to be her little sister."

"Sammy said that too, but to be honest I don't know how I would have managed without her. I was shy, but she made everything easy. She always told me exactly what to do."

He gave a little grunt. He was a good listener, watching with silent intensity as I talked. When I got to the part about Cake Sisters, he reached across the tub and turned me, wrapping his arms around my chest so we were spooned together in the water. I could feel him breathing against my back, but it was easier to talk when he couldn't see my face. He listened silently, stroking my arms gently as I told him about

Genie insisting we do the thirty-thousand-dollar cake. How she stayed up all night working on it, never sleeping. I got to the part about Beverly's wedding and the speeding Jag coming around the corner. "Then I dropped out of school and came to New York" — the water had grown cold by now — "and you know the rest."

Mitch reached across me to pull the plug and turn on the tap. "That's really hard, Billie," he said. The hot water splashed into the tub, a burst of steam warming the liquid around us.

He turned me then, so he could see my face. "But you're beautiful too. And talented."

"Talented? At what?"

He stared at me, as if I was missing something so obvious he didn't think it needed to be put into words. "Last I heard, you were the girl with the perfect palate, the only stranger Sal Fontanari has ever allowed to work in his precious shop." He turned off the tap, and in the silence his voice was louder. "You're a talented writer too. And, if I'm not mistaken, you're about to put a book together. You sound pretty good to me." He leaned back in the tub and closed his eyes. "I'm so comfortable, but we should get going. Let's meet at The Pig for dinner tonight, okay? I've got a lot to do before we go to Akron."

"You're coming with me?" When did that happen? Was it even a good idea? We were so new, and I had no idea what I'd find there. "Aren't you busy with . . ." I stumbled before I got the words out. "Pickwick House?"

"I am busy." He picked up my left foot and massaged the sole. "But I'd like to help."

"I could take Sammy."

"That" — he dropped my foot — "would be a terrible mistake. Consider how much more useful I'll be."

"Why is that?"

"Because" — he picked up my right foot and began to massage it, sending ripples through my body — "Sammy has no idea how to do this kind of research."

"And you do?"

Now he dropped my right foot. "That's what historians do: research. Do you even know where you'll begin?"

"What would you suggest, oh, great historian?"

He was unperturbed. "Go to the library. Ask for the old phone books. Begin with the forties and work your way forward. Look up the address of everyone she mentions in

514

the letters."

"That's a lot of people. Swans, Strohs, Cappuzzellis . . ."

"Don't forget mean Miss Dickson. She might prove very useful. Or not. Research like this is time-consuming. And you'll hit mostly dead ends. But that's how you do it."

"Then what? Knock on doors? Ask if anyone remembers a family that used to live there seventy years ago?"

"No." His voice was matter-of-fact, as if anyone with a brain would know this. "First you call."

"Old phone numbers? That's insane!"

"You'd be surprised." He'd gone back to my left foot. "I've called seventy-five-year-old phone numbers and hit the jackpot first try. Akron being a small town is a bonus; a house will often stay in the family for many generations. You could get lucky and save a lot of time. C'mon, take me with you. Besides . . ."

I looked at him, expecting a little romance. What Mitch said was, "Didn't you say Mrs. Cloverly lives in Cleveland? Close to Akron? I want to meet her."

A TRICK OF THE MIND

I walked up Essex, noticing how the neighborhood changed once I crossed Delancey. As I moved north, the old establishments become more hip, hardware stores and bodegas morphing into bakeries, boutiques, and gourmet ice-cream emporiums. The pedestrians I passed kept getting younger. It was warm but still April, and the people who'd left home without their coats were hugging their elbows, pretending they weren't cold.

My phone was buzzing in my pocket, and when I pulled it out I found six messages. Three were from Aunt Melba. One was from Dad. One was from Jake, who had somehow heard that I'd quit. And the most recent was from Sammy: "Come at once! Breakfast awaits. Plans must be made."

I decided not to bother changing and kept walking uptown. By the time I got to Sammy's, it was almost ten, and I couldn't tell if he and Anne were just starting breakfast or if they'd been there for hours, eating toast and jam. Anne sat at the foot of the table, holding Sammy's grandmother's sterling teapot as if she'd been born with it in her hands.

"Did you get the job?" I asked, taking a seat.

"Of course." She handed a cup across the table; it clattered musically against its translucent saucer. "Mr. Pickwick was extremely pleased when I offered to catalog the letters. His lawyers apparently think it will prove a tax advantage, and normally he'd have to pay a handsome fee for a job like this."

"So the letters will be saved?"

"Indeed." She smiled serenely.

Sammy sat at the other end of the table, wearing his Chinese gown. Fresh cinnamon buns steamed before him. He held out the plate.

"I had breakfast with Mitch."

Sammy smiled benignly at this, nudging the plate in my direction. "*Pazzesca!* These are irresistible."

"No, really, I'm not hungry."

His hand hovered over the plate, and then he took another for himself. "What are your immediate plans?"

"I'm going to Ohio tomorrow. Come with me?"

Sammy shuddered and put down the bun. "I have no desire to fly in one of the minuscule planes that will undoubtedly convey you there. I have no desire to spend my time poking around a dismal provincial metropolis. And as I assume that Mitchell will be accompanying you, I have no desire to be a third wheel. In any case, I very much doubt that you will unearth Lulu."

"You're probably right." There was no reason to believe she would have stayed there. "But we still might find out where she is."

"Precisely!" He aimed the half-eaten cinnamon bun in my direction. "Should Lulu still be whinnying with us, I will pounce on a plane the moment you discover her whereabouts. You have my solemn promise."

"I wish I could come along." Anne frowned slightly across the table. "Unfortunately, I have a great deal of work to do here. I intend to start immediately; I'm not about to give young Mr. Pickwick a chance to change his mind."

"What do you expect to find?"

"No mystery there: ordinary people writing about their ordinary lives. But those are

518

precisely the documents that tend to be discarded. It's what I find so thrilling about this project; quotidian letters can tell you far more about real life than the work of any scholar."

"You're doing this for Bertie, aren't you?"

She lifted her chin. "Why would you think that?" The suggestion obviously annoyed her. "History is the story we tell the future about the past, and we have an obligation to get it right. A chance like this comes along once in a blue moon." She gazed at her distorted reflection in the silver teapot. "On a professional level, I'm thrilled to have an opportunity to comb through these documents. But on a personal level . . . well, working is the only thing that keeps you young."

I glanced over at Sammy; I hadn't given any thought to what the end of my job might mean for him. What would he do now? He must have been thinking something similar, because he cleared his throat and looked at Anne. "Might I perhaps be of some assistance?"

"I've been counting on it." Anne said this so easily you would have thought they'd known each other all their lives. "You'll find that historical research is extremely sooth-ing. When you spend all day among old

519

papers, the people come alive for you, and you begin to see the present through different eyes. You'll see. You view young people knowing that this is only one moment in time and it's passing very quickly. It's comforting. You begin to understand that time is no more than a trick of the mind; some days I'm convinced that my young self is still here, somewhere, just walking down a different street."

That thought stayed with me the whole way home. The sun was directly overhead now, so there were no shadows. I liked thinking of Genie walking down some other street in a parallel universe, tossing her hair in the wind. As I waited for a light to change, I tried to fast-forward to the future, tried to imagine myself as an old lady. What would this corner look like? Would there still be cars? What would people wear? The elasticity of time made me dizzy, and I was glad to reach Rivington, where Ming was pleating dumplings in the window of his shop. He looked up and waved, solidly in the present, and it brought me back.

I had a lot to do when I got home. But first I had to call Aunt Melba.

"I was so involved with telling you that I'd quit that I forgot to tell you that I got a haircut. And contact lenses. Wait, I'm taking a picture." I turned the phone around, smiled, and took a short video, scanning from top to bottom. I pressed "Send" and listened to the sound of the picture flying through space.

There was a waiting silence, and then something that sounded almost like a sob. "Oh, Billie!" Aunt Melba's voice cracked. "Look at you! You look fantastic! And where'd you get those clothes?"

"Do you like them?"

"Like them? No, I don't like them. I *love* them. It's how I'd dress if I were a little younger. Who put that outfit together for you?"

"Hey." I found that I was annoyed. "I'm not that pathetic. *I* put my outfit together."

"Of course you did!" The triumph in Aunt Melba's voice erased my irritation. "I always knew you'd have your own style if you'd only learn to trust it." There was pride too. "Wait until your father sees this video. Let's surprise him! We could come this weekend —"

"I'm not sure I'll be back from Akron. I don't know how long I'll be there. It all depends what I find."

She sighed, disappointed. But then she said, "Probably just as well. I think Bob's traveling tomorrow too. But let us know the minute you get back. Seeing you like this is going to make him so happy. And email me your itinerary, okay? Just so we know where you are. You know we're here if you need us."

Aunt Melba's reaction was what I'd expected. Counted on. But until last night, when Mitch had talked about his family, I hadn't realized my luck. He hadn't said much, but it was enough to let me know he'd never taken love for granted. I always had. Genie had left me, but she had not left me alone. How could I not have known how important that was?

I Googled flights to Cleveland, excited about the trip. Still, in the back of my mind I kept wondering if it was a good idea to take Mitch with me. We were so new.

The question stayed with me all afternoon as I planned. Akron felt familiar. I could picture Lulu's house on Lookout Avenue as I printed out the map of Elizabeth Park Valley. I put it into a folder, along with maps of North Hill. I plotted a route to St. Anthony of Padua Church, circled North High, and Google-mapped the way to the old Goodyear Airdock and the main library downtown. I even mapped the route to Mrs. Cloverly's place on the east side of Cleveland. It was called Wade Manor, which made me smile. Such a grandiose name for a trailer park! I tucked the folder under my arm, changed into the chiffon dress, loving the way the fabric whispered around me, and left the apartment to go meet Mitch.

I detoured to Fontanari's. It was almost closing time when I got there, and I pushed through the jostling crowd, making my way forward. Gennaro was waiting patiently near the front, and his eyes grew wide when he saw me. Without a word he took my hand, tucked it into his bent arm, and walked me formally up to the counter.

He cleared his throat loudly. Sal didn't look up. "I know you're there, Gennaro. I'll get to you next, my friend. That's a promise." Gennaro cleared his throat again. Sal looked up. "What?" His voice was irritable now. He looked directly at Gennaro, who simply pointed at me.

For the first instant Sal didn't recognize me. Then he made a theatrical gesture, hand to his heart, and pretended to fall down in astonishment. "Willie! You got your hair cut!"

Rosalie emerged from the back kitchen, looked me over, pulled me behind the counter, and spun me around so she could see the back. "And she got new clothes!" she chided her husband.

"I noticed," he said. He was clearly not impressed.

But Rosalie was taking it all in. "They make her look so . . ." I waited while she searched for the right word. Crazy, maybe? Hip? Nah, not a Rosalie word. New York? Possible. California? Also possible. The word she chose rocked me back on my heels. "Feminine." She gave Sal an arch look.

"If you say so." Sal's voice was skeptical. "I thought she looked fine before." He turned back to the customers, who were growing restless. "Coming, coming."

I stayed to help with the last-minute rush, and when the final customers had reluctantly departed, I told Sal and Rosalie that I was no longer employed by Pickwick Publications. "I'm going to Akron," I said. "And —"

"— and you have a new boyfriend." The words came rushing out of Rosalie's mouth before I had a chance to say them.

"Do we know him?" Sal demanded.

"Of course we do." Rosalie gave him another one of those looks. "Didn't Mr. Complainer reappear the other day? And haven't I been telling you he was perfect for Wilhelmina?"

I stared at her, amazed. "But I haven't

524

even told you who he is!"

Sal turned to me. "Are you saying she's wrong? That it's not Mr. Complainer?" I shook my head and laughed. "Rosie doesn't need to be told." Sal's voice held pride, love, and admiration. "Somehow, she always knows."

"So go." Rosalie pushed me toward the door. "What I know now is that you're meeting him for dinner. And I'm guessing that you're late."

Sal handed me a twenty. "Take a cab," he said.

Climbing into the taxi, I thought of the first time I'd made the trip between Fontanari's and The Pig and how Sal had said so contemptuously, "A cab? To go a couple miles?" They'd been the longest two miles of my life.

Mitch was sitting at the bar when I arrived, and when he turned and saw me, I remembered what Lulu had said about Mr. Beard: "I thought that when people spoke of someone's face 'lighting up,' it was merely a figure of speech."

He stood and leaned down to kiss me — when I was not with him, I forgot the sheer solid presence of the man — and I tasted gin. He held up his glass. "Want one?"

The taste was so seductive. With the first

sip, I remembered that I hadn't eaten anything but a bite of pancake, but it was already too late, and the liquor was rocketing straight to my brain. Why be cautious? I took another sip, and another.

"The Pig won't run out of gin." Mitch took the glass from my hand. "You're drinking as if you're afraid this is the last martini on the planet."

"It tastes so good." Feeling reckless, I pulled the olive from the drink and sucked the gin from it.

"So what time's our plane?" Mitch moved closer and pressed his leg against mine. He was looking at me curiously in the dim twilight of the bar. "Right now your eyes look almost violet. Does that scare you?"

"Scare me?"

"You said your sister had violet eyes."

I took my martini back. "She did. But why would that scare me?"

"Don't you sometimes worry," he said softly, almost tentatively, "that you'll turn out like your sister?"

I knew the liquor had gone to my head then, because I couldn't understand what he was saying. Be like Genie? As if. If only. There was no way, not ever, that was possible.

"I don't know what you mean."

"The drugs."

"Drugs?" Mitch was speaking a foreign language. I needed subtitles. "When did I say anything about drugs?"

"You didn't. Maybe I misunderstood you." He ran his hands through his hair, the words coming so reluctantly that I knew he wished he hadn't brought this up. "But what you said . . ."

"Are you out of your mind? Genie would never touch drugs!"

Mitch stroked his beard, and I could see he was being careful as he reconstructed the conversation in his mind. "You said she drove down to Santa Barbara a lot but that you were never sure why."

"She did." I remembered how frightened I'd been when Genie went off to college, how I'd dreaded being left behind. I'd expected to close the bakery, and even when we kept it open, I was always sure she'd get tired of the long drive down from Berkeley. But there she was, every other weekend, almost as if she'd never left. "What does that have to do with drugs?"

"You said" — he was still speaking with slow deliberation — "that Genie stayed up all night while you were making that wedding cake. You said when you got up in the morning, she was in the kitchen, still making flowers. You said she was always edgy. And that she was the one who needed the money. You said she went to the bathroom a lot. It sounded like you thought she was using cocaine."

"Of course I didn't think that!" I stared at him, incredulous. "Where on earth did you get that idea? Genie never did drugs! She graduated summa cum laude, for Christ's sake!" The rage and turmoil were making my heart beat very fast.

"Okay." He was swiveling uncomfortably on his bar stool. "Then I did misunderstand what you were saying. All I meant about not becoming like your sister was that it must have been quite a strain for her, always having to work at being so perfect."

"Genie didn't have to work at it!" Mitch made little hushing motions with his hands as people turned to look at us, and I realized that I was shouting. I lowered my voice. "It was just how she was. She did everything well. And believe me" — I glared at him — "if she were here, you'd fall in love with her. Like every other man she ever met."

Mitch took a drink of his martini. "You don't know me well enough to be sure of that." He put the glass down. I could see him trying to control himself. "Are you even aware that you insulted me? I tell you that I love you, and you say I'd really rather have your sister? Can you hear yourself?" The muscles in his face worked, but his voice went very quiet. "I'm sorry, Billie. The truth is, I have no idea if your sister was doing drugs. And, frankly, it's not my business. Forgive me if I'm being presumptuous, but I think that somewhere, deep down, you've got bigger issues with your sister than just missing her because she died too young."

In that moment I absolutely hated him. "I do not have issues with my sister! You're the one who made it up, dredged it out of your own stupid subconscious."

"You know best." He sounded tired. "But I can't help feeling that you're competing with a ghost."

I pushed my stool away from the bar. "I've got a lot to do before I go to Akron. And, no, I don't want you to come with me."

"No surprise there." He pulled out his wallet and put a couple of bills on the bar. "It's clearly something you want to do alone. That's why you've picked this ridiculous fight."

Out of the corner of my eye, I could see Thursday setting a plate of chicken-liver toasts on the bar. She gave it a shove, her aim so accurate that it came skidding to a halt in front of me. I picked one up and took a bite.

"Hungry?" Mitch had caught me. "I guess you fall out of love pretty easily."

I flinched. "You think you know so much about me, Bernard Mitchell." I was speaking between gritted teeth. "Well, you don't. But I know something about you. You're the little 'M' boy in a 'B' family, and it hurts." I saw the words register on his face. How had we gotten to bitterness and rage so quickly?

"You're half right." He said it softly. "I am the family misfit. I always will be. And you're right: It's a lonely feeling. But the thing is, I deal with it."

Mitch had trusted me with his story, and I'd used it against him. I'd betrayed him in the easiest, cheapest way. "I wish I hadn't said that." I pushed the plate of toasts away.

"It's just as well you did; I'd rather be angry than sad. It's easier." He stood up. "Good luck in Akron. I hope you find what you're looking for. I hope . . ."

He stopped himself, turned, and left.

AKRON

I tried not to obsess about Mitch on the flight. It helped that we flew through stormy skies. The woman next to me grabbed my hand, clutching it so hard her knuckles went white. I tried thinking about Lulu's father and how the pilots used turbulence to make ice cream, but my mind kept going back to Mitch.

Why had what he'd said made me so furious? I remembered the rage that had gone shooting through me the instant he'd said Genie was doing drugs. I'd felt as if he'd violated my sister in some horrible way, and I couldn't forgive him for it. It was as if he'd stolen something from me. And he had: He'd destroyed the image I carried in my head, replaced it with someone I did not recognize. Last night I'd thought I was angry about what he'd done to Genie, but that wasn't what had made me so mad: It was what he'd done to me.

He was wrong about Genie, of course, but that had been my fault. I'd told the story wrong, led him down a false path. What else had he said? That I'd insulted him by claiming he would have fallen for her? Maybe he was right; maybe this time was different. Maybe for the first time in my life I'd met someone who would pick me over Genie. I thought about that long night in his apartment, how perfectly in sync we were, how comfortable we'd been together. Not just our bodies but our minds. It had felt so right.

The plane dropped suddenly, taking my stomach with it. My neighbor's hand dug into mine, and when it jerked me into the present, it was a relief.

"I think I'm going to be sick," my neighbor moaned. I reached for the paper bag in the seat-back pocket, but she shook her head. She had paled to the shade of paper. "Talk to me; please just talk to me."

Without realizing quite what I was doing, I channeled Sal and began to talk about Fontanari's: the customers, the cheeses, the streets of New York. I was still talking when we landed.

The plane filled with the sound of clapping, hooting, and whistling. It was such a relief to be on the ground. I helped my seatmate weave a wobbly path down the aisle. Outside, she turned to give the plane a last, loathing look. "I'm driving back to New York."

It was a cool gray morning, and I threw my suitcase into the rented Camry and followed the signs from the Cleveland Hopkins Airport to Akron. It took only forty-five minutes to reach the city, reminding me that Lulu's Akron was a pre-highway town, where antique cars and rationed gas had turned small distances into major obstacles.

I turned off the highway, driving slowly through a city that felt old and exhausted, lacking the energy for change. Elizabeth Park Valley was pretty, the streets winding past neat, tidy houses that looked as if they'd grown organically among the trees, each one individual, distinct. A small square of yard was laid out in front of every house, some enclosed by unfriendly fences, others open, inviting. Lulu's house no longer had the flagstone pathway the postman had used when he brought his letters from the war department, and the grape arbor was gone, but it was still a charming small-town American place, straight out of a black-and-white TV show. I convinced myself that if I squinted I could almost see Lulu banging the screen door, books in her arms, Tommy at her side, setting off for school.

I followed them in my mind as I drove to North High. It was a good uphill walk; they would have had plenty of time for talking. But when I reached the school the image faded, and I drove disconsolately around a vast parking lot, staring at the enormous brick buildings that made it look more like a college campus than an urban high school. These buildings were new, and in this large modern complex I couldn't imagine Lulu. I looked at the leaden sky, feeling the air grow thick around me; it was going to rain.

I drove slowly back toward Lulu's house, skirting the freeway as I went up one curving hill and down another. I headed toward North Hill, expecting to find Little Italy, but as I approached Tallmadge Avenue the buildings became drearier and more commercial. I drove past tire stores, thrift shops, and storefront churches. Italian North Hill seemed to be a thing of the past, and I was afraid that the changing demographics would have transformed St. Anthony's into a Baptist church, a synagogue, or a mosque.

But the church was still there, the modest building dwarfed by its large, empty parking lot. Mine was the only car, and when I got out I found myself walking up a sloping wheelchair ramp. The door was locked, and

I made my way around the building, trying to find another way in.

One small side door was open, and I crept into the darkened building, inhaling the scent of candle wax and hope. As my eyes adjusted, I saw that the interior was made entirely of inlaid marble, and as I took in the colors — cream, red, yellow — I had a brief moment of wishing Mitch were here to see this. He'd know where each stone had been quarried. I found myself counting the colors, saving the story to tell him later. I'd gotten to thirteen before I stopped. There would be no later.

I walked toward the altar, trying to recall what Lulu had said about midnight Mass. She'd come with the Cappuzzellis, and I closed my eyes, trying to see them sitting here in a church filled with candles and choir music. It must have been something wonderful. Then I remembered that Mother had been here too — and how surprised Lulu had been that she liked the service. In those days it would have been in Latin. Had Mr. Jones been with them? I thought he had.

There was a rustling beside me, and I opened my eyes to find a pair of elderly nuns surveying me with kind and curious eyes. When I asked if they remembered a family called Cappuzzelli from the 1940s, they smiled, looked at each other, then shook their heads. "We were not here at the time you're speaking of," said the first nun in a whisper. "That was in the time of Fathers Marino and Trivisonno."

"None of our sisters were here either," said the second nun.

"Emidio would have known," whispered the first nun. "He opened his pizza parlor back in the fifties, you know. But he is with Our Lord. He was over ninety."

"She should go ask at DeVitis."

"Yes. You should go ask at DeVitis. It's not far."

Driving to DeVitis & Sons deli, I had fantasies of an old man who would hand me chunks of warm mozzarella and regale me with tales of Cappuzzellis past and present. Instead, there was a fat teenager behind the counter, and when he asked what I wanted, I almost said, "Not you." I left with a very large sandwich wrapped in white butcher paper.

I sat in the Camry, devouring every bite of an enormous, garlicky meatball hero drenched in tomato sauce and sprinkled with cheese. It was delicious. Then I licked my fingers, remembered to text Aunt Melba with my itinerary, started the car, and headed for the Akron public library.

Cappuzzellis began to fade from the Akron phonebook in the fifties, and by the sixties not a single one remained. I wondered where they'd ended up. I imagined Mrs. C. making pasta for a group of grandchildren, then remembered that Massimo, Mauro, and Mario would have grandchildren of their own by now. I moved on, looking up Swans and Strohs, Joneses and Dicksons, writing all the numbers down. Then I left the library; the calls could wait until tomorrow. I'd promised Mrs. Cloverly I'd be there in time for tea.

Mrs. Cloverly's neighborhood was grander than the one Lulu had grown up in and much more urban. Looking for a trailer park, I drove right past the Wade Manor, then circled back and almost passed it a second time. The last thing I'd expected was this stately old hotel; the ornate lobby could have doubled as a set for *Brideshead Revisited,* and it made me hastily reconsider everything I thought I knew about Mrs. Cloverly. I'd suspected, almost from the start, that the failed recipes were a lonely old lady's excuse to reach out to the world, but I'd been certain she needed the small checks we sent her way. From the looks of this place, probably not.

The doorman summoned a uniformed porter. "Please escort Mrs. Cloverly's guest to her suite," he said grandly. The porter led me to an elevator even more luxurious than the lobby, all gilded wood, with a velvet sofa for anyone who preferred to ascend in seated splendor. When the elevator creaked to a stop, the porter opened the door and led me down one long, thickly carpeted corridor after another. They were lined with wooden doors that bowed outward, and when I tapped one lightly, it rang like a muted drum. "Those are old." The porter stopped. "Don't see them anymore. It's a double door with shelves inside. See" — as he pulled one open, I thought how much Mitch would have liked this — "it opens from out here so we can slide deliveries in. In the old days it was glass bottles of milk and cream. Nowadays it's mostly medicine. These may be the last ones in the world."

He moved on and tapped respectfully on a door farther down the hall. "In the twenties, this was the finest hotel between New York and Chicago." He tipped his hat and vanished quietly down the carpeted corridor. I braced myself as the door inched slowly open.

The woman standing there resembled the Mrs. Cloverly of my imagination as much as the Wade Manor resembled a trailer park. I took in this small poodle of a woman and stepped backward.

"Billie!" Her platinum hair was all curls, her small face was fully made up, and her perfume was strong. She gave me a limp hug, then pulled away so she could see me. "You're not at all the way I imagined you."

"You took the words right out of my mouth." We both laughed a little nervously. "What did you imagine?" I asked it quickly, before she could ask it of me.

"I'm embarrassed now." She gave me a coy look. "But I never thought that you'd be so pretty." She eyed me up and down, as if trying to replace the Billie in her head with the one who stood before her. "I thought you'd be plump and rather unkempt. I imagined glasses. To be honest, dear, you sounded very nice but rather . . . hapless. What could I have been thinking? Come in, come in."

Mrs. Cloverly led me into an airless living room crowded with a lifetime's accumulation of goods. The theme was blue and white, and every ornate piece of furniture shouted "quality." I was beginning to understand that nothing I'd thought about Mrs. Cloverly had been right. There were silver-framed photographs on every surface, and when she went off to make tea, I walked slowly around the room, discovering her at various stages of her life.

She had been pretty, and in every picture her husband was gazing proudly over at her, seemingly dazzled by his luck. There were no children in any of the pictures, but as the couple aged, the look on his face never varied. Even as an older man, Mr. Cloverly maintained an expression of slightly stunned pride.

Mrs. Cloverly returned carrying a large silver tray, which she set on a Louis XIV coffee table. When she saw that I was admiring the pictures, she emitted a deep sigh. "Elton passed away fifteen years ago, but I still miss him every minute of every day. Come sit down."

She handed me a cup decorated in a fussy flower pattern and passed a plate of madeleines. "Have one." She smiled proudly. "I made them myself."

"Uh, no thanks, Mrs. Cloverly." I stared at the plate. The little cakes looked nice enough, and they smelled wonderful.

She laughed. "Call me Babe — all my friends do. And please do try a madeleine." She thrust the plate in my direction. "You might be surprised." There was no gracious way to refuse, so I reached for one and took a polite bite. Babe was watching me intently, and I was careful with my face. But the cake was delicate and airy, the flavor rich, buttery, not too sweet. "It's delicious!" I could not manage to keep my voice neutral.

Babe laughed again, delighted. "Surprised?"

I blushed and nodded.

"Well, dear" — she held up the plate again, and I took another madeleine — "until Elton passed on, I'd never known a moment of loneliness. I'd never even slept alone, not one night in my entire life. When I was growing up, my sister Susie and I shared a bed, and after I was married, Elton and I were never apart. But that wasn't the worst. The morning after he died, I woke up and didn't know what to do with myself. I was at a complete loss. Elton loved to eat, you see, and I'd filled my days with cooking."

"So you can cook?"

"Oh, yes." Babe displayed not a trace of embarrassment. "I'm quite good." She stopped, staring across the table, and I knew she was not really looking at me. "It was what I could do for Elton, and I always did my best."

The voice was the same, but I couldn't reconcile Babe with the dithering Mrs. Cloverly I had known on the phone. It was oddly disconcerting, listening to her voice and seeing this person. "Can I ask you something?"

She inclined her head, a queen granting a favor.

"Did you actually cook any of those recipes you called about?"

"Of course I did!" Babe was indignant. "Let me just go get those English muffins." She returned carrying a plate covered with small rocklike lumps. The words that floated into my mind were "horrid little hockey pucks."

"Take one," she urged. "I know a bad recipe when I see one." She picked up one of the rocks and turned it in her palm. "And now that Elton's gone, this is how I amuse myself. I have no one to cook for."

"No friends?"

"Gone." She waved a ring-covered hand, indicating a host of departed friends standing somewhere offstage. "All of them. We had no children, so there are no grandchildren either. I go to yoga every day and to the occasional concert. I attend lectures at the library. But let me tell you, longevity's not all it's cracked up to be, even when you have your health. Life's not much fun when you're the last one standing. I suppose I shouldn't have bothered you people at *Delicious!*, but it seemed harmless." She allowed a small moment to pass and then added, "The truth is, I could never believe that you took me seriously."

"How did it start?" I reached for another madeleine.

She looked pleased. "Oh, it was innocent enough." She patted an errant curl back into place. "One day, about a week after Elton died, I was feeling very low, and I decided to bake a cake just to cheer myself up. I didn't have much in the way of ingredients, and I was too upset to go to the store. But I found a recipe that called for powdered milk and margarine, which I always have on hand for an emergency. I wasn't expecting much, but the results were extremely disappointing, so I called to complain. Talking to that young woman — her name was Victoria — cheered me right up. So the next week, when I got lonely, I deliberately looked for a bad recipe and called again. After a year or so I ran out of the truly vile recipes; that's when I began to make substitutions. It was my little game, talking to the young women at *Delicious!* It gave me something to look forward to."

"But you're nothing like that batty old woman who calls the magazine!"

543

"Thank you." She rubbed her lips together. "Thank you very much, dear. But, don't you see, that was the fun of it! The recipes got sillier and sillier, but you never questioned them. If you want to know what I think, it's that young people have such contempt for the old that you'll believe any foolish thing we do. In some sense, you might say that you made me up. I was exactly what you were expecting."

My face got red as I remembered Jake saying he'd be eating out on that story for weeks. I don't know what Babe saw on my face, but something made her stand up abruptly on her tiny feet. "Come with me." She held out a hand. "I want to show you something."

She was leading me toward the kitchen, and I had a horrible moment of thinking she was going to ask me to cook with her. I hung back, making up excuses, but she stopped before we got to the kitchen door. "This used to be a hotel" — she gestured toward the kitchen — "and the kitchens weren't intended for serious cooks. I can't begin to fit all my equipment in there." She flung open a door and switched on a light, revealing a large, square pantry stuffed with pots, pans, and utensils.

"You should open a store!"

What looked like dozens of cake tins were stacked in neat rows of diminishing size. There were dozens of pie plates and muffin molds galore. Fish poachers in three sizes lounged along one shelf, while another held tagines, beautiful ceramic Japanese rice cookers, and at least ten woks.

"When I told you" — she was reaching for a box — "that people were always giving me cooking equipment, I was telling the truth." She extracted a stringed instrument that resembled a medieval lute. "I bet you've never seen one of these."

"Actually, I have." I took it from her. "It's a chitarra for handmade pasta. We sell them at Fontanari's. Do you ever use it?"

"Of course." She was pulling down another box. "There's nothing here I haven't used. But I prefer my good old pasta machine." She pulled a battered object with a well-worn handle out of the box. "Elton did love his pasta. . . . Why, whatever is the matter?" She was following my eyes. "What are you looking at?"

"It's nothing." But my strangled voice gave me away. I was staring at the label on the box. In bright red script, it said, *The Cleveland Cookshop.* And underneath, in smaller letters, *Lulu Taber, Proprietor.*

Babe looked at the box. "I told you that

people were always giving me presents, didn't I, dear? A bit irritating, if you want to know the truth; how much equipment can one person use? I was constantly returning duplicate pots and utensils. When the shop closed — oh, ten years or so ago — I still had a large outstanding credit." She shook her head, annoyed. "I guess it was my own fault; some of those credits went back years. It was such a shame, their closing like that. . . ." She stopped, clearly puzzled. "Whatever have I said? You're giving me the queerest look."

"It's the proprietor's name." I couldn't stop staring at it. "The reason I'm visiting Akron is that I'm looking for a Lulu."

"Lulu's a common name around here," she said. "Or it was in my time. Every Lucy, Lucille, and Louise was shortened to Lulu. I must know" — she stopped to correct herself — "I must have known at least five Lulus."

"But the Lulu I'm searching for was very interested in cooking." I could imagine that Lulu might have opened a cookware shop. "It's probably not the one I'm looking for, but it can't hurt to check." I handed the box back, but not before I'd copied the address into my cell. "How long will it take me to get to Market Avenue?"

"The shop's gone," she protested, "I told you. There's no point in going over there." It was the querulous voice I knew so well, a reminder that Babe had invented that silly old lady for a reason. She was lonely, and she was loath to let me slip away.

"It's time I was leaving in any case." I turned toward the living room. "I need to check in to my hotel; tomorrow's going to be a long day. But I think I'll drive by Market Avenue if it's not too much out of the way. You never know; somebody might know something about the Cookshop. Or Lulu. It's worth a try."

"You'll stay in touch, won't you?" Her voice was anxious.

"Don't worry, Babe." I bent to kiss her. "I may no longer be at *Delicious!,* but you won't get rid of me so easily."

"Take a madeleine for the road." She wrapped one in a napkin and thrust it into my hand. "To remember me by."

A Whole Lot of Medicine

The girl working the counter at the Flying Mango had never heard of the Cleveland Cookshop. "Maybe you should ask over at the West Side Market?" She handed my coffee across the counter. "It's one of the oldest markets in America, and I've heard that some of the stalls have been in the same family for a hundred years." She looked at her watch. "They close soon. But it's only a couple blocks away."

I sat down at one of the small tables, remembering how the end of the day felt at Fontanari's, how eager we always were to get the last customers out the door. It could wait until morning. Babe was probably right: Even if I found someone who remembered the Cleveland Cookshop, chances were slim that it would have anything to do with my Lulu.

I pictured Babe, alone once more in her fussy little palace. She was nothing like the dithering old lady I'd been expecting, but the loneliness was real. It was pathetic — she'd had to make up an entirely different person just to reach out and make friends. The last line of that Randy Newman song Genie used to like kept running through my head: "You know I just can't stand myself; It takes a whole lot of medicine, for me to pretend that I'm somebody else."

The lyric was caught in my head now, and it stayed there like a stuck record, playing over and over as I thought about Babe. What if Lulu turned out to be like Babe? If that was the case, I'd rather not find her.

I finished my coffee, got back into the Camry, and headed toward the hotel. I was glad I'd decided to spend the night in Cleveland, but when I got to the Hyatt Regency I discovered an added bonus. As the valet took my car, I looked up and saw Cleveland's huge marble library right across the street. I'd go over first thing in the morning to see what I could find out about the Cleveland Cookshop.

I picked up my traveling bag and walked into the lobby, only to find a distressingly long line at the registration desk. I wanted a bath, a room-service burger, a huge pile of fries, and a mind-numbing television show. I didn't want to think. Somewhere in the back of my mind, Mitch and everything he'd said were waiting for me. I'd deal with it, I would, but not tonight. The song kept repeating in my head, and all I could think was how glad I was to be alone for the moment, among strangers.

I stood in line, so wrapped in this invisible cloak of solitude that I didn't register the voice saying, "Billie? Billie?" Nobody knew me here. Even when I turned and saw the attractive silver-haired man standing right behind me, it took a few seconds.

"Dad?" There was my father, still trim at fifty-something, wearing a conservative navy suit. I looked at his plaid tie, realizing it was the rather garish one I'd given him for his forty-third birthday. "What are you doing here?"

"Oh, Billie!" He seemed so stricken that I wished I'd been more welcoming. But what was he doing in my hotel? And why was he staring at me with that strange expression? "I'd forgotten" — his voice was so thick he could barely speak — "how beautiful you are."

He didn't even seem to register the haircut or the fact that I wasn't wearing glasses anymore. To him, I think, I'd always looked like this. "Me?" I said.

He reached out to touch the wisps of hair

around my face. "Don't you ever look in a mirror?"

I could feel the words engraving themselves on my heart, and for one moment I pitied Genie. They could never have meant to her what they meant to me; she had been too accustomed to them.

"Thanks, Dad." I grabbed his hand. "But what're you doing here?"

Dad looked down. Eyes on his shoes, he said, almost shyly, "I had a deposition in Chicago. And Cleveland's a short hop. Melba said you were here alone, and she thought you might welcome a little help." He offered an embarrassed half smile. "Did I do the wrong thing? It's been a while since you and I spent any time together."

Suddenly I was flooded with happiness. "Thanks, Dad." I leaned over and gave him a quick kiss. "I'm glad you're here."

"Really?" He let out his breath.

"Really." I was thinking about Mitch now — I couldn't help it — and what he'd said about his parents. When Dad reached to put his arms around me, tentatively, as if he was afraid I'd push him away, I pulled him close. "You're making me think that we might actually find her." My voice was muffled in his jacket.

I could feel his muscles losing their tension. "That's why I came." Behind us, a man coughed impatiently; the line had moved forward. It was our turn.

Dad handed over his credit card. "I'm paying." When I protested, he said, "You're unemployed now, remember?" We took our keys and walked to the elevator. "You hungry?" Dad punched the button for the eighth floor. "There are supposed to be some good restaurants nearby."

"It's been a long day. I was planning to hole up with room service and a juicy television drama. Want to join me?"

Dad looked at me, shoulders slumped with relief. "I was on a five forty-five flight to Chicago this morning, which means I've been up since three. Room service sounds like heaven."

We ate in Dad's room, each on our own full bed, passing a bottle of Merlot back and forth as we watched a rerun of *The Sopranos.* "Just like old times," Dad said, leaning back against the pillows. For a brief moment a shadow fell across the room, because of course it wasn't.

Dad fell asleep halfway through the show. I stayed awake until the end, then slid both our trays outside the door, removed his shoes, turned off the light, and left him sleeping in his clothes.

■ ■ ■ ■

In the morning, wearing jeans and a T-shirt, Dad looked ten years younger. "I was so tired last night, I never even asked whether you'd turned up anything useful." Dad poured milk into his cup of coffee.

"I might have." I dipped a slice of toast into my poached egg and took him through my day, ending with Mrs. Cloverly's box. "It's probably not the right Lulu — Babe says the name's very common around here — but still . . ."

"We begin with the box!" Dad sounded excited, and it hit me that he wasn't doing this only to be supportive; he was relishing the chase. Aunt Melba must have known that when she encouraged him to come.

"And if that turns out to be a dead end, we'll go back to Akron. But the box sounds very promising. What time does the library open?"

The main branch of the Cleveland Public Library, a distinguished temple to literacy, opened at ten. As we walked up the steps, past the imposing marble columns, I felt hopeful; the solid building was reassuring. The woman at the information desk was knitting a long green scarf, but she put her needles down and asked how she could help.

"I can certainly tell you about the Cleveland Cookshop. Any Clevelander could — it was a local institution. I learned to cook there; they used to give these classes for kids that were great fun. We all took them."

"You mean like cake decorating?" I said. Dad shot me a worried look. I patted his arm.

"No!" The librarian seemed almost offended. "None of that cutesy stuff. Mrs. Taber — she ran the Cookshop — didn't believe in that. She taught us how to make real food. After my first class, I went home and cooked dinner for my parents; I think I was ten or eleven, and I was very proud of myself. But she was mostly known for her foraging. She'd take us to parks or for walks along the lake, and we'd come back with enough food for dinner. It wasn't the usual mushrooms and watercress; it was weird stuff."

"Weird stuff?" Dad asked. "Like what?"

"Knotweed. Lamb's lettuce. Milkweed."

"Milkweed?" I hadn't meant to exclaim so loudly.

The librarian shot me a sympathetic glance. "I know it sounds odd, but it's really quite delicious. To this day I go out and col-

554

lect the floss in the autumn. It's the oddest thing; if you didn't know different, you'd swear it was cheese."

I squeezed Dad's arm, and he patted it in a don't-get-too-excited gesture. "Why did the shop close?"

The librarian looked down at the green scarf she was knitting. "I don't remember," she said slowly. "But I think it was something dramatic. Did the owner pass?"

"No!" Dad and I said it in unison, and the librarian's head jerked up. "Were you related to Mrs. Taber?"

"No." Again we said the word together. Dad added, "But we were hoping to meet her."

She took a pair of glasses out of a case. "I could be wrong." She put them on. "I remember that something happened, but I can't recall exactly what. Let me see what I can find." She stood up. "I'll just be a minute."

She returned empty-handed. "I was wrong." She sounded more cheerful. "There was a fire some years ago. The entire shop went up in flames, but as far as I can tell, no one was hurt. And I did find something that may be of interest to you: before the fire, Mrs. Taber made a donation to the library. Documents of some sort — they have yet to be cataloged, but we could call them in if you like. They're stored in our remote facility, so it will take a day or two. I've brought a request form, should you want to do that. But in the meantime, why not look up the fire in *The Plain Dealer*? It was eleven or twelve years ago, and I'm sure the paper ran a story. As I said, the shop was a Cleveland institution."

"In that case," I was thinking out loud, "there'd be an obituary if Mrs. Taber has passed away. Wouldn't there?"

"Without a doubt. The computers are over there. Good luck." She looked beyond us to the next person in line. "Can I help you?"

There was no obituary for Lulu Taber.

"But that doesn't mean she's alive." Dad was still typing, still scanning the screen. "She might have moved away. Wait" — his fingers stopped — "I think I've found something. Look at this. It's an obituary for a Peter Taber. Fourteen years ago. Maybe he's related."

Dad clicked a few times, and an elegant older man, quite thin, with white hair and a kind face, was staring out at us. I liked him immediately. " 'Doctor Peter Taber,' " read Dad, " 'is survived by Lulu Swan Taber' —"

"Lulu Swan Taber!" I shouted. Heads all

over the library swiveled toward us, frowning.

"— 'his wife of forty-six years,' " Dad continued, " 'three children, James Swan Taber of Cleveland, Joanna Taber of Manhattan, and Francesca Taber Cappuzzelli of Los Angeles, and eight grandchildren. The family asks that, in lieu of flowers, donations be made to the Food Bank.' "

"It's Lulu." I felt dazed. "She didn't marry Tommy. And she had three children!"

"Dr. Taber sounds like quite a guy." Dad was still reading. "He was a general practitioner, a published poet, and an authority on birds."

"We found her." I could not quite believe it. "We actually found her. She named her son for her father. And one of her daughters married a Cappuzzelli! I wonder which son? Oh, please, let her still be alive."

"There's no obit." Dad superstitiously touched the top of the wooden desk, banishing bad luck. "Let's see if the phone book can tell us anything."

Lulu Taber wasn't listed. "Well, she wouldn't be." Dad was still tapping the computer. "Widows rarely take the trouble to change the name on their utility bills. She probably left the phone in his name.

557

And . . ." He clicked a few more times. "Here he is! Dr. Peter Taber. Damn!"

I looked over his shoulder. "What?"

"Address and phone number both unlisted." Dad tapped some more, then let out a sigh of satisfaction. "There we go: the son, James S. Taber — address, phone number, the whole nine yards."

I sat down heavily in a chair. I felt slightly dizzy. It had taken Sammy and me months to locate Lulu's letters, and after our long, crazy chase, this seemed so fast. Dad and I had been in the library less than an hour. "We found her," I kept saying, over and over like a mantra. "We actually found her."

"Don't you think you're jumping the gun?" Dad was watching me, worry in his eyes. "We haven't really found her. We don't even know that she's alive."

"But now we know how to find out. She's not a ghost anymore." I shivered as I said this; I'd unconsciously used Mitch's word. "We know her name; we know what she did with her life; we know where to find her children. It's all happened so fast!"

"You sound disappointed." Dad took his fingers off the keyboard and sat back in the chair.

I didn't know what I felt. Excited and let down, both at the same time.

"I wonder how long it would have taken if you hadn't seen that box of Mrs. Cloverly's?" He was thinking out loud, but Dad had made his point. If I hadn't seen that old box at Babe's, we might have spent weeks looking for Lulu; it had been a fortunate shortcut. "What now, Sherlock Holmes?"

"Call James, I guess."

The library was no place to have a conversation, so we went outside and stood on the steps. It was a bright morning, and the light bouncing off the marble columns was dazzling. Somewhere, an answering machine clicked on. "The Tabers aren't home now, but you can leave a message for Clara, Jim, Pete, or Sophie, and we'll get back to you as soon as possible."

I didn't leave a message. "It would be good to know if Lulu's alive before we start throwing questions at her son. Let's go over to that market and see if we can find someone who knew her."

We crossed the street and walked through the Arcade, an ornate glass-covered Victorian building that had been transformed into an indoor mall. But half the shops were out of business, and our footsteps echoed mournfully through the beautiful empty space. Dad pointed to one of the boarded-up shops. "I imagine the market will be a lot like this. We'll be lucky if we even find anyone to ask about Lulu."

"I won't get my hopes up." I was remembering the shabby old public markets of New York, only recently making a comeback after years of neglect. We left the Arcade, walking north toward the market. "It'll be a miracle if anybody's there." As we walked down sparsely populated blocks, I was thinking about James Taber, wondering what I should say when we called. Would he even know about his mother's correspondence with James Beard? Deep in thought, I barely noticed that the streets were beginning to fill with people carrying bags of produce, and it was a shock to turn a corner and see the clock tower over the West Side Market and the streams of people pouring out its doors. From a block away you could feel the vibrant energy of the place, and by the time we walked into the huge, brightly lighted building, we were thrumming with anticipation.

Even so, the West Side Market, with its tiled and vaulted ceiling, came as a surprise. It was a beautiful old building, so filled with people munching, exchanging money, and exclaiming as they went from one well-stocked stand to another that we had to shout at each other to be heard. There seemed to be hundreds of purveyors, selling every imaginable edible from every corner of the world.

Dad squared his shoulders and began to walk purposefully through the market, a man on a mission, eyes taking in the various vendors. He looked at butchers, cheesemongers, fish men. Finally he strode toward a stall displaying a tangle of pink and brown sausages with strange, unpronounceable names. "Csabai kolbász." He struggled with the syllables. "Kielbas." He pointed to a weathered white-haired man in the adjoining stall. "Over there," he said. "We'll ask if he knows Lulu. He looks like someone who might." Above the man's head, a sign proclaimed, OUR FAMILY HAS BEEN SELLING SMOKED MEATS HERE SINCE 1912.

We approached the stall, and the old gentleman's faded blue eyes warily inspected us as he considered Dad's question. Then he picked up a pale-pink loaf, carved off a couple of thin slices, and handed them across the counter with gnarled fingers. "It's our secret family recipe. Lulu likes this; she never comes to the market without picking up some leberkäse."

Dad squeezed my shoulder so hard it hurt; the man had used the present tense! I took

561

a bite, and the flavor filled my mouth — pungent, slightly spicy, with the tang of onions and just a hint of . . . What was it? Marjoram! The taste was strong, primal, comforting.

"Never misses a week." The man handed me another slice. "She was here yesterday. She's loyal, is Lulu. It was a shame about her shop, but she had a good run. She doesn't complain." He looked across the counter, his pale eyes still penetrating.

It was the right moment; I could feel that. "Do you," I asked carefully, "know how we can find Lulu?"

Dad touched my arm softly, a suggestion of restraint.

But the old man was unfazed. "I must have her number here somewhere." He began riffling through little strips of paper on the counter behind the meat case. "Let me look. She doesn't live far, still in that place she and the doc bought years ago when they first came to Cleveland. Her kids keep trying to get her to move someplace more convenient — all those stairs! — but Lulu won't budge. What I say is, good for her."

He rummaged about, muttering to himself and shaking his head. "It's no use." He sounded apologetic. "Can't seem to find it.

Never call, myself; just stop in now and then on my way home."

"Then perhaps you could give us her address?" I hated the way my voice trembled.

"No trouble." Taking a flat stub of pencil from behind his ear, he turned one of the bits of paper over and wrote an address on the back. "Just over there on Bridge Avenue." He pointed out the door. "You tell her hello from Wally."

My hands were shaking so hard I couldn't close my fingers around the strip of paper he held out to me. Wally looked at me strangely. Then Dad's hand reached across my shoulder. "Good thing I'm here," he said drily.

STRUDEL

Lulu lived in a large colonial that sprawled comfortably across a corner lot, its faded bricks soaking up the sun. The house was surrounded by ancient trees, their branches spread across the roof; in summer it would be sheltered by a canopy of leaves. A crooked wrought-iron fence meandered casually around the house, protecting a large garden. The windows looking down on it were framed by black shutters, flung open so that we could see a big orange cat curled in a patch of sunlight on the second floor.

"I like the angle of that roof." Dad looked up at the single window just below the eaves. "I bet the kids fought over who got that room."

We strolled around to the side of the house and found a gate opening onto a little porch. "I wonder if the doctor had his office here?" There was a separate entrance. "It's certainly big enough. Patients could have come and gone without disturbing the family."

We walked around the corner, then back again, secretly hoping Lulu would open the door, let out the cat, take out the trash. But after a few minutes of this, Dad said, "The neighbors are going to think we're casing the joint."

The doorbell was a set of chimes, and a voice called out, "I'm coming, I'm coming." The footsteps coming toward the door were far too rapid for an old lady. I had a moment of doubt. Was this the right house?

But it was too late. The door was open, and a small, vigorous-looking woman in old blue jeans and a plaid shirt stood before us.

"Hello. Do I know you?"

It was Lulu. Almost exactly as I'd imagined her.

"You're Lulu Swan," I blurted out.

"I am." She stood calmly at the door, unperturbed by strangers. "Or at least I used to be. I've been Lulu Taber for a while now." She looked us over and said again, "Do I know you?"

I just kept staring, not quite believing we'd found her. Her face was quite round and still pretty, and she had a forthright air. She wore no makeup, but her face was almost unwrinkled and her back was very straight. The gray eyes were lively and intelligent, and her hair was thick, white, and cut off below the ears, as if she'd simply sheared it with a scissors. In her simple clothes, she looked almost boyish.

Words deserted me.

Dad stepped into the silence. "You don't know us." He held out his hand. "At least not yet. I'm Robert Breslin, and this is my daughter Billie. She's been trying to find you for quite some time."

She stood in the middle of the doorway for half a second and then stepped aside. "Come on in, then." She opened the door wider. "I'm in the middle of baking and I can't stop now."

Dad put out a hand to stop her. "You're going to let a pair of strangers walk into your house? Don't you even want to know why we're here?"

She turned to him. "Young man." I looked sideways to see how Dad was taking that. He seemed pleased. "As I see it, I have three choices. I can slam the door in your face, which would be rude. I can stand here and ask for credentials, but while you're giving them to me, my dough will dry out. Or I can trust my instincts. You don't strike me as serial killers. So, if you don't mind, we'll go into the house now and I can get back to my baking. Strudel won't wait!"

Walking briskly, she led us down a hall. I took in Early American furniture, old glass lamps with gleaming brass fixtures, hooked rugs. We entered a dining room dominated by a painting of a pumpkin patch. "I don't usually bake in here" — she reached for the rolling pin on the wooden table in the middle of the room — "but strudel requires a great deal of space. And this is the only round table in the house." She began to circle the table, rolling out the dough, stretching it thinner as she walked. "You have to keep rolling until you can read right through it." She was working with quick, efficient strokes. "I can talk while I work, though. Please sit yourselves down" — she gestured with the rolling pin — "and tell me again who you are."

Her eyes moved from the dough to me as we repeated our names. "And now I guess you'd better tell me why you're here." She was matter-of-fact, as if having strangers turn up at her door was an everyday occurrence.

"I've been working at *Delicious!*"

"Yes?" She looked down at the dough, continuing to roll. "I thought they closed the magazine."

"They did. But they kept me on to honor the *Delicious!* Guarantee. And one day . . ." I looked over at Dad, who smiled and nodded his head, urging me on. I took a breath and started again. "And one day I went up to the library and found a secret room."

Lulu kept walking around the table, rolling out the dough. "Yes?" Her voice was polite. Distant.

"It was filled with files and letters."

Lulu's feet came to an abrupt halt. She carefully set the rolling pin down on the table. "Letters?" she asked softly.

"Yes," I said. "And I found the ones you wrote to Mr. Beard during the war."

"Oh, my." She sat down suddenly, as if her feet had just come out from under her. "All of them?"

"I don't know if it's all of them. That's one of the things I wanted to ask. But there are quite a lot."

Lulu pushed her chair back and stood up decisively, rubbing the flour off her hands. "This is not going to be the best strudel ever made. But it will have to do; the dough's thin enough." With a few deft motions, she brushed the dough with melted butter, spread it with chunky poppy-seed paste, and rolled it up. Curling it into a ring, she set the cake on a baking sheet and disappeared into the kitchen. The entire operation had taken less than a minute.

When she reappeared, her face had undergone a subtle change, and the easygoing woman who met us at the door had become distant, wary. "How did you find me?" It was more accusation than question.

"It was Billie." Dad did not seem to have noticed Lulu's changed demeanor. "She's turned into quite the sleuth. But it was Wally who gave us your address." At that, her face relaxed, just a little.

"Oh. Wally." She hesitated for a moment, then made up her mind. "I'll put the kettle on." She went back into the kitchen.

When she returned, she had arranged her face into a tight, polite smile. She was carrying a tray with a teapot, cups, and a high-domed golden bread. "Is that Mrs. Cappuzzelli's panettone?" I was fishing, trying to lure back the Lulu who'd written all those letters. "The one you made when Marco died?"

Lulu started, and I noticed her hands shaking as she set the tray down. "Yes." She said it curtly. "I suppose you want the recipe." She cut three slices and shoved a plate at each of us. Her hands had steadied. I took a bite; the bread was sweet and airy, rich with eggs and laced with lemon and dried fruit. " 'We still have his memory.' " I was remembering the letter. "That's what Mrs. Cappuzzelli told you. And that you had each other."

Lulu's smile slipped; she appeared to be having a hard time controlling her face.

"I read that your daughter married one of the Cappuzzellis," I ventured, again trying to make contact with the Lulu I thought I'd known. "Whose son was it?"

"Massimo's son Lucas," she said stiffly.

"That must make you happy."

She gave me a cold stare. "Why would that make me happy?" She seemed to be hoarding her words.

"What I meant" — I was struggling now — "was that during the war you were like a member of the family. And knowing that you really had become part of her family would have pleased Mrs. C."

"We have no way of knowing how she would have felt." Lulu's words were cool and clipped. "Both the Cappuzzellis had passed on by the time Frankie and Lucas married."

Why was she making this so hard? With each passing minute, the Lulu I had known retreated a little further into the background, leaving this cool stranger in her place. I began to wonder if it would have been better if we had never found her. Maybe the Lulu of the letters no longer existed.

Desperate to bring her back, I pushed my luck. "Did you ever find out what happened to your father?"

The air in the room changed. Dad ran his fingers anxiously through his hair, looking horrified. Lulu dropped her fork, and in the silent room it clattered loudly onto the porcelain plate. "I'm sorry" — she was glaring at me now — "but I'm going to ask you to leave."

"Oh, no, please . . . I've come so far, I've been looking so long, and I have so many questions."

She watched the fork still vibrating on the plate, and I could feel her gathering her thoughts. Then she met my eyes. "I want you to go. Now. This is terribly upsetting. I don't know you, but you seem to think you know me. And for some reason you believe I owe you something." She hesitated for a minute, then balled her fists. "Who do you think you are, coming in here like this?" Her cheeks were flushed, her eyes flashed, and, despite her hostility, her spirit made me think of the young girl I knew. "Try to imagine how you'd feel! One fine day, without any warning, someone knocks on

571

your door and starts asking questions, churning up a past you'd just as soon forget."

I didn't know what to say.

Dad did. Moving smoothly into lawyer mode, he put his teacup down on the table and stood up. "Please forgive us, Mrs. Taber." His voice was filled with remorse. "You're quite right, we've been extremely thoughtless. We'll leave at once. But I wonder" — he stopped, glancing at me, as if asking my permission — "if we might take you to dinner? Not tonight, of course, but later, when you've had some time to get accustomed to the idea."

It was the perfect thing to say. Lulu looked up at him, seeming almost apologetic. "It's been quite a shock. You might have given me some warning. Called before coming."

"Of course we should have," soothed Dad. "Anyone would feel that way." He eyed me, silently urging me to chime in.

"I'm so sorry," I managed, trying to put myself in her place. We had come barging in. I looked straight at her, trying to mask my disappointment. I'd expected too much. "It was inconsiderate, coming in like this, throwing questions at you. It's just that . . ." I couldn't help myself. "You see, I've been reading your letters for months now, admir-

572

ing your courage, feeling that you'd become my friend. And I do feel that I know you. Or" — I gave her a rueful smile — "I did."

Her face relaxed. A little. Now that we'd agreed to leave, she seemed more comfortable. "I wonder if any of us ever really knows another person?" she replied, sounding wistful. In that moment I heard the voice of the Lulu of the letters. Then her voice hardened again. "I never imagined that Mr. Beard would save those letters."

This was hardly the time to tell her that Mr. Beard had not saved her letters. It might, however, be the moment to ask if she'd saved his. Giving me a warning look, Dad put up his hand, and before I had a chance to ask, he went rushing in. "Would you permit us to take you to dinner?" he repeated. "It would be an honor."

"Maybe," she said uncertainly.

"When do you think you might be ready for that?" he persisted.

"Give me a day or two." Lulu stood up.

"Tomorrow, then?" Dad was in full lawyer mode now, pressing his advantage.

"All right." He'd won. "Tomorrow. But let me make dinner for you." She gave Dad a mischievous smile and said bluntly, "I know you're going to ask a lot of fool questions, and I'd just as soon have the home advantage. How do I reach you?"

She showed us to the door, and when it had closed firmly behind us, Dad shook his head. "I blame myself." We could hear the bolt ram home. "I should have known better than to come rushing over here. Think how shocked you'd be if strangers showed up out of nowhere and started asking questions. And what on earth possessed you to bring up her father?"

"I knew it was a mistake the minute it was out of my mouth. I'd meant to wait, ease into it. But I couldn't help myself: I blurted out the thing I most wanted to know."

"Nobody ever suggested that you'd make a litigator." He gave me a lopsided smile.

"Did you think she was hiding something?" It had seemed so strange. "All that stuff about a past she'd rather forget?"

"Don't be silly." Dad shook his head. "If she had something to hide, she wouldn't have agreed to see us again. But, to tell you the truth, I don't understand why she did agree to it."

"Because you're so persuasive." I took his arm. "What now?"

Dad opened the car door. "I'm going back to the hotel to try to get some work done. And I've got to rearrange my schedule; staying until tomorrow wasn't part of the plan.

But let's have dinner tonight, okay? Melba gave me the name of some restaurant near the hotel. The Greenhouse Tavern — it's supposed to be good. I'll make a reservation. Eight okay?"

I left the car with the valet and went to my room to call Sammy. When I told him how Lulu had kicked us out, he heaved a melodramatic sigh. "How enormously distressing. I am overcome with chagrin. Had I envisioned the possibility of your operating with such an utter lack of finesse, I would have accompanied you and averted this disaster." He sighed again. "Imagine her sentiments!"

"But, Sammy, she said we were churning up a past she'd rather forget. It was almost like there was something embarrassing in her past."

"I imagine that there is," he said mildly. "Any soul who has survived to the age of eighty-two with nary a secret would be extremely dull. I, for one, would have very little interest in making their acquaintance. We all have something to hide. Do not neglect to procure an excellent wine to present upon your return. And I" — his voice became more cheerful — "shall dispatch a floral offering on your behalf."

Consoled by this happy thought, Sammy hung up.

With time to kill and no one to kill it with, I turned on my laptop.

Dear Genie,
    We found Lulu, and she is

She is what? I looked at the words on the screen and slowly erased them. My sister was dead. And now Lulu might be gone as well. After all this time I'd finally found her, but I'd stupidly expected her to be thrilled that I'd found the letters, excited to meet me. What now? The article would surely never happen. I had no job. And I'd ruined whatever relationship I might have had with Mitch. What was I going to do?

I put my head down on the varnished desk, feeling empty. I must have slept, because dusk had fallen when I woke, and my neck was stiff. I glanced at the clock radio — less than an hour until I had to meet Dad. I got up, gingerly rubbing the top of my back, trying to get the blood flowing.

I went into the shower, made the water as hot as I could stand, and stood for a long time, letting it pour over me. But the water brought a memory of Mitch, and I heard his words, over and over. "You're competing with a ghost." I turned off the water and dressed for dinner. My neck, at least, was better.

I found Dad at the bar, nursing a glass of Scotch, and I stood for a moment, watching from a distance. He was wearing his suit, and he looked solid, safe, dependable. I was glad to have him here. But the truth was that he'd always been there, every time I'd ever needed him. When my second-grade teacher called him in to discuss what she called my "persistent shyness," he'd caressed the top of my head and said, "When Billie has something important to say, she says it." Then he took me to La Super-Rica for tacos with extra salsa. As we ate them, he said, "You don't have to be like everyone else. You're the best you that ever was."

I slid into the seat next to him and said, quickly, before I could change my mind, "Was Genie doing drugs?"

He didn't look up from his drink. "Why are you asking?"

"You haven't answered my question." But he didn't have to; his face told the truth. "Did you know?" My words came out in a whisper.

He shook his head. "But I should have. All the signs were there." Suddenly he frowned. "Did you?"

"Of course not!"

"So what made you ask?"

"A . . ." I didn't know what to call Mitch, and I stumbled on the word. "A friend."

"A man friend?" Dad missed nothing.

"Yes. A man friend. When I told him about Genie, he said it sounded like she was doing drugs. I was shocked. I got angry and told him he was being ridiculous."

"And what did he say?"

"That he must have gotten the idea from what I'd told him."

"That's how obvious it was? A friend of yours, a stranger who never met Genie, could read between the lines? How could we have been so blind? Melba and I keep asking ourselves that, over and over again."

"But how do you know it's true?" I still had a tiny shred of hope.

"Remember Eli Pierce?"

I remembered Eli. Remembered sitting in Genie's room, watching her get dressed for the senior prom. That was the night she'd suggested keeping Cake Sisters going after she went off to college. I remembered my relief as Genie said, "It's not like I'm leaving for the ends of the earth," in her don't-be-stupid voice.

Then, from that deep place where I'd buried it, another sentence came bubbling up. "I could really use the money."

"What does Eli have to do with it?" I asked.

"He was arrested last year for dealing drugs, and it turned out he'd kept meticulous records of all his sales. Can you imagine anything more moronic? The prosecutor came to see me because Genie was one of Eli's best customers. He let me see the books; she'd been buying cocaine from him for four years. Just a little at first, but by the time she graduated college she'd built up quite a habit. It was all there in black and white. I managed to keep Genie's name out of it, but the evidence was indisputable."

"Oh, Dad." I could barely stand to see the pain on his face, and I hugged him, burying my face in his shoulder. "How horrible for you. You should've told me."

He kissed the top of my head. "You had enough troubles. Melba and I didn't think you needed one more."

"But maybe I could have helped you! At least I could have tried." They'd only wanted to spare me pain, but, still, it made me angry; they'd treated me like a child, kept me from sharing their grief. "We're family.

We need to help one another, and we shouldn't keep secrets. Especially one as big as this."

Dad lifted my chin so he could see my face. "You were so ready to blame yourself for Genie's death, and we thought knowing about the drugs would make it worse. Her death was an accident, but we keep wondering if the drugs were a contributing factor. You would've felt the same, and we wanted to save you from that. We weren't trying to hide anything from you."

"But you did hide it from me!"

Dad swiveled on his stool, turning away, and I knew I had to stop. I reached for his arm. "I know you wanted to protect me. Thank you for that." But I had to ask the next question, even if it hurt him. "Do you think we could have stopped her if we'd known?"

I could see him weighing his answer, wondering if he should tell me what he really thought. Finally he said, "If I'm honest, I have to admit that I don't really know. We could have tried. And I know this: Anything would have been better than nothing. But she hid it so well. She was such a paragon; everyone was always congratulating me for her grades, her talent, her industriousness. How do you know when someone as perfect as Genie's in trouble?"

"Maybe," I said, "you recognize the price of perfection." The words came flying out of my mouth, and I understood that they'd been with me ever since the fight with Mitch.

Then I saw the anguish on Dad's face and touched his arm. "You know everything you said to me after Genie died? How it wasn't my fault? I think you need to say them to yourself now. Nobody ever had a better dad. Genie and I were two lucky girls. You were always there for us. Always."

Dad drew me to him again, hugging me hard. "Thanks, sweetie," he said. "You're not so bad yourself."

"We have a lot more to talk about," I said, "but right now I need to make a phone call."

"Melba?" he asked.

"That call can wait till morning. This one can't."

Mitch was distant at first, limiting his answers to yes and no. But as I stumbled on, explaining that he'd been right, the iron finally went out of his voice. When I ran out of words, he said, "I'm going to ask you two questions, and I want you to be straight."

"Okay."

"Are you drunk?"

581

"Not this time. What else do you want to know?"

"If you are actually apologizing." I thought I heard the beginning of a smile in his voice, or at least the beginning of a thaw.

"Yes."

There was a small silence. Then Mitch said, "You know, I think I'd like to meet your father."

I woke up the next morning with a knot of pain centered somewhere in the middle of my chest. The signs had all been there, and I'd ignored them. Mitch was right: I hadn't wanted to know. Any more than I'd wanted to admit that Genie was dead. I pulled out my phone and dialed Aunt Melba.

When I heard her voice, I pictured her sitting in her green kitchen, surrounded by her daisies and the omnipresent halo of smoke. "Dad told me about the drugs."

"I know," she said. "I wish he hadn't; I don't see what good it will do you."

"It's not about doing good. I had a right to know the truth. And I think it might have been better for us — all of us — if we'd faced this together. Maybe I could have helped you. Did that ever occur to you?"

"Oh." She sounded so surprised. "You know, I forget sometimes that you're grown up. Forgive me, Billie. I'm sorry."

"Now I feel like I never really knew Genie. I'm trying to understand, but I can't. Why did she need drugs? She had everything."

"Apparently it wasn't enough." I heard Aunt Melba take a pull on her cigarette, holding the smoke for a moment. "Genie reminded me so much of my sister. So talented — and so dissatisfied. Like your mother, she held herself to very high standards. Impossible standards. Maybe it was too much for her too."

"What do you mean too?"

"No matter how well Barb did something, she always thought she should have done it better. It's not an easy way to live."

"But Genie did everything so easily! And everyone loved her."

"Billie, you were her little sister. No matter how she behaved, you thought Genie held up the sky."

There was so much heartbreak in her voice, and I thought it was as much for me as for Genie. And maybe a bit for herself too.

"Do you think there was anything that could have stopped her?" I don't know what I expected Aunt Melba to say or even what I wanted to hear. But her answer was totally unexpected.

"If you're asking if I think there's anything we could have done, from what I've read, probably not. The only one who could have stopped Genie was Genie. But I will tell you this, Billie Breslin, and it's something I know as well as I know anything in this world. If Genie had known how much her death would hurt you, I think she would have done anything to prevent your grief. She would have hated how hard this hit you. Hated it" — her voice broke — "even more than I do. And let me tell you, that's a lot."

"Oh, Aunt Melba." A great wave of tenderness swept over me. "I had no idea."

"Your father feels the same, you know. We love you very much." I sat there holding the phone, not knowing what to say next. And then, all at once, I did.

"Aunt Melba" — I hoped she could hear how much I meant this — "don't you think it's time you and Dad got married?"

TRUTH AND CONSEQUENCES

I lay in bed long after Aunt Melba hung up, clutching the phone to my chest like a stuffed animal, unwilling to get up and face the day. I was falling back to sleep when a knock on my door jerked me awake. "It's me." Dad's voice. "Mrs. Taber just called."

"Has she changed her mind?" I got up to let him in. "Decided she won't talk to us after all?"

"Not that." He walked in, clothes rumpled as if he'd been up for hours. "She'll see us, but she doesn't want to wait until tonight. She wants us to come this morning. Right now, in fact."

"I wonder why?"

"No use in speculating," he said. "We'll know soon enough."

Lulu came to the door looking so polished that it put me off; whatever she was about to tell us, she had prepared for very carefully. Today she wore a beautiful poppy-colored sweater over tailored gray wool slacks, and her hair had been curled into thick white waves around her face. Her lips were redder, and there was color in her cheeks. Yesterday she'd looked almost boyish; today she could have passed for one of those Fifth Avenue ladies who terrorized Maggie. "Good morning." She seemed almost formal. "Please come in."

Walking toward the dining room, I noted that the furniture, while old, had a grace and simplicity I'd missed on our first visit. As I passed a Shaker bench, I reached out to touch the warm cherrywood; it was soft against my palm.

Today the dining room's large round table was set with beautiful antique china, and an arrangement of sweet peas, violets, and lilies of the valley nodded from the center. "Thank you for the flowers." Lulu brushed a hand across them so that the scent of the lilies came wafting toward us. "It was very thoughtful."

We sat, exchanging polite comments about Sammy's flowers and the weather. After a few minutes the conversation fizzled out and we descended into an awkward silence, fidgeting uncomfortably. "Are you hungry?" she finally asked. "I'm making a cheese soufflé. All air, which must be why it seems like such a perfect brunch dish."

"The only thing that will make a soufflé fall," I said it reflexively, the way I always did when someone mentioned the dish, "is if it knows that you're afraid of it." Remembering where I'd first heard the quote, I gasped and began to apologize.

To my relief, Lulu gave a small gurgle of laughter. "That's one of my favorite of his sayings. I think of Mr. Beard so often — sometimes when I'm cooking, I feel as if he's right there with me, standing at the stove. I was so lucky to have found him; I honestly don't know how I would have gotten through the war without his letters. They gave me something to look forward to. I often wonder what made him continue writing to me all those years. He was so kind."

"Anybody would have," I said impulsively. "Your letters are amazing. So full of life. I don't think anyone could have resisted them."

"Really?" The look she gave me was truly surprised, and I saw that she had never considered them anything but ordinary. "You haven't said how you found them."

I went back to the beginning, to the locked library and Sammy's discovery of the room we would come to call Anzio. I told about the library ladies and then about Bertie and Anne.

Lulu listened quietly. "That's quite a saga," she said when I'd finished, "and you've gone to a great deal of trouble to find me. But you have yet to tell me why."

I knew this was important, that I had to get it right. Dad gave me a little nod of encouragement. "As I said, your letters are so full of life that Sammy and I felt we knew you. When they ended and you vanished from us, it was like losing a good friend. We weren't ready to let you go. We wanted to know what happened next. We wanted to know that you were all right."

She stared at me for a long minute, trying to decide whether to believe me. "But there's something else, isn't there?"

"I wanted to know how everyone's life turned out. Not just you — also your mother and Mr. Jones, the Cappuzzellis, Tommy Stroh. But most of all I wanted to know if your father ever came back. It was so frustrating, not being able to know."

"Like losing a book before you come to the end."

"Exactly!"

"But I don't think that's all. There's something more you want."

There seemed no reason to deny it. I nodded.

"You're wondering if I still have Mr. Beard's letters. You're in publishing, and you probably feel they'd make a fine article, maybe even a book."

She was no fool.

"And then," she continued drily, "there are all those lost recipes." She straightened her shoulders and looked directly at me. "I'm sorry to tell you it's all gone — the letters, the recipes, everything."

"You didn't save them?" I couldn't hide my disappointment.

"Of course I saved them." Her voice was sharp. "They were very dear to me. For safety's sake I kept them in the shop. I was aware of their value, and I decided it was safer than keeping them here. Ironic, isn't it? They vanished in the fire along with everything else."

"Oh, no!" My response was so immediate, so obviously heartfelt, that she stood up quickly, pushing her chair carefully back beneath the table, and said, "I can tell you the end of the story. But not until I get our brunch. Mr. Beard wasn't entirely right about fear: Soufflés do fall."

When she'd left the room, Dad leaned across the table. "I don't think —" he started, just as Lulu returned, the soufflé rising with majestic grandeur above its dish. He bit off the sentence as we watched it collapse.

I accepted a piece, although I had no appetite, and then a second because the flavor was so rich, the texture so light. Lulu was not always what I'd expected, but she certainly was a wonderful cook. "More?" she asked, and I said, "Well, just a tiny piece," thinking that no cook can resist an appreciative eater.

"So what would you like to know?" The soufflé was gone. Dad shot me a glance, and I knew he was warning me to ease in slowly.

"What happened to Tommy?" It seemed a safe place to start.

"He passed away almost twenty years ago. Heart attack. But we remained good friends all his life. He was the closest thing I ever had to a brother."

"He wasn't your boyfriend?" I couldn't help asking.

"He was, but only because in those days we couldn't imagine a boy and girl just being friends. People are so much healthier today; my grandchildren are very sensible about all that. But Tommy and I spent months trying to find the courage to tell each other goodbye. It was comical, really.

We were both in love with someone else and both convinced the other would perish when we told them. So stupid. Tommy's wife, Gayle, was much better suited to him."

"What about the Cappuzzellis?" I watched her across the table to see if that was all right, but her gray eyes were clear and untroubled. "I looked them up in the Akron phone book, and there isn't a single one still living there. The store's gone too."

"The boys all went to college on the GI Bill. Mario became a pharmacist, Mauro started a contracting business, and Massimo, the artistic one, went into advertising. Mr. and Mrs. Cappuzzelli were so proud! One by one they all went west, and sometime in the early fifties Mr. C. sold the store and they moved to California, closer to the grandchildren. We all thought Mrs. Cappuzzelli was immortal — she was never even ill — but one Thanksgiving morning she dropped dead as she was taking the lasagna out of the oven. She was almost a hundred."

"How perfect!" I could see it. "That's how I want to die."

"It's how we all want to die." She said this so naturally, so easily, that I forgot about being cautious, and the question foremost on my mind slipped out.

"Was your father a spy?"

Lulu's eyes grew wide and her left hand flew to her mouth, trying to hold in furious little choking sounds. Dad shot me a horrified look. I had blown it. I was frantically trying to formulate an apology when I realized that this wasn't anger: Lulu was trying not to laugh. She finally succumbed to mirth, and Dad and I watched, bewildered. At last she wiped her eyes. "He was many things, my father, but certainly not a spy."

Dad's look of relief, I knew, mirrored my own.

"Where did you ever get such a crazy idea?" she asked.

"From Bertie. Anne said he had some notion that the letters might be code of some kind."

"I'd expect nothing less from a person who goes to all that trouble to hide a few old letters. Surely you realize the man must have been quite mad?"

"But in the most wonderful way." The lightness of her tone gave me courage. "But your father — did he ever come home?"

Lulu's laughter faded. "He never did." Something about the way she said it suggested there was more.

Dad heard it too. "But he didn't die in the war?" He asked it matter-of-factly, the way you might inquire if it was raining or if a recipe called for one tablespoon of sugar instead of two.

"No. He didn't."

"He survived, then." Dad said it without any emotion.

"It's not a pleasant story. I've never told anyone — not even my children."

"But I think you'd like to tell us. I'm guessing it's why you asked us back," Dad conjectured.

Lulu was quiet for a moment, deciding whether to trust him. Her face was easy to read — you could see the conflict, then the resolution. "I do want to share this story with someone. I need to get it off my chest. Having it bottled up inside has been awful. If Peter were still alive . . ." She stopped, gathering her thoughts. "But I need your word that none of this will ever leave this room."

"Of course. I'm a lawyer. You're not my client, but I'll consider it privileged information. And Billie can keep a secret."

Lulu folded her hands on the table and took a deep breath.

"The letter came five years ago next week. The postmark was French, and I didn't recognize the handwriting. The first words were, 'Hello, my sister.'

"The writer began by apologizing for waiting so long to contact me. She said that her father — my father — our father, I guess — had told her his terrible secret as he lay dying. She'd spent years trying to summon the courage to contact me, but now she was very ill, and her priest insisted that she do it while there was still time."

Lulu was looking down at her hands, talking very fast. "The odd thing is that I wasn't surprised. In a sense I'd been waiting for that letter all my life. When Father didn't come back from the war . . . I knew he wasn't dead. I just knew it. And after all this time, reading that letter, what I felt was primarily relief. I finally knew the truth. And I was grateful that Mother was gone and would never have to hear how he'd betrayed us."

She turned and gazed out the window, avoiding our eyes, talking mostly to herself now. "I try to understand how it must have been for him. He was wounded twice, shot out of the sky. A Frenchwoman saved his life — and they fell in love. I imagine it happened more often than we know."

"Did you meet her?" I couldn't help asking.

She took a sip of water. "My sister? Lucette? By the time I got to France, she was gone."

"Lucette!" I had promised myself to stay silent, but it burst from me. "That's terrible!"

Lulu smiled briefly. "It made my skin crawl too. I tried to convince myself that he was thinking of me when she was named, but I never quite managed that. In any case, by the time I got there, Lucette had already passed. But she had three girls and two boys, and they told me stories about the man they called Grand-père. If I'd had any doubts that it was really Father, they vanished pretty quickly. One of my nieces, Claudine, told me that Grand-père took her out to the woods and showed her where to find morels. It was just what he'd done with me.

"They showed me the house too, and when I saw it . . . well, it wasn't hard to understand why he'd stayed. It was stone and very old. Beautiful. How does the song go? How you gonna keep them down on the farm, after they've seen Provence?"

"Have you forgiven him?"

"Forgiven him?" Her eyebrows went up and her hand went to her cheek. "Forgiven him? Of course not! I am furious. Even now, all these years later, just thinking about it

595

makes my blood boil. How dare he abandon us like that? How dare he abandon me? And do you want to know what makes me angriest of all?" She tossed her head. "He didn't have the courage, even at the end, to tell the truth and say he was sorry that he'd hurt us, to beg our pardon. I can't forgive him for that. I never will."

"But you told Mr. Beard that you hoped he was happy!" I remembered how I'd felt when I read those words in her final letter, recalled admiring the eighteen-year-old Lulu for her extraordinary generosity.

Lulu looked at me with something I can only call pity. "I was very young, and I was trying to be heroic. It seemed like what I should be feeling, what a truly good person would feel." She met my eyes. "That's one of the best things about writing letters, you know: You get to be the person you wish you were. I can see that I've disappointed you, and I'm sorry for that, but it's the truth."

"I'm not disappointed, Lulu." I wasn't. "I'm *glad* you're angry at him. It makes me feel less selfish about how I feel about my sister. She was hit by a car, killed in a stupid accident, and when I think about that, I'm furious at her. How dare she be so careless with her life? How dare she go off and leave me here alone? And then I feel terrible about feeling like that. After all, she's dead and I'm still here. How can I be angry at her?" To my horror, I began to cry.

Dad got up to comfort me, and I let myself go limp in his arms. When I looked up at his face, I saw relief, as if he'd finally gotten the answer to a question. Lulu stood, left the room, and returned with a box of Kleenex.

"You're right, of course." Lulu spoke as if she were picking up the thread of an ongoing conversation. "When you're young and you lose someone you love, it doesn't matter how and it doesn't matter why. What matters is that they're gone and you're still here." She folded her hands again and put them on the table, as if in an effort to keep them still. "But I want to be fair. So many men came home broken by that war. I think about Tommy's brother, Joe, and the bitter man he became. If Father had left someone he truly loved behind and come back to us . . . Maybe we had a lucky escape."

She stopped, looking out the window. "Mother was very happy, you know, with Paul Jones. I think that in many ways they were much better suited than she and my father ever were."

"Then," Dad finally hazarded a few words,

"why not tell your children?"

"That their grandfather — their real one — was a sneak and a liar?" She turned on him. "Oh, no, thank you very much. I don't want them to know that the 'hero' they've always heard about was really a man without a shred of decency. Is that something you'd want your children to know?"

Dad considered the question, unconsciously stroking his chin. He looked tired. "It would be a difficult conversation. . . . The truth is often uncomfortable, but that doesn't give us the right to hide it." His eyes shifted to me. "I'm just learning that myself. There are things I kept from Billie. . . . It was for the right reasons; I was trying to protect her. But now I see that it wasn't up to me to decide what she could bear. I don't think you have the right to make that decision for your children either. They'll find out sometime; better that they find it out from you."

"You may be right. Sometimes, in my imagination, I discuss it with Peter, and he agrees with you. But what makes you think that Frankie, Jo, and Jim will ever find out?"

Dad pounced. "If I'd had a lengthy correspondence with one of the most famous chefs in the world, I'd find a way to leave my children that legacy. They'd be so proud of you."

I was a little slow, not quite sure I understood his meaning. Lulu, quicker, gave him a steely glare. "I told you: The letters are gone. They vanished in the fire."

"You did. But I don't believe you."

"And why is that?" She sounded amused.

"We were at the library yesterday. They said that you had donated some documents. Before the fire."

Admiration and dismay played across Lulu's face. I watched her struggle, wondering which would win. We sat there in silence, the three of us. "I did give the letters to the library," she finally conceded. "But I left instructions that they're to remain sealed until twenty years after my death. You may be correct that I should tell the children about their grandfather, but I see no reason to share our story with the world."

"But no one would ever have to know!" I cried.

Lulu turned on me. "And how long," she asked, "do you think it would be before people found out? You came looking for me, and you wouldn't be the last. No, I'm sorry; I can't do that to my children. Or to my father, for that matter. It's not a very nice story, and I'd prefer to keep it in the family."

She got up then and removed the plates. She returned with coffee and cookies, but as far as she was concerned, all discussion of the letters was at an end. "You haven't told me" — she passed the plate of cookies — "how you managed to find me."

"It was serendipity." I told her about Mrs. Cloverly and her closet.

Her eyes flew to my face. "She's still alive?"

"You know her?"

Lulu colored. "I'm sorry to say that I do. She was one of our best customers for many years. But when her husband died, she changed, and we began to dread her visits. She was so difficult that every time she walked into the shop, salespeople would mysteriously vanish, one by one. Nobody wanted to wait on her."

"She was a legend at *Delicious!* too," I admitted, "but it was probably different on the phone. I looked forward to her calls." I told her about Babe's letters, and by the time I got to the scallop mousse, Lulu was shaking with laughter.

"She substituted canned clams for scallops?"

"And I believed her! That's the thing. But she did it all on purpose. She made up this totally ditzy alter ego so she could call and complain."

"Pathetic, really," said Lulu, "to be that lonely. I suppose it was the same with the shop; I've often wondered who she found to torture once we were gone. If I were a good person, I'd give her a call."

"That would be very kind."

Then came a smile so full of mischief, it was as if the Lulu of the letters had finally decided to join us. "Someday, when the urge to play Good Samaritan strikes, I'll invite that poor soul to supper. But for the moment I've used up all my Good Samaritan points. On you."

Her playfulness emboldened me. "Did you ever see James Beard again?"

"Just once, after that first trip."

"How did that happen?"

"I can see that getting rid of you is not going to be so easy. I don't have time for more questions now, but I'll make you a proposition: You come back tonight for that dinner we planned. By then I'll have figured out a way to fob you off."

Dad cleared his throat. "Would you be very upset if I declined your kind invitation? I've been in Cleveland longer than I'd intended. It's time I went home."

"Just us girls, then," said Lulu.

GINGERBREAD GIRL

Lulu opened the door, looking harried and holding a whisk. "Sorry" — she handed it to me — "I was giving a foraging class and I got a late start. If we're to eat at a reasonable hour, I'm going to need your help."

"I'll try," I said, following her down the hall. "But I'm a little nervous about cooking for you."

"Why does everybody always say that?" Lulu swept me into the kitchen. "It's so ridiculous!"

Lulu's kitchen was calm, the cheerful disorder reminding me a bit of Aunt Melba's style. A bookshelf took up one entire wall; the jumble of books was so dense that half the volumes were in danger of tumbling to the floor. Pots of herbs waved gaily from the windows, and an Aga stove sat in one corner, filling the room with gentle heat. A long, well-worn wooden table stood in the center of the room, and Lulu went over and began gently shoving at the big orange cat stretched luxuriously across it.

"Get down, Stanley." She pushed at him again. "Billie will think we have no manners." The cat gave her a baleful yellow look before slowly deigning to abandon his perch. I watched him leap from the table, and then a wave of dizziness came over me. I reached out, trying to steady myself; I could feel my body begin to sway.

"Billie! Are you all right?" Lulu's voice seemed to be coming from a great distance. "You've gone stark white. You'd better sit down. You look like you're about to faint." She pulled out a chair. "Try putting your head between your legs."

The panic attack was so sudden, so unexpected; I'd thought I was beyond them. For a moment I forgot how to breathe naturally, and I concentrated on pulling air in and out of my lungs. Lulu watched me with concern.

"I'll be okay," I said. "Sorry."

"Nothing to be sorry about," she replied, calmly reaching for a glass. She filled it with water from the tap and handed it to me. I drank slowly, centering all my energy on the sensation of the cool liquid sliding down my throat. Lulu took the glass, and the water splashed in, loud, as she refilled it.

Lulu put her hand out and felt my forehead. "They say this new flu comes on fast, but you don't have a fever."

"It's a panic attack." I said it a little too quickly.

Lulu was completely calm. "Have you always had them?"

"No. Only since my sister died. That was almost two years ago, and I thought I'd gotten past them. It's just when I go into a kitchen . . . I miss her so much."

"Tell me about it." She pulled out a chair and sat down facing me, then took both my hands in hers. Looking into her earnest gray eyes, I saw Lulu, my Lulu, and I began to talk. I told her about Cake Sisters, about Genie, about the Jaguar. And then, finally, about the cocaine. Lulu kept her eyes on me, nodding her head now and then as I spoke, saying nothing. "I always knew that car was meant for me," I ended. "But now that I know about the drugs, it's worse. I was so stupid. I should have known! I should have stopped her!"

Lulu's face was full of sympathy. "That's the most terrible thing about being a child: you're convinced that it's all your fault."

"Did you feel that way?"

She nodded. "I was certain that if I'd been a better daughter, Father would have come home. The young feel omnipotent. All through the war, I was sure that as long as I kept Father in my mind he would be safe. I felt so guilty whenever I forgot and went on with my life. And when he didn't come back . . . well, I knew it was my fault. I tortured myself with every single time I'd disappointed him. I was convinced he would have come home to us if only I'd been better, nicer, more generous."

"But it wasn't your fault!"

"Of course it wasn't!" She brought her palm down on the table; the noise made me jump. "But until you know that, really know it, you can never let it go. I thought I'd done that, but when Lucette's letter came, I understood that deep inside I'd been clinging to the guilt. Going to France was what made the difference; I finally understood that nothing I could've done would have brought my father home. Nothing. It was not my fault. I was free."

"So why protect him? If you're truly free, what difference does it make what the world thinks of your father?"

"Oh, Lord! I set myself up for that, didn't I?" Lulu stood up.

I looked around the kitchen. The dizziness was gone. "Genie will never get to know you." I said it out loud.

"No." She seemed to understand. "She

never will."

I closed my eyes, and for just a moment I was back at Cake Sisters. Genie was at the table, drawing a new cake, and I watched her pencil move across the paper as I conjured the recipe in my head. I opened my eyes and the vision evaporated. Lulu was watching me, sympathy etched across her face.

"There are many kinds of crime." Her voice was gentle. "I've always thought the most unforgivable is to have a gift and turn your back on it."

Had she hit me, it would have hurt less. People had said the words before — Sammy, Diana, even Thursday — but I hadn't been ready to hear them. Now I took them in, knowing it was finally time to stop running from the best in me. Cooking was my gift, and Genie's death didn't change that.

I got to my feet and looked at Lulu. "Got any ginger?"

"What else will you need?"

"An orange. Butter. Flour. Eggs." Lulu pointed to the cupboard, and I reached in for cardamom, cinnamon, and clove.

Lulu went to look for bourbon and I took in the kitchen, trying to memorize this room. I wanted to store this peaceful place away so the next time the panic came, I could remember how I was feeling now.

I picked up the orange and grated the peel, enjoying the lovely citric scent filling the air. I squashed the ginger, feeling the quiet explosion beneath my knife. I sifted flour, watching the patterns drift onto the wax paper.

Dusk was falling, the fading light making the kitchen glow. Somewhere, off in the distance, Lulu had turned a radio on, and gentle music wafted into the room. I creamed the sugar into the butter, watching two substances become one. I cracked the first egg, mesmerized by the deep marigold color of the yolk. As I began to stir in the spices, Stanley leapt back onto the table and stuck his nose inquisitively into the bowl.

"You know you're not supposed to do that." Lulu handed me the bourbon. Stanley gave her a disdainful stare and walked away, tail held proudly in the air.

I buttered the cake pans, dusted them with flour, and filled them with batter. I smoothed the tops and set the pans, very carefully, into the oven. As I closed the oven door, I whispered, "No earthquakes now," knowing that I was, at last, on solid ground.

THE LAST LETTER

Dear Genie,

It's been a year, exactly, since Dad and Aunt Melba tied the knot. It was no big deal, just the four of us at the house, but it felt right. I missed you, but, then, I always do. What's different is that whole hours go by now when you're not with me. What I'm trying to say is, I'm still in mourning, but it's become bearable.

Here's the worst thing: You'll never know Mitch. I think you'd love him almost as much as I do. (He'd love you too, but that doesn't scare me anymore. Those days are over.)

And here's the best: Every day brings a moment when I know that I am happy.

Lulu's here a lot; she can't get enough of New York. Now that she and Sammy have become so close, she says it would be a shame to waste the opportunity. She sometimes stays with us, but she'd rather be with him. I think they stay up all night talking. He's still trying to argue her into doing the book. Good luck with that.

If there is a book, it will be Sammy's. I'm way too busy. When I got back from Ohio, Sal had a proposition for me: He wanted to start Fontanari's Bakery, and he wanted me to do it. What he said was, "Rosie thinks this is what you were meant to do. And she's never wrong. Stop wasting your talent."

For the first few months the bakery did really well. Then MJ's opened, Jake asked me to supply their pastries, and all hell broke loose. Maggie's in the kitchen, Jake's out front, and the place is so crazy successful I'm having a hard time keeping up. Next month Diana's moving back to New York to help me out. Ned might come too, but Diana says if it comes to a choice between Ned and getting her hands on the gingerbread recipe . . .

Mitch and I will probably get married. Someday. He gets cold feet every time he thinks about inviting his family. And I'll never go to another big wedding. (Fontanari's Bakery doesn't do wedding cakes. Not for any amount of money.)

There's some sad news too. Anne Milton passed away last month, just after she finished cataloging the *Delicious!* letters. It happened the way I always knew it would: She went to sleep and didn't wake up. Whenever I miss her, I think about time being a trick of the mind, and I know that she's here somewhere, walking down another street. And when I think that, I know you're there with her.

xxb

BILLIE'S GINGERBREAD

I have so many memories wrapped up in this cake. All I have to do is start grating ginger and I'm ten years old again, in the kitchen with Genie and Aunt Melba learning how much I love to cook. As I pick up the oranges I think back to that first day at *Delicious!* when Jake asked me to bake for him, grateful that I'm no longer frightened. By the time the cake is in the oven, sending its rich, spicy aroma into the air, I'm thinking about Lulu, and how lucky I was to find her.

This cake is great when it's just been glazed, but it's even better the next day: spicier, richer, more forceful. When I put a little sliver into my mouth, its friendly intensity reminds me how much I like my life now, and I turn to offer Mitch the second bite.

Is my gingerbread as good as the one my mother made? How could I possibly know?

But I do know this: it's good enough.

Cake
whole black peppercorns
whole cloves
whole cardamom
1 cinnamon stick
2 cups flour
1 teaspoon baking powder
1 teaspoon baking soda
1/2 teaspoon salt
3 large eggs
1 large egg yolk
1 cup sour cream
1 1/2 sticks (6 ounces) unsalted butter, at
  room temperature
1 cup sugar
2 large pieces fresh ginger root (1/4 cup,
  tightly packed, when finely grated)
zest from 2 to 3 oranges (1 1/2 teaspoons
  finely grated)

Preheat oven to 350°F. Butter and flour a
6-cup Bundt pan.

Grind your peppercorns, cloves, and cardamom and measure out 1/4 teaspoon of each.
(You can use pre-ground spices, but the
cake won't taste as good.)

Grind your cinnamon stick and measure out

1 teaspoon. (Again, you can use ground cinnamon if you must.)

Whisk the flour with the baking powder, baking soda, spices, and salt in a small bowl.

In another small bowl, whisk the eggs and egg yolk into the sour cream. Set aside.

Cream the butter and sugar in a stand mixer until the mixture is light, fluffy, and almost white. This should take about 3 minutes.

Grate the ginger root — this is a lot of ginger — and the orange zest. Add them to the butter/sugar mixture.

Beat the flour mixture and the egg mixture, alternating between the two, into the butter until each addition is incorporated. The batter should be as luxurious as mousse.

Spoon batter into the prepared pan and bake for about 40 minutes, until cake is golden and a wooden skewer comes out clean.

Remove to a rack and cool in the pan for 10 minutes.

Soak
1/2 cup bourbon
1 1/2 tablespoons sugar

While the cake cools in its pan, simmer the bourbon and the sugar in a small pot for about 4 minutes. It should reduce to about 1/3 cup.

While the cake is still in the pan, brush half the bourbon mixture onto its exposed surface (the bottom of the cake) with a pastry brush. Let the syrup soak in for a few minutes, then turn the cake out onto a rack.

Gently brush the remaining mixture all over the cake.

Glaze
3/4 cup powdered sugar, sifted or put through a strainer
5 teaspoons orange juice

Once the cake is cooled, mix the sugar with the orange juice and either drizzle the glaze randomly over the cake or put it into a squeeze bottle and do a controlled drizzle.

AUTHOR'S NOTE

This is a work of fiction. Although James Beard wrote for many magazines, he never worked for Pickwick Publications. I like to think that if Lulu Swan had written to him, he would have written back (he was extremely generous to many, many correspondents). Mr. Beard did, indeed, say that the only thing that will make a soufflé fall is if it knows you're afraid of it, and the particulars of his life during World War II are all accurate. But if he ever wrote to Lulu, those letters have not been found.

ACKNOWLEDGMENTS

Writing, for me, is a waiting game. I go out to my little studio, light a fire in the wood-burning stove, turn on my computer, and stare at the screen. I switch the radio on. I switch it off. I fidget in my seat. And then, on the good days, I vanish for a while. The writing happens, and I am in it.

I've never written fiction before, and I have no way to explain the process. But my first thanks go to the characters — to Billie and Lulu, Sammy, Mitch, and Jake — who simply gave themselves to me.

My next thanks go to Susan Kamil. She has the extremely rare quality of the born editor: the ability to be simultaneously critical and encouraging. She falls in love with your characters. She is thinking about them even when you're not. And she won't let you stop until the book is as good as it can be. I couldn't have written this book without her.

I also owe a deep debt of gratitude to my agent, Kathy Robbins. When I found myself abruptly out of work she said, "You've always said you wanted to write a novel. Now's the time." Then she took my hand and held it through the process, reading endless drafts.

Thanks to my husband, Michael Singer, and our son Nick. They endured endless dinners when I was not really with them, but wandering through the Timbers Mansion in my head.

The incomparable Ann Patchett read a draft and gave me thoughtful notes. I will never again forget the Rule of Chekhov. I hope the day we spent talking about the background of the book was as much fun for her as it was for me.

The MacDowell Colony offered me the perfect place to work on this book, and I am deeply grateful for the peace, time, support, and friendship that I always find when I am there.

I also want to thank: My assistant, Francesca Gilberti, who keeps track of my projects. Robin McKay and Maggie Ruggiero, gingerbread experts, who consulted on the cake. All the people at The Robbins Office — David Halpern, Louise Quayle, and especially Arielle Asher, who is always cheerful, enthusiastic, hopeful, and helpful. The wonderful team at Random House, starting with Gina Centrello, who named the book before it was even written. Sam Nicholson, Molly Turpin, Avideh Bashirrad. Thanks to Barbara Bachman, who did the lovely design. And I am indebted to the extraordinary copy editors, Loren Noveck and Kathy Lord, who pored over every word, untangling the chronology.

Finally, I want to thank the many food people who were the inspiration for this book. I've learned so much from the talented butchers, bakers, farmers, chocolatiers, and cheesemongers I've been fortunate enough to meet. And, of course, endless thanks to all the cooks. Feeding people is an act of generosity — I don't think it is possible for a great cook to have a stingy soul — and I have done my best to honor that.

ABOUT THE AUTHOR

Ruth Reichl was born and raised in Greenwich Village. She wrote her first cookbook at twenty-one, and went on to be the restaurant critic of both the *Los Angeles Times* and *The New York Times.* She was editor-in-chief of *Gourmet* magazine for ten years.

She now lives with her husband in upstate New York.